MOSAICS

A Track Presius Mystery
E.E. Giorgi

E.E. Giorgi

MOSAICS

Printed in the United States of America
ISBN: 978-0-9960451-3-1
Print Edition

MOSAICS

Also from E.E. Giorgi

CHIMERAS

GENE CARDS

**Subscribe to the author's newsletter
to be notified of forthcoming books:**
http://eepurl.com/SPCvT

E.E. Giorgi

PRAISE FOR MOSAICS

"Giorgi's prose is full of pithy, witty, comic, tragic, and merely memorable lines."
Carol Kean, Perihelion Book Critic

"Author E.E. Giorgi weaves a quick-moving page-turner that is hard to put down."
Indie Reader

" The story is suspenseful from the first page to the last. The writing is well crafted and the descriptions of Los Angeles make me feel that I'm there, watching things unfold with my own eyes."
Mysterysequels.com

"This novel is filled with great scenes, great characters and great lines."
Carol Kean,
Amazon Vine Voice and Perihelion Book Critic

PRAISE FOR CHIMERAS
A Readers' Favorite Book Award Winner

"A riveting and entertaining read."
Dr. Rob Brooks
author of *Sex, Genes, and Rock 'n Roll*.

"A great debut novel and has a satisfying ending."
the Kindle Book Review

"E. E. Giorgi has created a fine ensemble of professionals pursuing what might happen if biotechnology and the desire to overrule nature clash."
Dr. Ricki Lewis,
author of *The Forever Fix*

MOSAICS

E.E. Giorgi

For my mentor Bette

MOSAICS

PROLOGUE

The eyes.

The first to burn are the eyes. They crackle and hiss inside their sockets until there's nothing left but two gaping holes. The nose dissolves next, skin receding over cartilage flaps.

Then the lips.

Flesh liquefies.

It bubbles and oozes and evaporates, leaving behind clean, white bones.

He tilts his head and smiles.

Such pretty cheekbones.

For you, Laura, he thinks, gripping the scalpel. The next toast will be for you.

ONE

Sunday, June 20, 2009

The air smelled sweet, the vaguely rotten reek of algae mixed with drenched wood, *toyon*, and yucca pollen. The fog had dissipated and the wind was starting to pick up now that the sun was out. My boat rocked, Will growled. The poor mutt had the stomach of a kitten when it came to water.

I patted him on the head. "Almost there, buddy."

He wagged his tail, licked my hand, then resumed his post by the gunwale, his wet nose stuck up in the air, sniffing.

Dawn had been perfect for angling. No other boats on the lake at five a.m. — just the distant lilt of crickets, a full moon, and bass feeding in deep waters. I'd driven the boat up to the dam and dropped a heavy sinker and frozen anchovies. The weight carried them into the cool waters. I caught three stripers within the hour.

The hardest part was to keep Will from barking and scaring the fish away.

Dogs were meant to hunt, not fish.

The sun was high now, the cooler full with our limit of stripers plus two large catfish and a couple smallmouth bass. Despite the mucky smell of lake fish, the thought of grilled fillets for dinner made my mouth water.

I drove to shore, the wind behind me, and docked. Will jumped on the pier and went running on the beach.

In just a few hours the place had changed completely. Kids had gathered by the launch ramp to fish. The lull of the waves lapping against the docks was now covered by the roar of the jet skiers and the loud stereos of the sunbathers. The wind carried the familiar reek of humanity — beer, different brands of lotions, fried food, and gas exhaust from the motorboats.

There wasn't a single cloud in the sky and the temperature was already in the seventies. An F-150 started beeping loudly as it backed up into the launch ramp with its boat trailer, getting ready to launch.

I tied the boat and lifted the cooler on the dock.

A small kid came running to me as I climbed out of the boat. "Look what my big brother got." He stretched out skinny arms that smelled of sunscreen and mosquito repellent and showed me the small perch in his bucket.

"You're missing some scales," I said.

The kid blinked. "What?"

"You didn't count the scales? If some are missing, you have to throw the fish back."

I winked. The kid stuck his tongue out at me and ran away.

You're an asshole, Ulysses.

I stooped down to pick up the cooler. Something bit at my ribs—a small pain I'd never felt before. I inhaled, waited. It passed.

Man, you're getting old, Ulysses. Can't sit in a boat for too long no more.

The cooler felt heavy in my arms, yet I kept grinning at the kids watching from the ramp and pretended I was carrying a feather pillow. The mutt trotted behind me, wagging his tail.

By the time I got to my pickup I was out of breath. I set the cooler on the ground by the boat trailer and dumped the bag of leftover anchovies for Will to finish up. As I stood up again, my head spun. Pain clutched at my chest, burning. I leaned against the truck and clenched my teeth.

What the hell's going on?

My cell phone rang. I inhaled, the pain now seeping to my throat, not letting go. The cell phone kept ringing. Will licked up the last of the anchovies and came to snuggle against my legs.

I reached for the phone in my pocket, the pain quietly ebbing off.

Satish Cooper, I read on the display.

I took a deep breath and the pain was gone, just a dull ache left in my ribs.

"Yello," I croaked.

"May I ask you where the hell you are, Detective Ulysses Presius?"

I took a minute, readying myself for the pain to come back.

It didn't.

Satish's words rang in my ears—it was nice to hear the old man's voice.

"Silverwood Lake," I replied. "And you must be in a

load of shit to be calling me by my full name."

Satish's creamy voice melted into a chuckle. "How you doin', Track?"

Back when I was in Gang and Narcotics, I could smell a closed thermos full of sherms faster than the K9 units. Dipped in PCP, the brown cigarettes stink like hell in open air, but once sealed in a thermos, even the police dogs have a hard time finding them. The dicks in Gang started calling me Track, and the nickname stuck. These days, only the rookies called me Ulysses.

"Not bad," I replied. "Life's a bit slow. Can't complain, though."

Since I'd started freelancing six months earlier, ninety percent of the calls I got were for lost pets and cheating brides. The remaining ten percent paid too little for me to survive on.

Satish clicked his tongue. "Your badge's still sitting on your desk."

The pain was gone now. My muscles started to relax. I unlatched the tailgate and let Will jump up in the truck.

"I cleaned up my desk last fall. I don't miss my badge."

I heard a loud honk, then a jazz tune playing on a radio. He was in his car, driving.

"How long we been partners, Track?"

"Five years, give or take."

"Hmm. Five years, and you still can't shoot a damn lie to my face—not even through the phone. You been away, what? Six months now? The guys over at the Force Investigation Division are bored. Their workload has been cut in half without you. Ours has doubled."

"Very funny, Sat. Undetermined leave means I don't know when I'll be coming back."

It was more complicated than that. And I was a bad liar. Hell, I missed my job. I put the phone on speaker, set it on the truck bed, and picked up the cooler. The pain bit me again, just a nibble, a subtle reminder it wasn't done with me yet. I shrugged it off.

Nothing a double espresso can't heal.

I hopped on the pickup bed and tied the cooler at the back. Will wagged his tail and yapped.

Satish's voice came amplified through the speaker. "I take it you haven't been watching the news lately, Track. Somebody's been on the prowl again."

I grabbed the phone. "Wait. Say that again?"

"On the prowl, Track. Watch the news."

And with that, he hung up.

Damn, the man knew how to get me.

* * *

The jacaranda trees were blooming, shedding slivers of purple on the hills. Blue skies loomed over the oaks and sycamores bordering Chevy Chase Drive in Glendale as it climbed up the San Gabriel Foothills. All around, houses perched on the slopes like seashells on rocks.

I lived in one of those houses.

It was noon when I backed the boat trailer into the open shed on my property. Will paid his respects to the neighbors' dogs, yapping and howling to his heart's content, then trotted inside the house and conquered my couch.

"Thanks a lot for the help, buddy!"

I hauled the cooler inside the garage and set it on the washboard at the back. I squeezed between my workbench and the 1980 Porsche 911SC I'd been fixing, and almost stepped on the heat gun I'd left on the floor next to the fuel tank.

I should learn to clean up the garage before going fishing.

I'd acquired the 911 from a mechanic friend last March.

No other baby can tear up the track like a Porsche turbo engine, so when my friend told me he had a 1980 model in need of a little fixing, I jumped on it.

A guy's gotta have his toys.

Over the past few weeks, I'd removed the gears, disassembled the crankshaft and cam, and gotten everything reground, rebuilt, and resurfaced.

The engine now lay in pieces on the floor next to the body, waiting.

I patted the hood. *We'll get you back in shape, babe.*

In the kitchen, my answering machine blinked with five new messages, which I had no intention of listening to. The King, my antisocial cat, came mewing and purring as soon as he smelled the fish on my hands and clothes. I normally would've played Pat Metheny on the stereo, but Satish's words had teased some fuse at the back of my head. If I knew my partner well—and I did—the prowling he'd mentioned over the phone came with one or two complimentary stiffs. I brought the radio to the garage, tuned it to one of the local news stations, and let it blabber in the background while I set out to clean the fish.

The King hopped up on the workbench, on standby for scraps, and watched me with his tail swaying.

"Your Majesty's on a diet," I said, giving him a couple of spines and dumping the rest in a bucket.

The headlines on the radio skimmed over a couple of shootings, a bank robbery, a high-speed chase, and then rambled about the economy and how the new president wasn't going to bail us out of our misery. Stephanie Lazarus, the highly decorated LAPD detective arrested on June 5 for a twenty-three-year-old murder, dominated the rest of the news. Reporters were already speculating about cover-ups, insider jobs, and all the like.

The LAPD cracks the case, and the LAPD gets egged in the

face.

I deboned and filleted the fish, set a couple aside for tonight's grill, and stored the rest in freezer bags. Some of the innards I froze for The King, the rest I dumped in trash bags. By the time I was done, my hands and nails were dirty with blood, my armpits stunk, my back was damp with sweat, and I had dinner for two weeks. I was the happiest guy on earth. Let the rest of the world fill their kitchens with polyester, plastic bags, and chipboard boxes. I get my food at the source.

I washed the knives and buckets, scrubbed the sink, hauled the trash bags out. When I returned, I turned off the radio and padded back to the living room to try the TV. Lieutenant Al Gomez stared at me through the screen, round eyes bulging out of his toad-like face. The camera zoomed out and panned over the media conference room in the new Metropolitan Communications Dispatch Center. It was still as new and shiny as the day they inaugurated it, in 2003.

Detective Satish Cooper was sitting next to the lieutenant. The minute I laid eyes on him, the man smirked, as if satisfied I'd finally tuned in to watch him. I turned up the volume and dropped my ass on the couch.

Gomez appeared to have already delivered his spiel, which, from the banner at the bottom of the screen, was about a Montecito Heights medical doctor found murdered in her home.

A reporter from the very back of the room shot his hand up in the air. "When will the victim's identity be released?"

Gomez scratched his wide forehead and cleared his throat. "As soon as we're done rounding up every possible witness."

"Can you tell us if you already have a suspect?"

"We're leaving no stone unturned."

Diplomatic non-answer.

Another eager reporter raised her voice. "But why was the case transferred to the Robbery and Homicide Division? The division only handles *famous* crimes, like the Grim Sleeper or the Cosby case—"

Magnificent question.

"The RHD has assumed the primary investigative role on this case," Gomez interjected. "We've put together a task force of detectives from both the RHD and the Hollenbeck station. Again, this is a collaborative effort between LAPD divisions."

On that note, the lieutenant invoked his right to remain silent, waved off all other questions, and marched out of the frame, followed by two officers as stiff as Swiss guards, and a still smirking Satish Cooper. The camera panned to the right and showed a view of the dispatcher floor fanning out below the media room. I turned the TV off, trudged to the bedroom, peeled off my camos and T-shirt, and started the shower.

Fifteen minutes later, skin dripping and hair steaming, I came out of the bathroom, picked up my cell and dialed Satish's number.

* * *

The face was gone. Holes gaped where the eyes and mouth had been. Shreds of charred skin clung to the white plate of a cheekbone, the flesh eroded all the way down to the ear. Naked teeth were locked in an eerie grin. Black hair framed a surviving strip of forehead and fanned over the red and gray pattern of a rug.

A tag at the bottom of the photo read, "Amy Liu, age 34, Case ID AZ3964."

The next page offered more photos of the victim

sprawled on her back in a red tube dress. No gunshot or defense wounds, no slashes across her body, no blood pooling on the floor—just the eerie mask of her non-face. A close-up of the back of her head showed the area where the killer had carved a flap of skin and hair—a four-inch long triangle cut out of her scalp. I wondered about the possible meaning of removing scalp from the victim—I'd never seen it before.

A black, U-shaped indentation scarred the neck from side to side. A ruler held next to it marked the distance from the jaw.

Except for Satish sitting at the desk across from mine, the squad room was deserted. All its old smells were still there, though—mold, rust, a banana peel left in one of the trashcans to rot, the infectious odor of old office furniture.

It was late June, and the Glass House—the old LAPD headquarters—was already a boiling cauldron. The building was so old the AC had become a historic relic that served a purely decorative function. Two fans swooshed quietly from the ceiling, pointlessly blowing hot air against the dusty Venetian blinds. Honking and gas exhaust from Los Angeles Street leaked from a window left ajar. And yet, as my eyes skimmed the crammed desks—some clean and tidy like Satish's, others strewn with piles of blue murder books, crime scene sketches, and smiling pictures of spouses and children—I felt a little something tighten up in my throat.

A squad room is like a woman you've slept with too many times. The excitement is all gone, yet you always end up coming back.

I returned my attention to the murder book. The next photo showed the vic's naked feet, a pair of black thigh-high stockings neatly folded next to the body. Nice lace garters, the kind you'd want to peel off a nice pair of legs. The killer left the stockings but took something else—skin, again, judging from the lesions at the base of the victim's toes and down the sole of the foot: two wide incisions to remove a flap of skin, five millimeters deep according to the notes typed on the side, and several other small cuts all around. No apparent pattern. Failed attempts to make the proper incision? It seemed improbable.

"Was there anything missing? Belongings, clothing—"

Satish left his chair and came over to lean against my desk. "None that we could tell. We did a walk-through with the victim's mother, and she didn't notice anything missing from the house. Except for the stockings, the victim was fully clothed. No apparent sexual activity in, out, or around. Whatever this loon had in mind, it wasn't sexual."

"What about the acid?"

Satish crossed his arms. "Acid is a powerful weapon and relatively easy to find. You can buy either the muriatic or the sulfuric kind at any hardware store. Sulfuric acid is found in lead-acid batteries, liquid drain openers, household cleaners, pool chemicals—the list goes on."

I closed the murder book. The clean surface of my desk looked as desolate as an empty fridge on a Friday evening. I opened the first drawer and a small paperclip rattled inside—a last remnant of my presence there. I picked it up and stuck it between my teeth. "Nobody's claimed this spot yet?"

Satish smiled. "It's *your* desk, Track. Besides, we'll all be moving soon."

I propped up my feet and grinned. "It's finally happening, huh? The new Parker Center, all shiny and sleek."

They had promised us a new Police Administration Building for years, as the current one was outdated and didn't even comply with seismic regulations. They finally approved the project in 2006 and broke ground on First

Street in 2007, right across from the City Hall. I hadn't been inside yet, but old owls like Detective Oscar Guerra claimed it was as beautiful and new as a first wife. Since he'd been married five times, I figured he would know.

Satish cocked his head to the side. "How would you like to clutter up one of those brand new desks, Track? You'll even get your own overhead cabinet."

"Nah, not for me. Got my PI license and everything. I'm the Glendale Philip Marlowe now. Lotsa perks. Gotta try Armenian food, Satish."

I kept my grin up for as long as I could until it miserably dissolved under Satish's hard stare. Who the hell was I lying to? I missed my job. Hell, I even missed *him*, my partner. I missed his old man's stories he'd drop whenever I needed them the least, only to wake up the next morning slapping my forehead and thinking, "That's what the hell it meant!"

Satish wobbled his head, an Indian custom carved on African American features. He looked thinner than I remembered, his temples whiter. Other than that, he was just the same, his part Indian part African American heritage well mingled in his gestures and inflection. The bullet that skewered his right lung last fall had dented his reflexes, not his wordiness. I hated to admit, but my days felt empty without his stories.

"We're swimming in hot water again, Track."

I made a face. "Sat. That Lazarus woman will be on trial, not the LAPD. This ain't another Rampart. She screwed up and she's gonna pay for it."

"That Lazarus *detective*, Track. A *seasoned* detective, one of our own. This ain't another Rampart, and yet the names Javier Ovando and Suzie Peña are coming up all over again. People are throwing pitchforks at us. This is a test case."

I shrugged, feigning indifference.

He tilted his head and stared at me. "Come on, Track.

You know you want to nail the bastard. Look at what he did to her."

I pushed the murder book away. "Not my problem."

I dropped my feet to the floor and stood up. I adjusted the holster hooked on my waistband and for once felt cocky in my shorts and T-shirt. To hell with the LAPD monkey suits.

I patted my partner on the shoulder and walked off.

I expected another couple of words. None came.

I slowed the pace.

He still said nothing.

Come on, was he giving up so easily? What happened to all the prep talks about us being the good guys, getting paid to play cops and robbers with real robbers, and making the world a safer place?

I got to the door, wrapped a hand around the jamb, and turned around. "Okay, Sat. What aren't you telling me now?"

He smiled, the Indian way, his profile outlined by a shaft of sun poking through the blinds. "Why, Track. I thought you'd never ask."

He hopped off my desk, hooked his jacket over his shoulder and walked with me to the elevator lobby. "We think he tossed the acid while she was still alive this time. No sign of forced entry. He probably attacked her as she opened the door. Oh, and you'll love what he left behind."

"Did you say, 'This time'?" I said as the elevator doors closed on us. "Was there *another* time?"

* * *

The sun was setting when Satish parked in the driveway of 453 Santa Fe Terrace. The first city lights blinked through the sunset, a loud Latino pop song poured down the valley.

I got out of the car and studied the neighborhood. Montecito Heights was an oasis of green rising above the expanse of suburban L.A. Purple jacaranda trees, frazzled palm tops, and red roofs speckled the wavy profile of the hills. The air was cool and it bore the scents of early summer: wisteria, freshly mowed grass, and barbecues.

Across the street, still wounded from last spring's heavy rains, the hillside spilled over a row of shattered wood planks and into the curb. A dog barked in the distance. A pick-up truck rattled by, spilling out the fragment of an old rock-and-roll tune. All around, homes were nestled in the folds of the landscape, hidden by firs, oaks, and evergreens.

Blooming rosebushes crawled along the yellow walls of Amy Liu's house, a one-story ranch-style faced in red brick. A magnolia tree shaded its east side. Flanked by birds-of-paradise flowers, redwood stairs climbed up to the front door. It was all very peaceful and cozy, had it not been for the yellow crime scene tape crossing the garden gate. Satish lifted it and motioned toward the back of the house. "Let me show it to you now, before it gets too dark."

The backyard consisted of a nicely sized lawn hemmed in by a metal chain-link fence.

I donned a pair of gloves, smacking the latex against my wrist. "Any wits?"

"Only if you count the nine-one-one caller. Some joe who didn't ID himself. He must've had some really good reason to be in her house at one a.m. and *not* be the killer."

"Some killers are nice enough to call nine-one-one."

Satish shrugged. "That'll soften the prosecutor once we catch him." He pointed to the patio, a square of gray paving stones set around a circular mosaic pattern. Concentric rows of blue and aquamarine tiles framed a red and yellow sun, its jagged rays cut out of stained glass. Satish pulled a transparent evidence bag out of his pocket, crouched, and dropped it next to the sun pattern.

"He left them by the body," he said, tilting his chin toward the bag.

I crouched opposite to him and emptied the content of the bag in my hand: four small glass tiles, each half an inch in size. Except for the green one, the other three colors—red, orange and aquamarine—matched the ones in the sun pattern. Not the shapes, though. The tiles in my hand were regular squares, all identical. The sun mosaic instead was made of unevenly cut bits and pieces with jagged edges.

I aligned the squares in two rows, orange and green at the top, and red and aquamarine at the bottom. "That how you guys found them?"

Sat nodded. "They're called tesserae. Square glass tiles used for decorations. Most common in patios, decorative benches, bistro tables, swimming pools—anything with a mosaic pattern. As you can see."

"Maybe some kind of artist?"

Satish gave me a lopsided smile. "Crime's an art, Track. I thought you'd come to appreciate that."

"Yeah. And crime fighting is the shit that happens after that."

Satish sighed, his smile gone. "No tiles missing here, and the shapes are all irregular. Turns out, they all come in squares. They're cut on the spot as needed. Vic's mom told us she had this done pretty recently—couple of months ago."

I raised a brow. "Do we know by whom?"

"Katie's been looking into that."

I picked up the green tile, stood up, brought it to my nose.

Tesserae.

Aluminum dust was the first thing my nostrils detected. The forensic team had left it, attempting to catch the faintest

21

smudge of a fingerprint. Their effort had not been rewarded—the tiles were clean. There were other smells, mingled, vaguely sweet, and vaguely acidic, a distant memory of being sick, the foul taste of medicine in my mouth—

Satish squeezed my shoulder. "Come on. Let's go take a look inside."

We walked back to the front. Satish unlocked the door and pushed it open. It had a peephole.

She stares through the hole, recognizes the face — familiar enough to feel safe. She opens the door. Does she smile, murmur a greeting? A moment of disbelief and then the agonizing pain, flesh burning off her face. She tries to scream, blinded, but acid is scorching her from the inside, seeping down her throat...

I waved away the crime scene sketches Satish offered, stepped inside and inhaled.

The olfactory landscape changed abruptly. The place was cold, the air stale. Summer evening smells gave way to ninhydrin and fingerprint powder. New scents enveloped me—alcohol, food, expensive perfumes—all fading, swallowed by the sting of death and abandonment.

I paced into the open-space area. Right off the foyer, fluorescent cards had been taped to the floor to mark where the body—and the rug she'd been lying on—had been found.

The kitchen was straight ahead, with its lingering scent of fried foods and Asian spices, separated from the living area by a long, curving breakfast counter. The sink was cluttered with dirty dishes and trays, the counter crowded with cocktail glasses. A trash bin under the sink had been emptied.

"Dirty plastic cups and plates from the party," Satish said. "Trace Unit tested everything. Plenty of DNA and fingerprints—enough work for a year. All prints analyzed so far go back to either the victim or her guests. No extraneous sets found."

I opened the fridge, took a peek inside, inhaled, closed it back. "How many people?"

"Six, all co-workers from UTech. Last ones to leave the scene swear she was alive and well when they drove off."

I smelled the cabinet doors and knobs. "Do we have statements from all of them?"

"We do. A few agreed to be polygraphed, too."

"And I bet all the polys were inconclusive." I've never been fond of polygraphs. I trust my nose better. "You said the other one—the man found in Silver Lake—he'd been strangled first, *then* scarred with acid?"

Satish had filled me in during our ride to Montecito Heights: there had been another victim, a young homosexual from Silver Lake. The similarities between the two murders had put the brass on edge and motivated the case transfer to the RHD. The rumor spreading through the agency was that a new serial killer was on the prowl.

Behind the breakfast counter was the dining area, which extended into the living area and foyer. An abstract painting hung above the mantelpiece, one of those pictures a two-year-old could draw, yet it came with a six-figure price tag in snobbish art galleries where it's legal to rip you off and make you feel good about it.

Satish stood by the door, hands deep in his pockets. "Track, there's general dissent on whether we're dealing with a serial or not. Could be a copycat. Could be that Amy Liu's ex finally wanted payback and found it convenient to follow on the footsteps of another killer. Whatever this is, it's heinous, and nobody wants another heinous offender on the loose. Especially one that targets nice neighborhoods, if you know what I mean. But yeah, the M.O. is different in this one."

Yes, I knew what he meant. A homicide in a place like Montecito Heights weighed more than ten slayings in South Central. Always had.

The coffee table was cluttered with used glasses, dried up wine spatters, and tortilla chip crumbs. The sofa, buried in a wide assortment of pillows, smelled of a cat that no longer lived there. I stuck my nose everywhere, picked up everything and sniffed. A dirty plate on a chair, an open book, the TV remote. A bunch of keys and a row of coins on the console in the foyer, the glass top sprayed with fingerprinting powder.

She staggers back and clings to the wall, one hand on the console, the other one on her face.

"Traces of acid have been found on her fingertips," Satish said. "Both victims were strangled from behind. Both were found in or near their homes with their faces mauled by acid. The victim in Silver Lake, though, had bits of his own skin underneath his fingernails."

I came back to the foyer, got on my hands and knees, and perused the ground where Amy's body had been found. "He tried to pry the ligature away," I said.

"Correct, and that's how his own skin ended up under his fingernails. Also, the acid spilled down the sides of his neck, erasing the ligature marks. That would be consistent with liquid poured on him while he was lying down, not standing up, as in Amy's case. At the autopsy, the M.E. concluded the acid had been poured on the Silver Lake victim after his death. There were no traces of acid in his airways. On the other hand, there were droplets of splashed liquid on Amy Liu's neck and chest—at least on prelim— and inside her throat."

"The attacker splashed her while she was standing by the door?"

"That's our hypothesis so far, yes. Her finger pads were

burnt, most likely from touching her face. Definitely alive when she was attacked."

Satish shook his head. "If it is the same killer, his hunting grounds are quite broad, the cooling off time is less than a year, and the violence is escalating—which makes him very dangerous. If, on the other hand, it's a copy cat, the motive is unclear: why copy the mode and manner of death, and then take the time to remove the skin flaps?"

"What kind of MD was she?" I asked.

"Internal medicine at UTech university hospital in Boyle Heights."

"Family practice?"

"No, HIV specialist. They have a large clinic affiliated with the medical school."

Satish watched me sniff the floor with vague interest. We'd been partners for almost six years now and my modus operandi no longer surprised him. I inhaled, followed the vic's path from the door back to the console, where the killer pounced on her, wrapped the ligature around her neck and pulled, leaving a smooth, almost anonymous indentation. No telltale of rope, chain, fibers—none visible to the naked eye at least.

"You said we don't have telltale marks on the first victim?"

"Only partials, nothing conclusive. The damage done by the acid in that case was too extensive."

"Why erase the ligature marks on victim number one but not on victim number two?"

"Maybe he found a better ligature, one he felt confident it wouldn't give him away. I tell you Track, if it's the same guy, he's getting better at this."

I sniffed the floor where her body had been found. "What were the M.E.'s thoughts on the skin carvings?"

"Smooth blade, firm hand. He knew what he wanted."

A med, I thought, impulsively. And then I remembered the care with which I dress my game when I go hunting.

Or a butcher.

Anyone with some practice with animals could do that.

I let my thoughts wander back to the night of the murder. The clatter of conversation, the laughter, the music from the stereo. Did one of her guests come back after the party was over? Or maybe they never left? I could only imagine the bedlam of fingerprints, fibers, and what-have-you the Field Unit must have collected from this scene. Six guests, plus the victim, plus—or including—the assassin. Or assassins.

I said, "Did you listen to the nine-one-one tape?"

Sat crossed his arms and looked down at the tip of his shoes. "Fairly calm voice, given what he was supposedly looking at. One word he said, though—*abraded*. About the face."

"Interesting word choice."

"Agreed. We got a couple of blue suits trying to trace this guy."

"And six likely candidates."

"We're keeping tabs on each one of them. We taped their voices and sent them off to Electronics. They're all some kind of medical professionals."

"All quite familiar with the word *abraded*."

He shook his head sideways. "Suppose Joe Party Guest forgets something. A pair of reading glasses, a salad bowl, or maybe a question. Joe comes back, finds her dead and makes an anonymous call because—"

"Because he's got something to hide. Either he did it or he's holding back."

Satish's phone buzzed. "Gomez," he mouthed, taking the call. "Yeah, we're at the scene."

I took the chance to explore the rest of the house.

A dark hallway with no windows opened to the right from the foyer. The smells changed — the staleness of a vacant place and the victim's scent — feminine, ambitious, seductive. The wall displayed wrought-iron sconces and a collection of photos of Amy: Amy in her graduation gown, Amy with friends, Amy with her cat.

Her bedroom was orderly. There was a half-empty birth control kit in her nightstand drawer, but no boyfriend in her life, according to the friends and relatives interviewed, only an ex-husband who now lived in Oregon. Toiletries on her vanity table, regular clothes in her closet, a few garments in her drawers that told me she was no nun, but no distinctive masculine scent anywhere. If she shared her bed with somebody, she'd done a good job at hiding it. The sheets smelled freshly washed.

The next door led to her home office, a small carpeted room with a couple of white bookcases, a table with a desktop and printer, a metal chair, and, on the opposite side, a futon, a laundry basket, and an ironing table folded against the wall. Through the window, the hills of Montecito Heights glowed against the evening sky, a wavy fabric of glimmering lights.

I inhaled. The bookshelves were crammed with medical books, the desk buried under stacks of papers.

The sweet, foul smell of the tiles…

I sat at the desk, checked the drawers, sniffed the keyboard, then the computer screen.

Not here. Close, though.

The papers. He went through the pile of papers.

I rummaged through the folders not knowing what to look for, just tailgating a smell. Gloved fingers had brushed through printouts and graphs, tables, essays, research proposals…

Did he find what he was looking for? And if so, what?

Article after article of scientific jargon, each title some random permutation of the words immunodeficiency, vaccine, study design, therapy, antiretroviral.

"What are you gonna see in the dark?"

By the office door, Satish flipped the light switch.

"Smells."

"On paper?"

"Yeah. And patterns, too," I said. I sniffed the top right corner of every paper in the pile. I could follow the gloved fingers searching through the stack, most likely a left thumb holding up the top ones so he could read the titles, and a right index flipping through. Until the trace stopped.

He found what he was looking for. Probably took it with him.

I inhaled and gave one last look around. Everything else seemed untouched. "What did Gomez have to say?"

Satish wobbled his head. "Autopsy's scheduled for Thursday morning. Just got an invitation. Wanna join the party?"

He smiled. Waited.

Amy Liu smiled too, from a silver frame on her desk, a man's hand draped over her shoulder, and a strand of black hair blowing across her face.

"Fine," I said, walking past him out of the room. "I'll keep you company on Thursday, but—"

"Uh-uh, Track." He switched the lights off and followed me back to the foyer. "First things first. Tomorrow you pee in a cup and get your LAPD badge back."

"I pee in a what?"

We locked the house and made sure the yellow crime scene tape was back in place. Outside, the air was tainted with a hint of humidity and the scent of jacaranda blooms. A handful of pale stars dotted the sky, the glow of downtown beneath them like a disoriented dawn. A broken streetlight strobed from farther down the street. The Latino music persisted.

Yo sufrí mucho por ti, mi corazon…

Satish unlocked the car and slid in behind the wheel. "Union mandated drug test. Your leave of absence was longer than ninety days. Welcome back to regulations, Detective Presius."

I made a face.

"Look at it this way. Whoever handles those cups has it way worse than you." He started the engine and backed out of the driveway. "Shit happens, Track. Never forget that."

"Hard to forget on days like this."

I rolled down the window and let cool air blow in my face. The freeway droned in the distance, as another night descended upon Los Angeles. Another murder, another killer on the loose.

It was June 2009, the beginning of summer.

Killing season had just started.

TWO

I left my Charger in the driveway, clambered out, and smelled freshly baked *lahmajoun* — Armenian pizza. It came from a white plastic bag hanging by the door. Besides the Armenian pizza, wrapped in paper, the bag contained a yellow envelope.

Will jumped on me as I unlocked the door, yapping and licking. I set the *lahmajoun* on the kitchen counter and tore open the yellow envelope. Inside was the picture of a sixty-something lady, proudly smiling in front of a water fountain. The back read, "Please find her. SKL," in slanted handwriting.

I told him a scarf, damn it. A hat, a shoe, a sweater — something I can fucking smell.

Katya Maria Krikorian, age sixty-two, had vanished on

May 24. She got into her car in the early afternoon to visit a friend in El Sereno, spent about an hour with her, then left and never made it back home. Her brother had hired me to find her, but he kept missing the point that in order to find people I need to know what they smell like.

I tossed the picture on the dining table, together with the rest of the photographs, and served the boys—Will and The King—dinner. I didn't feel like eating, so I grabbed a Corona and a lime from the fridge and walked to the living room. Ass in recliner, feet on coffee table, laptop on lap. Will's adoring eyes on me, The King settled on his windowsill, despising us both. I took a long swig of Corona and typed, "mosaic tiles."

Google's my best friend.

My browser told me that mosaics had been around for a long time. The Greeks and the Romans used them to decorate their homes until they became the primary Christian art form. Interestingly, whereas the Greeks and the Romans used mostly stone tiles for their mosaics, it was the Byzantines who introduced glass tiles for the first time.

Glass tiles—the kind our killer seemed to like. I downed the rest of my beer. Four tiles, four different colors. Christianity had a fixation with the numbers three and seven. What was the meaning of four? Four cardinal directions, four limbs, four elements, four states of matter.

The Byzantine Strangler.

My eyes fell on the painting propped against the wall, between the bookcases. A red woman lay naked in the grass, her bosom dappled with black stars, a cougar emerging from the shade behind her. Artist, friend, occasional girlfriend, Hortensia had given the painting to me four months earlier and I still hadn't gotten around to hanging it. I flipped the cell open and punched in her number.

"Still not available, Track."

"Hort. It's been six months already. You don't need to remind me every time I call."

She puzzled over that. "You mean you're not calling to have sex? That's not flattering."

I resisted the urge to hang up. "I need an art lesson. On mosaics."

There were noises in the background—glass jars clinking, water running. "I don't do mosaics. I paint."

I missed the time when we had sex instead of talking. "Well, that covers it. Do you know people who do mosaics in L.A.? Would you know where they get the tiles?"

"In the recycling. Broken bottles, colored glasses, crocks, what have you. Even pebbles. Artists are creative people. Hey, I have a friend who does pistachio shells on wire mesh. That's pretty cool."

I thanked her and hung up, making a mental note to call her again should I find pistachio shells at the next crime scene. I got out of the recliner, trudged back to the kitchen, and tossed the Corona bottle. My answering machine was still blinking. I hit the play button.

"Yeah. This is Joe from Jiffy Lu—"

Skip.

"Mr. Presius, your results are in. Dr. Watanabe wanted me to schedule—"

Skip.

"Hey."

I froze. My finger retreated from the skip button this time.

"Thought you'd be home," Diane's voice crooned through the phone. "Guess not."

The answering machine's beep at the end of the message rang like a long amen.

I shuffled to the fridge, grabbed another Corona and slumped back in the recliner, my fingers itching to dial

Diane's number.

She said not to call. Not to call, Ulysses, can you follow one simple direction?

Yeah, but then she called me.

She left a message.

I punched in her number on the cell phone. It rang once. Twice. Then her voice, snappish, nothing like the message she'd just left. "I still need time, Track."

"You left me a message."

"I didn't—Sheesh, Track, how often do you listen to your messages?"

I swallowed, squeezed the beer bottle in my hand. "Once or twice—a month... maybe..."

A sigh, a hand going through her hair and materializing in a rustle of static through the phone. Where was she? Pacing in her living room, or maybe lying on the bed, coiling strands of hair around her index finger...

"Do you ever make mistakes, Track?"

"Lots of them. You were never one."

She considered. "It's not you, Track. It's me. I'm going through things. I need—I need to find myself again."

She'd been saying that for the past three months. How she wasn't sure about stuff anymore. How she hated her job, hated Los Angeles, hated everything about her life.

I told her to give it some time. Being held at gunpoint twice in one week is not something that goes down as smoothly as bourbon.

Her reply had always been the same: "You don't get it, Track."

I *didn't* get it.

"You need to give some love to that pretty Sig your dad got you. The range stays open till late on Wednesdays. I could pick you up at - -"

"I can't. I'm sorry."

She wished me goodnight and hung up.

I brought the Corona to my lips, took a sip, and swished the chilled beer in my mouth.

Women are like whiskey, I thought. If you have too much you get drunk. If you have too little all you're left with is a bunch of regrets.

THREE

Monday, June 21

The air was heavy with the smell of rain—an unexpected change from the usual bouquet of smog and wildfires. Crows sat quietly on high branches and waited. The treetops swayed and the boughs groaned. The first drop hit me in the face as I unlocked the Charger. By the time I got on the freeway, the storm was pounding.

There's something ominous about rain in Southern California. Black, fat clouds fill the sky and mock the all-year-round flip-flop crowds. They hover over posh hairdos, convertibles, and the sports car fanatics who wash and wax their vehicles every other day. News reporters with a sadistic eye for meteorological catastrophes gain more airtime than infomercials.

Chaos spreads. Highways jam. Traffic lights flash.

Honking horns trail off.

After all, we *are* Southern Californians. We're prepared for earthquakes, fires, and flash floods. We're *not* prepared for rain.

Red brake lights blurred across my windshield, the wipers squeaking with the rhythm of a nighttime lullaby. Mozart would've written a symphony out of that. The pavement turned into slosh. A trailer truck passed me on the left and gave me a free shower.

A siren wailed. Traffic stopped. Red and blue bar-lights flickered ahead in the weaving stream of taillights, courtesy of the usual idiot who forgot that brake distances increase on slick roads. Like toads and slugs, they're a subspecies of drivers that comes out with every storm.

I slowed down and smiled.

I'd peed in the fucking cup, tomorrow I was getting my LAPD badge back, and Dave Brubeck was playing on my car stereo.

As far as I was concerned, the world could stop for a few drops of rain.

* * *

By the time I got to South Oak Knoll, in Pasadena, the rain had tapered off. Faces braved the sidewalks of Lake and Colorado again. The clouds had dissipated, and a bright sun poked through a canopy of dripping oaks. I entered a long driveway that parted the front lawn of a two-story colonial house, inclusive of all accessories: white portico, white pillars, white stucco all around, and gray shingle roof just so it wouldn't look like a bridal cake. I parked my Charger under the carport, next to a well-preserved W140. Mercedes cars are like divas from the Fifties — they never fade.

The sodden lawn shimmered in the sun. Different scents

of dampness mingled in the air: grass, bark, soil, cobblestone.

A little anxiety.

Oh, come on, Ulysses.

This was where all the fine lines blurred together: killer, cop, predator. Patient. *Privileged* patient, who got to see his doctor in the comfort of his home office, chatting over genetics and DNA as if they were some abstract philosophical concepts.

As if it weren't my life.

I rapped on the door.

What if the Byzantine Strangler can't help himself?

Hell, I could. I made a choice.

But you still kill, Ulysses, don't you?

Dr. Watanabe's office would've been a decent size if only he hadn't crowded it with a mismatched assortment of furniture. His wife poured us *sake* in small cups while I sniffed books. One by one, I slid them out, flipped through the pages and inhaled. Some smelled too old, some smelled too new, and some smelled just perfect.

Watanabe's wife dismissed herself with a bow. Being at least two decades younger than her I should've bowed lower, but I'd come to the conclusion a while ago that Japanese customs had not been invented for people over six feet tall. So I smiled and waved my hand.

Watanabe handed me a cup. "Have a seat."

I didn't. I stood by the window and sipped the *sake*. It was strong and pungent and I figured it was going to help.

Watanabe was a small man with puffy eyes, saggy jowls, and the shiny black hair of a child despite his sixty-something years. His skin had the creamy color of a glass of Baileys and the vaguely foreign scent of a wine whose origin you can't quite pin down. He drank his *sake* in small sips, smiling through his eyes. When he was done, he got out of his chair and reached for the Newton's pendulum sitting on top of a file cabinet. He propped the pendulum on the desk and then flicked the first ball to set it in motion. The balls started clicking. Watanabe sat with his hands laced across his stomach and a wide, lipless grin sprawled across his face. The metal balls clicked against each other, the first and last ones rocking back and forth at alternate times.

"What do you know about pendulums, Ulysses?"

I licked the last drop of *sake* and wished Japanese cups came in larger sizes. "Is this going to be a physics lecture?"

He scratched a thin brow. "It would've worked better with a traditional pendulum, but this is the closest thing I could find in the house. You see, I just happened to remember that these cute gadgets have two points of equilibrium, not one." He touched the balls and stopped them. "One's stable, and the other's not." He held the first ball out and rotated it around the fulcrum until it reached its highest point, vertically above the others. "According to Newton's law, if you give it exactly the right amount of energy, the ball will swing all the way up and stop at its highest point. However, it will fall again at the minimum perturbation." He let go, the ball swung back down and hit the other ones. The ticktack of five balls hitting one another resumed.

I set my cup on one end of the desk, dropped into one of the armchairs, and smiled a what-the-heck smile. Granted, I'd had Dave Brubeck keeping me company all the way to Pasadena, but I hadn't braved a flooded freeway to watch some balls rock back and forth.

"Fascinating," I lied, scratching my chin.

A satisfied chortle escaped his throat. He picked up the pendulum and delivered it back to the file cabinet. "I believe the same holds in genetics." He sat back at his desk, donned a pair of reading glasses, and slid a hand inside a yellow

Manila folder. "Most variations can only push us this far from our stable equilibrium point. We swing and come back."

"Or we die," I interjected.

He pressed his lips together, considering. "Hmm. Yes, some phenotypic changes can be lethal." He pulled a long printout from the folder and carefully flattened his hands over it. "But once in a million, maybe a billion times, something extraordinary happens." He was peering at me over the rim of his lenses. "The ball will hit that one point up there and, almost miraculously, will stop there. Waiting."

Ha. I cocked my head and gave him a half smile. The other half I kept for myself. "Waiting to crash?"

Watanabe heaved the slightest of sighs. "Not necessarily." He grabbed a pen and pointed it at me. "*You* are extraordinary, Ulysses."

"I don't take credit for that."

My wit washed off Watanabe's face like waves on wet sand. "You survived a deadly brain tumor when you were only six years of age. The virus that killed the tumor turned on chimeric genes that now coexist within your DNA in *chouwa*—harmony. Together, they form the balance that allows you to exist."

"And you're now telling me this balance is unstable."

He passed me the lab printout from the yellow folder, his small eyes scrutinizing me as I stared at the list of acronyms and numbers.

"I don't know what these mean, Doc."

"Your antinuclear antibody levels are off the chart."

"What the hell are those? Weapons of mass destruction?"

He gave out a shrill little laugh that died as quickly as my sense of humor. "No. They are antibodies that bind specifically to components inside the cell nucleus. We all have them in low concentrations, but when they get past a certain threshold they start to draw concern. That's why I want you to stop by the lab one of these mornings and do another draw. I just submitted a standing order in your name." The pen wagged at me. "Have you been feeling well, Ulysses?"

I frowned. "Of course!"

I was fit, reasonably young, and moderately addicted to caffeine and ethanol, but hell, who isn't?

I stretched my lips in a lopsided smile. "I'm great, Doc. Really," I insisted.

Watanabe wasn't impressed. "No joint pain? Fatigue? Rashes?"

I leaned an elbow on the armrest and scratched my jaw. "Doc. You didn't call me to your home just to tell me about some screwed up blood count."

A blade of sun poked through the curtains and glinted on his jet-ink hair. He leaned forward on his elbows, hands steepled together. "The way your chimeric genes coexist with the rest of your DNA is remarkable. We need to keep an eye on it, understand the mechanism. Make sure the balance that allows you to exist—"

"Doesn't break." I finished the sentence for him.

He stared at me for the longest time.

And then he nodded.

FOUR

Thursday, June 25

"Oh, come on, Track. It's like smelling raw chicken."

"I don't *smell* raw chicken. I grill it."

Satish looked comical all garbed in an oversized surgical gown, paper cap, and facemask. He shook a couple of booties out of a dispenser and leaned against the wall to slip them over his shoes. "Don't want no souvenirs on my shoes this time."

I tied the laces of the gown behind my back. "Don't tell me you get in there—" I pumped my thumb at the autopsy room "—and all you smell is chicken."

He shook his head sideways. "I'm odor blind."

"*Odor* blind?"

He stepped in front of the mirror and adjusted the paper cap on his head as if it were some sort of military beret. "You go to India once, inhale, and when you come back you're odor blind. The streets in Kolkata smell of gasoline, fish fry, betel leaves, sweat, monkeys, mangoes and chutney." He patted me on the back and shouldered through the doors to the autopsy room. "Not for the faint of heart—I mean *nose*. You wouldn't survive a day."

I took a deep breath, pulled up the facemask, and followed.

A chrome faucet dripped in one of the sinks. Air vents hummed gently from the ceiling. The body was draped, an anonymous hump on a stainless steel table. An assistant pushed a cart of instruments to the table and lined up the tools for the cut. Clipped against the glass of a view box were Amy Liu's dental records and a couple of pictures from the other victim, Charlie Callahan, found strangled six months earlier outside his home in Silver Lake. His face had also been marred with sulfuric acid, though in his case the damage had been inflicted postmortem.

"I don't believe it! Detective Presius!"

Robed in green, Dr. Russ Cohen looked like a giant M&M rolling toward me. He pulled down his facemask and shook my gloved hand a little too enthusiastically. "Where I grew up they say, 'Only the dead don't come back.' Of course that's not true in my line of work, is it?"

He slapped me on the shoulder and roared with laughter. "I see you're well prepared this time—paper cap and booties, too. Cuz you know, *If you've got a T-shirt with a bloodstain all over it, maybe laundry isn't your biggest problem.*" He winked and nudged me in the ribs.

I stretched my lips and faked a smile without putting too much effort into it.

Satish leaned closer and whispered, "Seinfeld joke, Track. You forgot all about that, didn't you?"

"Gladly," I replied.

Cohen wiped the grin off his face and cleared his throat.

"So. We've all had our share of mutilated bodies." He waved at the assistant and she lifted the drape off the body. "But I confess this is a first for me."

The room fell silent.

The crime scene pics had not prepared me for the sight of Amy Liu's disfigured features. Her face had peeled off the skull. In its liquid path, sulfuric acid had etched grooves along her cheeks and simmered in her orbs.

All bodies are naked. Yet, deprived of a face, Amy Liu felt more than unclad to me: she was bare, exposed, stripped of her persona.

The killer wants to erase his victims' faces.

In my whole career, I could only remember one case that offered a worse sight—a John Doe found on the street. He'd loaded up with semi-jacketed hollow points and eaten his gun.

Cohen walked to the cart and picked up a magnifying glass. "Let's start from the feet." He stood at the end of the table and moved the surgical light to the victim's feet. Bending the toes all the way back he pointed the beam at the right foot plantar.

"See these? Multiple lacerations, one-to-two centimeters long, only a few millimeters deep. You'd think he'd tortured her, but—"

"But there are no signs of restraints on the body," I said.

"The cuts were inflicted postmortem," Satish concluded.

Cohen nodded, his eyes grave. "They're not deep enough to think he was attempting to mutilate her. Still. They don't seem to serve any purpose." He leaned closer and examined the whole plantar under the magnifying glass. "Was she wearing socks?"

Satish dipped a hand under the surgical gown and retrieved pen and notepad. "No. Sheer stockings."

"Black?"

"No, Doc. Skin colored."

"Interesting." Cohen traded the magnifying glass for a pair of tweezers and retrieved a fine, black and curly filament from the edge of one of the cuts. He held the tweezers against the light and we all squinted at the filament.

Satish slid the tip of the pen under his paper cap and scratched his head. "Hard to tell if it's a hair or a fiber."

Cohen turned the tweezers until he'd examined all sides of the filament. "Right. I'm not seeing a root. The lab will be able to tell us." He carefully passed the specimen to the assistant and added, "Did you see what he did to her scalp?"

We all walked to the other end of the table. Cohen turned Amy's neck all the way to the right and exposed the scalped area behind her left ear.

"See this? This is a meticulous job. Shallow incision behind the ear and transversal to the back of the neck, forming a V."

Satish took notes.

"He peeled the skin off starting from the lower edge, up along the temporal bone, and severed a triangular flap."

Around the scalped area, bits of dried blood and tissue hung to the skull like red crumbs.

Satish leaned closer. "Have you ever seen something like this before, Doc?"

"Other than old Western movies, that is," I added.

Cohen turned Amy's head the other way, looking for more lesions. "Actually, the movies had it all wrong, you know? They made it look like scalping was a Native American custom, but it turns out, the white settlers were scalping even more than the Indians." He checked the back of Amy's head then reached for the laryngoscope. "Anyway, the answer to your question is no. The only case on my table happened by accident. A worker from a Santa Monica manufacturing plant got her left scalp ripped off by a the rotating bar of a spinning lathe. Couldn't pull her out of the machine fast enough."

I swallowed. "Now that's a happy image."

"Yeah, it wasn't pretty." Cohen sighed, waited for the assistant to return to the table and then pressed the record button on his handheld voice recorder. "Ok, let's get started. Victim's name is Amy Fang Liu, five-foot-two-inches long and weighs one hundred and five pounds. Asian descent, age thirty-four. Small tattoo, one and a half centimeters long, on the right shoulder near the collar bone. Red birthmark on left breast, adjacent to the areola. No evidence of sexual assault and no defensive wounds." The M.E. dictated the general appearance of the corpse, describing the gory details of her facial injuries and the numerous lacerations on the soles of her feet. He handed the recorder to the assistant and proceeded to insert the laryngoscope down Amy's throat.

"The tissue inside the oral cavity is abraded. Vocal cords are seared." He waved, and the assistant paused the recorder. "We'll examine closely the bronchi and esophagus for confirmation, but it looks like she swallowed the acid. Probably inhaled it, too." He pointed a penlight down her throat. "In a way, he spared her a lot of pain by strangling her. I'm guessing he surprised her with a first splash, then poured more once she was dead."

He palpated her neck and examined the ligature mark. "See how close to the jaw the ligature came? We're looking at somebody at least a foot taller than her." Cohen applied pressure at the sides of the scar and pinched it. "Black ligature mark. Straight line with raised edges," he dictated into the recorder. "Except for the indentation, the skin around it is smooth and clear. No discoid bruises. Gail, pass me a scalpel number four, please."

While he waited for the blade, Cohen pointed to the fine cloud of dark specks above and around the ligature mark. "These are *petechiae*," he said. "In death by strangulation you usually find them in the eyes, too—tiny bruises that form when the capillaries break. Too bad we don't have much of the eyes left in this case." He took the blade from the assistant and started making a transversal incision about a quarter of an inch above the ligature mark. As he cut deeper into the tissue, a gooey smell of rust and decay stuck to my palate and refused to let go.

"First thing I always look at—fluid from the eyes. I can see everything through vit electrolytes. Time of death, general health, sexual orientation..." His eyes peered at us from behind his surgical goggles for a second to see if we'd caught on the last joke. He chuckled, we smiled politely. "Once I had a sudden death with no medical history. Young fella in his late thirties. Guess how I found what he'd died of?" He kept talking while smoothly working around the incision, carving out a triangle around the ligature mark on the left side of Amy's neck.

"You asked?" I said.

Satish elbowed me in the ribs.

Cohen didn't even notice. "The eyes. Exactly. From the vitreous electrolytes it was clear he'd died of non-ketotic hyperosmolar diabetic coma. You wouldn't believe how common undiagnosed diabetes is." He dropped the skin section from the ligature mark into a new tissue cassette and pointed to the photo of Charlie Callahan's neck clipped to the view box on the wall. In Callahan's case the killer had poured the acid not only on the victim's face, but also on the neck, burning away most of the ligature mark. Cohen drew our attention to little crescent-shaped incisions on the side of his neck spared by the acid.

"See those marks over there? They're semicircular and one-to-two millimeters in length. Those are nail marks. Callahan tried to pry the ligature away from his neck. No such marks on Amy Liu's neck. No skin underneath her nails, either."

Satish nodded. "What about telltales? I can't see any to the naked eye."

Cohen shook his head. "None whatsoever. Smooth indentation, blanched out at the bottom, with clear edges. No fibers, either."

The assistant leaned forward and measured the depth of the indentation with a probe. "One-point-five, Doctor," she said.

Cohen pondered the information. "One and a half millimeters. Shallow, compared to what a nylon string or wire would normally cut into, but deep compared to a scarf." He frowned. "I can see bruising in the tissue, all the way down to the strap muscles of the neck."

He made a new incision starting from above the thyroid and running down across the ligature mark. He then came down to the side and cut out a triangular flap of skin, exposing the larynx in its full length. "It's mind boggling, really. Usually one can pin it down to a group of ligatures, you know? Strings, ropes, scarves. This, however, has me scratching my head. Can't be wire, as it would've cut through the tissue. You need something thicker to compress the carotids without severing them. A rope or a scarf will do, but those leave fibers and telltale marks. Ah, but see here?" He brushed his gloved finger along the U-shaped bone at the top of the larynx. It was cracked in the middle. "Fractured hyoid bone. There's your cause of death—asphyxiation—and manner—strangulation."

Satish scribbled on the notepad and blew through his facemask. "Now we just need to figure out the mode."

* * *

A telephone cord, a nylon scarf, a computer cable, shoelaces, a fishing line, a climbing rope—all used at some point as lethal weapons. Next to each one, Satish placed a sticky note with the description of the corresponding ligature: telltale marks, depth of indentation, type of bruising. Rumors of the puzzle spread quickly across the squad room, and soon a small crowd of detectives ringed around our desks. The fact that Presius was back after a six-month sabbatical also added to the general curiosity.

The heat enhanced the overhanging concerto of male sweat, testosterone, gun oil rubbing against leather holsters, and cheap Formica furniture. Two rows of desks faced one another over old, linoleum tiles. All around, yellow walls were plastered with the ghastly faces of L.A.'s most wanted.

A smile dangling from his black mustache, Detective Oscar Guerra dragged a chair across the room, straddled it, and stared at the eclectic collection on Satish's desk. He plucked a cigarette out of his breast pocket, stuck it between his lips, and spoke carefully around it. "What about a computer cable? Wouldn't leave any telltale, would it?"

Satish clicked his tongue. "Too large."

"A nylon string?"

I replied this time. "Too deep. We need something that has no fibers, leaves a perfectly smooth indentation, but doesn't get too deep into the flesh."

Oscar flipped his unlit cigarette up and down with his lips, thinking. "What if it didn't get deep enough because your guy didn't apply enough pressure?"

Satish shook his head. "The pressure is measured by the bruising. Our guy pulled to kill."

Oscar sucked on his unlit cig, then leaned across the

desk and gave me a brotherly slap on the shoulder. "Asshole," he said. "Should've left this one to Satish. Let him puzzle over it for another six months, then you come back, as fresh as a quartered chicken."

The door to the lieutenant's office clicked and we all turned. Silence filled with anticipation fell over the room. Hands buried in pockets, Gomez shook his head. "Just got a call from the UCLA Med Center. They pronounced him dead at two-twenty-six. Michael Jackson is dead, guys."

Oscar's mustache swallowed the smile on his face. "Wow. The King of Chicken Hawks left us. I bet all those child molestation victims will come forward, now."

Jo Kertrud, another seasoned detective who'd been with the RHD since the early Nineties, said, "Who knows. Maybe one of them just did."

The LT waited for the general murmur to subside. "Heart attack, they think, but you know the drill, guys. Mayamoto and Garrison—let's have you two go to the hospital and talk to the docs. I want you to report back immediately after. Next two on the callboard stand by."

He bobbed his head, looked around if there were any questions. There weren't, and he retreated back into his office. We shuffled back to our spots, all except Satish, who detoured to the vending machines in the hallway. Katie Cheng was sitting on my partner's desk, casually fiddling with the strangulation props. She was a young Chinese-American officer permanently loaned to our division. She helped us deal with the estimated five thousand Chinese who lived in L.A. and didn't speak much English beyond hello and thank you. Katie loved the homicide table so much that even when she wasn't needed as a translator she kept herself busy doing desk work for us dicks.

"Wow," she commented. "Jackson was going to turn fifty-one next month. Gee, I grew up with his songs."

I stared at the paper in her hand. It bore the warm, acidic smell of fresh-out-of-the-printer ink. "What's up, Katie?"

She blinked. "Oh. Sorry. This is for you and your partner." She handed me the printout, together with a whiff of body lotion and mint chewing gum.

* * *

Satish slid inside the Charger. "Where are we going?"

"Vernon Motel on Fifty-six. Couple blocks west of South Fig." I whipped the car up the One-Ten ramp, merging into the steady flow of traffic. I had a Glock 17 tucked in my waistband holster and a five-inch M327 revolver for backup. I was wearing a tie and dress shoes as the brass gods demanded, and my badge, all polished and shiny, was safely stowed into my wallet. Little uncomfortable in the shoes, and already sweaty in the nice shirt, but other than that, I made one hell of an RHD dick. Satish wasn't too bad either.

Not that anybody cared. In South Central what most people care about is survival. A ghetto of dilapidated apartment buildings, body shops, liquor stores, and cinder-block walls decorated in layers of graffiti, South Central has always been ruled by the Main Street Crips, the Hoovers, and their various street factions. Summers get pretty damned hot in this part of town.

"So, what's the deal in South L.A.?" Satish asked.

"Katie found the guy who did the mosaic art on Amy Liu's back patio. The work was done two months ago. Guy's got no priors, but his nephew, who helped with the mosaic, is a Eighteenth Street with a tail. Ricardo Vargas, age nineteen."

Satish tapped the car window. "A gang homeboy with a record. Interesting. What did he serve for?"

"Fly-by shooting when he was fifteen. Shot a guy in the face to prove to his gang he was a man. His prize was a ten-dollar bill — that's all the vic had in his wallet. Been on parole since last January. His uncle's trying to keep him off the street by having him help out in his handyman business. They redid Amy Liu's back patio last March. Uncle claims he's been keeping an eye on the boy and he's clean."

"I'm sure his Eighteenth Street pals are keeping an eye on him, too."

Half an hour later, we left our vehicle and stepped into the sweltering heat of the small parking lot of a dingy, hot-sheet motel. By the street, skinny palm trees bowed under the sun. A man in a wheelchair peered at us from the sidewalk, his weathered face caked with layers of street life.

"Bro," he called. We ignored him. "Hey, bro!" He wheeled toward us across the parking lot. "I got information for you. You uh… you got a buck or two?"

Satish dipped a hand in his pants' pocket and fished out a card. "We don't handle information. Here's the number to call."

Black fingers gingerly reached out to pluck the card. He stared at it, not too troubled by the fact that he was holding it upside down, then gave us a toothless grin and turned his wheelchair around.

Satish sighed. "Cashed out. My last buck went into the vending machine at Parker."

"A buck for a bag of stinkin' Cheetos." I turned my pockets inside out, found a crumpled dollar, and walked back to exchange it for another toothless grin. I got a *God-bless* as an extra bonus.

"There's a reason it's called City of Angels," Satish said.

"Yeah." I nodded. "Only angels around here ain't got wings and ain't wearing white, either."

I glanced at the two story-building spread out along the

three sides of the inner court: pink, chafed stucco, tears of rust and bird droppings, green doors alternating to dark sliding windows, and the lingering smells of sweat, dog urine, and tired humanity. A maid in pink scrubs came out of an open door on the second floor, dumped a heap of dirty laundry into her cart, sent a disapproving glare at the wheelchair, now on the other side of the street, then vanished back inside.

"Luxurious place," I commented.

Satish tipped his head toward the lobby. "Parole doesn't make you rich." He adjusted his belt and holster, put a hand on the door, and gave me a stern eye. "Now, the guy being a parolee and all, we have some leeway. Still, I'd like to talk to him alive."

I flashed him my most innocent smile.

The lobby was as dingy and gray as the outside. Under our shoes, linoleum tiles popped with old grease stains. Yellowed photos of the Rose Parade randomly decorated the walls. The frames were all crooked and looked like they hadn't been straightened since the '94 earthquake. A full ashtray sat beside a brass plate claiming that smoking wasn't allowed. Stale coffee percolated on a Formica countertop covered in blotches of maple syrup and jam. A radio blabbered in Spanish from somewhere at the back of the office.

I hit the brass bell on the counter. An annoyed voice replied, "We're full."

I flipped my badge wallet and held it up. "Try again, dude."

Bored eyes came forward from the back door and squinted at the badge. They rolled unhappily in their orbs and disappeared again. Papers rustled, drawers closed, the radio shut up. I inhaled, but didn't smell anything alarming other than rusty pipes, tobacco wads, and the lingering tang of refried beans.

The eyes came in full view under a strip of forehead beaded with sweat. Black brows shot up with a pinch of anxiety. "The place is clean," the man said, wobbling to the counter. "And my papers are all in order." He made a vague gesture toward the back.

I propped my elbows on the counter. "You the manager here?"

He brushed a nervous finger along the sides of a mustache that had seen blacker days. "Yes, sir."

"We're looking for a man named Ricky Vargas," I said.

The manager's shoulders relaxed, his brows came down a notch. "Never heard of him."

Satish pulled out the mug shot. "Never seen him either?"

I rapped the countertop. "You know, maybe we should take a look at those papers you mentioned—"

"No." He pointed at the photo. "Him—He goes by Ralph. Owes me a full month."

"He in?"

His eyes darted back and forth between us. "You make him pay, yes?"

Sat and I exchanged a quick glance. "Get the key and take us to his room."

"I can't leave the desk! I have to answer the phone, and—"

I patted my holster. "I hope you have a good locksmith, then."

His face swelled up like a puffer fish. "One second." He sank back in his chair, swiveled it around to a cabinet drawer and retrieved the key from one of the drawers.

We followed him outside through the back door. The sun glistened off the car roofs parked in the court. Two kids were playing hopscotch in the driveway of the adjacent apartment building. Everything else was as still as a postcard.

I scanned the windows of the upper floor as we filed up the stairs. "Do the rooms have back doors?"

The manager shook his head. "Windows and fire stairs. And smoke detectors. All compliant, eh? All in order." His words turned into wheezing as he huffed up the stairs. "Your friends, last time they came, they reported this and that, and safety hazards, and —"

"They're not our friends. Which door?"

He lifted his *first* chin and pointed ahead. "Room two-eighteen."

We covered the sides of the door. Satish banged once. We heard nothing. I inhaled. "With goods," I confirmed. I flattened myself on the hinge side and drew my Glock. Satish banged again.

A feeble "Yeah?" percolated through the door.

"Management."

There were steps, padding over carpet. Something dropped. Then more steps, away from the door this time.

Satish beckoned to the manager. "Hey, I hear a moan inside, don't you?"

"Huh?"

"The door," I growled. "You want it to go bang?"

The man fumbled with the key in the lock. As soon as the lock clicked I kicked the door and yelled the customary "Freeze, asshole!" A draft from the open window at the back of the room made the curtains billow. On top of the fridge, the microwave's door hung open and yawned a familiar reek of burnt plastic. A heap of bed covers was piled on the floor, and the mattress still smelled of human heat and the last remnants of crack smoke. A lamp had fallen off the side table.

I ran to the window, Sat checked the bathroom.

"Careful with the TV," the manager mumbled over short breaths. "I just replaced it. And no messing with the carpet. Blood especially —"

A square had been cut out of the window screen. I leaned out and spotted the asshole running down the emergency ladder.

"Fire stairs!" I yelled. Man runs, cops split. I holstered the Glock and climbed out on the windowsill. The drop was about twelve feet—not worth the risk. To my right, the metal frame of the fire escape rattled with Vargas's steps. I grasped the lintel with one hand, reached for the railing with the other, and swung over. Pain shot up my spine. I ignored it.

Feet dangling, I grasped the top banister with both hands, pulled myself up, hopped onto the fire escape and started down the stairs, the wall behind me radiating heat like a nervous animal. I cussed the dress shoes and fucking business attire.

Vargas jumped down the last flight, landed on a heap of abandoned tires, and vanished into a narrow alley lined with corrugated metal sheets and the slashed skeleton of an old couch. I jumped over the railing and leaped after him, following his adrenaline trail over the reek of urine and trash bins, the sky above me lined with cables and rusty clotheslines.

Pain gnawed my lower back. I ground my teeth and kept pursuit.

Vargas climbed over a fence, jumped, scrambled back up, spotted Satish at the end of the road, and doubled back across the street. A red Nissan was pulling to the curb. The driver barely had the time to unbuckle before Vargas opened the driver's door, yanked him off the wheel and shoved him to the ground. He didn't get very far after that. Pain hammering through my chest, I pounced from behind and brought him down, face eating the pavement and Glock pressed against the back of his head.

"Don't shoot," he squealed.

I swallowed, barrel unmoving.

The pain was making me blind with rage.

I clutched Vargas's arms with my left hand and blocked his lower body with my right knee and leg. Satish came from behind and snapped the cuffs around one of his wrists.

"Track," he said.

I shifted. Vargas slowly peeled his face off the pavement. Blood crept down his nose. "Tell 'im not to shoot. I ain't done nothin', man..."

I stepped aside and leaned against the fence, breathing heavily, waiting for the pain to ebb off.

Same pain as last time.

Satish pulled Vargas to his feet and pressed a handkerchief against his forehead. "Hold this to your head and take a good look at what we found in your room." He shoved a baggie of rocks in front of his eyes. "This how you support your mama? Your parole agent will be thrilled."

"No, man—"

The Nissan owner scrambled back to his feet and watched us from a cautionary distance. A few more faces emerged along the sidewalk, a residential block of pink and gray bungalows fenced by black metal railings.

I inhaled, waited for the pain to wane, then leaned inside the Nissan, turned the engine off, and tossed the keys to its owner.

"Show's over!" I yelled to the rubberneckers.

Satish was already walking back toward the motel, towing a limping Vargas by the cuffs. The rubberneckers dispersed. I stood under the sun, catching my breath.

It's the heat, I told myself. I thought of Watanabe's little chat on Newton's pendulum, I thought of genes, and then I thought of the heat again.

That's all it is. It's just the heat.

I took a deep breath and sprinted after my partner.

Satish shoved Vargas in the back of my vehicle. The manager came out of the lobby to inquire about the status of his finances. "He payin'?"

"Not this time. His deal just fell through the cracks," I replied. "Pun intended."

He made a face and retreated to his haven.

My partner stared at me. "The hell were you thinkin'?"

"What d'you think I was thinkin'?" We have a broad vocabulary, us coppers.

He shook his head, Western way this time, and held up the bag of crack rocks. "What are we gonna do with these?"

I loosened the knot of my tie. "What d'you mean? We violate him. We got him for possession."

"No probable cause, Track. That's what I mean."

"So? He ran. Even if we get a reject, his parole agent can still request a hearing."

"You could've blown his head off."

"He could've been armed! You got one to the chest last year for a caper like this, you forgot that?"

"And you must've missed the Force Investigation Division pretty badly."

I hooked my hands on my belt and shook my head. I hated the FIDs as much as they hated my guts for every time I'd squeezed the trigger on duty. In fact, they were the very reason I'd been away from the LAPD for so long.

"Track, we nab Vargas for a couple of rocks, the hell he cooperates. We cut the guy a little slack, treat him nice and smooth, and he might give us somethin'."

"And confess to murder?"

He gave me one of his Satish looks.

"Don't give me the Vaseline crap," I said.

He grinned. "You know it's the perfect metaphor."

"What if he doesn't give us any juice?"

"In that case, we've used the Vaseline and we can all go home happy." He flashed me one of his smiles, white teeth framed by chocolate lips. "Get in the car and have a cig. I'm gonna handle this."

I tossed him the car keys. "I don't smoke."

"Then maybe it's a good time to start."

"Fuck off, Sat."

FIVE

Ricky Vargas rocked in his chair. He had the rugged smell of somebody who'd been on the run long enough to consider the street his home and a daily joint his pacifier. From time to time, he'd slip forward, lose his balance, and then slide backwards again, pulling himself up as if somebody had just smacked him out of a trance. His left brow was split open in the middle and his nose was purple and swollen from when he'd eaten the pavement. A tattooed red and green lizard spilled out of the back of his black A-shirt onto his tanned shoulders. Its red eye ogled me sternly. On each arm he had the insignia of the Eighteenth Street gang — the numbers one and eight in black ink.

Satish pushed a tape recorder toward the middle of the table. Vargas bulged his eyes.

"What's that for, man?"

Satish's voice was as soothing as a lozenge. "Just so I don't forget our conversation. I'm old and I tend to forget things. Want a Coke?"

Vargas nodded and asked for a cig, too.

"Tell you what. We start chatting, you and I, then you can have a cig." Satish leaned forward across the table. "But you gotta answer my questions, Ricky. My partner's pissed off already."

Vargas shot me a nervous glance. We'd gotten him into one of our interview cubicles at the back of the squad room. We didn't mention his drug caper, he never complained about his beauty treatment. Over two bottles of Coke, Vargas told us about the job his uncle and he did at Amy Liu's house.

"Who designed the mosaic?"

He frowned. "You mean the artsy thing? My uncle did that. He's real good with that stuff. The lady gave him a picture."

"What did you guys do with the leftover tiles?"

"We left them there. She'd bought the stuff herself."

Satish sent me a sideway glance. There was nothing in the garage or backyard. She could've already gotten rid of it, though.

I stopped pacing and sat at the table. "You ever go back to her house at night, Ricky?"

His eyes widened. "No, sir. Me? Why?" His knees rattled. He wrung his tattooed arms, hands cracked and tanned beyond their nineteen years of age.

I leaned on my elbows. "Why? I'll tell you why. Because the lady was pretty, for one thing. And she had money. And the two things together are usually appealing to a piece of scum like you. You know what we found on her body? A hair. Our guys are extracting DNA as we speak. Makes me want to have a chat with your parole agent—"

"No! I—"

"Okay, let's take a breather." Satish laid a hand on the

table and locked eyes with Vargas. "Ricky. You wanna make me and my partner happy? You want us to forget that you gave us a sweat over a bunch of rocks?"

He nodded.

"Then give us something, okay? The lady's dead. You worked on her yard. There's something puzzling about the way she died and about that sun your uncle made for her."

"Remember how pretty she was?" I said, opening a folder on the table. "This is what she looks like now."

Vargas's eyes fell on the picture and then skid away like bullets bouncing off metal. "Whoa. I ain't done that, man. No way. No way I'd do somethin' like that." He swallowed hard, then stared at us, heavy eyebrows slanting up like the head of an arrow. His childish features were darkened by a two-day stubble and polluted by street life.

"Make us believe you," I said.

He ground his teeth and mused. "Suppose a guy was there to—uh—take a stroll or somethin'. But he ain't done nothing," he quickly added. His eyes strayed back to me. "That hair ain't mine, man."

Satish stretched one corner of his mouth. "Suppose the guy gave us something useful."

He wrung his arm harder. "No, man, I—Look. She was nice to us, okay? Even offered me a cig from time to time. She'd come out and share a drag. Not like those rich ladies with all the stink up their noses. Yeah, she was pretty. She got somebody to warm up her sheets at night. Why don't you look *him* up?"

Sat and I exchanged glances. Maybe Ricky was going to be useful, after all.

"You take a good look at her man, Ricky?" Satish asked.

"I saw his car. Was there that night—" He caught himself short, then stared at us like a deer stunned on its path. I knew that look. "The stuff," he said softly. "I ain't—"

"What stuff?" Satish replied. "Tell us about Amy's man."

"I never saw the guy. I'd see the car parked in the driveway. Audi, A8, one of the pretty ones."

"What color?"

"Silver, I think…"

I slammed my hand on the table. "You think? Sat, this turd thinks he can fool us. I say we send him back to the joint and wait for the DNA results."

Satish indulged in his brotherly smile. "Give us something Ricky, or else we've got no choice."

Vargas's voice cracked in shrills. "Look—Silver! Definitely silver."

"And how do you know it was the boyfriend if you never saw him?"

He sneered, and for a moment, the adrenaline in his perspiration ebbed off. "I got ears, okay?"

I leaned back in my chair. "That's hardly anything we can work with, buddy. You gotta give us something more if you want those rocks to go down the toilet."

His perspiration spiked again. He rubbed his cheek, forehead shiny with sweat. I inhaled. Sour, spiced with the nice cocktails he smoked and sold. "I was with a girlfriend. She can tell you I ain't done nothing."

I passed him a pen. "Write your friend's name and number."

He took the pen and fiddled with it. "That night. The car was there. Not in the driveway. A few yards down the road. My friend saw it, too."

"What were you doing there, you and your friend?"

He shrugged one shoulder, gave us a pale little smile. "I told her the lady was nice. Lived in a nice house. She said she wanted to see it. So we grabbed the bike and went. You know. Just to do somethin'."

Satish pointed to the pen. "Your lady friend's number."

He wrote it down. Satish grabbed the piece of paper and walked out of the cubicle. Vargas frowned. "Where's he going with that?"

I smiled. "Some girlfriends have a short memory—better to catch them early. You sure it was the same car?"

He shrugged. The lizard on his shoulder winked. "It was an Audi. Nice cars those are. They make a smooth rumble, Audis. They do."

"Yeah, we all love 'em. Keep talking, dude."

"It was kinda late, but the lights were on in the lady's house, and me and my friend—we just wanted to take a peek inside the fine car, ya know? So I stop, and the streetlight ain't working, but my girl starts screeching that there's a dead body inside the car."

I blinked. "In the car?"

Vargas started playing with the label on the Coke bottle. He nodded. "I only took a glimpse. Saw a shadow in the back. Maybe somebody's sleeping—dunno. My girl gets scared and wants to leave. I tell her to get ahold of herself. The dude in the back of the car probably high or somethin'. I turn around the bike just the same and ride around the block. Then I go back, cuz I want to take a better look, ya know? Right as we're rolling by the house, this other dude comes out of the lady's house. Running. Gets in the car and guns off. Must've been drunk or something. Almost took the curb away with him."

"The other dude being Amy's boyfriend?"

He nodded.

"You're sure about it? Same guy you saw at her house other times?"

He nodded again.

"What time was it?"

"'Round two. Only crickets out that early."

"Yeah. Crickets and loons looking for trouble."

And us coppers love our loons. Especially when they start talking.

* * *

I dropped in my chair, opened the drawer—now properly replenished with my usual junk—grabbed a paperclip, bent it, and stuck it between my teeth. An officer from Northeast Community Station had delivered the Callahan murder book a few hours earlier, so I took the chance to examine it. Charlie Callahan, age twenty-eight, found dead behind the dumpster of his apartment building in Silver Lake, his face and neck mauled with acid, and the side of his head whacked. There were traces of meth in his pockets, but the tox results from the autopsy came back negative. The autopsy also determined the head injury had been caused from falling against the cinder brick wall after he was attacked. An eyewitness, a neighbor from the building next door, testified he'd seen Callahan exit from his apartment door to dump the trash. A few minutes later he saw a tall, blond man walk away from the driveway, though no car had come in.

Two days after Callahan was found dead, a forty-two-year-old man who lived two blocks down the street was arrested on domestic violence charges. Sodden drunk, Malcolm Olsen had beaten his wife to a pulp. Investigators found numerous homophobic statements on his Facebook account and immediately raised a red flag. Another neighbor came forward saying he'd witnessed a heated argument between Olsen and the victim during which Olsen had not been shy about his anti-gay views. Charlie Callahan was gay and Olsen fit the wit's description. His house and vehicles were turned inside out for a scrap of DNA. A loose telephone wire found in his trunk—compatible with whatever was left of the ligature mark on Callahan's neck—was also tested for DNA. All results came back inconclusive: "RFU levels too low"—science jargon meaning it was negative with a chance of doubt.

Olsen's wife originally said that the night Callahan was murdered her husband had gone out to walk the dog, but the dog had come back on its own. After being pulped by her husband, she retracted everything and claimed her husband never left the house that night. Olsen was booked for the assault and aggravated battery of his wife and was currently serving five years in Centinela. Despite not a single scrap of Callahan's DNA having turned up from Olsen's possessions, both the investigators and the prosecutor had no doubt he'd done Callahan in and let the case go cold.

I turned to the autopsy report.

With the exception of the fingernail marks, Callahan's face looked strikingly similar to Amy's. In both murders, the cause of death was strangulation, the mode homicide, and the manner unknown. Callahan's skull was fractured at the side, consistent with a fall. Hair and blood had been found on a cinder brick where he'd been attacked. The assassin had strangulated him from behind and let him fall and hit his head. Tox results on Callahan's face had yielded sulfuric acid, lye, and potassium hydroxide.

He'd been whacked with drain cleaner.

A note at the end of Callahan's autopsy report stated that the deceased was HIV positive and taking anti-retroviral drugs. Something at the back of my head told me this was an important detail, but somehow I couldn't come up with a specific reason, so I let it drift.

On the other hand, no tiles had been found near Callahan's body and no skin flaps had been removed from his body. Amy had been murdered in her house, while Callahan outside, in a well-hidden spot: the complex's dumpster was secluded in a nook between the south wall of the building, which only had frosted bathroom windows at higher levels, and a high cinder block wall that separated it from the next-door property. Still, if this turned out to be the same killer, in Callahan's case he probably felt in a hurry to leave and didn't have the time to indulge in any trophy collection.

I sucked on the paperclip and considered the odds. A gay man versus a medical doctor. Burnt alive versus spared the agony. The act itself was remarkably different: Amy's assassin tortured her and took pleasure in it. Callahan's killer went for domination first. An escalation in rage or a copycat? Could the similarities be just coincidences? And if it really was a copycat, why go through all the trouble of reproducing the crime almost identically, and then leave the four tiles as a distinct signature?

Vargas's rugged smell wafted my way. I watched a uniformed officer escort him out of the squad room. Hands deep in his pockets, Satish came to lean against his desk.

"The girlfriend confirmed his story," he said.

I rolled the paperclip around my teeth. "He coming back for a poly?"

"He said he'd think about it. We know where to find him. And we've got his voice on tape for comparison with the nine-one-one call. Worth a try. What'd you think of his story?"

I crossed my arms, my skepticism written in bold letters all over my face. "That she was no nun he could've figured out by himself. And at that point, he would've given us anything just to make us happy and not spill the beans to his parole agent. However," I clicked the paperclip against my teeth. "The streetlight wasn't working, I noticed that too.

He wouldn't make that up. He was there at night, for sure. To do what—that's what we need to find out."

Sat let out a long sigh, slid behind his desk, and opened Amy Liu's murder book.

I leaned forward and pressed my point. "This guy has a rap sheet, a prior, and worked at the vic's place. And yet we have nothing on him because the little we had we flushed down the toilet. We could've booked him and let his parole agent grill him."

Satish donned his reading glasses and flipped through the murder book. "He's not our man, Track. His second alibi checks, too."

I spit out the paperclip. "What *second* alibi?"

Sat tilted his head toward Gomez's office. "An old acquaintance of yours. Forensic psychiatrist Adam Washburn."

* * *

Dr. Adam Washburn wore a Darwinian beard to compensate for his shiny baldness. Heedless of the heat in our prehistoric building, he wore a long-sleeved shirt with no tie. And he didn't sweat. Not a drop of perspiration, not a hint of a scent other than the laundry detergent from his clothes. He sat at one end of the table and placed a notepad and a blue folder side to side in front of him. He waited for the rest of us to gather around the table while pinching the tuft of hairs sprouting under his lower lip, his pate glistening under the fluorescent lights.

Gomez's forehead looked like a mushroom top beaded with morning dew. He took the seat next to Washburn and rubbed one eye so hard I thought the other one was going to pop out of its socket. Satish and I sat across the table from the two of them, me still miffed about the inconclusive interview with Vargas, and Sat as unscathed as ever. I leaned casually toward Washburn and took a long sniff in his direction.

Nada. The man didn't have a smell.

Freaked the hell out of me.

Gomez tapped the table with his pen and checked his watch. "We're still waiting for Detective Courtney Henkins, from Northeast Community. She was lead on the Callahan murder case." He exhaled his usual whiff of halitosis and sighed. "Let's go over what we've got so far, shall we?"

Wobbling his head, Satish gave a brief summary of the crime scene, field interviews, and the declarations left by the witnesses on Amy's case, topping it with Vargas's profile and the little chat we just had with the guy. Over the whole account, Washburn pinched the hairs beneath his lower lip, eyes fixed on either his notepad or the crime scene diagrams in the open murder book. He spent a long time staring at the autopsy pictures and, from to time, scribbled a handful of words on his notepad in a convoluted and illegible handwriting.

Only when Satish had finally covered everything did Washburn raise his gray eyes, deep set beneath eaves of gray brows, and said, "I don't believe Vargas is your killer."

I straightened up, but before I could utter any word of protest, the door sprang open.

"Sorry I'm late." A short, hefty woman strode inside the room and noisily dragged a chair away from the table. "Henkins," she said, taking a seat. "Northeast Community." She peered through small, blue eyes, a defiant face parched like a fig after a drought. "So. What did I miss?"

She smelled of whiskey, dog drool, and lull days spent at the beach.

Jeez, I need to retire too.

Despite Washburn's icy presence, the temperature in the

room rose drastically. Lady cops are their own breed. They want to be treated equally, which means there's no way to handle them right. If you assume they're gay, turns out they're not, but if you don't, sure as hell they are.

Satish broke the silence. He wore his most polished smile, leaned across the table, and stretched out his hand. "Satish Cooper," he said, over Henkins's unconvinced handshake. "And this is my partner, Track Presius. We took over the Liu case and were hoping to learn more from you about the Callahan murder."

A classy man, my partner.

Henkins sized him up. "You a lady's man, ain't you? Sure, I can tell you about the Callahan case. It generated a lot of hoopla last January. It was a career case. The press was all over it, all the boys in the division wanted it, and I was the one in line to get the call. They stuck me with a gung-ho rookie who did his best to ruin the case, and then they all shrugged when it became yet another sixty-dayer to turn in." She leaned forward on the table and crossed her arms. "Anything else you'd like to know?"

I fetched a paperclip from my pocket, straightened it, and stuck it in my mouth. "Poodle?" I asked.

She cocked her head and studied my face. "Terrier," she replied.

"Female," I said.

Henkins indulged in a hint of a smile. "Name's Pearl. Got her from the shelter five years ago."

I reciprocated the courtesy. "Mine's a mutt. Half shepherd, half Labrador. Do you believe Olsen killed Callahan?"

The hinted smile disintegrated. "We all did at the time, didn't we?"

At the other end of the table, a long wrinkle bolted across Gomez's forehead. "Well, then," he said. "Now that we've greased our way across divisions and established a path of collaboration, maybe Dr. Washburn can proceed to expose his thoughts on the kind of offender we're dealing with."

Washburn cleared his throat. He took two pictures of the bodies, placed them side-to-side in the middle of the table, and said, "There's a good chance we're dealing with the same offender."

The wave of heat Henkins had brought in chilled instantly.

"Well that's good news," Henkins said. "You guys get to reopen my sixty dayer."

Eyes fixed on the two photos in front of him, Washburn pried open the killer's mind for us, and the more he talked, the more I became convinced the shrink had a secret admiration for the asshole we were trying to catch.

"This offender is organized and methodical. He's smart, possibly highly educated and well inserted in society. Think of individuals like Dr. Michael Swango, a physician and former U.S. Marine. Or Dennis Rader, the BTK strangler: he was in the air force for four years, happily married, and a deacon in his local parish. By destroying the victim's face, our killer dominates his prey. He wants to annihilate his victims' identity, make them a nobody."

A respectful silence followed. Gomez doodled pensively while running a hand across his wide forehead. Henkins bobbed her head in assent. Washburn drained his glass of water and resumed his spiel. "He probably takes his time after each killing. He's still rehearsing his ritual, as demonstrated by the escalation in the second killing. To offenders like this one, a crime scene is a work of art. It becomes his shrine. He's still practicing, though. He didn't get enough satisfaction from the first kill, not enough attention. So this time he leaves us a message, the four tiles.

Why four? What do the colors mean? I'm afraid we won't be able to answer these questions until he kills again.

"There's no sexual act. No rape, no sign he masturbates at the scene. His orgasm is reached with the kill. We're looking at somebody with a dominating mother and an absent or indifferent father.

"His interest in the second victim's feet and scalp is fascinating. I wonder if we're dealing with another foot fetish, like Jerry Brudos. I see a man who's struggling with his emotions. He wants more from each victim, exploring new ways to get greater pleasure. Searching for new ways to get his orgasm, if you will. I can see the violence escalating, moving up to full mutilation. Taking the scalp could be just the beginning. The cooling off period between killings may shorten. He's already gone from using the acid on the body to marring the victim while still alive. Next time, he might take the victim's feet as souvenirs, to relive the pleasure. When the police searched Brudos's home, they found two amputated breasts he was using as paperweights. This is how these offenders operate. Our killer is not there yet. He's still learning."

"One hell of a learning experience," I said.

Washburn shunned me with his glacial stare, while his index finger caressed the corner of one of the autopsy photos. "We're just seeing the tip of the iceberg, Detectives. This offender has killed before—maybe got to practice with pets, or prostitutes—and I have no doubt he will kill again."

From a dark corner in my head, a voice whispered in my ear.

Once a killer, always a killer.

The voice smelled of rusty metal and rancid food, of stiff air, moldy walls and ancient sweat, of—

Washburn snapped his folder closed. "Expect more killings. These offenders are predators and summer is their hunting season."

And with that, the temperature in the room dropped to freezing.

No wonder Washburn never yielded a drop of sweat.

* * *

Satish shook his head. "Breasts as paperweights. How sick is that?"

"By the end of the meeting I could've used my balls as a door stop," I replied.

"Still not getting along with Washburn, are you?"

"The man doesn't have a scent."

He lined the little boxes of Chinese take-out on his desk and laughed. Wafts of chicken, steamed rice and tempura tickled my nostrils.

"Come on," I said. "So Vargas's not our man and we need to look for an educated and polished guy with a double life. Are we supposed to take all this as gospel?"

Satish split his chopsticks and dipped them into his rice box. "I'm with Washburn on this one, Track. South Central was my beat for five years back when I was a street copper. People out there die for nothing. A carjacking, a drive-by, a dispute over dealing turf. They shoot and run. They don't do acid—*that* kind of acid anyway." He pointed the chopsticks at me. "This ain't a South Central crime."

The sun was coming down, blinking through the Venetian blinds and bathing the walls in a warm, pinkish light.

I dug into my box of teriyaki. Save for the watch commander, the squad room had already been vacated. A few Rape Special detectives were working late in the room next door, dicks like us beating the trail while still hot.

"For that matter," I said, plopping a chunk of beef in my

72

mouth, "this ain't a sexual crime, either, despite what scentless Washburn says. He may have all those books to back him up, and all those hours spent picking brains back at the joint, but I've got my practical experience."

"It doesn't have to be rape to be sexual."

"That's not what I'm saying. Think about the Broadway murder, two summers ago. Victim found sprawled on the floor, naked, stabbed twenty-nine times, of which fourteen in the groin. Her clothes were never found."

Sat took a long swig of Coke. "I remember that. The killer stabbed her eyes, too. There's no knife here, but there's acid, which serves the same purpose."

I made a face. "Yeah, but he takes off the socks and then backs away. What the hell, now that he's killed her he gets frigid?"

"You've heard Washburn. The guy's still exploring."

I swallowed another chunk of meat. "The Jane Doe down in Baldwin. Naked, again, stabbed in the groin and chest. Left breast missing, right nipple bitten off. Sat, these perps go for the stuff they can't get from women—that's why they kill them. Our guy isn't interested in any of that. He's got a different agenda, and he leaves the tiles behind to tease us."

Satish shrugged, my argument no more convincing than Washburn's. "He's just not there yet. He's got a repressed Oedipus complex."

"Bullshit. Guesswork based on some theory that we all want to murder our fathers and fuck our mothers." I scraped the bottom of my food box and sucked the last noodle. "Oedipus's myth isn't about that."

Sat squashed his box, drained his Coke, then tossed everything in the trash. "No? What's it about, then?"

"About a bunch of fools who thought they could get away from their own fate. Truth is, no matter how hard you try, your fate is always gonna come back to bite your ass."

Satish crossed his arms and leaned back, one of his dreamy smiles plastered across his face. "Sounds like somethin' my old man would've said."

He said nothing else for a little while, the skin between his brows pinched together like pizza dough. "You know what this reminds me of, Track?"

I rose and slid my jacket on. "Can't wait to hear it," I said.

He gave me a puzzled look. "Jeez. You missed me that bad, huh?"

"In some twisted sort of way."

Our steps resonated in the deserted hallway.

Strange night to be catching a faceless killer.

Satish was lost in one of his stories. "It reminds me of *prasada*," he said.

But then again, all killers are faceless and all summer nights have a tendency to be strange.

"*Prasada?*" I repeated.

Satish pressed the elevator call button and bobbed his head. "It means 'cooking for the gods.' It's a big deal in India. There's a whole ritual that goes with it: you have to thoroughly wash before and after cooking. You can't taste the food while you make it. You're supposed to meditate and pray as you cook. And you can't eat until after the gods have eaten."

"Good luck with that."

The elevator chimed, the doors slid open and we stepped inside. "As always, you miss the point, Track. Ma would make *rasgulla* to please the gods. She'd place two or three in a special plate and set the plate in front of the altar. After that, we'd all bow our heads and close our eyes while she'd recite *Om Namo Narayanaya* over the rumble of our empty stomachs. When done reciting all prayers, she'd return the food to the kitchen and we could finally eat."

"So, the gods wouldn't literally eat the food?"

Satish winked. "Except one time they did."

We exited the elevator. The lobby was dimly lit and had the distinct smell of old building material and wood decay, mixed with remnants of fried beans from back when the cafeteria was there.

Outside, hot air yawned in our faces. I jingled my car keys and pondered. It was past dinnertime, the honks of traffic had tapered off, and downtown was cloaked in a hazy sunset. Cruisers at the end of their shifts turned into the San Pedro parking lot, while others left to prowl the night beats. Pink clouds spilled into the sky and reflected off the glass façade of Parker Center.

"Ma threw a fit when she opened her eyes and one ball of *rasgulla* was missing. And then she started the investigation. Except, she already knew the perpetrator."

"She did?"

"Well, me and my brother, we always got excited about *rasgullas*. We helped Ma make them, but we were forbidden to even lick our fingers. It was torture."

"So you ate one?"

"Uh-uh, we did not. But Ma was convinced we did. Our hands were sticky and there was sugar on our cheeks. She sent us to our room. The gods were very mad at us."

I winked. "I thought the gods had eaten the missing *rasgulla*."

Satish walked to his car and unlocked it. "Not the gods. Our baby sister Rhani, who'd just started crawling. My old man came back from work, picked her up, and asked, 'Why is Rhani's face all sticky with sugar?'" Satish chuckled, unlocked his car and slid behind the wheel.

"I see," I said. "So your mom had the perfect profile for the perpetrator, except it led her to the wrong suspects."

Satish scrunched his brows together. "Perfect profile? What are you talking about?"

"You said this is what our meeting with Washburn reminded you of!"

He wobbled his head and started the car. "Oh, that. Nah. I just miss my old man is all." And with that, he backed out of his parking spot, bade me goodnight, and drove off, leaving me to cradle my own thoughts on profiling, murder suspects, and what the hell I wanted in life.

Once a killer, always a killer.

Danny Mendoza. I slit his throat when I was sixteen. And then stabbed his eyes. Except I recalled nothing of that. All I recalled was his slurred voice, his breath heavy with dope and nicotine, telling me how he'd tortured fourteen-year-old Lily Germano, how he made her beg for her life, before he closed a noose around her neck and strangled her.

The judge denied bail based on the cruelty of the crime. Every Monday of my one-month pretrial term, the jail psychiatrist came to the interview room with his perfectly knotted tie and clean-shaven face. He smelled of sugarcoated lies and ordinary mediocrity, of unexciting sex and conventional middle-class life, of a suburban two-story home with a blonde wife installed on the front doorsteps.

Of everything I never had growing up. And he was staring at me, judging me.

I have no doubt.

He smelled so damned normal.

The nights I'd spent curled up in a dirty cot, heavy steps echoing in the background. Keys rattling, inmates moaning, kids—just like me—screeching, sneering, snoring, crying, wrapped in vicious smells that crawled under my skin, into my bones…

You know nothing about it, I snarled. *Nothing.*

My rage churned a smile out of his thin lips. His finger

slid toward the panic button, poised.

Killing fulfills your anger, Ulysses, doesn't it?

I *did* kill again. As a cop, clean shootings. Yet that triumphant little smile of his came back every time I pulled the trigger, like a feather tickling the inside of my ego. To remind me what I am. And what I'll never be.

No matter how hard you try, fate is always gonna come back to bite your ass.

Like Oedipus.

It's in your genes, Ulysses, your fate switched when you were six... Every time you collect a new trophy, it reminds you of what you are.

And what you'll never be.

SIX

Wednesday, July 1

"I hear your man did it again." Malcolm Olsen squinted his small, beetle eyes trying to look earnest. He was trying too hard. A wrinkle on his left cheek curled around the corner of his mouth and came to rest on his chin like an old scar. He leaned back against the wall, laced his fingers across his stomach and smirked. A smirk never looks good in an orange jumpsuit, especially the kind that has CDCR—California Department of Corrections and Rehabilitation—embroidered over the breast pocket.

Satish sat at the long end of the table, facing the white cinder block wall, and I at the short end, opposite from Olsen. There were no windows, only a gray, heavy metal door, and a cc camera looking down on us from one corner of the ceiling. A bounty of disinfectant sprays lingered over all surfaces and yet failed to cover the stale smells of recirculating air, un-showered humanity, and general ripeness that permeated the place.

I undid the knot of my tie. It didn't help much—the nausea had already kicked in. It didn't matter that I was wearing civilian clothes instead of an orange jumpsuit, or that the hogs—jail guards—nodded at me instead of sneering and yelling to my face. The nausea kicked in as soon as Satish and I walked through the double metal doors and a correctional officer handed us our visitor badges.

Smells remain engraved in the brain like lovers' initials on a tree—long after the love is gone.

Satish plucked a pack of cigarettes out of his shirt pocket, opened it, and set the offering on the table in front of Olsen. "We're not sure, Mr. Olsen," he said. "A birdie told us *you* might have something to do with Charlie Callahan's murder."

Olsen squinted. He shot his chin up and regarded both Satish and me very carefully. His complexion had absorbed the dull and gray color of the walls. A sagging wrinkle across his neck was reminiscent of his pre-jail chubbiness. Brown hearing aids sat behind his ears—from a trauma or genetic condition, I guessed, as he didn't look older than fifty. He picked up the pack of cigarettes, plucked one out, and pocketed the rest. Satish produced a lighter and lit his cig. I inhaled and held my breath. I couldn't hold for too long and eventually resigned to yet another reek filling up the room.

"I didn't do the fag," Olsen said, sucking on his cig.

"We heard you weren't exactly fond of him, either," I interjected.

Olsen unplugged the cigarette from his mouth and blew smoke toward me. I made a face. He stretched his lips and showed me two rows of yellow teeth, too small for his big mouth. "You don't smoke, Detective?"

"Hate the smell," I said.

His lips stretched further.

Satish rapped his fingers on the table. "My partner gets easily irritated. I suggest you help us out, Mr. Olsen, so you can enjoy your cigarette and we can be out of here soon."

Olsen wiped the smile off his face. "What's in it for me?"

I shifted in my chair. "Besides the cigarettes?"

Satish sent me a sideways glance. "We can talk to people, Mr. Olsen," he said. "We're after Amy Liu's killer, whether the killer did it again, like you say, or he's just a copycat. Help us out and we'll help you out."

Olsen shook his cigarette and tiny flakes of ashes fluttered to the ground. "I already said what I know. To the other cops. They didn't help me out. Why would you guys be any different?"

Nausea crawled from my stomach up to my throat. I banged a hand on the table in frustration.

Olsen leaned forward and locked his eyes onto mine. "You hate it here, Detective, don't you? You hate it just like me. You hate the smells, I can tell from your face. The banging, the shouting, the moaning—I don't care for any of that." He shrugged and tapped the hearing aid behind his right ear. "I just turn these off and I can forget all of that. But the smells..." He sucked on the last bit of his cigarette, dropped it to the floor and crushed it with the tip of his shoe. "Can't tune out the smells. Urine. Shit, from when the smart asses clog the latrines. Sweat. Freaking disgusting."

"I hear Vacaville is better, Mr. Olsen," Satish said. "We can get you a transfer. Tell us what you told the other cops and we'll work from there."

Olsen lifted his chin and squinted. He dipped a hand in his pocket and plucked a new cigarette out of the pack. This time Satish didn't reach for the lighter.

I pushed my chair backwards and got to my feet. "We're

wasting our time, Sat," I said and walked to the door.

Olsen stuck the cigarette between his lips. "Nail polish," he said.

I turned and looked at him.

"It's your clue. I told the other cops, too, but they didn't believe me. There was a car that night. I saw it when I walked the dog. An Oldsmobile Alero, black, one of the older models. The driver was smoking. When I walked by, he rolled up the window and left. And I smelled nail polish after the car."

"Nail polish?" Satish repeated.

He snapped. "What do you expect from homos?"

Satish asked, "You got a plate number?"

"Arizona plates. That's all I remember."

I strode back to the table, turned the chair around, and straddled it. "What night, Olsen? If you're gonna help, you might as well try a little harder than some manicure bullshit."

His lips closed around the cigarette butt, his eyes smirked. "The night the fag got whacked, of course."

I banged a hand on the table. "Wrong," I said. "According to your wife, the night Callahan was killed you stepped out to walk the dog at least one hour before the murder. If you saw the car leave—"

"So? He could've driven around the block and come back. Like he'd done the week before. And the one before, again. Same car. Same vague nail polish smell."

Satish straightened up and leaned both elbows on the table. "And why do you believe this guy in the Alero was after Callahan, Mr. Olsen?"

Olsen bit on the cigarette and narrowed his eyes. "Couple weeks earlier. Car was there. Fag comes out of his house and sees it. He gets nervous. Starts walking away. Car follows him. They talk. Doesn't look good."

"You hear what they say?"

He flashed us a yellow grin. "Uh-uh. That's when I yelled 'Go away fags' at them and the car vanished."

The grin got wider and prouder.

My stomach knotted. I pushed the chair away from the table and walked to the door. The correctional officer waiting outside the interview room shot to his feet.

"Is everything okay, Detective?"

"Your closest restroom," I said.

I didn't bother latching the stall door behind me. I kicked up the lid, bent on my knees, and retched.

* * *

"A smell for a clue?" Satish protested.

"All my clues are smells," I replied.

"Oh, please. Nail polish? If at least he'd given us a license plate..."

"Smoked meth smells like acetone, nail polish remover. Weren't there traces of meth in Callahan's pockets?"

Satish shook his head. "To you it may smell like that. The only thing I smell around meth users is their armpits."

"I'm not the only one with a sensitive nose. The guy wears hearing aids. If he can't hear, chances are he's got a good sense of smell."

Satish shrugged. "Nail polish in a black Alero. He could've smelled it from some girl doing her nails with her feet propped against the window. That's as helpful as a cell phone without signal."

The foggy, cooler days of June were over. It was ten in the morning and downtown was a sweltering pot of metal, smog, and asphalt. In a few weeks, the wildfires would start raging the foothills, adding a new fragrance to the mix.

We left Starbucks at the corner with First and crossed

the street toward Parker Center, our headquarters, Satish sipping his iced latte, and I savoring the aftertaste of a double shot espresso.

I said, "The whole scalping and skin removal has me wondering. Why wasn't Charlie Callahan scalped? I'm not buying the theory that the guy had worked out a new ritual the second time around—that the first time he acted on instinct, and the second time he had more time to plan ahead."

"That's because that theory came from Washburn, and you don't like Washburn. Olsen will never admit to whacking Callahan. He knows we've got nothing on him."

"But then why risk it and give us a bogus story?"

We walked a few steps without saying anything.

"June's gone already," I said, squinting through sunglasses.

"You know," Satish replied, "Cohen was right about the scalping. I looked it up. Apparently, the colonists scalped Native Americans and sometimes even stripped them of their skin. Native Americans started it as retaliation."

I considered. "What he did to Amy didn't look like retaliation."

Satish sucked from his straw and nodded. "I agree. Cohen said it himself, it was a meticulous and careful job."

A DASH bus stopped by the curb. I raised my voice over the growling of the engine. "You said Katie looked up scalping in the databases and found nothing."

"She tried both VICAP and NCIC," Satish said, "and found a gruesome case in Montana. The victim was not only scalped but also skinned and partly mutilated. Her husband was convicted two years later."

The NCIC and VICAP were national investigative repositories for all violent crimes in the country. If scalping had been done before in some other crime or murder, all details of the case and the investigation would have been indexed and filed in at least one of the databases.

My eyes strayed from the bus, now closing its doors and attempting to merge back into traffic, and the shiny façade of Parker Center, a lonely cloud reflecting off its windows. A van from one of the L.A. news station was parked in front of one of our patrol cars.

"They're prowling again," I commented.

Satish nodded. Now that the Callahan case was back in the news, the news vultures had come back to the nest.

The rattling of a jackhammer joined the honks of downtown traffic. Workers were replacing the old memorial monument with a forest of metal tubes — some sleek concept by the firm Northrop Grumman Space and Missions Systems. Together with the new headquarters about to open up, it was all part of the beautification of our over one-hundred-and-fifty-year-old agency. Our façade was being polished and refreshed, yet the bureaucratic loopholes kept tightening, the brass was aging, and our crime labs were still understaffed and overburdened.

We walked past the fenced off area and inside the building. Under the skeptical brows of the watch officers, two cameramen were wrestling their equipment through the metal detector. Satish and I snuck right behind them and took the elevator down to Property Division, where all evidence from cold and closed cases was stored until they could either be officially released or used for court proceedings.

An officer checked our badges and scribbled our numbers on the visitor log. She looked neither black nor white, neither young nor old. Her inflection was from the valley, her stance from the city.

We walked down a long corridor. The waiting room to Jail Division was located at the opposite end, and we could clearly hear the bickering of family members in line to visit their relatives. A man shouted he'd been waiting for more than an hour to see his son. An officer replied his son had been waiting in the joint for more than one year, so he could wait a few minutes longer.

The evidence room was small and windowless. Four boxes sat on a round, metal table. They all bore the LAPD stamp and the additional labels, "Charlie Callahan, case ID XCV56, submitted by Det. C. Henkins."

"The evidence on the Callahan case, as you requested," the officer said. "All his personal items are here. We contacted the family to see if they wanted it, but they replied we could burn it all." She gave us a quick glance that meant, "Do you have any questions?" Relieved to see that we didn't, she took off.

Satish hooked his hands on his belt and took a deep breath. "Well—looks like we'll be in here for a while."

I leaned across the table and pulled one of the boxes closer.

"Look at the bright side," I said. "Chances are, by the time we're done, the news crews up on our floor will be long gone from Parker Center."

Satish flopped on the chair across from me, loosened the knot of his tie, and pulled out the field reports. "They'll come back," he said. "They always do."

We sorted through the victim's clothing, field notes, pictures, crime sketches. In the inventory, we found Callahan's apartment floor plans marked with all the places from where evidence had been taken.

"What's in the box that says 'Digital'?"

I craned my head and looked inside. "CDs. Couple of jump drives."

He reached for the box and looked for himself. "No laptop?"

I shook my head. "Does the inventory say laptop somewhere?"

Reading glasses precariously hanging from the tip of his nose, Satish flipped through the pages of the inventory. "Home desktop."

"Was it seized?" I asked.

Satish frowned, flipped more pages, then dropped his chin and stared at the boxes on the table from above the rim of his reading glasses. "Well, it does say they looked at emails and personal documents, but I don't see no computer here."

I sifted through the box of CDs, mentally counting. There were about a dozen data CDs and a couple of jump drives. "Maybe it's still at Electronics. Did they find anything interesting?"

"Personal emails to friends. Nothing out of the ordinary or raising flags. All data on the CDs was from work." He clicked his tongue. "Browsing history didn't raise any red flags either, apart from the usual gay and lesbian internet rooms and the men-seeking-men pages on Craigslist."

I pushed away the box with the digital evidence and went through Callahan's personal belongings. "Tell me something I don't know. I've seen those ads. Those loons, they hook up, get high on meth, and fuck for three straight days. When they wake up they have HIV. Where did he work?"

Satish went back to his notes. "*Used* to work for a local web design company."

"Positive on a drug test?" said judgmental me.

"Nope. Been laid off last fall. The company was going through a hard time. Track, there wasn't any meth in his veins and no drugs were found in his apartment. The only traces found were from his pockets."

"You're thinking planted?"

86

"I don't know what I'm thinking. It just doesn't add up."

I fished several things out of the personal belongings box: prescription drugs, a battered leather wallet with no cash but several credit cards, a box of condoms, an address book with only three entries. I brought each item to my nose. They smelled of overused deodorant and cheap perfume, of dog hairs and passive smoke. They smelled forlorn.

"No cell phone among his personal items. Who doesn't have a cell phone these days?"

Satish went back to his notebook. "The murder book says, 'Missing.' The killer probably took it. Phone logs were subpoenaed but all they got was the usual calls to friends, plus a couple of businesses."

"What about his family?"

"Family lives back in Georgia and hasn't spoken to him ever since he's moved to California."

"Loving family." I plucked the prescription drugs out of the box—four orange pill bottles—and brought them to my nose before examining the labels. They had all been issued by a J. Thompson, MD, except for the last one, which bore the name A. Liu, MD.

Ha.

The label had peeled off at the corner and the only surviving part of Callahan's name was the C. I opened it and sniffed inside. Didn't smell familiar.

"Hey," Satish said, "this is interesting. Callahan was laid off on September fifth, last year."

"Right around Labor Day. Very thoughtful of his employer."

Satish glanced me from above the rim of his reading glasses. "Here's the thing, though. According to his monthly bank statements, he's made bi-weekly cash deposits starting October twenty-first. Amounts vary, but they all seem to be around five-hundred, give or take a few bucks."

"Unemployment benefits?"

"Nah, those are much less. One-twenty, direct deposit from the state every two weeks. The rest are cash deposits he made himself."

"When was the last one?"

He turned the page over. "Looks like—January third."

I leaned back in my chair. "Hmm. He was killed on the thirtieth."

Satish tapped his notebook with the tip of his pen. "There are many non-kosher ways one can get by in L.A."

"Yeah, and most get you killed. What's going through your mind, Sat?"

He sneered, white teeth and all. "How 'bout a date at the Belmont, you and I?"

My left brow shot up. The Belmont used to be a gay bar at Fifth and Main—Satish's beat back when he was a street copper.

"I'm too picky to go on a date with you, Sat," I replied. "Besides, they tore it down five years ago."

He shook his head and sighed. "Skid row is not what it used to be anymore. At least the Regent is still there. You know, one day—"

"One day you chased a loon inside the Regent and it was all dark and your shoes were popping on the floor because it was covered in manly goo," I said. "Yes, Sat, I know. I think you told me that story a thousand times."

The Regent was a porn theater right next to the Belmont. Certain things come in pairs, like balls.

"Did I tell you that when me and my partner shouted, 'Freeze, asshole,' they *all* shot their hands up in the air?"

"Yeah, you told me that part too. Look. We should get ahold of Callahan's computer, find out what user name he had on Craigslist, post an ad in his name, and see what happens. In the meantime, will you look at the label on this prescription bottle?" I rolled the pill bottle from the Liu doctor over to him.

He smiled dreamily and picked up the bottle from the table. His eyes were still chasing memories. "Me and my partner, we started arguing on who was supposed to frisk the suspect." He chuckled. "His zipper was still—"

"Down" I leaned back in my chair and laced my fingers. "You told me that part too."

Satish stared at the label on the prescription bottle. "Man," he said. "Can't read anymore. As I grow older, I don't get any younger."

"Seems to be a common problem. Look at the doc's name in there—A. Liu. What do you make of that?"

"You're thinking *Amy* Liu?"

"Didn't you say she specialized in HIV?"

Satish checked the evidence log. "Hmm. Strange. The pill bottle doesn't seem to be logged in here. There's a lot of Liu's in L.A. If it really was Amy Liu, wouldn't Henkins mention the connection?"

I dropped my chin. "You sure about that?"

Antagonism between divisions was no secret, especially when cases got transferred to the RHD. Even in the hottest investigations, battles for turf often turned into hold-ups and innuendos.

Satish rose to his feet and put Callahan's bank statements back inside the evidence box. "Whether or not Henkins keeps her secrets, it's worth checking out. Let's go, I think we've seen enough for now."

Man, I love my agency. Old fashioned bureaucracy and solid spirit of cooperation.

* * *

The jagged skyline of Bunker Hill emerged through a film of haze. A chopper circled over Dodger Stadium, the Five below a ten-lane river snaking into downtown. All around, under a yellow dome of smog, treetops and palm fronds speckled the expanse of buildings and houses.

Another sizzling day in the City of Angels.

"Nice view," I said, tapping the windowpane. "The glass could use some cleaning, though."

Satish slammed a drawer closed and opened a second one. "We'll put a memo in the murder book."

The building was new—the latest addition to the UTech medical campus in Boyle Heights. It hosted genomics labs on the lower floors, and offices and conference rooms on the upper ones. Construction had begun five years earlier and stalled several times until one of the most affluent UTech alumni, philanthropist Amintore Schnell, poured a stunning fifty million donation into the completion of the project. Eight months later, the Schnell Molecular Genomics Core saw its grand opening—another sleek tower rising from the hills of Boyle Heights.

Amy Liu's office was long and narrow, with skewed walls that made the furniture sit at weird angles. The wall facing west was a floor-to-ceiling windowpane looking over downtown, a view Amy hid behind stacks of research papers, a printer and two computer screens. Somebody had left flowers next to her keyboard, and needles of dried-up petals spilled over her desk.

Having found nothing of interest in her drawers, Satish moved to a metal file cabinet standing against the north wall between two armchairs upholstered in red.

I knew Amy's killer had taken something from her home office. I'd detected the sweet, almost nauseating odor from the tiles on a pile of papers on her home desk. What if he hadn't found what he'd been looking for? What if he came back here, to her work office, searching for more? I perused the small room trying to detect the same scent, but all I got was fresh paint from the walls and formaldehyde from the brand new bookshelves. I sat in her chair, flipped through the stacks of papers and sniffed her keyboard, mouse, pens. Same result: only the victim's smell, mixed with the artificial scent of medical labs.

On one of the shelves was a picture of Amy Liu surrounded by a bunch of other docs, all in white coats, stethoscopes dangling from their necks, arms crossed, and confident smiles sprawled across their handsome faces. They looked like they'd come straight out of a highway billboard.

"Do doctors live in soaps?"

Satish fished some papers out of one of the cabinet drawers and leafed through. "Let me tell you something, Track. When I was eight, I told my mom I wanted to be a doctor. She laughed and I was hurt. I said, *Why, Ma? You think I'm not smart enough?*

"*Oh, you're smart all right.* She patted my head and kissed me on the forehead. *But doctors need to be handsome, honey.*"

"Of course," Satish went on, "she changed her mind ten years later when I told her I wanted to be a cop."

"She was happy, I suppose?"

He sighed. "She was devastated."

"What? Why?"

"People in India don't generally like cops. My old man, though, was thrilled. He thought a cop in the family is always a good insurance plan. I ended up being an ABCD cop."

I stood by the door and looked down the hallway. "ABCD?"

"American-Born Confused Desi."

The hallway was a long corridor with curving walls.

Whoever designed the place had an issue with straight angles.

"Hey, Sat," I said. "I'm gonna take a look around, 'kay?"

Satish didn't reply. He went on opening and closing drawers and mumbling within himself about India, cops, and strange alphabet acronyms.

The bending corridor converged into a lobby with tall windowpanes that once again displayed the same, hazy view of downtown and Bunker Hill. On the opposite side was a reception area enclosed by a sleek, semi-circular desk. Two rows of black leather chairs faced one another in the waiting area. A kid with a few chin hairs and a lot of pimples sat in one of the chairs. He stared intently at the screen of his cell phone tapping it with his thumbs. The thumbs were a blur, the rest of him was as still as a statue.

A hand slid across the reception desk and pushed a clipboard toward me. "Your name and who you've got your appointment with." A pen followed. "Insurance information in the second sheet."

And then *a scent* happened. It wafted my way in little, syncopated waves—the smell of salty, sun-bathed skin, and the balmy fragrance of an exotic beach. *She* appeared shortly after, hips humming and calves flexing under the hem of a lab coat. They were nice calves, the kind your eyes trip over when jogging at the shore.

The syncopated scent buzzed in my ears at the rhythm of Jobim's tune *The Girl from Ipanema*.

"Mr. Cress?"

Ipanema Girl stood with a clipboard clutched to her chest, the wake of her scent crooning in my head. From the row of black leather seats, a man raised his head, blinked a couple of times then returned his attention to the magazine on his lap. The kid with the cell phone froze his thumbs for a fraction of a second.

"Mr. Cress?" Ipanema Girl asked, squeezing the clipboard to her chest.

Her eyes rested on me, hopeful.

Hell, you don't disappoint a girl like that.

I smiled, she smiled back. "Right this way, Mr. Cress," she said, cocking her head to the side and letting a black lock brush her long neck.

And who was I not to follow?

She crossed the waiting room, heads turning as she *gently swayed* by the rows of chairs.

The tune hummed in my head and somehow escaped my lips.

"Sorry, did you just say something?"

I froze. "Me? Er—no."

Her black lashes fluttered and her brows knitted together, the faintest ripple crossing her forehead. She beckoned to a small room fitted with a chair, a scale, gray cabinets, and educational posters on safe sex, condom use, and HIV.

Very romantic.

"Since this is your first appointment," she explained, wrapping a sphygmomanometer cuff around my right arm, "Dr. Swanson will do a physical first." Her hands were cold and smelled of pineapple lotion, her breath of watermelon. The girl was a fruit basket.

"Actually, I'm not here for an appointment." I fished out my badge wallet with my left hand and flipped it open. "Presius, LAPD Homicide."

Her smile evaporated like rain from a dry storm. Her lips tightened. She said nothing and kept pumping air into the cuff until it was about to pop. My fingers went numb from lack of blood flow.

"Your BP's too high," she finally sentenced, before removing the cuff from my arm. "You could've told me.

Now I have to go find the *real* Mr. Cress." She flopped on the chair across from me and sighed. Her scent drifted my way, now spiced with the staccato of her adrenaline.

The girl's musical and *vengeful.*

She shook her head and bit hard on her lower lip. "It's about Amy, isn't it?"

I nodded, put away my badge and gave her a minute. Her name—Leilani—was embroidered on the front pocket of her coat.

She pulled a tissue from a box on the countertop and crumpled it in her hands. "Amy was so nice," she whispered. "What happened to her is chilling. Gives me nightmares. How could this happen... Everybody loved her here at work. *Everybody.*"

The pen she'd left by the clipboard rolled off the countertop and on the floor. She considered picking it up, then bit her lip again and didn't move.

"Did anybody love her a little too much?"

Leilani wrung the tissue in her hands. "You mean romantically? No." She shook her head, her hair releasing a cantabile of fragrances. João Gilberto started humming again in my head.

"Are you sure about that?"

She gave me the "women-know-better" look. "Amy was gorgeous. I'm sure she had her suitors. But she once told me she got her life back after her divorce. She loved her independence and wasn't going to make the same mistake again. Her life was divided between the lab and her patients. We're the busiest HIV clinic in L.A. county."

"What kind of lab work did she do?"

Her eyes widened. "You don't know about Dr. Lyons's vaccine?"

"I tend to be more up-to-date on murders than vaccines," I said.

She tilted her head and looked at me with a mix of pity and disappointment. "Dr. Lyons is the director of the clinic. He patented a revolutionary vaccine to cure HIV. It took him years to get it tested. The FDA wouldn't give him the approval until—I think it was two years ago—he made the news by injecting himself at Vaccine International, a yearly world conference on vaccines. It was all over the news." She paused, searched my face for some kind of recognition. It didn't come. "We started recruiting patients and high-risk subjects for phase one trials ten months ago."

"Patients? Aren't patients *already* HIV-positive?"

"Yes, but that's the point. We want to see if the vaccine can cure them from AIDS."

I considered. One doctor, a revolutionary vaccine, two murders.

"Did you ever meet a patient named Charlie Callahan?"

Leilani's dark eyes narrowed. "No. But I heard what happened to him. There's no words, really." Her lips curled. By then, the tissue in her hands had disintegrated.

"I heard he was a patient of Dr. Liu's," I said.

She tilted her head. "Amy's? No, I would have seen him personally—just like I should've seen Mr. Cress." She served me a long, stern glance. I thought of how she'd cut the blood flow in my arm with the sphygmomanometer and figured she wasn't one to argue with. "I'm not sure who was seeing Charlie Callahan, here at the clinic, but I know he had enrolled in our clinical trial. Patty said she recognized the name."

"Who's Patty?"

"Patty Roberts. She's in charge of enrolling patients in the study—when they agree, that is. She explains everything to them, does the paperwork, and hands them the questionnaires. Everybody here at the clinic was outraged when we learned he'd been killed by a homophobic. We all have friends, family members or patients who are gay."

I crossed my arms. "What did Patty tell you exactly?"

"That she remembered him because he told her he'd come in to see Dr. Lyons, but Dr. Lyons no longer accepts new patients. Callahan ended up seeing a different doctor."

"Do you know who?"

She shook her head. "Could've been either Dr. Swanson or Dr. Thompson."

Thompson, I thought. I remembered the name from one of the other prescription bottles in Callahan's evidence boxes.

"Could Amy have signed one of Callahan's prescriptions even though he wasn't her patient? Don't doctors in the same clinic sign prescriptions for one another when one's not available?"

She shrugged in the loveliest way. "That's possible."

I switched subjects. "Did Amy get along well with Dr. Lyons?"

"Like I said, Amy was very nice to everybody."

"What about Dr. Lyons? Is he nice to everybody?"

Leilani squirmed out of her chair and decided to pick up the pen from the floor right then. "Of course," she said, sitting up again.

"Right," I said. *Like I didn't register the spike in adrenaline in her scent.*

She ran her fingers along the back of her neck and studied me carefully. It was a nice neck, long and slender. "Look. *Mr. Cress*," she teased. "Dr. Lyons is known for making medical students cry. That's just who he is. But he's a good person. He fought really hard for his vaccine to be a success."

"Did he ever make Amy cry?"

Her shoulders drooped. She sighed and looked away.

I leaned forward, her scent singing in my nostrils.

"Leilani. Whatever you just thought of, you need to tell me."

"It probably has nothing to do with anything."

"If that's the case then I'll forget right after you've told me."

She looked down at the shredded tissue in her hands. "Okay. But please don't say I told you this."

I grinned. "I'm a cop, Leilani. I can keep a secret."

"Amy and Dr. Lyons had a heated argument the week she was killed. I don't know what it was about. All I know is that Amy was upset. She stormed out of his office and asked me to wait a few minutes before sending in her next patient. She needed time by herself."

Now the girl was talking. "She didn't say anything about the subject of their discussion?"

Leilani shook her head. "No, but I'm guessing it must've been about the vaccine trial. Like I said, it had become her priority. We're one of six clinics in town recruiting people and handing out consent forms. Especially after the conference two years ago, we've had volunteers pouring into the clinic. Amy cared very much about the study, and Dr. Lyons..." She brought a hand to her earlobe and fiddled with a long earring. "Dr. Lyons has a strong persona but a generous heart. I'm sure whatever disagreement Amy and he had, it was probably nothing. It's a—"

"Look who I found roaming in the hallway."

A nurse in floral scrubs and pink clogs stood by the door. She smelled of soda pops and latex gloves and she tried to look sociable but didn't try too hard. Behind her was a fragile looking little man a hundred and ten years old, give or take a month.

"Mr. Cress went to the loo and couldn't find his way back," the nurse explained. She then looked down on me, scrunched her fine brows together, swayed a large hip to the right and said, "And if this is Mr. Cress—who are you?"

SEVEN

"Heated argument? What heated argument? We brainstormed over the next budget report, that's all. Who gave you that kind of misinformation?"

"We prefer to ask the questions, Doctor," Satish replied.

Dr. Fredrick Lyons walked fast and in long strides. A gaudy Hawaiian tie and the neon green of the reading glasses swinging from his neck intentionally clashed with his white-shirt, black-suit attire. He had longish gray locks, a short beard trimmed close to the jaw, and shrewd eyes that sized us up impatiently, yet found the time to linger over a nice pair of legs as we strode across the curving corridor back to the office suites. He looked too wealthy not to be opinionated, and too smart to be unpretentious.

"I already told you everything: I was the first one to leave the party that night. The other guests can confirm. I was home by midnight. No, I didn't notice anything strange inside or outside her home. She was a pleasant host, cheerful and happy as always. I assume that's what everybody else told you."

"We're not exactly looking for originality, here," I replied. "Just plain old useful information will do."

He stopped and gave me a long, condescending look. "If she and I had such a nasty disagreement the day before, why would I even show up at her party?"

I could think of about a dozen reasons but decided to keep them to myself for the time being.

Lyons shared the front office with Amy Liu—a small corridor where a parched assistant with oversized glasses and a gray hair bun made an anachronistic mismatch with the computer, printer, fax machine and other electronic gadgets she was surrounded with. Her monitor bloomed with so many fingerprints it would've made the Trace lab guys ecstatic.

There was a tall and narrow window facing down on a lateral street. Next to the tall and narrow window were three upholstered chairs, the kind that come in a row, and if the guy sitting at one end has a twitch, you either join the twitch or you go sit somewhere else.

The guy sitting at one end didn't have a twitch, though. He didn't have much of anything, really, he just sat there looking like somebody who's been waiting for so long he's forgotten the reason he got there.

Luckily, Lyons remembered. "What are you doing here, Medina?"

Medina raised his head slowly, almost lethargically. His eyes squinted as if staring into too much light then settled on the reading glasses dangling from Lyons's chest. "I c— came to ask you about the new s—sequences, sir. They're not a—aligned, and if I include them in the s—sample—"

"Of course they're not aligned. That's what I hired you for, to align sequences." Lyons opened the door to his office.

"Did you reply to the crap from reviewer number three?"

Medina rose from his chair and leaned against the wall. He was tall and lanky and kept blinking at the floor as if the light from the ceiling were too bright. "N—not yet. I n— need to include the new s—sequences to r—run the additional tests he asked for."

Lyons stood so close to Medina's face their noses almost touched. "Then go—align—the sequences," he hissed.

Medina blinked at the floor one more time then scuttled off.

Lyons motioned us inside his office. "The man only stutters when he's nervous. Drives me up the wall." He stepped inside and strode to his desk.

Lyons's office was at least twice as large as Amy's, with a hazed view of the San Gabriel Mountains. He retreated behind a curved mahogany desk that smelled as new and expensive as his clothes, and pretended not to be concerned while Satish and I took our time perusing the room.

The place was a bouquet of smells. It took me half a second to pin Lyons's aftershave—poppy and fig fragrance, Italian brand, sixty bucks a bottle. Then came the secretary's perfume, as antiquated as her hairdo. Several other scents weaved in, probably from daily meetings with staff and collaborators. And finally something totally new and foreign, a mix of dry soil and leather, of spiced perspiration and bags of rice...

Two djembe drums sat in one corner of the room. On the shelves, between the numerous books on virology, immunology, microbiology, and a bunch other -ogy's, were wood statuettes of elephants, antelopes, and giraffes. From the wall, next to Lyons's degrees and certifications, stared a row of black African masks, with slits instead of eyes, and long horns coming out of their heads. Woven baskets in vivid colors—bright yellow, red and blue—decorated the desk and coffee table.

The pictures on Lyons's desk displayed images of African children playing barefoot in a dirt lot. In one of the photos, I recognized Lyons standing in front of a hut, next to a tall, skinny man. Half of the man's teeth were missing, as well as most of his hair, yet that didn't deter him from grinning from ear to ear. The next frame depicted a blonde woman in her early forties, heavily made up. She had plenty of hair and teeth, and yet her smile wasn't even half as heartfelt as the grinning guy's standing in front of the hut.

Hair and teeth don't make happiness.

Go tell dentists and hair stylists.

Satish took a seat in one of the leather armchairs. "We understand you and Dr. Liu worked together and discussions came up all the time. We just want to know exactly what it was that you two discussed the day before she was killed."

Lyons shot both hands up in the air in mock surrender. "Fine, fine," he said. "I'm easy, okay? I manage a lot of people and a lot of grant money and as you know, guys managing a lot of people and a lot of grant money don't usually win popularity contests. I don't care, okay? I'm not in this to win a popularity contest. I'm in this to stop a pandemic. So, yes, I'll tell you what our conversation was about. Like I said, despite what you'll hear elsewhere, I'm easy."

I smiled and sat in the chair next to Satish. I had yet to find a witness who admitted to being difficult.

"It was about the vaccine trial." Lyons brought a hand to his mouth and carefully brushed the corners of his goatee. "Amy wanted to change some of the wording on the informational packages we hand out at enrollment. A lot of people come in because they've heard of our study in the news. Amy was worried the wording wasn't clear enough on what they were getting and *not* getting when they enrolled."

Satish took notes.

I raised my opinionated brow. "Of course, injecting yourself in a room filled with paparazzi was a great move to make sure you got a lot of coverage, Dr. Lyons."

The man regarded me with contempt. "Do you know how many years I've waited to see my vaccine finally tested on humans, Detective? Twelve. Twelve long years, during which the number of people living with HIV rose from twenty-five million to thirty-three million. My vaccine was created on a computer instead of harvested from somebody's plasma. I had to perform dozens of tests to show that my strain was viable, stable, and safe." He rolled up the sleeve of his shirt and showed me the inside of his arm. "I poked myself. Yes, it generated a lot of buzz in the news. It was for a good cause."

Satish raised his eyes from his notebook. "Yet Amy was worried?"

"Cautious, I suppose. When people come in they get randomly assigned to either the control group or the study group. So they may or may not get the vaccine, but they're not told what they get. Amy was worried that people could be misled."

Satish's pen squeaked on the notepad. "Her request seems reasonable. Why the altercation, then?"

His right brow shot up. "We go out on a limb to make sure our volunteers get all the information they need. They sign a waiver clearly stating they may not get the vaccine but only a placebo, and even if they get the vaccine, it's still an experimental trial and there's no guarantee it will be protective. And it was not an altercation! We discussed, like we often did."

"Amy was quite upset after your 'discussion'," I

interjected.

Lyons exhaled. "Look. I don't know who you've been talking to. She didn't look upset to me. She didn't like my answer, either—that was clear. Amy is—" He swallowed, inhaled, then tuned his voice down a notch. "Amy *was* a brilliant physician, but sometimes she wanted to do things her way. Well, I happen to be the principal investigator on this study, so she had to back off. I told her so, and we left it at that. No harm done. If she was upset, it wasn't because of something I said."

"And you're pretty certain about that?"

"Absolutely."

I laced my fingers across my lap and smiled my polite smile. I love folks like Lyons. Men who thrive on certainties, whose vocabulary is peppered with phrases like absolutely, most certainly, without any doubt; whose world is split between black and white, liberal and conservative, religious and agnostic, straight and gay. No shades in between.

One of the djembe drums was standing next to my chair so I gave it a little try with the ball of my thumb. It made a nice, round tone.

"Careful with that, Detective. It's handmade."

"You've got a lot of handmade stuff in here, Dr. Lyons."

A proud smile grew on his face like a bad habit. "Souvenirs from my trips to Africa. The southern part of the continent has been hit hard by AIDS. Entire villages spread thin because of the pandemic. Kids orphaned by HIV who are raised by her grandparents. Babies born HIV positive."

"You travel often to Africa?" Satish asked.

"I wish I could go more often. Last time I was there was two years ago. I visited my colleagues in Johannesburg then toured around the villages. I go there thinking to give some hope and the people end up giving *me* hope. We can beat this. We *have* to."

"What can you tell us about Charlie Callahan, Dr. Lyons?"

He blinked at me, pretending he hadn't recognized the name.

"I believe he enrolled in your study about a year ago?" I insisted. The hell he didn't recognize the name.

"Oh. Mr. Callahan." He took a glass paperweight from a stack of papers on his desk and passed it from one hand to the other. My eyes fell on the first paper on the stack. Somebody had scribbled comments all over the first page. One table in particular, had been circled numerous times, next to the word "NO," followed by several exclamation marks. Interestingly, Amy was the first name in the list of authors, Lyons was the last.

Dr. Lyons is known to make medical students cry.

"You have to understand," Lyons said. "We don't go by patient names, and—"

"I know. The usual HIPAA crap. I'm sure you were informed when Mr. Callahan became suddenly unavailable for your study?"

Satish shifted in his chair. "What my partner's trying to say—"

"I get the question. Yes, when the news came out, I was informed about Mr. Callahan's participation in the study, but just because of the way he died. Of course, I was shocked when I heard. We're all quite sensitive about the subject. Homophobia is something we despise. Many of my patients tell me they're scared. Under any other circumstance, participants remain anonymous. People drop out of studies all the time and we don't keep track of where they end up or why they stopped showing up for samples—we have statistical tools to account for that."

I shoved a hand in my pocket and fished out a paperclip.

"Do you think Amy may have died for the same reason?

Homophobia?" Satish asked.

Lyons's hand froze around the paperweight. His lower lip trembled, a nerve in his temple twitched. I blinked and the imperturbable, self-confident Dr. Lyons was back, no trace of hesitancy in his baritone voice as he said, "I've no idea. It's something I—I can't even begin to comprehend. Amy was a great asset to our group. A fine scientist and a good—friend." He choked out the last word.

There was a moment of silence, before the paperclip flew from my hand and skidded under the desk. I delved to retrieve it and on my way back I took a good sniff at the paper.

I smelled Amy on it. And something vaguely sweet, enough to perk my interest. I leaned forward for a second sniff, but our time was up. Lyons swiveled away from the desk and shot to his feet. "I'd love to chat more, but I've got a meeting in five minutes."

He shook our hands as if we'd just sealed a million dollar deal.

As we walked to the door, I took one last peek at the children framed in Lyons's photos. They were dressed in rags, playing with broken sticks and a deflated ball, and yet their smiles were happy and full.

They end up giving me *hope.*

I turned and met his eyes. "Do you think you'll nail it, Doctor?" I asked. "The vaccine—do you believe it'll eventually stop the pandemic?"

He'd already lifted the receiver of his phone. He put it back down and gave me a condescending smile. "I've no doubt we will succeed. We owe it to those kids you're staring at."

I nodded, stepped out, and closed the door behind us.

* * *

"Interesting character, this Dr. Lyons," Satish said once we were back on the street. Hot air blew in our faces like a drunkard's breath. A crane rattled above our heads, a truck idled by the curb. Men in hard helmets and yellow vests spilled out of the fence surrounding the construction site across the street, UTech's next fifty-million-dollar project. They settled on the sidewalk with their lunchboxes, a radio tuned to pop music to keep them company. Others formed a line outside Einstein Bros, mingling with students in flip-flops and skimpy tops, doctors in white coats, and a couple of campus security guards.

"Guess what it reminds me of, Track?"

I grinned. "Mangoes? Elm trees? Bicycles?"

"Pistachios."

"Jeez... so close."

We zigzagged around street cones and orange tape.

"My old man used to be addicted to pistachios. *You see, Satish*, he used to say. *There's three kinds of pistachios. The breakable ones and the unbreakable ones.*"

"That's two."

"That's what I said. *Pa, that's two.* He said, *The cracked ones are a whole species on their own. They trick you into thinking they're breakable, they show you a peek of their fruit inside, but you either never get to break them, or if you do, you learn somebody else's already got them.*"

"Hmm. You think Lyons is the cracked kind?"

"No. I'm thinking I just don't want to dig through the pile of pistachio shells and find that somebody else's already eaten all the fruits."

We cornered an old apartment complex, now converted to office suites—probably where all the folks who didn't get their grant last year got sent to pay for their sins, judging from the rundown appearance of the building.

The asphalt exuded whiffs of hot air.

I eyed with envy the row of vehicles stationed around the corner, the gate arm at the entrance bearing the warning that access was reserved for the faculty in the Schnell building. We'd parked our vehicle two blocks away, by the Chavez campus entrance.

Satish didn't seem to mind the heat. Jingling loose change in his pockets, he kept walking and musing. "What struck me of our doc, actually, was how emotionally detached he wanted to appear."

I stopped by the sidewalk and stared at the cars in the reserved lot. The spots in the first row were assigned by name.

Dr. J. Salmad, Dr. K.H. Kurt, Dr. Hoon…

I said, "He almost lost it when you mentioned Amy's murder."

Dr. F. Lyons.

Interesting.

"I noticed," Satish replied. "Now, if one of your best physicians had been brutally murdered, wouldn't you make sure you showed some kind of shock, whether you felt it or not? Track? Where the hell are you going?"

I walked around the parking gate arm into the lot. "Would I show some shock? Depends, Sat."

He followed me and we both stared at Lyons's car. A white Audi A8, same 2006 model Vargas had seen at Amy's house.

"Depends on whether I'm innocent or guilty."

I crouched to look at the tires. There was dirt in the grooves, and the fenders were dusted with dried soil. I took out a handkerchief and brushed it along the wheel well.

Soil had spilled onto the street from the barriers along the hillside by Amy's house…

I rose, cupped a hand around my right eye and stared

through the window.

"And there's your guy sleeping in the backseat," I said.

I took a step back and motioned to Satish to come closer to the car. "Look at the backseat and tell me what you see."

He leaned against the window, hands around his face to shield off the glare from the sun. "I see a blanket, a duffel bag, and a white lab coat."

"The lab coat is sprawled across the back seat, giving the impression of a—"

"Track, I know what you're thinking. The car is white, though, not silver."

"The street light by Amy's house wasn't working. It was strobing. And Vargas wasn't sure about the color. Silver could easily be mixed up with white. Now imagine taking a peek inside this car and the light going off in flashes. All you get is a quick glimpse of the interior, the whites jumping at you—"

"...in a way that you might mistake the lab coat for a person."

A campus security van stopped by the curb. "Can I help you?"

I flashed my badge and the driver waved back. "Should've guessed," he mumbled. "Do you need any help, Detective?"

"How much for your silence?" I asked.

He laughed and drove away.

Satish shoved both hands in his pockets and stared at the dirty handkerchief in my hands. "Even if you get a match, dirt's still dirt pretty much anywhere in L.A."

"But if we get the dirt, *and* Vargas's statement, *and* the nine-one-one tape..."

He nodded. "And we've got fibers sitting at the lab. Let's wait until we hear back from the forensic labs. We might have some leverage at that point."

"You never know," I said. "Even the hardest pistachios eventually crack."

We started back down the sidewalk. A web of scaffolding and cranes reflected off the glass façade of the Schnell building. A siren wailed in the distance. The workers made their way back inside the fence. The crane started rattling again. A faint breeze blew warm air in our faces.

I craved air conditioning.

"A doctor would've no problem with scalping," I said, once we got to our car.

Satish unlocked the car. "Which reminds me —"

"More pistachios?"

"No, no. The first American serial killer, H. H. Holmes. He skinned, scalped, deboned his victims and sold their organs."

He slid behind the wheel and I in the passenger seat. "*Doctor* H. H. Holmes. Brilliant association, Sat."

The back of my seat was hot and made my skin tingle. Satish jammed the key into the ignition, and I turned the AC knob all the way to the max. As we merged into traffic, we once again fell silent.

"What are you thinking, Track?"

"João Gilberto."

"I thought you were a Bill Evans kinda guy."

I stared out the window, ramps of freeway braiding and looping in front of us. "I am. Though I get distracted from time to time."

Satish whipped the car onto the Five and smiled. "I love Brazilian jazz. It's sexy."

"Sexy is deceiving."

"No, Track. *Deceiving* is sexy."

I rapped my fingers against the window. "Darn it, Sat. Why do you always have to be right?"

MOSAICS

EIGHT

Thursday, July 2

"Human hair, scalp. Human hair, facial. Human hair, arms."

Fiber analyst Gustavo Salazar slid his thick lenses off his fleshy face and wiped them on the sleeve of his coat. He sighed heavily, as if every action cost him a great deal of energy, took three more pictures out of the blue folder he'd been holding and set them on the workbench between us, below the three he'd just shown us.

"Doberman hair, poodle hair, terrier hair—all breeds covered. Horse, cat, rat, house pets—tried those too." He squinted at the pictures and shook his head. "Tried 'em all."

He crossed his arms and leaned against the cabinets behind him, waiting for us to draw our own conclusions. My eyes shifted from the picture in my hand to the ones on the counter in front of us.

Satish scratched his brow. "And you're positive we're

talking animal hair?"

Salazar cleared his throat, opened his mouth, gave it a good thought, and then clicked his jaws together again. He retrieved an inhaler from his coat pocket, squeezed it in his mouth, swallowed hard, and flashed us a pitiful smile. "Seasonal allergies. All those summer pollens drive me nuts."

He coughed in his sleeve and punched a fist on his breastbone, his shiny tear ducts grossly enlarged by the thick lenses of his glasses. His breath reeked of medicine, washed down coffee, and the last cig drag he had outside, right before meeting with us.

I nodded. *Blame the trees.*

"Definitely animal fibers. Filaments of alpha-keratin, shaft only, both ends blunt, as if they'd been clipped. No root. The color's black, consistent with Asian, if we're going with human source, though the diameter's too thin. A hair that thin I've only seen fair, like body hair from northern Europeans. This one's too long to be that kind, though."

The acidic smells of lab dilutions and gels lingered in my nostrils. I rose from the stool I'd been perched on and looked out the window. The Hertzberg-Davis Forensic Science Center, home of the LAPD crime labs for two years now, sat on the southeast end of the Cal State L.A. campus, nestled between the Ten and the Seven-Ten. From where I stood, I could see the busy ten lanes of one of the Interstates, snaking below the Eastern Avenue flyover. All lanes were clogged, and the haze over downtown was as thick and colorful as the tiers of a wedding cake.

My brain felt as if it were wrapped in the same kind of haze.

Salazar was telling us that the fibers Cohen had found in one of the cuts on Amy's feet were of animal nature but no standard comparison yielded a match. In other words, we had no clue *what* species the fibers belonged to. Nothing else had turned up from Charlie Callahan's files, either. On top of that, we were still in complete darkness as to what kind of ligature had been used to strangle either victim.

The more I thought about it the more I was convinced Lyons was hiding something about the night Amy had been murdered. Vargas was no saint, but he had no reason to lie about the car he'd spotted at Amy's house. Even if he was wrong about the exact night it had happened, the car had been there at an unconventional hour. *Lyons* had been there. I wanted to know why and I wanted the fiber to pin my suspect to Amy's murder.

I said, "So this hair is too thin to be black, too long to be fair, and too freaking weird to be anything we know."

Salazar stared at me through his thick lenses. He raised a pinky to his lips and stuck the fingernail between his front teeth. "Pretty much," he said, moving his lips around the pinky.

Satish crossed his arms and wobbled his head. "Look. The hair was found on a victim. No other hair like it was found on that body. You'll agree it's gotta come from somewhere, right?"

Salazar plucked his pinky out of his mouth and wiped it against the front of his lab coat. "We're going blind with no root."

I rolled a stool over and sat down. "Fine," I said. "Tell us what you found and we'll figure out the rest."

He wheezed again, adjusted the lenses on his nose, and began his lecture. "I looked at the medulla, scales, and pigment granules. Let's start with the medulla. It makes up less than a third of the diameter of the hair, which is typically an indication that we're dealing with human hair. Except—"

"Except?"

"What we see in this sample is a *continuous* medulla, which almost never happens in human hair."

"Almost doesn't mean never."

"Fine. But there's more. I created a cast of nail polish around it and then examined it under the microscope to see the pattern of scales. Overlapping coronal scales. Not found in human hair."

Satish drummed his fingers on the countertop and stared at the pictures. "Some kind of fancy garment? Have you excluded silk? Wool?"

"Not even alpaca wool matches these characteristics."

"Farm animals?" I insisted.

"Done those too."

"What about exotic pets? Tiger cats, bobcats, opossum, squirrels—"

Salazar's black brows steepled above the thick frame of his glasses. "Whoa," he said, raising his hands up in the air. "We don't have reference samples for that many animals. If you think it could come from any of those we can send a field officer to fetch samples, but it takes time and money, and you know how it goes with money…"

My head spun. I felt a tingling pain at the small of my back. "Yes. We know how it goes with money."

Only two years old, the forensic labs were equipped with state-of-the-art technology and expensive machineries. Despite all this, our job requests continued to be backed-up, DNA results took ages to come in, and only a few months earlier Latent Prints had fired a bunch of people over yet another misidentification that had ended up in court.

Satish wrapped a hand around my shoulder. "Thanks for your time, Sal."

Salazar collected all the photos neatly lined on the workbench and shoved them back inside the folder. "Anytime."

The pain at the small of my back got sharper. I slammed a hand on the workbench and walked out of the room.

"It's not Sal's fault he couldn't find any match, Track," Satish said as we walked down the stairs and out of the building. "I thought he'd done a pretty good job with those comparisons. I mean, if nothing matches—"

"He pronounced the word 'inconclusive' with the sympathy of a squirrel chewing the wiring of a pickup truck."

Satish chuckled.

A few black and white Crown Vics were stationed in the parking lot. On the other side of the building, the Ten roared with its steady flow of vehicles, dictating the pace of a hot summer day. A siren blasted from somewhere in the distance, maybe the high-speed chase the earlier helicopter had picked up. From the university cafeteria on the east side of the parking lot came a whiff of French fries and fast food. On any other day, the scent would've made me ravenous. Today it made me nauseous.

Satish smelled it too. "How about lunch? There's a great prime rib place near the golf course…"

I didn't reply. My eyes fell on the billboard advertising the L.A. zoo and got stuck there.

Satish jingled his car keys and cocked his head. "Pork is tastier than zebra, Track."

I slowly peeled my eyes off the billboard. "Yeah, but zebras are in Africa. When was the last time Lyons was there?"

Satish's facial expression dwindled between worried and amused. He decided for worried. "Two years ago. Not enough to justify collecting fibers from the whole entire zoo and running an indefinite number of tests. It would be smarter to look for fibers on the African souvenirs he keeps in his office."

"We need a subpoena for that, and we can't get a subpoena unless we put him at the crime scene."

The usual catch 22.

Satish opened his car door. "C'mon, Track. You're low in sugars. Let's go eat. I'll drive and drop you off to pick up your vehicle after lunch."

I wasn't low in sugars. I was having an epiphany. "You go ahead." I trotted back toward the entrance of the Forensic Center. "Get me a double burger with French fries and all the junk that comes with it. I'll see you at Parker."

Satish shrugged, shook his head, and drove away. The man's used to my quirks.

* * *

Forensic scientist Diane Kyle removed the lid of her lunch container, stuck it in the microwave, and pressed the start button. While waiting, she softly hummed an off-key version of *Eleanor Rigby*, her scent mingling with the fragrance of her lunch—chicken cacciatore, I guessed from the scent, which wavered out of the break room and down in the hallway, where it found my nose.

I leaned against the open door. "Hey," I said.

She turned, surprised to see me. "Hey."

I tried to forget the pain at my back and grinned. "You said not to call. You didn't say anything about showing up in person."

Her eyes softened, her lips cracked into a smile. "Sal told me he'd run some analyses for you and Satish." The microwave beeped. She retrieved the pasta, covered the container, and then turned to stare at me, an ethereal look about her eyes and a divine scent exuding from the collar of her shirt. "So. You're back to duty."

Damn, I missed her.

I shoved both hands in my pockets and nodded. "Did Sal tell you what the analyses were about?"

The ethereal look hardened. "Of course," she muttered, walking past me and out of the door. "All you care about is work. Some things will never change."

Man.

"D. — wait!"

Her gait didn't slow down a notch. I tailed her to her office. She stopped by the vending machine across the hall, one hand holding the container with her lunch, the other fumbling inside her coat pocket. I fished a dollar from my wallet, flattened it, and inserted it into the money slot.

"Thank you," she said, pressing the Diet Coke button. She grabbed the can, opened her office and walked inside.

"Did you already have lunch?" she asked, grabbing a fork from one of the drawers.

"I'm not hungry."

Diane sat at her desk and popped open the lid of the food container. "Satish said you'd be back to work," she said, mixing the noodles.

I hadn't eaten since breakfast. The fragrance of tomato sauce and chicken would've normally enticed my taste buds, yet the dull ache at the small of my back deprived me of any appetite.

I grabbed the chair by the door, sat next to Diane, and inhaled her instead of the pasta. Old Bill Evans tunes started playing in my head. I grabbed a pen from her desk and clicked the retractor.

"How are you, D.?"

Her eyes switched to bored. "You know how I am. Overworked. Disillusioned about life. About *men*," she added. The sting in her voice didn't go unnoticed.

I put the pen down, leaned forward, and touched the pendant on her neck. It was black and bulky and I knew it opened up to a push-knife. "Since when are you wearing this?" Her skin was warm and smelled like the poem you've always wanted to write and never got around to writing.

"I'm taking a self-defense class," she said. "Makes me feel safe."

I let go of it and leaned back in my chair. "D., nothing makes you feel safe like a loaded puppy bulging from your waistband. What happened to that Sig your dad gave you? I thought you had fun last time we took it to the range."

She scraped the last of her pasta with the tip of her fork. "It's heavy. I get tired of carrying it everywhere." She put on her business face and took a sip of Diet Coke. "What do you need, Track?"

"What makes you think I need something?"

"You came in to see Sal, not me."

I picked up the pen again and clicked the retractor. "I've got a puzzle for you. One not even Sal could figure out."

She snapped the lid back on the food container. "You got fibers from the crime scene?"

"One. Very thin and very subtle. All Sal could tell us is that it's a hair from an animal, but couldn't match it with any species on file. Hell, he wasn't even sure if it's human or not."

The news didn't trouble her. "Send it in for DNA."

"It's got no root."

"Send it in for mtDNA."

"What the hell is that?"

"You've never heard of mitochondrial DNA?"

"Of course I've heard of mitochondrial DNA. It's the mt-stuff you just named I've never heard of."

A smirk escaped her lips. "That's what it stands for — mitochondrial DNA. Cells in hair shafts don't have chromosomes because they don't have a nucleus. But they have mitochondria, small organelles that contain

119

mitochondrial DNA, or mtDNA. Thirty-seven genes that can't tell you exactly who your suspect is, but they can at least tell you what species the hair comes from. If it is a hair."

I scratched my head. "But you can't even run it on CODIS."

CODIS, or Combined DNA Index System, was the DNA database maintained by the FBI. Any DNA record found on crime scenes had to be logged into CODIS. However, mitochondrial DNA was routinely collected—when available—for missing persons.

"That's because it's not unique to one individual," Diane explained. "It's inherited from the mother's side only, and it may be identical from mother to children to siblings."

I clicked the pen and pondered. "But you said you can use it to figure out whether it's human or not."

"Correct."

"And if it's not human, whether it's monkey, zebra, elephant—what have you."

She made a face. "Why would you find a zebra hair on a crime scene?"

"Could be lion, giraffe, antelope..."

"Those are big animals, Track. They wouldn't have thin shafts."

"Some small African animal, then? How about insects?"

"Insect hair aren't really hair and they wouldn't look animal. Why are you so fixated with Africa?"

I grinned, she jacked up her brow. "You've got your suspect in mind, already." ·

"I have a witness on a suspect's car. I just need a little more. My guy travels often to Africa."

She cocked her head and gave me a skeptical look. "And he'd leave an African fiber at a crime scene?"

I liked that smile. I wanted to kiss that smile. Just one

more time, like a box of chocolates you save for a gloomy day, only to go back and find there's only one left. Dark chocolate, the bitter kind that sticks to your mouth and makes the flavor last longer, with a drop of alcohol in the middle, enough to make you want more, yet hardly enough to give you a high… And man, I wanted to get high…

Diane swiveled her chair to the file cabinet by the window. "I'll get the order sheet." Flipping through folders, she casually added, "I interviewed for a job in Boston."

"Boston? You're joking, right?"

The earlier smile evaporated from her lips. "I'm *dead* serious," she replied, handing me the form for the DNA analyses.

I winced. "Boston is — east. And north. Northeast."

"Oh, don't be so freaking Californian, Track. I don't mind winters. And I don't mind snow, either."

"Hell, Diane, I *love* winters. I get in my truck, drive up to the Sierras, get plenty of winter, and when I'm tired of it, I leave. Don't need no Boston for that."

She fiddled with the push-knife hanging from her neck. "The job is with the Harvard School of Health. I'd be doing genomics for epidemiological studies. No more picking through crime scenes."

She gave me the *dead* serious look. I didn't have much to add to the fact that Boston *is* north and east and if that wasn't a convincing argument, then what else would've been? So I got up, took the form to drop off the fiber at the Serology lab, told her one more time I wanted her to take care of it personally, she promised she would, and dragged myself out of the door.

I was about to close the door behind me when I yanked it open again and blurted out, "Saturday afternoon. I'll pick you up at two."

And then I stood there like an idiot, waiting for her to

send me to hell.

Instead, she blinked a couple of times and said, "This Saturday? It's the Fourth. I'm going to a barbeque for dinner."

I swallowed the pang of jealously I felt and rebuked, "We're not going to dinner. We're going to the shooting range."

NINE

From CalState, I didn't go back to Parker Center. Satish called me to remind me about the lunch he'd bought me, now waiting on my desk, together with a stack of bank statements and phone logs from Amy Liu's murder book. I told him to put the lunch in the fridge and took the Ten westbound instead, all the way down to South Central. Joe Mustache, the owner of the hot-sheet motel in South Central, wasn't too happy to see me back on his premises.

I reciprocated the courtesy.

"I need another chat with your favorite client," I said, my shoes still popping on the linoleum floors of the stingy lobby.

He squinted and exhaled. I smelled his lunch of refried beans, frijoles, pico de gallo, and Tums. Or maybe early dinner, since it was four already. "He's no longer here. He wasn't paying rent. I called his parole agent and he was moved."

Damn it. These guys go through relocations like cops go through wives.

"Do you happen to know where?"

"What am I, his keeper? I'm still waiting for my late rent, now you guys come and ask questions. Call his agent." He slammed a sign "Ring the Bell" on the desk and vanished at the back.

Fucking cooperative, the citizen.

I stepped outside in the afternoon heat and reflected on the human condition.

Hell, *my* human condition.

The working day was coming to an end and I still hadn't had a bite to eat. I was after an assassin who left plenty of traces, except we couldn't decipher them. I'd flirted with João Gilberto and sought redemption in Bill Evans's solos. I'd found half a suspect and lost a quarter of a witness.

And I still hadn't had a bite to eat.

The thought that good ol' Doctor Watanabe might've been somehow right about me not being super-healthy lately did cross my mind for a very brief moment. The Pain was there, subtly reminding me of its presence, whether I chose to ignore it or not, yet I still hadn't turned up at the lab for the blood tests he'd ordered.

I slid behind the wheel of my Charger, turned the stereo on, and forgot all about that.

It's called jazz, and it's my therapy.

It worked. By the time I got home I was ravenous.

And felt too lonely to eat by myself.

* * *

"You look thinner."

I swirled the glass of Bordeaux. *Deep ruby, as it should be.*

"Thinner compared to what?"

"Thinner than last time I saw you."

I brought the glass to my lips and took in the wine in small sips, letting the flavor simmer on my tongue before swallowing.

A touch of berry flavor, as rich and velvety as Eva Cassidy's voice.

I was fed, rested, and particularly happy over the choice of wine for the evening.

Hortensia couldn't care less. She sat on the board floor of her porch, holding a jar filled with glass shards on her lap. "Do you think there's too much green?"

I took another sip and swished it in my mouth. "You've crushed green bottles to make that. Of course there's going to be green."

The evening was crisp and carried the rugged scent of the ocean. Fifteen miles away from downtown, the relentless heat of July had melted away, swallowed by the sea breeze. The nocturnal voices of the Venice Boardwalk came and went in waves, making a lazy background, like a tune you don't really enjoy but somehow grow accustomed to. Yellow streetlights projected onto the sky, hiding the stars. Only a pale moon poked its lopsided grin through the fringed tops of the palm trees.

Hortensia tipped her head to the side and drummed her long nails against the jar on her lap, pondering. She'd pinned her hair up with a pencil, and her neck was pale and inviting like an icicle on a hot day. I'd kiss it, but then she'd give me the *boyfriend* Gary crap all over again.

"It's an Amazon parrot," she said. "Amazon parrots are green."

"Why d'you ask, then?"

She turned and gave me a weary look. "You're so thick about these things, Track. I just want you to tell me you like it."

125

I downed the rest of the wine and poured another glass. "I like it," I said.

Hortensia clonked the jar on the floor next to her masterpiece and got back to her feet. "Thanks a lot, Track. That was heartfelt."

"Jeez, Hort! I said what you wanted me to say," I yelled over the slam of the screen door. "Besides, you told me you don't do mosaics."

I heard her pad inside the house, sulking. I shrugged, sipped my wine, and watched the kids zip by in their skateboards.

Truth was, her mosaic looked nothing like a parrot.

She'd glued glass shards from broken bottles onto a baseboard she had previously cut in the shape of a bird. Aside for some blue and red on the wings, the rest was a jumble of green glass shards mangled together.

The screen door squeaked again, followed by the jingle of Hortensia's bangles.

"I don't *normally* do mosaics," she said. "But you brought it up the other day, so I thought I'd give it a try. Here. Mix this." She took the wine glass from my hand and passed me a wooden spoon and a bowl with a peanut-butter-like paste inside.

It smelled awful. I made a face. "Dessert?"

"No. Grout."

Thank goodness.

Hortensia drained the rest of the wine in my glass as if it were a schooner—a blasphemy to drink a Bordeaux like that. She sat on the floor again, leaning with her back against my knees. She plucked the pencil off her hair, and used the tip to shift the glass shards closer to one another. As it fell on her shoulders, her hair filled the air with the zesty scent of her shampoo. When she was done, she donned a pair of blue rubber gloves, spooned a blob of grout onto her hand, and smothered it on the parrot with a palette knife.

"How long have you been on a diet?" she asked, her fingers carefully coaxing the grout into the grooves between the shards. Her voice was tuned to cheerful and casual.

I love Hortensia. To her, the world is divided into things she believes and things she *doesn't* believe. The rest is irrelevant.

"What the hell are you talking about, Hort? Did you not see me eat?" I stabbed the grout with the wooden spoon. It smelled of acrylic and glue. Nothing like the sweetish, rotten smell I'd detected on the tiles left by the Byzantine Strangler.

Hortensia worked her fingers around the groves in the mosaic. She smoothed the edges, filling the spaces between the shards. "You look thinner."

I scoffed. "It's summer and I'm wearing less clothes."

"I've seen you with *no* clothes."

"I need more wine."

I left the bowl of grout on the floor, got out of the chair and leaned on the railing. Down the street, a blinking row of block after block of traffic lights hiccupped from red to green and then back to red.

"I'll get another bottle," Hortensia said. She took the gloves off, left them by the baseboard, and walked back inside, her bangles jingling with every step.

The parrot stared at me with its lonely, black eye. I crouched down and picked up one of the gloves Hortensia had left on the ground and brought it to my nose. The sharp smell of grout hit my nostrils first and then, as I inhaled more, I detected a new, familiar aftertaste.

Nitrile.

And something suddenly snapped into place.

The smell on the Byzantine tiles.

Something sweet, something rotten, something rubbery. *Nitrile* rubber.

It wasn't much, but it was *something*.

TEN

Friday, July 3

My shirt was drenched. A siren blasted in my ears, but I couldn't figure out where it was coming from.

The lower half of my body was tied.

The siren was still howling. It was in my head.

I tried to move and my whole body screamed in pain.

The Pain.

Awareness hit me like a sniper.

Will came licking my face, nudging me with his wet nose.

"One—second," I mumbled.

I crawled out of the tangle of sheets wrapped around my waist, saw the edge of the bed looming above me, grabbed it, and pulled myself up. The room spun, its edges blurred.

Bits of a nightmare clung to me. Pain reached my chest, crept up to my neck, and then slowly vaporized, carefully letting go its grip, like a toying lover. It finally ebbed off, and all that was left was its memory, echoing in my joints and muscles.

The walls realigned, the bed stopped running away.

Will stuck his muzzle between my legs and wagged his tail, thrumming against the mattress.

I heard the silence around me. The alarm clock read 3:17 a.m.

Have you been feeling well, Ulysses?

Hell, Doc. I've been having a blast.

I picked up the sheets from the floor and tossed them back on the bed.

So then why have you not gone to the lab to get those tests done, Ulysses?

That was my *other* self, asking.

I sent my *other* self to hell and shuffled to the bathroom to pee.

Nothing clears the mind like releasing your bladder in the morning. I filled the boiler of my little Moka espresso maker with water, set it on the stove, and pulled on a T-shirt and some work pants while it brewed. I drank the espresso straight and bitter, then went to the garage. It smelled of car oil and molasses from the last derusting job I'd done on the fuel tank. I opened the window a crack and inhaled the nippy night air wafting through. A staccato of crickets chirped outside.

Under Will's watchful eyes, I gathered my toolbox, wrenches and drills, and set to work on the Porsche engine. Manual work helps me think, and the Byzantine Strangler had given me a great deal of thinking to do over the past couple of weeks. Last weekend, as I puzzled over mysterious fibers and elusive ligatures, I'd put the crankshaft and connecting rods together and installed them in the case.

The next step was to install the pistons and barrels—a delicate task that requires a lot of patience, which, I soon realized, is not one of my best qualities at four in the morning. The first wrist pin went in just fine, the second took me a little wrestling, and by the third one I was swearing like a drunkard. The Pain came back instantly, like an awakened beast. I banged my fist on the workbench and growled.

Oedipus.

My *other* self came back too, with renewed fervor.

You're just like stupid Oedipus. Stop running away from your fate, Ulysses. The more you run away, the more it comes back to bite your ass.

I waited until the Pain let go of its grip, then left the garage, went back inside, peeled off my drenched shirt and briefs and stepped under a cold shower. When I returned to the bedroom the alarm clock on my nightstand read 4:55 a.m.

The lab opens in thirty minutes.

Time to get poked, Ulysses.

I picked a black suit and a black tie to go with it, treated myself to another espresso, and left.

* * *

I proceeded at fifteen miles per hour, windows down and shades on my eyes. Even the crows bickering on the treetops could tell I was a cop.

After stopping at the lab to get the blood draw Watanabe had requested, I called Ricky Vargas's parole agent and had a chat on Ricky's whereabouts. One hour and forty-five minutes later—gotta love morning traffic—I was cruising the winding roads of South Pasadena. In front of me unrolled tree-lined streets with manicured lawns and colonial houses with as many front windows as the number of digits on the annual household income. Hollywood crews had taken over a couple of streets, while Mexican workers were sweeping through the following two blocks, mowing, trimming, plowing and raking.

It was the kind of neighborhood where houses are statements, not homes. The kind of neighborhood where if you're skilled enough and down on your luck you might find some work, so long as you don't expect more than minimum wage and don't need medical insurance.

I set my eyes on two such down-on-their-luck guys, working on a retaining wall between the two levels of a front lawn. The house was a pink cottage with a gabled porch and matching planters decorating two sets of bay windows. I drove another hundred yards up the hill, parked by the street and walked back. By the time I got to the cottage, there was only one man laying down bricks.

Vicente Vargas dunked his trowel into the wheelbarrow and mixed fresh cement with damp and brisk swooshes. "See?" he said. "Not too soft, not too hard. Just like you'd want a woman's breasts."

Phlegm gargled up his throat like bubbles in a fish tank. He turned and spit on the ground.

I stood on the sidewalk and watched.

He didn't know I was watching.

He picked up a brick from the ground with the ease of a freight making a U-turn. His joints looked like they were about to creak and fall apart, yet they held together and pulled him back to a semi-vertical position. The brick seemed soft in his large, rugged hands. He tapped its sides with the tip of the trowel then smothered it with a blob of fresh cement that smelled cool and earthy.

Vicente, instead, smelled of tobacco and sunburnt scalp. He smelled of insomnia, hard labor, occasional sponge baths, and an old suitcase large enough to contain all his possessions.

He wiped the extra cement off the sides of the wall then reached for the level. "Gotta make these things straight, you do. Blocks need to be level on all sides. A sturdy wall can last through flood and fire. A crappy wall—"

"Who are you talking to, Mr. Vargas?"

He took his time turning, and when he finally did, he blinked, one eye looking at me, the other one going its merry way. I thought of going my merry way too but I had to talk to Ricky Vargas one more time, which meant I had to talk to his uncle Vicente first.

Once Vicente had me all figured out, he turned back to check on the level, making small adjustments with the tip of the trowel. "My wife," he said at last. "I talk to my wife. Been dead for thirteen years. Them ghosts are pretty hard to let go."

A second trowel lay abandoned on the ground next to the pile of bricks. Closer to the house, two parallel rows of two-by-four's marked the foundation for a walkway. I picked up the second trowel, brought it to my nose, sniffed it, and then let it drop back on the ground. A slap hammer stood on its head on the last tile.

"You building all this by yourself, Vicente?"

Vicente didn't seem to mind a stranger knowing his name. Like I said, he had me all figured out already. "If you don't count them ghosts," he said.

I smiled. Judging from the prints on the sand, *them ghosts* wore size eleven boots and smelled awfully familiar— adrenaline, sweat, and a midnight joint. Or two. With some company, most likely.

I knew exactly where Ricky was hiding. I could've bluffed, pretended I was leaving, only to blast into the shed and grab him by the back collar.

And then what?

I paced, feigning indifference. "Will you tell Ricky a friend came looking for him?"

The trowel dug into the fresh cement with a swish. "You're no friend of his."

I smiled. "Let's put it this way. I need his help. I'm very friendly with people who help me out. I can be very friendly with parole agents too, as a matter of fact. You can tell that to Ricky. Or, you can tell him to keep hanging out with his *real* friends from Eighteenth Street. And while he's doing that, you count the minutes until he gets back to the joint. With *no* friends, this time."

The straight eye stared at me like a chicken smelling danger. I shoved a hand in my pocket, found a paperclip with a bent end and stuck it into my mouth. Vicente sucked on his teeth, I sucked on my paperclip. You could hear the neurons working with all that sucking.

An airplane flew by, scratching a perfectly blue sky. A garbage truck turned into the street and clonked trash bins at the end of the block. A crow cawed from the top of a telephone pole.

"Very well," I said, and started back toward the sidewalk.

Vicente slapped the trowel in the cement. "Like I always says to my wife, a man's got no real friends, just good company or bad company." He let his last words hang in the air, clinging to a thin thread of phlegm, before turning to spit. "Those guys from the street—"

"They're good guys. They're my friends."

Ricky Vargas stood by the shed, half hidden behind the door. The one hand I could see was deep in his pants' pocket.

Adrenaline shot up my spine. It's a cop reflex: hand-in-pocket equals hidden gun. My right hand crept to my holster.

And just like that, nerves jumping in my arms and legs, and cold sweat condensing on my lower back, I examined the boy. He was lean and fibrous, strength dictated by sheer instinct and manual work. His small, dark eyes came down a notch at the sides so that his smiles looked melancholy even when they didn't mean to.

Women tend to fall for that kind of eyes. So do some men.

They were proud eyes, eyes that had seen everything and yet not enough, that had known life and death and had not cared, eyes that had been scared shitless because no matter how many times they'd come this close to death, those eyes still craved to see the world.

They were a survivor's eyes.

The white cinderblock wall.

A voice emerged from the dark well of my memory. The voice smelled of stale and it yelled in my ears, "Toes and eyes against the wall!" Over and over it yelled in my ears and face, because personal space had become a lost commodity... the white wall, the metal bars, the rugged cot, the restraint chair...

Never... never again ...

The white cinderblock wall in juvi.

Ricky had slammed his face against the white cinderblock wall.

And so had I.

Ricky Vargas killed at age fourteen over a ten-dollar bill.

He did it to prove to his gang he was a man.

The joint made him a man.

Just like the joint made *me* a man.

You got a second chance, Ulysses.

I was acquitted of all charges.

He deserves a second chance too.

From behind me came a low, monotone rumble. It hissed and mumbled and gargled, until it became words. "Don't do anything stupid, Ricky," the gargle said.

Ricky's hand came out of his pant's pocket. Slowly.

Something dropped on the ground.

A pocketknife.

"That's a good boy." The gargle appreciated. "Now talk to the cop. He's a nice cop." I turned. Vicente was pointing his trowel like a handgun, his eyes squashed to slits, and his voice coming out in wet gargles. He spit on the ground and tuned his voice a notch up. "My wife told me he's a nice cop."

"The dead one?" I asked.

He nodded. "The live one doesn't talk as much."

I'd thank the dead lady, but I was in no rush.

"Show me both hands, Ricky," I said.

He did. His hands were empty now.

"Step out of there. And keep showing me your hands."

Once he was out of the shed I said, "I brought a few pictures for you to take a good look at."

Vicente's trowel went back to the cement. Ricky Vargas sat on the finished end of the retaining wall and pointed his chin to the pack of cigarettes bulging from his left shoulder, under a rolled up sleeve.

"So long as you blow the smoke away from me," I said.

Ricky slid out a cig, lit it with a match, then brought it to his uncle who showed his yellowed teeth in appreciation. Ricky sat back on the wall and lit a second one for himself this time.

Vicente smiled around the cigarette butt. "You sure you don't want one, cop?"

"I'm good, thanks." I took the mug shots out of my pocket. "Ricky. You remember telling me and my partner you saw a man coming out of Amy Liu's house the night she was killed?"

He nodded. "Drove away in the nice Audi."

"That guy." I handed him the mug shots. "Can you see him here?"

He took the six-pack from my hand and stared at it while chewing on his cig.

Vicente blew misty smoke out of his mouth. "It's not bad for you. My wife, the dead one, says the stuff is bad for you. She says she don't smoke. She says she's gonna outlive me because she don't smoke. She been dead thirteen years now." He let the ashes dangle from the tip, teeth clenched around the butt and lips moving carefully around it. "Now I go to her grave and smoke myself a cig. She don't complain no more."

The photos in Ricky's hands were mug shots, all except for one, which I'd replaced with Lyons's driver's license photo. When Ricky came across it, he pointed to the doc with no hesitation.

"Are you sure?"

He took the cigarette out of his mouth and stared at it while blowing smoke out of his nostrils. "It wasn't the first time I saw him there."

"What other times did you see him?"

"He'd come in the evening, when we'd pack our stuff to leave. She'd get mad and say he'd come too early. That people would see him. But then she'd be happy." He sneered, his still boyish features emerging through unshaved cheeks and smudges of cement. Then his nineteen-year-old eyes became old again, the smile melancholy.

"Did you watch them?"

He grimaced. "No, man! That's sick!"

Like I haven't seen it before.

"How did you know they were lovers, then?"

There came the gargle again, low, then louder, until it became the rustling of an old, cracked laughter. "Some things you just know," Vicente said.

That was good enough for me. I put the mug shots back in my pocket.

Ricky scrutinized me from the tip of his cigarette. "I helped you out, man."

"Yes, you did. I might ask you to remember our conversation today. You might have to remember it in front of a judge."

His smile came back, and with it the shade of melancholy. "I helped you out, man," he repeated. He took another drag and blew smoke out of his nostrils. "I heard you guys are looking for the guy who did 'em both. The fag and the lady."

"And hopefully catch him before he does somebody else," I said.

He considered me through thin loops of smoke. "That's crazy, man."

"What is? Killing?"

He shook his head. The lizard tattooed on his shoulder winked. "You can kill a fag, if you don't like fags. You can kill a pretty lady in a pretty house, if she done somethin' to you. You don't kill both."

I wanted to ask why not, but my phone didn't give me the time. The display flashed Satish's number. As I flipped it open, Vargas pointed a finger at me. "You don't forget. I helped you out."

I answered the phone while walking back to the car. "What are you, a mind reader?"

Satish pondered. "You think I could make money out of it?"

"Not with minds. Palms, maybe, if you put some practice into it. Listen. I've got a wit on Lyons. Vargas. He puts him in Amy's house the night she was killed."

"After the party?"

"After the party."

"Well, that's interesting. You see, I happen to be at his house right now. Together with a stiff and an SID Field Unit."

I stopped cold. "Is Lyons the stiff?"

"No. His wife. Come."

ELEVEN

It was a box: a house with a slanted roof and a breezeway between the main building and the three-door garage. Still a box, if you ask me. One of those ultra-modern things that in a real estate listing would've had more bathrooms than bedrooms and enough zeros to make you feel astigmatic.

It was a *glass* box, really, with no hint of privacy. At night it must've glimmered like the top of the Empire State Building. Which is why a house like that came with an eight-foot-tall property wall covered in crawling ivy.

A swimming pool shimmered in the midday light, needlework of reflections wavering off the windowpanes of the first floor. I climbed up the cobblestone steps, walked through a maze of tapered fiberglass planters, snaked across the recliners on the poolside deck and admired the roses raining down the gazebo. The tall breezeway hung between the garage to the left and the glass-paned living area to the right. Its ceiling slanted up, hinting to a second floor at the opposite end.

A dog barked. A female officer held her on a leash. "Lily belongs to the home owners," she said. "She's in shock, poor baby. I'm keeping her out of the crime scene."

Lily was a golden spaniel, well groomed, with a pink ribbon on her head. And she was barking at me. "Was she inside at the time of the attack? Did anybody hear her bark?"

The officer patted her on the back. "I'm not sure. She was with the husband when we arrived. The neighbors didn't hear a thing. The husband was swimming in the pool when the wife was attacked. He didn't hear or see a thing either." Her eyes went back to the spaniel, who was now making a point of showing me her teeth. "She's such a sweetie. I bet she got scared and went hiding."

Funny how the *sweetie* got scared when she saw the killer, but kept on barking at me.

I turned my attention to the main entrance, a red metal door encased between glass panels. It was ajar. I pushed it open and examined the dead bolts and locks. Everything looked intact: no jimmies, no signs of forced entry.

"Aw, aren't you a beauty?" the officer cooed.

"Yeah. I get that a lot."

There was a disapproving pause. "I was talking to Lily." She pulled the leash and took Lily somewhere else to have their private conversation.

No forced entry, no dog barking. It made me eager to hear Lyons's story.

I left the red door and stepped between the box hedges and the windowpanes to take a closer look at the glass. It was thick, the bulletproof kind. I crouched, inspected all edges, and noticed a little brown box on one corner with a tiny LED light in the middle. If robbers really wanted to cut through the glass, they'd have to come prepared.

Inside the house, I spotted an SID tech standing at the bottom of a spiral staircase, dusting the shiny steel railing with a fingerprint brush. He saw me peeking through the windows and frowned while his right hand continued its dusting job.

Tires screeched from the street. The length and pitch of the screeching was vaguely familiar. The car stopped, the engine was cut off.

A door slammed.

I inhaled.

Past the chlorine of the swimming pool and the gas exhaust from the street, past the scent of the marina half a mile away, came a whisper of honeydew and lost childhood memories. A Bill Evans tune started playing at the back of my head.

I walked back to the property gate.

"What do you mean my name's not on your list? I called as soon as I was notified."

The watch officer stiffened. "Ma'am—"

"Can't you read my badge?"

"Ma'am, the Field Unit's already here, and—"

I grabbed the yellow tape and lifted it. "She's with me," I told the officer.

He had one of those square faces that narrows at the temples and widens at the jaws. The lower one opened slightly then clicked back in place. "Yes, sir," he mumbled, with the vacant look of somebody who's been given overriding orders and doesn't quite know what to do.

Diane sucked in air as if she was about to dive under water and ducked under the tape.

"Thank you," she said and scuttled up the cobblestone steps squeezing a large handbag under her arm. "How old is the stiff?"

"I love it when you talk business, D. If the Field Unit's

already here—"

"—means I wasn't called on this. Why do you think I had to yell at the guy?" Her logic was as flawless as a freshly ironed shirt. "Here, hold this." She shoved her handbag in my arms and started donning gloves and protective booties.

Lily and the officer were strolling by the swimming pool. They seemed to be getting along well.

Diane slid on gloves while surveying the driveway, backed up with two cruisers, the SID van, and the L.A. county coroner's van. "The M.E.'s already here. I want to see the stiff before they take it away. *You* got me into this, remember?"

"Me?"

"You gave me the hair to analyze." Her cheeks were flushed from the argument with the officer. It registered in a spike in her scent. My nose sang. Bill Evans played.

"Well, did you?"

"Are you kidding? Do you know how long it takes to run that kind of analysis?" She pushed the red metal door open with a blue-gloved hand. "Have you seen the body already?"

I shook my head and held the door open for her. "Just got here a few minutes ago."

We stepped inside, sunrays drifting through the window panels and glinting off shiny wood floors. The air was chilly, the AC blasting through air vents from the ceiling. Right off the door, we came down three steps and were enveloped in a living area, the first one of what looked like an open plan the size of a five-star hotel lobby. A tall chandelier came down from the ceiling and had me wonder if one needed a parachute to change its light bulbs. A spiral staircase coiled all the way to a loft.

I inhaled and smelled ninhydrin and fingerprinting

powder, wood floor wax and carpet cleaners. I smelled everyday life mixed with police procedural, I smelled the dog the officer was entertaining outside, and I smelled fear still lingering in the air.

All around there were few walls and all very white, with the sole apparent function of holding some kind of modern art artifact: a red canvas, a black vase illuminated by a receding light, a crystal sculpture.

Whoever designed the house was a minimalist.

Whoever lived in the house put up with it.

The first living space led to the second one through an archway and up a few steps, only to come back down again into a white kitchen with stainless steel appliances and shiny black countertops. A two-sided fireplace separated the kitchen from the rest of the open-floor space, flanked by a wet bar equipped with sink and fridge cellar.

Next to the wet bar, shimmering in the sunlight from the windowpanes, was the most exquisite creature I'd ever seen. She stood leaning on her right side, her left leg bent as if about to step forward, and her ethereal face tilted, looking past me, past all things earthly and mundane. A veil barely hung to her hips, and part of me wanted to help her lift it up, the other part wanted to wait to see if it would fall off.

"Wow." Diane stepped closer and touched her. "The Venus de Milo. I've never seen a life-size replica before."

"Me neither," I said. "Gorgeous at the Louvre, tacky in a place like this."

"I guess you're right." Diane shrugged and moved on to meet the stiff. I came to terms with the fact that Venus wasn't going to shed the veil and stepped into the kitchen.

Dr. Frederick Lyons was sitting on a bar stool by the kitchen island, his knotty hands wrapped around his head. Gray locks spilled between his fingers. An untouched glass of water stood in front of him.

I said, "My condolences, Dr. Lyons."

He didn't move. He didn't give away any sign that he'd heard me.

An officer from the Pacific Community station stood behind him. "Detective Presius?" he asked. I nodded, and we shook hands across the countertop. "We offered to take Dr. Lyons to the station, but he wishes to wait until the medical examiner is finished."

I tried to smell the man, but no emotion came through. No sorrow, no anger, no fear. I caught the odor of chlorine from the pool, faint, washed out by a long shower still lingering on his skin. And no booze, despite the nice assortment I'd glimpsed in the wine cabinet above the wet bar.

Diane emerged from a sliding door to the right and handed me a pen and clipboard. "Here, sign the log. Dr. Cohen just began his examination."

Hell, *her* I could smell.

* * *

When I die, I want to be alone. Like elephants. They sense their time has come, leave the herd and walk to a secluded place.

When the time comes, I want to know. So I can die alone.

No eyes staring at me.

No penlights shining in my eyes, no probes poking my butthole.

No smelling my dirty underwear as death inflicts its final bowel movement.

There's dignity in dying alone.

What I was staring at had no dignity. Homicide never does.

The room was filled with feminine fragrance, the glamorous and expensive kind. It was so strong it choked the first methane exhalations from the corpse and the reek of scorched skin.

Laura Lyons lay sprawled on the floor, her face mauled. A purple grin marked her throat from ear to ear. She was wearing a light blue robe. Pink slippers lay at her side, one next to the other the way some people leave them at night before going to bed. It all felt too orderly.

Cohen updated Satish and me on his preliminary findings. Despite the AC in full blast, his round face was red and pearled with sweat. "Body temperature's eighty-five. Given the AC, I'm guessing she hasn't been dead for more than five hours. He crouched by the body and pointed a penlight to Laura's head. "Her face is cooked."

Cohen retraced the ridges and valleys of Laura's face with the beam of the penlight. It was like looking at a hillside after a mudslide. Some of the acid had spilled onto the beige sheepskin rug she lay on and left blotches of scorched fabric. The tiles were next to her head. Three, this time, in a vertical row: aquamarine, green, and red. I let the photographer take the usual set of shots then crouched, picked up the red one and brought it to my nose. Sweet and rotten, like Amy's tiles. And a hint of nitrile rubber.

Satish was examining a second tile. He flipped it over and showed me the back. "Look at this. This wasn't on the set from Amy's house."

A string of characters and symbols was engraved on the back of the tile he was holding. I flipped the one in my hands and noticed the same letters and numbers, only in a different order: #w 0.9, #tks -0.4, #lw 1, #m 61. The third tile also had similar combinations of hashes, numbers and characters at the back.

"Could it be a store code?" Satish wondered.

"Or maybe a serial number?"

"Whatever it is, it's interesting. We'll run it by Electronics." He took out his notebook and copied the engravings.

Cohen held Laura's chin between his thumb and index fingers and turned her head. She was just starting to set. A flap of scalp had been removed from the back of her head, right above the nape. Cohen pushed away her long, blond hair, measured the area, and then exposed the right side of her neck. He waited for the photographer to take a few close-ups before speaking again. "The ligature mark looks exactly like the one on Amy Liu. Straight and smooth. A raised abrasion, purple in color." He held out his measuring tape. "Sixteen centimeters long, from three centimeters below the right lobe, to half a centimeter away from the left lobe." He shifted, his face reddening from the strain. "Hmm, this is interesting. Take a good shot at this area here," he added, beckoning the photographer.

Satish and I waited for the camera's flash to go off then squatted closer. Cohen's gloved finger pointed to the left edge of the ligature mark. The smooth indentation changed abruptly, almost cut off by an orthogonal dent less than half an inch long. The dent was less deep than the ligature mark, and it almost funneled out of it.

"A telltale mark," Satish said. "I've never seen one like that."

"So much for a telltale," I said.

Diane's scent drifted to my nose a second before her voice. "Have you examined her feet and hands, Doctor?"

Cohen nodded slowly, as if still pondering the telltale mark. "Only the feet. Will get to the hands shortly."

I flinched. "The hands?"

Satish replied, "We noticed as you were getting here, Track. The hands have the same lesions and skin excisions

147

as the feet. Washburn was right. The violence is escalating. He hadn't touched Amy Liu's hands."

Laura's left hand lay by her side, her right one on the chest. The hand was pale, with soft fingers that knew no or little housework. Cohen turned her palm face up and pointed the light. Straight, blade-inflicted lesions like the ones I'd seen on Amy's feet marked the base of Laura's fingers. Small flaps of skin had been carved out of the heel of her hand.

Diane's voice was anxious. "Do you see anything in there?"

Cohen's assistant passed him a magnifying glass. "Hmm. Can't see anything to the naked eye. Maybe we'll have better luck at the morgue."

"Are you sure—"

"Ah, don't worry, Ms. Kyle." Cohen held up Laura's arm and helped his assistant wrap a plastic bag around her hand. "She's in good hands." And then a smile sprawled across his large face. "In good hands! Get it? A pun," he giggled as the assistant wrapped Laura's hands.

He shook his head, the smile quickly vanishing, and got back to his feet. "You guys do realize this completely ruins our Fourth, don't you?"

"It's high priority, Doc. Serial killers don't go on vacation."

"Sadly not." He pulled up his schedule on his phone, and after he tapped through a few screens we had a date at the morgue for the next morning at eight a.m. "I'll confirm after I get all the paperwork in. Something tells me the schedule's still open for tomorrow."

He dropped the phone in his pocket and returned his attention to the body.

I rose to my feet and looked around the room. It was a large home office, accessible only through the sliding door that led into the kitchen. A birch desk sat between the beige rug and a wide window. The window offered a nice view of Playa Del Rey, with the marina's bobbing masts peeking through skinny palm tops.

"I don't like Lyons's story," Satish said. "He claims he and his wife got up around six a.m. He went to the pool for his morning swim, she came here to write. She's also an MD, working on HIV, just like him. She was finishing up a grant, the deadline was next Monday."

"Was she working in the same clinic as Lyons?" I asked.

"No. Different one, down in El Segundo," Satish replied. "Lyons wasn't involved in the grant, either."

"Still," I wondered. "There's a good chance she knew Amy Liu. And perhaps her killer, too."

I'd just learned from Ricky Vargas that Lyons had a relationship with Amy Liu. They'd been good at hiding it with some people—Ipanema Girl had sworn Amy wasn't involved in any relationship, so had all of Amy's friends and family members we had interviewed—but not all. What if Laura had found out?

Satish flipped through his notebook and reported Lyons's version of the events. "Lyons swims for half an hour—he's sure about that because he times himself. Comes back in the house, showers, gets dressed, makes her coffee. When he delivers the coffee he finds her dead. Before that, he doesn't hear or notice anything odd or out of place."

"What time was it when he found her?"

"He wouldn't say for sure. I'm figuring between seven thirty and eight, given the swim and the shower. Thing is, he didn't call nine-one-one until it was almost nine."

"I just walked by the pool," I said. "Anybody coming in would've walked the same way?"

"No, there's a second gate through the east wall. The intruder came through the front door, though. The back door was locked from the inside. Lyons didn't bother locking the front door. Still, that doesn't explain the gate. It opens with a combination. There's a keypad by the gate and another one inside the house that opens it remotely."

"So the intruder either knew the combination or somebody let him in."

Satish lowered his voice. "If it *was* an intruder, yes."

I pondered. "What did Lyons sound like on the nine-one-one call?"

Satish tweaked his chocolate lips in one of his wise smiles. "Don't know. But our next stop is Electronics, and we can both listen to the tape *very carefully*."

"Smooth move."

Especially after Vargas picked Lyons out of a six-pack.

I checked Laura's desk. It was strewn with loose papers—pages and pages covered in red pen marks. A computer screen was snoozing in the middle of the chaos. I touched the mouse and it came back to life. It was open on a word document, densely typed with a very thin margin all around. The last sentence hung unfinished: *To manufacture clinical lots of HIV proteins for efficacy evaluation of poxvirus/protein prime-boost regimes in*

The rest of the page was white, save for the very last line, which read, "THE END."

Diane came to look at it too. "Nobody finishes a grant with the words 'THE END'," she said.

I sniffed the keyboard and mouse. "Are you saying she couldn't have written those words herself?"

It was fainter than on the tiles, but it was there—the killer's smell. The Trace guys had done a good job flouring the computer and phone, but I already knew the answer to their efforts. Rubber gloves don't leave fingerprints.

Diane scooted in front of me and slid into the chair. "That's easy to check. I'll pull up the auto-recovery file."

Cohen picked up his tools and notes, snapped his bag closed and dismissed the photographer. His assistant brought in the tarp body bag and unfolded it on the floor next to the body.

Diane typed on a terminal shell, her gloved fingers squeaking at every keystroke. "There," she said, pointing to the screen. "This one was saved at six fifty-nine. It's the auto-recovery file."

She scrolled all the way to the bottom of the document. There were only blank pages after the last unfinished sentence. The words 'THE END' weren't there.

I turned to Satish. "What's the exact time on Lyons's nine-one-one?"

He checked his notes. "Eight fifty-two."

My eyes strayed to the body, her non-face frozen in Munch's silent scream. "Lyons swims thirty minutes, gets back into the house, showers, gets dressed, makes coffee. Claims he doesn't notice or hear a thing until he comes to her office to bring her coffee. He doesn't spill a drop of coffee, doesn't shout or panic. In fact, we have no friggin' clue what the man does for over forty minutes, until he calls nine-one-one."

Either the man had nerves of steel or he was full of it.

Diane swiveled away from the computer. "What if Laura died after eight thirty and the killer fiddled with her computer to let us believe she died earlier?"

"That's a question for Electronics," Satish said.

She rose from the chair. "I'll talk to the Field Unit guys. If they pack this up, I can bring it to Piper Tech."

Two more assistants from the coroner's office came into the room with a stretcher. They lifted Laura's tarp cocoon and carried it away.

A pained growl came from the kitchen as they left the room. Sat and I ran.

Lyons was standing by the breakfast counter. He was tall and imposing and the space seemed to bend around him. His hair was tousled, his face colorless. He kept his palms up and blood trickled down one of his wrists, soaking the cuff of his shirt.

Glass shards were scattered on the countertop and on the floor.

He tried to slit his wrists, my first thought.

"What the hell happened?" I yelled.

The uniformed officer pulled a wad of Kleenex out of a box on the kitchen counter and offered it to Lyons. "The glass," the officer said. "It just popped in his hand." He snapped his fingers. "Just like that, you know?"

"Call Cohen," Satish ordered him.

Lyons stared at his palms. His lips moved without making any sound.

Satish grabbed a kitchen towel hanging by the stove and wrapped it around Lyons's bleeding hand. I stood behind him, ready to either flip him if he became too aggressive or hold him if he fainted on us.

He did neither. He flopped like jello, leaned against the counter top, and cried like a baby.

Still holding the stretcher with Laura's body, the two coroner assistants stood frozen in the middle of the living room, looking dull and clueless like statues at the park.

I frowned at them. "Don't you have a first aid kit you can go grab from your van?"

The chubbier of the two shrugged. "Don't need one of those for the dead!"

He signaled to his partner, and the two carried on with their task, the stretcher wobbling between them.

Cohen walked into the kitchen and set his clipboard on the countertop. I thought he too was going to make one of his tacky jokes about not doing the living. Instead he remained quite composed and asked Lyons whether he thought he needed stitches. Lyons mouthed a feeble no. The officer came back with some bandages and a bottle of hydrogen peroxide he'd found in one of the bathrooms. Cohen helped Lyons to the kitchen sink, had him thoroughly wash his hands and then disinfected the cuts. He agreed they weren't deep enough to need stitches.

Satish's shoes crunched over the glass shards. "Dr. Lyons, maybe it would be better if you came—"

"No. I wanted to stay. I wanted to see her one more time. I—"

We settled him on the white couch in front of the two-sided fireplace, and he folded onto himself like a book too heavy to stay open. All his certainties had burst on the floor like the glass of water he'd just popped.

"Would you like a drink, Doctor?" I asked.

He unconvincingly shook his head.

Satish said, "Dr. Lyons, we can go somewhere else to talk. Some place where you would be more comfortable…"

I kept my ears perked and walked to the wet bar to fix the man a drink. Had I not been on duty, I would've fixed one for myself too. The statue of Venus stood by the wet bar, impassible and imperturbable. Shadows of palm tree fringes danced on her face. She looked as if she winked at me.

Hell, I'd fix her *a drink too.*

Ironically, she and the family dog were the only witnesses we had so far.

The wine cabinet had an interesting assortment of Cabernets, a couple of Brunellos, a few Chiantis. I figured Lyons would appreciate something with a stronger personality, so I closed the cabinet and went sniffing for whiskey. There was a half-full bottle up on the shelves, next to a grappa. I walked around the tall fireplace and back into the kitchen in search for a clean glass, careful not to step on the shards scattered all over the floor. There was an empty coffee mug in the sink. Could've been the one meant for Laura. The fluorescent bulbs beneath the kitchen cabinets were on, washing a cold light on the granite countertops. In a corner, between the coffee maker and a few kitchen appliances that looked like they'd just come out of the box, was a twelve-inch flat screen TV. It was showing a football game. It seemed surreal on mute. I reached for the remote and turned it off. My eyes fell on a bunch of coins next to the pedestal. They were just coins, smelled like coins, and yet I couldn't take my eyes away from them. And then I realized why. They were aligned in a row. Three quarters, two nickels, five dimes.

I'd already seen that. Where?

Amy's crime scene came back in a blur. Small details—wine glasses scattered around the house, a pile of dishes in the sink, trays of wontons and spring rolls. The smells, the chaos, the house: everything was so different compared to the cold, almost static crime scene I was staring at now—the shattered glass on the floor the only sign of entropy.

Except for one detail.

A row of perfectly aligned coins on Amy's console by the door.

That's where I'd seen it before.

I bent over and sniffed the money.

Metal, sweat, gloves.

Nitrile gloves.

I whirled my head around. Of all places, why did the killer come back here? Did he bring the coins or did he see them lying around and felt the need—compulsion—to order them? I brushed a hand along the countertop, crouched, and examined the reflection against the fluorescent light. Lots of mug rings but no fingerprints, not even gloved ones. The smell of nitrile became stronger.

I followed it.

I stuck my fingers underneath the countertop, found a panel that covered the gap between the top of the dishwasher and the granite. It felt loose, I pulled it. It came off easily, leaving a smudge of detritus on my latex gloves. Another smear was already on the floor. I groped with two fingers inside the groove until I felt something slide under my touch.

I pulled it out and brought it to my nose. It was drenched in Laura Lyons's nauseatingly sweet fragrance.

It was the picture of a woman, smiling, her face scribbled over with a pen.

The woman wasn't Laura Lyons, though.

It was Amy Liu.

"Dr. Lyons," Satish was saying. "I understand this is a very distressful time for you. Like I said, if you'd rather go somewhere else to talk…"

Lyons didn't reply. He rubbed his eyes until they were bloodshot. "What time is it?" he drawled.

"Time to take this conversation downtown," I replied, holding up the picture I'd just found.

TWELVE

"It was planted."

"There's a date and place on the back. It's in your handwriting, Dr. Lyons."

"So? It was planted."

I rapped my fingers on the table. The guy had more certainties than the Pope.

After being in Lyons's refrigerated house for over four hours, the squad room felt like a furnace. Satish loosened his tie knot. I undid the damn thing all together and let the tie hang around my neck.

Lyons hunched over the table in the interview cubicle and played with a Styrofoam cup filled with black coffee. After the latest developments, I'd changed my mind on the whiskey.

A greasy pizza box lay open on the table, Lyons's two slices still untouched. A stubborn fly stalked the pepperoni. Satish shooed it off, just out of habit. Unconcerned, the fly came back, just out of habit.

Lyons didn't move. His nose was stuck up in the air and his eyes were scrutinizing us, either pitying us or despising us, I couldn't decide which. I dropped my hand on the picture for the tenth time. It showed Amy Liu in a bikini and a sexy pose. Her face had been scribbled over with a pen, but it was her all right. And the fact that, of all things, her face had been scribbled over would've made any shrink like Washburn prickle with excitement.

Planted my ass.

Vargas put Lyons at Amy's house the night Amy had been killed. The kid was ready to testify that the two were romantically involved. The picture I'd found was drenched in Laura Lyons's perfume. What if Laura had found out about the affair?

I tried to get a whiff of nitrile gloves from Lyons, but any smell his hands may have carried earlier had been washed out after Cohen helped him clean his hands and cuts earlier at the house. All I could sense now was blood and hydrogen peroxide.

"Look, Doc," I said. "We wanna believe you, 'kay? But you've got to help us out. There's a bunch of holes in your story and we need to fill 'em up or else our boss is going to come after us. And if he comes after us, we have no choice but come after *you*."

Lyons said nothing.

Sat indulged in his broad, reassuring smile. It fell unnoticed. "*Numero uno*," he said. "We know you had an affair with Amy Liu. We have a witness who puts you at her house. He says you two were intimate."

I thought the news would surprise him. Instead, the man didn't even flinch. He looked down at the pen, bent the clip backwards and started twisting it. Swarms of freckles netted the back of his hands. They were interesting freckles, the kind that form patterns, and the more you stare the more patterns you see. Somehow I found it fascinating.

I didn't smell fear or sorrow. I smelled annoyance, impatience, regret. I smelled a life of overachieving and giving orders, of Harvard degrees and Ivy League recognition, of important handshakes and well-orchestrated battles of egos.

I tapped Amy's face in the picture, what was still visible of it through the inflicted scribbles. "You know what I'm thinking, Doc? I'm thinking Laura did this." Lyons flinched at his wife's name. "She found out about the affair and confronted you. You went alone to Amy's party the night she was killed—was it because Laura had a reason to hold a grudge against Amy? Did Laura kill Amy or did you? And then things got out of hand—"

"Stop talking about my dead wife like that," he snapped. "Laura didn't need to find out about Amy. Laura *knew* about Amy."

There was a pause. Satish and I stared at one another.

A crack as thin as ice came to Lyons's voice. "You don't get it, do you?"

I spoke nicely. "Help us get it."

"We filed for divorce two months ago. You can ask Laura's lawyer. It was a mutual agreement, and we were in friendly terms. Laura was working on the grant proposal— the grant was all she'd been doing for the past four weeks. That's why she hadn't started looking for her own place yet. We'd agreed I'd pay her half and she'd move out as soon as time allowed." He swallowed. "The grant deadline is next Monday, and—"

He gave me one of those looks that you feel like washing off your face like spit. "You don't understand. I still loved my wife."

Satish leaned back in his chair. His smile was

understanding and embracing and it wisely spread to a grin. "As a matter of fact we do, Doctor. Especially us cops. We love our wives so much we feel the need to have three or four at least. Ask my partner. How many wives does a cop have on average, Track?"

I got out of the chair and started pacing. "Two and a half. The half comes from people like me who'd rather exchange beds than wedding vows."

Lyons didn't register any of the words we'd said. He stared into his coffee cup, by now as lukewarm as the room. "You've got it all wrong. They're after me. Laura… oh god, this is despicable. First Amy, then Laura. Don't you see? They're after me. They want to kill *me*."

Satish and I exchanged a long glance.

I dropped back in the chair. "Why d'you think you're the target?"

Lyons straightened his back and put on a face like I'd just asked why he was wearing pants. "They've been after me since my research focused on the origin of HIV."

We welcomed the statement with a long, thoughtful silence.

After the long, thoughtful silence, Satish spoke. "Why would anyone be upset over a disease?"

Lyons's thin lips stretched. It was a sad, bitter smile. "We're scholars, right? You'd think research would be respected, whether it's stem cell research or gene therapy or disease epidemiology. You'd think we'd civilly discuss things among ourselves." He shook his head. "There's always somebody who knows better." He tapped the pen with the bandaged hand and twirled the Styrofoam cup with the other. "Have you heard of HIV/AIDS *denialism*?"

We hadn't.

"When the HIV virus was first isolated, back in the Eighties, a bunch of colleagues were skeptical. Their position was—still is—that drugs and certain behaviors cause AIDS, not HIV. Since so many years pass between the HIV infection and the onset of AIDS, for a while these claims found quite some support in the scientific community. Robert Wilner, an MD from North Carolina, went as far as to inject himself with blood from an HIV-positive patient to prove his conviction. He never got AIDS, by the way. He died of a heart attack one year later."

"I suppose that could work too," I commented.

Lyons didn't take notice. "Conspiracy theorists claimed HIV had been engineered by the U.S. military. Some theorized it came from the polio vaccine, others from the smallpox vaccine. In the meantime, HIV-positive people carried on with their lives, which included high-risk behaviors that caused the number of infections to rise. HIV-positive pregnant women in South Africa were denied anti-retroviral drugs that could've prevented their babies to become infected. All because of the denialist movement." Lyons twisted the clip of the pen until it broke. "Ideas are powerful. They can give life and they can take it away."

For a few minutes all we heard was the intermittent buzzing of the fly and the drone of traffic down North Los Angeles Street.

Satish shifted in his chair and made it squeak. "It's been almost ten years, though."

"And the conspiracy theory hasn't died," Lyons retorted.

"What conspiracy?"

He sighed, his eyes hardened. "For some people it's more feasible to believe in some genetically engineered disease mysteriously introduced in the environment than a fast mutating virus that jumped from monkeys to humans less than one hundred years ago. I've dedicated my entire life to proving them wrong. Denialists hate people like me.

They send us threat letters and emails on a regular basis. I delete them and that's the end of it."

"You never filed a complaint with the police?"

Lyons made a brisk gesture as if annoyed by the question. "Of course I did. I even hired a private bodyguard back in 2002. I was traveling a lot, giving talks and participating in board meetings. I don't take chances with my life."

The fly had finished its tour of all the pepperoni slices. It crawled along the cardboard then flew on Lyons's Styrofoam cup. He stared at it vacantly. It never occurred to him to shoo it away. There were a lot of things that had never occurred to him before.

I got up and looked out the window. The workday was coming to an end, and the One-Ten droned its evening commute. From the squad room, I heard chairs drag and murder books snap closed. Laughter, yawns, a pat on the shoulder. A "Hey, wanna grab a beer?" that tapped into a web of solitude we don't always have the guts to face.

"You're staying for dinner, Dr. Lyons, right?" I quipped.

The man considered the proposal while chewing on his lower lip. "Actually, I'd rather go home, now. It's been a long day."

His voice was plain, his manners calm. I no longer smelled adrenaline. The guy really wanted to go home and have a good night's sleep. And maybe wake up tomorrow and find it was all a bad dream.

I gave him my best smile. "I understand, Doc. It's been a long day for me and my partner, too. You wanna know why? Because some people deny AIDS, others deny murder. That's why."

That put him right back on alert mode. He flattened his palms on the table and stared at us. I couldn't tell if he was shocked or outraged by my remark. "I told you everything," he said.

"Actually," Satish said, "I never got to *numero dos*."

"What?" he said.

"You haven't told us what you did when you found your dead wife in the study. At least forty minutes went by before you finally picked up the phone and called nine-one-one."

If Lyons was feigning surprise, he was doing it remarkably well. "Forty minutes? What are you talking about? I saw her on the floor and I—I—" He swallowed, his hand lost in the air as if trying to weave back memories. Then he dropped it on the table. "I called nine-one-one. That's all I did. I was in shock."

So shocked he has the presence of mind to put the mug back in the sink and rinse it.

Satish leaned forward and pushed the pizza box toward him. "Have some food, Doctor. We're gonna be here for a while."

He shook his head and put on a strained smile. "I thought of reviving her. She wasn't breathing, and—and there was nowhere to blow air into. She just wasn't there anymore. I—" He swallowed hard. "I had this patient, once, in my residency. He shot himself through the chin and missed the vital organs. He blew off his face, but he was still alive. He couldn't see, he couldn't talk. It was horrific to watch. The idiot couldn't even kill himself. What were we supposed to do? Let him live with no face?" He stared at the fly then out of the blue shooed it away. His anger rippled the air and drifted to my nostrils.

He drew in a sharp breath and tuned down his voice. "Laura—when I saw her this morning—her face looked like that. But she wasn't breathing. She didn't have a pulse. And that—that was good. In a twisted way, but it was good."

A thought occurred to me then. I felt goose bumps

prickle at the back of my neck, and they brought my temperature down a few notches. "You didn't—did you wait for her to die?"

His sharp, icy eyes felt like a burn on my skin.

"She wasn't breathing," he said. "There was no pulse."

It was getting chilly. Or maybe it was all that snow in the middle of summer.

"Is that what you found out when you went back to Amy's house the night she was killed?"

He bristled. "I—Why do you keep bringing back Amy? I'm here because my wife was murdered this morning!" He lost it. He slammed a hand on the table—the one he hadn't injured—and rose from the chair. "I did not go back to Amy's house. Amy's dead, and so is my wife. Now do your fucking job and catch the bastard who did this before he comes and kills me too!"

Satish's eyes gave me the cue. We both rose. "Please sit down, Dr. Lyons," Satish said.

The man flopped back in the chair like a used magazine. That last spur had taken all his energy. I walked back to the squad room, grabbed the brown paper bag Katie had left on my desk, and returned to the interview cubicle.

Lyons's eyes darted. "What's that?"

I took the recorder out of the paper bag and put it on the table. "So you never went back to Amy's house that night?"

Lyons straightened up and perched on the edge of the chair. Something was finally biting that cool ass of his. "No. I did not. Why? What's this about?"

I pressed the play button. There was static, then the operator's voice,

"Nine-one-one, what's your emergency?"

At the other end of the line someone breathed into the receiver. "I'm at 453 Santa Fe Terrace, in Montecito Heights."

Keystrokes, from the operator. "What's your name and emergency, sir?"

A long sigh, then the answer. "A body."

"Can you state your name, sir? And are you sure it's a body—"

"It's dead. Definitely dead. Her face is... abraded."

"What? Sir, can you repeat that last word? What happened to her face—"

There was a long beep and the operator telling the dispatcher she'd lost the line. I stopped the tape. Lyons's face was as white as a full moon.

"Would you like to hear the next tape, Dr. Lyons?"

"What next tape?"

"The call from your home. We got that one, too. And you know what we did? We brought both tapes to our guys at Electronics. They're smart, the folks down there. They have this cool software that can match voices, even when they're strained through a handkerchief. And guess what they found?"

He closed his fists and bit his lip again. "You're bluffing. They can't—that wasn't my voice you just played."

"You're so sure, Doctor, aren't you?" Satish said. "Would that be because you'd put a handkerchief over the mouthpiece?"

I pressed on. "That's such an old trick. You know computers can get around that stuff." I leaned closer and locked my eyes on his. "You see, we've got your voice on tape and a witness. You better tell us what happened, Doc, or you're going down for double murder."

"Double—What? What the hell are you talking about?"

I smelled fear for the first time. High pitched and loud, sour perspiration pearling his wrinkled forehead. Gray locks plastered his temples.

His eyes darted from me to Satish then back to me. He

swallowed hard, dug his nails into his arm.

"This is… This is when I ask for a lawyer. Cut the crap and get me a fucking phone."

Damn. It's always like that. Right when you think you've pressed them into a corner, they sober up. I looked at Satish. He shrugged and shook his head.

* * *

The lawyer came—a distinct, mature man with round, intellectual eyeglasses, or maybe I should say spectacles, and a bowtie sitting below his throat. The rusty red of his hair strained into gray at the temples. His white shirt smelled of starch and old-fashioned things—pipe tobacco, Beethoven and Wagner LPs, and a black cat curled on an old, tartan throw. His posture was staged yet casual, and his brown linen blazer ran a little long on the hips, with carefully arranged wrinkles. He spoke softly, which is not unheard of among defense lawyers, his well-intoned diction tampered with the subtlest accent of all—the lack of one.

Satish showed both the law doctor and the medical doctor into the Captain's office, which was a far more appropriate accommodation than the dingy cubicle at the back of our squad room, and left them there to confabulate. They called us back after about half an hour. Lyons looked reinvigorated. The lawyer hadn't changed a bit.

"My Client wishes to cooperate," the lawyer said, in his whispery voice. How he could capitalize the word "client" every time he pronounced it, I couldn't tell. He just did. His eyelids hung halfway across his lenses as he steepled his hands neatly in front of him. "I advised him not to, but he still wants to talk to you."

Satish leaned forward and crossed his arms. "We're happy to hear that."

The lawyer didn't reciprocate the enthusiasm. "My Client has nothing to hide," he said. "He's choosing to cooperate because he wants you to get the perpetrator as much as you do."

I pulled a chair and sat down. "Let's hear it."

Lyons bobbed his head forward and cleared his throat. "I made the nine-one-one call from Amy's house," he said. Two sets of brows in the room shot up. "But I didn't kill her."

"Why did you lie about it, then?"

His eyes turned the color of water under a stormy sky. "Because everybody had already seen me leave. I couldn't —" He inhaled. "Look. That was the plan. Leave before everybody else did, drive around for some time until everybody left the party, then come back."

"You had plans for the night?"

He nodded wearily.

"Why keep it all hushed up if Laura knew and you two had already filed for divorce?"

"Amy didn't want the news to spread at the clinic. Not until Laura had moved out, at least."

"How long had the affair been going on?" Satish asked.

The icy look in his eyes resurfaced. "Six months."

I looked at the lawyer. He sat quietly next to his Client, his features as expressive as Abraham Lincoln's statue at the National Mall.

I was getting tired. "Amy never hinted at wanting to put an end to it?"

Lyons shook his head. "We were — happy." He swallowed, licked his lips. His fingers played with a piece of paper. "Amy — she liked the secrecy. She said it made it more exciting."

I scratched my brow. "Amy didn't mind the fact that Laura was still living with you?"

"No."

"Did you?"

His glare was as sharp as a paper cut. "You may not understand this, Detective, but I loved my wife. And Amy, too—"

"May I remind you, Detective, that my Client has no Obligation to answer that kind of Question."

The Lawyer was getting pissed. Now he capitalized all nouns.

I leaned back and crossed my arms. "Fine. Tell us what you saw when you returned to Amy's house."

"The door was ajar, which was strange. All lights were on." He inhaled. "I didn't see much, really. I saw her feet on the floor, first, and then the rest. When I saw her face, I—"

If it were a show, it was a damn good one. Lyons brought a hand to his face and sobbed like a child. The lawyer, pardon me, the Lawyer took a handkerchief out of the front pocket of his blazer and offered it to his Client. "My Client saw nothing," he said. "He needs to go home and rest. He's been through a lot. If he can think of anything to help the investigation, we will call."

The Lawyer stood up. We all followed.

"Catch the bastard," Lyons said, choking on his own words.

We shook hands. They were soft hands. I waited until their scents vanished down the hallway and into the elevator, then retrieved the pizza box from the cubicle, dropped it on my desk, grabbed a slice and bit into it.

Satish leaned on his desk and watched me with a frown sculpted across his forehead. "A fly has walked all over those leftover slices."

I shrugged. "I've eaten far worse than pepperoni walked over by flies."

Sat grinned. "You're right, there's always worse than

flies. Frank Armand, from Van Nuys, used to frisk bums and whores with his bare hands. Never bothered washing them before eating, either."

I spoke with my mouth full. "That's nothing. It's after he frisks stiffs that he has me grossed out."

Satish smiled without really meaning it. He stared at the ceiling without meaning that either. I munched down the last slice of pizza, then walked to the water fountain, drank, and returned to my desk. It's a nice feeling to be hungry, one that shouldn't be taken for granted.

I opened a drawer, plucked out a paper clip, and stuck it between my teeth. "So, you buy his story?" I asked.

Satish crossed his arms and wobbled his head. "Some pieces are still missing from the puzzle. He could've done Amy in because of the argument they had at work. But why do the wife?"

I worked my tongue around the paperclip. "Laura's lawyer confirmed she'd filed for divorce." I'd made the call while Lyons and the Lawyer were confabulating in the captain's office.

Satish wrapped a fist around his chin. "And what about the clues? The fibers, the tiles…"

"The fibers could be from the African artifacts," I said. "I've got Diane working on that."

"Why the tiles?"

"To veer us."

There was some silence. After the silence, Satish said, "Lyons strikes me as a womanizer, not a killer."

"Okay," I said. "Okay. Forget Amy, for a moment. Focus on the wife. Even if he didn't kill her—he found her clinging to life and waited until she was dead to call nine-one-one."

Satish walked around his desk and picked up the phone. "You can't prove it."

"You heard him, didn't you? Why did he tell us the

story of the faceless guy at the ER? Hey, who are you calling?"

He raised a hand and talked into the mouthpiece. "Hi, Pacific Station, this is Satish Cooper from Parker Center." He clicked his jaw and wore his charming smile. Female watch officer at the other end of the line, no doubt. "I'm good, how are you, kid?"

The kid said something. Satish laughed politely. "It's good to talk to you too. Listen. I know things get tight over there, but when you got a minute for this old cop friend of yours, would you mind doing me a favor?" His voice rose and bobbed like a boat on a lull. "You got time now? Well, that's fabulous. I know I can always count on you, baby!"

The baby giggled and the giggle crackled out of the mouthpiece.

Satish winked at me and made his request. "U-huh. You can pull it up? Uh-huh. Yeah, I can wait. No problemo, babe."

Detective Cooper charmed his way through the terminals of the Pacific Community Station while wearing his imperturbable smile and examining his polished nails. I could hear the clicking of a keyboard from the other end of the phone. He laughed, from time to time, asked about the kid's kid. When he was done, he bargained a promise to have everything sent through email and then hung up. He opened up his notebook and scribbled down some notes.

"May I be part of this investigation too, partner?"

Satish tapped the notebook with his pen. "Lyons wasn't lying about one thing."

"Which is?"

"The hate mail. He filed two complaints in 2002 and 2004. There are letters and emails on record. Jade's going to send me a copy of the report. She pulled it up and gave me a sneak peek: Lyons filed a third complaint while at a conference in San Francisco in 2002. He claimed a stranger approached him with a knife and told him to retract his positions on HIV. After the incident, Lyons requested a police escort but all he got from the PD was a list of names and numbers of private companies. We can call them up and find out which one he ended up hiring."

"The origin of the threats was never ascertained?"

"No. Some emails bore the signature 'Continuum,' a denialist group, but the IP addresses turned out to be bogus." He scratched his jaw. "What do you know? Maybe he's right. Maybe they're after him and he'll be the next victim."

"Hmm." I moved the paperclip around my mouth. It made nice, clinking sounds against my teeth. "It's been five years, though, since his last complaint."

"And nine since the Durban declaration, a document signed by over five thousand scientists asserting that HIV causes AIDS. Apparently, the denialist movement hasn't died yet."

"You can kill people, not ideologies."

"There's two reasons why people are hated. One is money, and the other is opinions," Satish said, checking his watch. "We should go get a print-out of Laura Lyons's assets. The bank's closing in five minutes, but a buddy of mine who works there said he'd be waiting for us."

I got to my feet and rolled down the sleeves of my shirt. "So Lyons gets in trouble because of his opinions?"

Satish started to the door. "You know what this reminds me of?"

"Cucumbers." The first thing that came to mind.

"Yeah."

I pulled out a face. "Seriously?"

He smiled. "Nah. It reminds me of my old man's Chevy."

"Right. You can tell me all about it tomorrow."

Satish ignored my comment. "I kept telling him, *Pa, you're too old to drive. You can't see no more.* But no, sir. Stubborn old man, he'd still drive his Chevy all over town," he said, as we walked out of the squad room.

I nodded at the watch sergeant down the hallway and called the elevator. I said, "Sat, old people are like that. They don't wanna hear they're old."

"No. They don't *believe* they're old. One day — "

The elevator chimed and the doors slid open. "Did you just trick me into listening to one of your old man stories?"

He grinned. "You didn't see it coming, did you? So, anyway, I had to drop off my own car for a tune-up. I tell him, *Don't worry, Pa, I'll get the bus.* He says, *Nah, I'll come pick you up.* We go back and forth a few times then I drop it and tell him where and when."

"Did he show up?"

"Yeah, he did. He drove by in the old Chevy he loved so much and didn't stop."

"What d'you mean he didn't stop?"

We crossed the lobby downstairs, our steps echoing in the empty hall of Parker Center. Outside, downtown yawned its warm breath of gas exhaust. Swirls of heat evaporated from the asphalt. My shirt stuck to the small of my back.

"He didn't stop," Satish insisted. "He drives by, looks at me, and drives away. I take the bus, get home, and find him on the porch, drinking a Budweiser. I say, *You didn't stop.* He winces and replies, *You weren't where you said you'd be.*

"You looked right in my direction. I waved at you.

"I can't see that far away.

"Then you should've stopped, I yell.

"Why would I stop if I didn't see you! he yells back."

I laughed. "Guess you couldn't argue, huh?"

Satish dipped his hand in his pocket and fished out his car keys. "Think about it, Track. You can't argue with denial. People are much better at correcting others than they are at correcting themselves." He opened the driver's door. "Are you driving or riding?"

"Driving," I said. "I'm heading home once we're done at the bank, hoping to beat rush hour." It'd been a long day since I'd awakened on my bedroom floor in a pool of sweat.

He nodded, slid behind the wheel and started the car.

I wiped the smile off my face and climbed into my Dodge.

You can't argue with denial.

Can you, Ulysses? Said a voice inside my head.

"I'm fine," I replied to the voice. "There's nothing wrong with me. I feel *just* fine."

THIRTEEN

The dark chrysalis on the white wall hits him like a punch in the face.

A spit of black on his pristine walls.

He puts a hand on the doorframe, then slowly slides his fingers closer, without touching it. He can't get himself to touch the hairy thing.

He stares, pondering.

A dark shell of exoskeleton, with a head, a thorax, two antennae encased inside. And soft, whispery wings waiting to come out.

He could squash it in one swift movement. The thought of the yellowish blotch it would leave on the white wall disgusts him, though.

"Hector! Close the damn door, it's blowing a draft."

He moves his hand away, closes the door. It'll be a few more days before the moth ecloses, he muses, taking his shoes off. He dusts off the tip of his loafers, sprays them, places them in their box, and then the box on the top shelf of the shoe rack by the entrance. He retrieves his slippers.

The pupa can stay one more day. He'll decide later when to get rid of it.

"You're late. Rachel left an hour ago. Where the hell have you been?"

He keeps thinking about the gypsy moth chrysalis as he thoroughly washes his hands, rinses, then washes them one more time, lathering under scorching hot water. Gypsy moths are diurnal. It'll pupate in one-to-two weeks, he figures.

"I was supposed to have Bonefos half an hour ago. But of course, you had to be late. What do you care about your mama anyway, huh? I'm stuck in bed for the rest of my life, and you don't give a fucking shit."

The kitchen is too hot. The sun's been filtering through the tall windows all day and now it feels like a balmy greenhouse. He draws the curtains and cranks up the air conditioning.

"Did you just turn the AC on? How many times do I have to tell you it gives me a headache? How can I have a headache on top of everything else, huh?"

Gypsy moths sometimes lay their eggs in shoes and clothing. He'll have to check all closets, maybe drop a few balls of camphor here and there, even though he hates the smell.

He starts the kitchen faucet and lets the water run as he lines up syringes, spoons, and a bowl on the countertop. The pantry shelves are filled with boxes of latex gloves, paper towels, cans of formula and protein powder, sterile gauzes and feeding bags — everything sorted by expiration date. Makes it easier to find things. He gloves up, pours two cups of formula and one of protein powder in the bowl, adds warm water, one spoonful of sugar, then stirs. He rips open the wrapping of a feeding bag, pours the brownish batter inside, places the bag onto a tray together with the syringe, more gloves, a roll of gauze, the bottle of Roxanol.

"There you are, you scoundrel. You look well fed, you do."

The smell is revolting. The sweet stench of decay and urine, purulent bedsores whose reek can't be covered by any amount of hydrogen peroxide, bleach, or disinfectant.

"Why are you late again? Oh, forget it. You'll never tell me."

He stoops by the bed, pulls up the covers. The urine bag feels warm even through the gloves. He snaps it off, replaces it with a fresh one, caps the full one and seals it away in the medical waste bin in the bathroom. When he comes back, he's wearing a new set of gloves.

"It's not that girl again, is it? You can't marry her, Hector. You just can't. She's such a spoiled bitch, that one. How is she ever going to take care of me, huh? You need somebody who's loving. And caring. Not like Rachel, who sits here all day doing crossword puzzles and blabbering over her phone. You gotta fire her. And you gotta come home earlier, because she doesn't care if you're back or not. She just leaves. Ouch, gentle there, now."

Hector stares at his mother's taut stomach, riddled by raised, purple veins. Everywhere else, her skin is a papery, transparent film over brittle bones. As if the sarcoma sucked all the flesh and collected it on the lower abdomen, making it swell up like a ripe watermelon. A J-peg feeding tube sticks out of her side like a long, misplaced phallus. He soaks some gauze with disinfectant and cleans the skin around the port, before applying dabs of antibacterial ointment.

"I said gentle, do you hear me when I speak? Or do you simply not care? Stuck to a hospital bed for the rest of my life, and my own son doesn't give a fucking shit."

He fills the syringe with a dose of Roxanol and squirts it down the tube. By reflex, she starts sucking on her gums, making little smacking sounds like a baby.

"What's it gonna be tonight, Hector? Cannelloni or lasagna?"

The bloated stomach quivers with the spasms of forlorn laughter. It rattles into a cough and then ebbs off. He flushes water down the tube, hangs the feeding bag on the IV pole, and connects it to the J-peg. He tosses the syringe and gloves in the bin, then hauls the trash bag to the dumpster outside. When he comes back, *he lathers and rinses his hands three times.*

"Do you remember the lasagna your mama used to make, Hector? Ah, those were the days. The house would fill with the aroma of simmering ragú and onions. Nobody makes lasagna the way I did. I bet you miss it, Hector, don't you? Hey! Hector! Where the hell are you going now?"

The office is the coolest room in the house. That's where he keeps the computer. It chimes as he boots it, his thoughts drifting again to the moth pupating on the wall. How did he miss the larva crawling around the house? Disgusting creatures, all covered in hairs.

"Hector! I'd told you to turn off the damn AC! Why don't you ever listen to me, huh? You cursed me, that's what you did. You cursed me to this fucking bed hoping you'd get rid of me, but you're wrong. You hear me? You're dead wrong!"

He inserts his jump drive into the USB port, clicks on the icon and waits, excitement prickling at his fingers.

"You're a fool if you think I'm gonna die this easily. I'm gonna make your life a living hell. I'm gonna die... long and... slow, I'm... gonna... Fool."

The house is silent now, save for the soft whirring of the computer and the crackling snores drifting from the bedroom. He stares at the monitor and beams. Thin lines of colors and gaps crowd the screen, so densely spaced together the eyes get lost and feel jarred.

Not Hector's eyes, though.

To his eyes, every line is a code to decipher, a new language with which he can dominate the world. It's his newly found key to glory, fame, and, finally, revenge.

A long awaited revenge.

FOURTEEN

We had three more tiles. They were identical to the old ones, except for the code at the back. Same shape, same color, same subtle smell—rotten sweet, like a sugary fruit starting to ferment.

It was past six when I got home. I found the usual note at my door—my still unresolved missing persons—but no *lahmajoun* this time (the Armenian pizza), only the words, "Please find her."

Something edible would've been nice too.

I guess I'd slacked on my P.I. job and no longer deserved provisions.

I tossed the note on the couch, opened the fridge, took out the largemouth fillets I'd left to marinate, and turned the oven on. I fed Will and The King, then walked to the bedroom, removed my holsters, guns, cell phone, handcuffs, and all the paraphernalia I carry around my waist, and dumped it all on the bed.

I stripped off my clothes and stepped into the shower.

The tiles kept nagging me.

Aquamarine, green, and red. Why not orange this time?

Maybe he just ran out of those.

What about the lesions he inflicted on the victims: scalp and feet on Amy, scalp, feet, and hands on Laura. *I can see the violence escalating, moving up to mutilation,* Washburn had said. Was there a meaning for the feet and hands? Was there a reason why he wrote THE END at the bottom of Laura's grant draft?

I let chilled water wash down my face.

Two victims, maybe three, plenty of traces, and still no clue.

I stopped the water and sat on the edge of the tub, naked and dripping.

The asshole is no idiot. He's teasing us.

I pulled on a shirt, a pair of shorts, and padded back into the kitchen. The oven was nice and hot, but somehow I felt a strange apathy inside, as if my head were in a different time zone than the rest of my body.

My eyes strayed to the table, overflowing with unread *Fish and Game* issues, unopened junk mail, and an elderly lady smiling from underneath a mop of silvery hair, next to a brown envelope, the one delivered a couple of weeks earlier together with another loaf of *lahmajoun*. I opened the envelope and fished out a black scarf, which I brought to my nose. I smelled the *lahmajoun*, of course. *Brilliant.* And then hairspray, talc, lavender.

Six weeks and I still hadn't found the lady. I hadn't put too much effort into it, either.

Damn it, some evenings are meant to make you feel a failure.

How about you start over and try to do something right, Ulysses?

I turned the oven off and placed the fillets back into the fridge.

Will looked at me in dismay.

"Come on, buddy. We're going for a ride."

That was enough to make him loll his tongue in contentment again. I grabbed the cell phone, the leftover *lahmajoun* from the day before, my Glock, and left.

It's dinner on the freeway tonight.

I still had a couple of hours of daylight and intended to use them.

* * *

When I can't solve a puzzle, I let it sit for a bit and muse over something else, possibly another conundrum I've set aside a while back. And my last unfinished puzzle was Katya Krikorian, the Armenian woman who'd vanished after visiting a friend in El Sereno. Katya's car—an old Honda Civic from the early Nineties—was found parked a few blocks away from her friend's house, one mile south from Huntington Drive.

And that's exactly where I left my Charger.

The friend Katya had just visited—Lyanne Norris, age fifty-nine—had terminal cancer and spent her days in bed. Her nurse had answered the door when I went to see her. She told me Lyanne was sleeping and confirmed that Katya used to visit her once or twice a month. She typically spent about an hour and then left.

When I asked Lyanne's nurse if she had any idea why Katya would leave her car one mile away from there she replied she'd overheard Lyanne recommend a good hiking trail up a set of stairs in that neighborhood. The police had already canvassed all trails within a two-mile radius from where Katya's car had been found, before the case had gone cold and Katya's brother had resolved to hire me.

Turns out, there are a lot of stairs in El Sereno. The ones I'd found back in June led to no trailhead. I'd resolved to check out the rest in the next few days, but my resolution had been sidetracked by the Byzantine Strangler.

Tonight I was determined to find the trailhead.

Rows of trashcans were lined up against cracked stucco walls. Eucalyptus and palm trees poked out of the wavy landscape, and gray antenna dishes craned their faces from red shingle roofs. *For Lease* signs and rusty pick-up trucks were embedded in the bushes and had become part of the landscape. The air smelled of barbecue and fresh laundry tumbling in the dryer.

Dogs barked, kids screamed, a mower droned.

Will trotted ahead of me while I mused. Why would Katya park two miles away from her friend's house?

I walked up the street, the hillside to my left a yellow incline overflowing from a concrete slab wall. The high-pitched laughter of a comedy show spilled out of an open window. Bearded palm trees drew long shadows on the pavement. The sky turned sunset orange. I found myself at the bottom of a steep staircase climbing up the hillside.

Golden sunrays shimmered down the steps, and up at the top all I could see was sky.

Another staircase to nowhere.

It didn't look familiar, so I decided to check it out anyways. I whistled, Will doubled back and flew up the stairs skipping three steps at the time.

I need an extra set of legs, too.

By the time I got to the last step I was drenched in sweat.

There was an unpaved, rutted road snaking through dry land covered in rock, yellow weeds, and the occasional oasis of dogwoods, oaks, and intricate shrubbery. I didn't know what the heck I was doing there, but sometimes you feel like you're part of some greater plan and you just need to play along.

Bullshit, I just needed to convince myself I was doing something useful. So I followed the ruts like Dorothy followed the yellow brick road.

The sun lowered on the horizon and shimmered with hues of pink and yellow. Evening came with its soft smells of grass, wild melon and eucalyptus leaves.

Will had a ball marking the trail with his stuff. Makes you wonder if dogs' bowels and bladders ever run dry.

I could hear the drone of the Ten in the distance, and the humming of the million voices of the City of Angels. A snake swished across the weeds, next to an empty can of soda, a few cigarette butts, a flattened box of condoms, a slab of rock spray-painted in blue.

The place was far from abandoned.

Ulysses, you're wasting your time. This is not where a sixty-two-year-old would hang out for a stroll.

Ulysses, shut up.

The road narrowed to a trail and the vegetation started closing in. Vines of wild melons choked old pieces of junk: a rusty truck fender, a slashed tire, black shreds of tarp. No longer baked by the heat, the soil released new scents only I could sense. I stopped, crouched and inhaled.

A smell, distant, oily, earthly, vaguely reminiscent of molded cheese.

Will stepped on his tracks and looked at me. I nodded, he took off.

I followed him, past a tree stump, past a pile of branches in a sea of weeds, and into an intricate jumble of shrubs. On the ground, three small rocks of the same size had been lined up in a row.

A mark.

Next to the rocks, low branches had been recently

snapped. I crouched, pulled them apart and uncovered an opening through the canopy of twigs and dead leaves. I got to my hands and knees and crawled inside.

The smell peaked. It was strong and foul and I had to swallow several times not to gag.

By my side, Will whined impatiently. He smelled it, too.

I snapped branches, pulled out weeds and shoved away dead foliage until I exposed one end of an old sheet of corrugated metal. I grabbed it with both hands and tried to pull, but it didn't yield. No way to tell how deep underground it was buried. Will barked, the smell clearly doing a number on his senses. I brushed my hand along it and uncovered something that looked like a second mark— three painted tacks along the edge.

I found a splintered two-by-four nearby and used it to break the soil around the panel. I dug with my bare hands, prodding and tugging with the two-by-four until it yielded. An old, screeching smell of decay rushed to my face, so strong it made my eyes water.

Even Will retreated.

Corpse wax.

I shoved the panel to the side and sent it sprawling against the shrubs.

Buried in the dirt was an old concrete cistern, about two feet wide and six feet long, probably a remnant of back when this part of town was farmland. The bottom was covered in black trash bags. One was torn open. Suddenly exposed to the light, from its gaping hole crawled out little creatures with multiple sets of legs: centipedes, beetles, spiders, scorpions. They ran in circles over the trash bags like a crowd of underage drinkers busted out of a bar.

"Party's over, guys."

I prodded the torn bag with a stick, but it felt empty. I shoved the stick in the hole and pulled. The bag came up offering no resistance, only a handful of dirt and sticks spilled from the hole. I prodded the other bags, and this time I felt something inside.

Katya got chopped up, my first thought.

The pit looked old, though, older than six weeks, when Katya Krikorian had disappeared.

I'd had enough experience with corpse wax to know that if it gets on your skin the reek will stay with you for days—corpse wax doesn't wash off, you need to sweat it away. I gently poked a hole in the nearest bag and pried it open. What came out wasn't a piece of sixty-two-year-old Katya. It was a charred little hand, no wider than an inch, one flimsy finger falling off right as I gently pulled it out of the bag.

A hand no wider than an inch… Damn it.

FIFTEEN

The red ember of a cigarette breathed deep into the night then turned into ashes. Detective Ruben Ganzberg, from Hollenbeck Station, inhaled, a suspended look in his dark eyes, as if he were holding the woman of his dreams. He savored the cigarette in his mouth, laces of smoke curling up against the streetlight shafts.

I sat on the stairs at the bottom of the trail and rapped a finger on my knee. The medical examiner on call had agreed to meet us here at the trailhead so we could all drive together to the water tank.

Will sat patiently next to me, his nuzzle nestled on my lap.

"And you said you came to investigate a missing persons?" Ganzberg asked.

I nodded and waved to some indefinite point down the road. "Her car was found in this neighborhood."

"Man. Life's a bitch," he said and took another drag. He

smoked the cig all the way to the butt, then tossed it on the ground and crushed it with the heel of his shoe.

I kept digging my nose in the collar of my shirt and smelling corpse wax even though I hadn't touched any of the bags. I was ravenous and stinky, and I tend to be in a bad mood when I'm ravenous and stinky. A little jazz in the background would've helped, but my car was too far and I doubted Ganzberg's car stereo would've been equipped with anything different than Bruce Springsteen.

The headlights of a patrol unit washed on us. The driver's window came down and a copper with a shaved head and a child's face saluted us. "I brought the lights."

"We're still waiting for the coroner," Ganzberg said.

The copper's forehead corrugated. "Do you want me to radio the watch commander and try to locate him?"

"Hell no," I said. It was no turf of mine, but I had no problem acting as if it was. "Listen to me, buddy. I want you to forget you even have that radio hooked to your belt, okay? The minute you touch it, the news hawks get here, and the minute the news hawks get here you can forget catching your perp."

Ganzberg sucked in air. He let out a nice, complimentary swearword, and then added, "I'll wait until I see those bodies, Presius, if you don't mind, before deciding we even have a perp on the lam. I've seen enough shit in my career."

I showed him my teeth with no effort to smile. "I don't mind at all. You're the one on call tonight, not me. I counted six, by the way. I'm sure your super will be thrilled."

His foot went looking for the cigarette butt on the ground and started playing with it. "Park the vehicle, officer," he said. And then, when the copper was out of earshot, "You know what they say about you, Presius, in the divisional rows? They say you're an asshole. You know what else they say about you? That you're brilliant. A *brilliant* asshole. Now, I have no friggin' clue how you got ahold of six bodies of—you say—infants. You say you were looking for a sixty-two-year-old lady, and that's what got you to a part of town where bums set up their cardboard beds at night, whores get fucked, and junkies get fixed. You say she liked to hike, and that's how she walked straight into a body dump, and you after her. Let's say I believe you. I want to believe you, Presius. After all, life's a bitch to every one, you and me alike. All I ask is that you talk to me alone. I've seen enough shit in my career. All colors of shit, you get me? You *do not* address my officers. This is *my* part of town and *I* give the orders around here, understood? That way we all get along nice and smooth, and I'll reciprocate the courtesy when I'm loaned over to your part of town. How's that for starters?"

I pondered his nice little speech. Well delivered, I considered. I never heard of this guy, and here he comes, calling me asshole. *Brilliant* asshole.

I loved it. I really did. I imagined a fellow cop coming over and saying, "Hey, that dick over there? He's a brilliant asshole." It makes me instantly smile and want to shake the guy's hand. It takes a lot of butting heads with the brass to get that kind of reputation in the LAPD. I'd done my part well.

I grinned, nice and slow. "Ganzberg," I said. "What do they call you, Ganz?"

"Gaz," he replied, studying me.

"Gaz. Whoever dumped those bodies is going to come back, and when they do, they better not find a welcome mat of yellow tape and news crews, you agree?"

He nodded, his brows knitted together in an elaborate ripple of furrows.

"So, here's what I'd do if I were you. I'd get there,

remove the corpses, then cover up the pit, spread around dead leaves and twigs, and pretend we've never been there. Leave a well-hidden surveillance camera, maybe two, and station a couple of blue suits out here twenty-four-seven."

The ripple in his forehead deepened. I could almost hear the electrical flickering of his neurons. "You said one body had gone to dust. That means the pit's pretty old."

"It looked untouched for a few months. But somebody's been there more recently. Visiting."

What if Katya really walked straight to the dump? What an excellent reason to make her vanish…

A white van with the county coroner's seal on the side pulled in front of us. The driver's window came down, uncovering a familiar thirty-something face, unshaved, sleep-deprived, with blondish hair thinning at the temples. The face scanned us over, rested on me, and produced a thin sneer.

"Presius! What's up with you and cadavers, eh? Is it you finding them or them finding you?"

I got up, walked around the vehicle, and opened the passenger's door. "Shut up, Matt, or next time I'm gonna have you chase a zombie." I let Will scramble to the back seat. "I hope you got AWD on this thing because we're getting on a dirt road."

* * *

The next four hours were hell. Emptying the cistern while leaving little traces was a pipe dream. Our first priority was to document everything and pull the remains out as intact as possible. I had to leave Will in Matt's car—the mutt was sure to mess things up in the excitement of a concerto of rocks. We all got into the white LAPD coveralls and each one of us worked one side of the burial site. It was like walking on eggshells.

The stench was nauseating.

Ganzberg kept a handkerchief over his mouth whenever he could and held his breath every time he couldn't. I stopped counting the times he'd muttered, "Life's a bitch" under his breath.

Awakened by the lights and smells, crows came to watch the show. Perched on high branches, they cawed and bickered for the best view. Moths fluttered in our faces. Beetles crawled over the plastic bags, every flash from the photographer's camera sending them in frenzied circles.

Matt kneeled by the cistern and unrolled his measuring tape. "Never apply to a job ad that says, 'Enjoyable outdoor working conditions,' Track. There's always a catch when they say that. This side is three feet, four inches."

Ganzberg jotted down the information on his notepad, sketching the shape and location of the cistern.

I shone a flashlight on the tiny hand poking out of one of the bags and we all fell silent.

"Oh, shit," Matt said.

"Life's such a bitch," Ganzberg felt the need to add.

The torn plastic bag was still there, on top of the others. I retrieved the stick I'd used earlier, fished it out of the pit, and let Matt vacuum the handful of dirt left inside.

"Now, here's the thing with corpse wax," Matt said, lying on his stomach by the edge of the tank. "Babies have enough fat that, given the right conditions, they easily turn into adipocere—what we commonly call soap, or corpse wax. To have a whole body turned into soap, though, is pretty rare. Most I've seen is body parts. Legs, arms. One time a whole torso and head."

He used tongs to delicately pull the first bag onto an extended plastic pan attached to a long wooden rod.

"That must've been pleasant," I said.

"It's really like looking at a wax statue. The thing that gets you is the stench."

Matt set the pan on the ground and pulled the edges of the bag apart with the tip of the tongs.

Ganzberg swallowed hard and took a deep breath as if about to go underwater. "Can you tell how old they are?" He gulped down air and covered his face again.

"That's up for the examiner to say," Matt replied. "I'm just an assistant. Problem is, corpse wax stops the tissue from decaying. The biological clock stops and there's no way to tell how long they've been there. The process can take from months to years. Let's see what we've got." Matt cut through the polythene—two sealed bags, one inside the other—and for a moment I closed my eyes to let the wave of foul smell wash away. When I reopened them the sight wasn't any more pleasant than the smell.

"It's turned into soap, all right," Matt said. "Which is good news, the internal organs should all be intact."

The flash flared over the small body. We held our breaths, not for the reek this time, but rather taken by that sort of stupefied reverence you feel when in front of something sacred.

The body in the bag was perfectly preserved except for one thing.

There was no head.

Ganzberg's shadow loomed over the corpse. I craned my head back and yelled at the officer, "Can you move the lamp closer?"

The light shifted and washed over the remains. The body was covered in a gray, waxy cast, with a round, pear-shaped belly and tiny legs still bent in a fetal position. If it weren't for the smell, I would've said it was a broken doll a child had tossed away.

I examined the plastic bags. They were thick and sturdy

trash bags, and while the outer one was faded, the one inside still had the *Glad* logo printed on it. The plastic looked ordinary polyethylene, black, thick and sturdy, with the usual wear and tear of time. Hard to tell how long it'd been dumped in there. I put the outer one in an evidence bag and labeled it for the Trace labs.

Ganzberg mumbled, "You think it could've been born like this?"

Matt took out a measuring tape. "Maybe. It reminds me of partial birth abortions, where they destroy the head in the uterus before delivering the fetus. Could be something like that. Or, it could be that only the lower body turned into wax and the bugs got the head." He measured the length and girth of the body and wrote down the numbers on his clipboard. "If that's the case we should be able to recover some of the cranial bones in the bag."

Ganzberg and I looked inside the bag but there was nothing to the naked eye. Matt vacuumed the inside anyway and stored everything in evidence bags.

One by one, we took all six bodies out. They were all headless.

Like Matt had predicted, not all of them had completely saponified. Along the internal walls of the cistern, green lines of dried up mold accounted for past water levels, likely from flooding over the rainy season.

We tagged all bodies and zipped them up in blue bags that were too big for them. We placed the panel of corrugated metal back over the pit and covered up our tracks as best as we could. I made a few recommendations to my friend Gaz. He assured me he'd have a patrol unit on watch twenty-four-seven and issued a gag order for the press. He concluded with a final reminder what a bitch life was.

I rode with Matt back to my car, both our windows

rolled all the way down. Crickets chirped low, monotone songs. Under the light of a crescent moon, the hills weaved the landscape in a cantabile of arcs.

Matt put the headlights out.

I flinched. "What'd you do that for?"

"Look at the moon, Track. Look at it." He shook his head. "Those kids in the back, they'll never see a moon like this."

I inhaled and stared at the lights of downtown blinking in the distance. "They'll never cry again, either."

We wobbled down the rest of the dirt road at a lazy five miles per hour, neither of us speaking another word.

SIXTEEN

Saturday, July 4

Two weeks earlier I had one missing person and one murder. Now I had one missing person, three murders, and six infanticides—possibly seven if Serology found DNA in the dust collected from the first, torn bag I'd pulled up.

I got home, dumped my clothes in the trash, and showered. It helped some.

There was no way to sleep. I tossed and turned but couldn't get the image out of my head—a headless corpse, folded onto itself in a fetal position. Defenseless.

At five the jays started screeching. At five thirty the first light of dawn crawled through the slats and reminded me I had a date with Cohen at 8 a.m.—Laura Lyons's autopsy.

As if I hadn't seen enough bodies in the past twenty-four hours.

I flung off the bed sheets, pulled on a shirt and some

pants, shaved, and brewed two Mokas. I played Ahmad Jamal's *Stolen Moments* on the car stereo as I drove to downtown while musing over all the stolen moments in my life.

The Five was blissfully deserted.

I found Satish pacing under the modern portico in front of the autopsy suite building, his usual latte in one hand and jingling car keys in the other.

"You look like you haven't slept in twenty-four hours," he said.

"I haven't."

I told him about my sleepless night. "I chased a ghost, found zombies instead. Maybe I'm in the wrong business."

"Oh no, the business is right. The approach is wrong. You're collecting murders rather than solving them."

"Very funny, Sat. Are any of Laura's family members coming for the show?"

He drained the last bit of his latte and tossed the cup in a trash bin. "Her sister's coming down from Sacramento. I'm picking her up at the airport once we're done here. Don't think she's interested in seeing the body, all she wanted to know was when she'd be released for the funeral."

"That's it? No father, mother, children?"

"She had no children. The father's long gone and the mother's paraplegic, lives up in Washington State."

Laura Lyons's autopsy wasn't much different from Amy's. Cohen found another fiber, on the left hand this time, which was promptly labeled and shipped to Diane's lab. The scalp and skin harvesting had the same appearance as the ones found on Amy's body, and the laceration of the face and neck were again consistent with an attack while still alive, followed by strangulation from behind.

The funneling indentation on the left edge of the ligature mark had our attention for a good ten minutes. Cohen measured its depth, width, shape—everything, and yet we couldn't come up with anything that could possibly match it. A synthetic scarf with a brooch or large bead was our closest bet, though that would've likely left other telltale marks rather than a smooth indentation.

I stepped out of the autopsy suite to breathe in fresh air, yet the smell of corpse, now mingled with corpse wax, kept following me. It filled my car when I slid behind the wheel, it lingered in my nostrils even when I rolled all the windows down and blasted the stereo to numb all my senses. I got home, started a new Moka, drank my espresso, then brewed another one. Which is *not* the equivalent of one mug of Americano. *Never.*

I was groggy and still in a bad mood. The fact that it was Saturday and, coincidentally, the Fourth of July, didn't help.

I picked up the paper from the driveway and sat on the back porch waiting for the caffeine to percolate to my brains. Will wrapped himself around my legs and stared at me lovingly.

Every man needs an admirer. It's an ego thing.

Caffeine or not, you try putting a warm, purring thing around your legs and, assuming you've had a really rough night, and a really rough day before that, count the seconds before you fall asleep...

* * *

Get the phone.
The phone kept ringing.
Get the damn phone.
The phone quieted down. I dozed off again. Then it rang again, and the ring was louder and angrier. It made me jump.

"Damn it." I opened my eyes. Will had vanished and left

a cold spot on my lap. I wondered what time it was, but in order to find out I had to get the phone. Which was still ringing. I staggered out of the chaise and back inside.

"Yello?"

"You better have a good excuse, Track. You're forty minutes late."

Damn it. It was Saturday, July 4, 2:40 p.m.

* * *

Diane Kyle wrapped her firing hand around the grip and lined her arms with the barrel. The sun glinted off her eyeshades. Her stance was solid, her knuckles too white.

Loosen up the grip.

After she'd been attacked twice last year, her dad bought her a Sig Sauer P226. A fine piece, but with a five-pound trigger squeeze and over two pounds on the waist when tucked into a holster, I could see how Diane was having a hard time falling in love with it.

She inhaled, held her breath, and squeezed five rounds out.

Other than a light breeze it was a fine day. Behind the steel targets, the hills of the Angeles Forest weaved against the backdrop of an evenly blue sky. The range wasn't too crowded, given that it was a holiday: only two other folks shooting at the ten-yard line and a bunch of show-offs at the black and concrete benches.

I took my binos and squinted at the silhouette. "You got two in the scoring ring," I said, though she was unlikely to hear me through earplugs and earmuffs.

When I turned, she'd put the gun down and was shoving her things back in her bag. "Break," she mouthed. I yanked my earmuffs off.

"Where are you going?"

"It's not my day," she scoffed. She swung the bag across her shoulder and marched inside the lobby.

I gathered mags, ammos, and guns, and followed her. She wasn't in the lobby anymore. I stopped at the vending machine, got a couple of Cokes, and chased her scent. That wasn't hard to do. Bears have no problem tracking down honey.

I found her sitting at one of the picnic tables outside. A tear of sweat wept down her cheek. It smelled salty. It smelled of all the things I wanted in life and couldn't have. She brought a stainless steel bottle to her lips and I followed the rise and falls of her neckline as she chugged down the water.

"Drink this instead." I sat next to her and pushed the chilled can of Coke toward her.

It was a regular Coke, not diet. She looked at it the way a vegan would've looked at pork chops. It didn't discourage me from flipping the tab. I popped the can and took a long swig.

"Last time I got all rounds on target. Twice," she complained.

"You're out of practice."

"I haven't been shooting for a month—that's not too long." She sighed, checked her watch. "It's five twenty. I need to be home by six. Ellie invited me to a barbeque at her boyfriend's. Wanna join us?" There was no particular expectation in her voice.

Ellie was Diane's *feminazi* friend who could find testosterone-driven contempt in a handshake.

"I better go to bed early tonight," I said.

She took a mouthful of water and almost choked on it. "Who? You? On the Fourth?"

"Flattered. I didn't sleep at all last night. I was dozing off in the backyard when you called."

Diane took the unopened can and rolled it against her neck. Her skin raised in tiny goose bumps. "Friday night partying?"

I fiddled with the soda tab. "Yeah. You know who else came to the party? A detective from Hollenbeck, a county coroner assistant, an SID photographer, and six bodies. The bodies were too young to drink, so they just hung out in black plastic bags."

Diane put down the soda can and drew in a sharp breath. "How young?"

"Infants."

"Shit. Six infants? Where?"

"Up in an undeveloped part of El Sereno. They were down at the bottom of a dried up water tank. One was completely soaped, the others only partly. And they were all headless."

"Jesus. Stuff like that gives me the shivers. Are you and Satish going to investigate it?"

I shook my head. "Hollenbeck got the case. A guy named Ganzberg. He's okay. Bit passive aggressive at first, but quieted down once he saw the bodies. Matt, the guy from the coroner's office, said they could be partial birth abortions."

Diane drank some more of her water then brought a thumb to her mouth and nibbled it. "Those are done in clinics. Clinics, whether illegal or not, are smart enough not to dump bodies in open spaces. Ganzberg should be looking at the households nearby the dump, instead."

I took a swig of Coke and considered. "It's an isolated area. Not many houses around. Why do you say that?"

She shrugged one shoulder. "Statistics. Mothers are the most likely perpetrators in infanticides. Wanet Hoyt killed five of her children. Marybeth Tinning killed nine. There was a recent case, a few years ago, in Germany. The woman hid the bodies in flowerpots in her garden."

"Jeezus."

Hard-boiled dicks like me have this mental image of serial killers as males. It's how we're wired. And yet, there was something even more disturbing than a faceless killer attacking his victims with sulfuric acid. And that's a killer with a *familiar* face — the face of a parent.

The one who gives you life, takes your life.

The Spartans threw unfit newborns down Mount Taygetos. The Romans had the power of life or death over their children. Agamemnon sacrificed his daughter Iphigenia to the gods, Orchamus had his daughter buried alive, Medea killed her two sons for revenge over their father. These weren't just myths. Of all children murdered under the age of five, sixty percent are killed by one of the parents.

What I'd found wasn't just a body dump. It was a shrine.

I drained the can and crushed it. "I'm hungry," I said. "Wanna go grab a bite before I drop you off?"

Diane smiled for the first time since I'd picked her up from her house. "Only if you promise to keep both work and guns away from any conversation."

Her cheeks were flushed, her hair tousled. Her scent was jazz for my nostrils, as thrilling and enticing as the drum solo in Dave Brubeck's *Take Five*. I leaned forward and kissed her cheek.

Man, she was fast. She grabbed my chin and dug her nails in it. "I don't want a one-night thing, Track, you understand?"

I nodded politely and she retracted her claws. She brushed her fingers against my stubble, gently this time, and briskly kissed me on the lips. "Let's go, then. I need coffee."

And so I followed. Again.

And no, there was no one-night thing.

There was no night at all.

I dropped her off at her place and went to Parker to review the murder books. I wasn't sure what to look for, so I just picked aimlessly at Amy's and Charlie's last days: bank accounts, phone logs, friends', neighbors' and family's statements. Charlie continued to cash his weekly five hundred bucks, give or take twenty, until the beginning of January. His family had estranged him eight years earlier. Neighbors claimed he was at home a lot more since he'd been laid off, but nobody had noticed any special visitor or anything weird in his lifestyle. He had dated for some time a man in the same complex, and they had remained on good terms, according to the same neighbors.

I wondered about Olsen's story—the black Alero that smelled of nail polish. Weird clue. If he were making that up he would've gone for something more sensible.

I read the hardware scan done on Callahan's personal computer. A lot of activity on Facebook, social networks, and the lesbian-gay pages of Craigslist, where he hung out under the screen name "Code7."

Interesting choice. Code 7 is the police radio code for "lunch break." A coincidence?

Nothing else raised a red flag.

Nothing particular in Amy's lifestyle either, except for what I knew already—her relationship with Lyons. I found it hard to believe nobody else except for Laura Lyons knew about it. Somehow I couldn't imagine a wife being quiet about her husband's extra marital relationship. Somebody close to her must've offered a listening ear.

I went through the list of contact numbers on Laura's cell phone, left a half a dozen messages, got ahold of a couple of coworkers who knew very little about her, and finally found a gal on maternity leave who seemed eager to share a few thousand words. Most of the words got swallowed by the screeching and howling of what I guessed to be a brood of toddlers running and spinning around her.

"Laura was very private about her personal life," she told me. "She resented being known as the wife of the *famous* Dr. Lyons. She strived to push her work forward, to be known for what she'd done, not who she was married to—hold on, honey, the milk is almost ready."

"Did she succeed?" I asked.

Something beeped, maybe a microwave. "Detective, in order to stay afloat in our line of work you have to either be smart and clever or act as if you were smart and clever. Does that make sense?"

"Perfectly. And Laura was neither?"

"Laura's problem was that she didn't believe in herself. She felt she was her husband's shadow—one second, hon. Oh, please don't step on Rufus's tail!"

"She must've been angry when she found out her husband was cheating on her," I hollered over the crying and the rattling and the barking.

"She was, but they'd already grown apart. They just happened to still live under the same roof. Laura and I jogged at the park together, before, you know, *this* happened." I heard the bawling and assumed "This" was unhappy about the milk. The conversation got lost for half a minute, then the bawling magically stopped and she came back to the phone. "There was this guy we'd often see jogging. Laura said she found him sexy. I told her she should start dating again. She laughed and said why not. I was happy when she told me they were finally going forward with the divorce papers."

"Do you know if she ever talked to this guy at the park?"

"If she did, she never mentioned it."

I asked for a description of the sexy guy, took note of where they'd jogged and when, then thanked her and wished her all the best with her brood. Something crashed on the floor. A child howled. A dog barked. She didn't run. She breathed into the receiver then replied, "What brood? I've got only one, he's two and a half."

"Good luck raising him," I said. "Sounds like he's ready to manage the LAPD."

Next on my list were Laura's close relatives, which weren't many and were scattered all over the country. Aside from the sister coming down from Sacramento, Satish had mentioned a disabled mother who wasn't going to be able to leave her home for the funeral.

I flipped through my notes and found a phone number, area code from Olympia, Washington. I dialed and waited.

Mrs. Fawn picked up at the third ring. "I was expecting your call," she said once I identified myself. She had one of those soothing voices that had climbed the rises and falls of life. A voice that had cried a little, laughed a little, and then settled on a low croon, like a scratched LP that had been loved and played one too many times.

"I'm sorry for your loss. Mrs. Fawn."

"I'm not the only one who lost a child that night, Detective. Whoever did this to her is a lost child too."

I stared vacantly at the wanted faces decorating the walls of the squad room and tried to picture them as lost children. I shrugged. They still looked like the usual bastards to me.

"Mrs. Fawn, did your daughter tell you she'd filed for divorce?"

There was a pause so long I thought I'd lost the line.

"My daughter wouldn't share things like that with me. Last I'd seen her was the day after Christmas. She came by herself, she said Freddy—"

I heard a rustle—old fingers brushing over paper, or maybe a table. "We still call him Freddy. I suppose he'd be Dr. Lyons to you."

I said he would. She carried on. "Freddy was too busy to make it. He's been too busy to come for the past five years."

I sensed the scratches in her voice deepen. I figured I could get something out of it, so I dug further. "Do you think Freddy killed your daughter?"

Again, she took a long pause before replying. "Would I be surprised he did? The older I get, the fewer things surprise me." I heard her swallow. "But then again, the way she was—"

I heard a rustle, then a lot of static. When she came back her voice had changed. "Did you look into her bank account yet?"

I frowned at the question. The papers were on Satish's desk. "We just started," I said. "Why?"

"I don't mean the one she had with Freddy. I mean her stock portfolio. Ah, never mind, he's probably going to inherit everything because they weren't divorced yet, isn't he?"

"I'm not sure, Mrs. Fawn. Why d'you ask?"

"She borrowed money to buy these stocks. Freddy talked her into it. I'd like to have my money back."

My ears perked up. "What kind of stocks, Ms. Fawn?" I wedged the phone between my ear and shoulder and opened the laptop on my desk.

"Jan-something. I think. Hold on." She set the phone down. When she came back something like a paper folder was rustling in her hands. "It's right here… there. *Jank*, spelled like Bank, with a J. That's the company."

The name sounded familiar. I Googled it. CEO's name was Robert Kunst. Executives, lab directors—no trace of the name Lyons anywhere.

"Are you still there?"

"Yes, Mrs. Fawn, I'm listening. Laura borrowed money from you to buy stocks from Jank—how much?"

"A lot. The exact amount is irrelevant. Laura said it'd beat my retirement plan. She said the stocks would make us both rich. I'm sure Freddy got her into that."

"Did she ever mention anything else about this company? Why was her husband so confident it was a good investment?"

"No idea. All I know is that it had to be his idea. She'd never done stocks before."

"I gather you didn't get rich?"

"I got tired of waiting, Detective."

"Mrs. Fawn?"

"Yes."

"Your other daughter said you won't be coming for the funeral."

She thought it over before replying. "She told you I'm paraplegic, didn't she? Yeah, that's my official excuse. Haven't been out in ten years. I suppose I could come down, if I believed in all that. Don't you wish you believed, sometimes, Detective?"

I let the question drift.

"My daughter's looking at me right now. Laura is. She's holding a lollipop and her lips are red and shiny from the sugar. She's been fussing all day about that lollipop. I told her no, we've got to stop at a few more doors. People are happier to buy when you show up with a child. And my, she's a cute child, she is. The books don't sell, but I buy her the lollipop anyway. Because sometimes you just gotta follow your gut. To hell with encyclopedias, look at where they are right now. Nobody wants them anymore, it's all on the Internet anyway. But the lollipop, that one lollipop makes her happy. And me with her. That's my Laura, looking at me and smiling. There's no other way I want to remember her."

The scratches in her voice mended. She wished me good night and hung up.

I stared at the screen of my laptop.

Jank Biologicals had been a small corporation until its main objective became HIV vaccine design. They bought Lyons's vaccine patent in 2003. Lyons was listed under "benefactors" in the company's "About" page. Under "Recent News" I found an article from 2005 that announced Jank's IPO. I checked the dates on Google: the company went public the day after Lyons injected himself with his vaccine. It raised close to two billion dollars on the first day, selling over fifty million shares.

Smooth move, Doc. I'd inject myself too for that kinda money.

I got up and retrieved Laura's bank statements from Satish's desk. She'd made a $200,000 investment in shares from Jank in January last year. I opened Amy Liu's file. March last year, $80,000. Jank, again.

Neither lady had a history of buying stocks before. This was their very first investment and it was huge.

I'm sure Freddy got her into that, Laura's mother said.

I checked the market. Jank's stocks had been doing exceedingly well. There were blips, here and there, as it often happens with stocks, but since 2007 the shares had over quadrupled their value.

Why was Mrs. Fawn so sour?

She probably never got her money back from Laura...

Being the Fourth of July, there wasn't even the slightest chance of getting ahold of Lyons's bank assets. I wrote a note with my findings, dropped it on Satish's desk, then flopped back into my chair.

A faceless killer. A maniac. The Byzantine Strangler.

No. Psychopaths don't follow patterns. They kill randomly.

Two docs in a row, both working on HIV... too much of a coincidence.

I looked at Amy Liu's phone logs. She called one number twice a week—her mother. I spotted several other regulars: friends, a hair salon, colleagues. Lyons's cellphone number never appeared, which didn't surprise me. They probably had more than one occasion to arrange their meetings in person. I kept scanning the log from beginning to end and then all over again from the beginning. I found one instance of Lyons's home number. Strange, not his cell. I flipped back, but out of a whole month, that was the only time the number appeared. The call lasted five minutes and forty-two seconds, and it took place four days before she was killed. Maybe it was just the invitation to the party.

Maybe.

I left the squad room. Save for a few patrol cars on call, Los Angeles Street was deserted. I could hear the music and drums from the celebrations down on Olivera Street. It made me all the more desolate, so I drove through skid row just for the company. That part of town never misses its crowds.

Back at home, there was no *lahmajoun* at my door, no envelope under the mat, no scarf, no nothing. My mood was as flat as a slashed tire. Thanks goodness for my two boys: Will did his usual "I'm so excited to see you" welcome dance as soon as I opened the door, and The King actually dignified me with a mew. They both followed me to the kitchen, where I served them dinner and opened a bottle of Brunello. The King gave two bites to his dinner then hopped on the countertop and stared intently at the wine.

"Best company on lonely nights," I said.

He agreed.

I poured myself a glass, twirled it, then sipped. The King

kept staring at me, the tip of his tail bending ever so slightly.

"Fine," I said. I took out a saucer and spilled a few drops of Brunello on it. Damn cat of mine licked it all up in two seconds. He licked his whiskers, too, then hopped back down on the kitchen floor and returned to his dinner bowl.

"Alcohol is bad for felines," I said.

He chomped on his dinner and ignored me.

I shrugged. "You're too smart even to be a feline."

The answering machine was blinking again. I left it blinking, took my glass of wine and settled in the back porch to watch the fireworks from the Dodger Stadium. They crackled, hissed and whistled and turned the sky into a canvas of shimmering lights.

The Brunello was ok.

Damn it. The hell with the Brunello. It's Diane I wanted. You can't stop at just a sip of good wine, that's a blasphemy. You have to get tight.

Diane had given me just sip. And man, did I want to get tight.

SEVENTEEN

Dr. Frederick Lyons leans over his desk and squeezes his temples between the heels of his hands. He looks tired. He looks tired and old. Shards of shattered dreams lay all around him, their edges as sharp as a scalpel.

What happened to you, Dr. Lyons?

"What do you want?" *he snarls, without bothering to lift his head.*

Some things haven't changed.

Just give him time.

"You're b – back to work, D – Doctor. I didn't think – "

"What do you want, Medina?"

Medina stiffens. He swallows bitter hatred. To the rest of the world, it looks like he just cleared his throat. To the rest of the world, he looks like a turtle peeking out of its shell. "The new draft, sir," *he says, softly. This time he manages not to stutter.*

Lyons dignifies him with a stare. "What draft?"

"The PNAS p – paper. The s – second r – rev – "

"Reviewer," *Lyons snaps.*

"Yes. He w-wanted to s-see more tests, so I r-ran those and —
"

"Right." Lyons draws in a sharp breath and leans back in his chair. His eyes glaze over. They seem sad, almost soft. What a heartbreaking view. *"I asked Marianne to cancel my trip to Duke."*

"I understand — "

"And then I told her not to."

Medina doesn't reply. He squints and looks at the world through the small opening of his shell.

"They can't stop me," Lyons says. *"Not like this. They won't stop me like this."*

"Yes, s — sir."

Lyons's eyes focus back, sharply. *"I need a dozen slides by next Wednesday."*

Medina stiffens. He swallows, again, then tiptoes to the desk, where he leaves the paper draft he's brought along.

"A dozen should suffice," Lyons goes on, his eyes glazing over again. Outside, a jackhammer rattles. A crane looms over the scaffolding across the street. *"Show a couple of your neat graphs. Explain the algorithm, you know it best. The usual stuff."*

"Yes, sir." Medina shuffles back to the door. *"Oh, and s — sir?"*

"Yeah?"

"My deepest condolences."

Lyons frowns, taken aback. It's just a moment and then he turns away, his eyes lazily following the block of cement dangling out the window.

My deepest, deepest condolences.

Medina limps down the hallway. His feet hurt, his hands prickle.

Damned moths, they suck the life out of me.

A dozen slides, your usual graphs. Explain the algorithm, you know it best.

Of course I know it best. It was my idea to begin with.

He shuffles down the hallway back to his office. Nurses walk by. Lab technicians chat in the elevator lobby.

Nobody talks to Medina. Nobody seems to even notice he's there.

Until they need something from me.

Medina the stutterer, the loser, the poor dude with the invalid mom.

Medina, the one they all pity.

He sits at his desk and logs into his machine.

The alignment he's been working on opens up, mismatched columns of colors.

Four colors.

He reads the first line.

CAATTGTGGGTCACAGTCTATTATGGGGTACCTGT GTGGAAAGACGCAACCACCACTCTATTT...

No, wait. His eyes run back to the beginning of the line. He starts reading again.

CAAATTGTGGGTCAC...

That can't be right. He jumps to the next line.

CAAATTGTGGGTCAC...

Damn it, an insertion. Stupid insertion made the whole region a stutter. Screwed up the whole alignment. Fucking software, if only there were one that did the job right. What's the point of having machines if all the dirty work has to be done by hand?

He clicks on the edit tab and starts typing. Then he stops. A bright red drop sits on the A key. Another one drips on the G. The Space key is smeared.

Damn it.

He reaches for the Kleenex box, plucks out a tissue, wraps it around his left hand.

Damn it, damn it, damn it.

He wipes the keyboard clean, starts over. Menu, edit, insert gap column.

He stops, again. His hand hurts. He opens his fist, the Kleenex on his palm a clump of bloody shreds. Carefully he peels them off his skin and tosses them in trashcan. He examines the inside of his hand. Tiny lesions crowd at the base of his thumb and pinky. He balls his hand and fresh blood oozes out.

He squints.

Fresh blood and crawly, hairy legs, tiny spider legs, thousands of them, oozing out of his open skin like —

Argh!

He jumps out of his chair and leaps to the door.

Breathe. Just. Breathe.

A beep from the computer makes him turn back to the screen.

"New message from lj66: Hey, would you look at this?" he reads on the monitor.

Medina takes a deep breath, shuffles back to his desk. He keeps his injured hand closed into a fist, while with the other he opens his inbox.

"Confidential data, I'm not supposed to send you this stuff," he reads off the first line. John Wood, an old bloke from college. He works at TYU Labs now. They chat, from time to time. Nothing special.

What does he want now?

"Pseudogenes," the email goes on. "I bet you've never seen them like this. You're gonna love it."

Medina clicks on the attachment. His jaw drops, his hand no longer hurts. He lets go of the Kleenex he's been squeezing and picks up the phone.

"I knew you'd love the data," he says. "It's unbelievable, isn't it? I wonder what it feels to have all this stuff going on in your body. You know, the normal genes, and then all the extra genes overlapping. It's like — like that documentary on the Discovery Channel, the real superhuman, remember that?"

Medina thinks about it. Of course he remembers. Seems almost too good to be true. All he's been looking for, for years …

What perfect timing.

He licks his lips and whispers softly into the mouthpiece. "Wh-who's the data f-from?"

John doesn't reply right away. He lowers his voice. "Um, listen. Blood came from a client, a geneticist down in San Marino. One of his patients. He wanted some dendritic cell tests, antibody titers, and peripheral blood PDCs. I found the gene expression tests from assays done on the patient last year. So, you know. I'm not supposed to share this stuff. It's just a curiosity, I thought you might like it. Besides, the guy's screwed. Look at those test results. He's a battlefield of antibodies attacking all the tissues that express the supergenes. He's toast. Nothing like what the documentary made you think."

John chuckles, Medina doesn't join in.

Medina's thoughts are elsewhere right now. His fingers click on a terminal window, his brain fires with ideas.

Nothing's anonymous once on the web, he thinks.

Nothing, not even firewalls.

And deep inside, he smiles.

EIGHTEEN

Dr. Cohen pointed the surgical lamp to my face. "What did you die of, Track?"

I squinted at the light. "I don't know, Doc. I thought it was *your* job to find out."

Cohen laughed his bubbly little laughter. It trailed off as quickly as a New Year's Eve toast. Water ran from one of the faucets by the wall. The air smelled of formaldehyde, bleach, and cytological stains. It smelled aseptic and cold, a metallic tang that clung to the air like a hangover. It smelled of death.

"This is going to be fun," Cohen said, hovering over me with the Stryker saw.

It didn't look promising. It didn't look fun, either.

"It's the first time I get to actually talk to one of my

patients. *If* you can call them patients, that is." Cohen laughed and dug the saw into my breastbone. If the water of the Styx had a sound, it had to be that of a Stryker saw. Blood and warm chunks of flesh spattered on my face. I licked my lips. They tasted salty and rusty.

The hedge clippers came next. They cracked through my ribs like nutcrackers. Cohen's puffy face pearled with sweat. "Sheesh, Track. You always loved to give me a hard time."

I thought of apologizing but didn't quite see the point.

He wiped sweat off his forehead with the back of his sleeve and stared into the hole he'd dug into my chest. It occurred to me then that he wasn't wearing a facemask. "Now, that's interesting," he said.

I felt a little apprehension. When it comes to doctors, I don't want to be interesting. I want to be as dull and boring as a Sunday mass recited in Latin.

Watanabe emerged through the darkness of the backlight. His face was yellow and grave and didn't look too healthy either. He stared at the hole Cohen had dug through my chest and pursed his thin lips.

"Where's his heart?" he asked.

Cohen craned his head. "I can see only some of it."

"Makes sense," Watanabe replied. "His antinuclear antibodies were off the chart. His immune system started attacking his heart until it eventually destroyed it."

"A-ha," Cohen said. He shoved his gloved hands inside my ribcage and pulled out a bloody mass. It was still pulsating, though slowly, its red walls rising and falling in long, tired sighs. "Well, of course. Look at that, it's half-eaten. Why didn't you tell me before, Track?"

"Tell you what?" I asked.

"It's in V-Tach," Watanabe said.

"That's too bad," Cohen sighed. "A strong heart. Strong indeed."

"Tell you what?" I yelled.

Cohen tipped his head. "You didn't have a human heart. You had a predator's heart."

A predator's heart.

A predator's...

I sprang my eyes open. A faint light crawled through the curtains and wavered on the ceiling. I inhaled. Sweat, my own. Carpet, dust, wood. *My* dust, *my* wood. A jay screeched outside. A neighbor rolled the trash bin down the driveway.

I brought a hand to my chest. It felt smooth—intact skin, a few hairs, no hole. My heart was still there, thumping against the breastbone.

My heart.

A predator's heart.

The autopsy was a nightmare, but the conversation at Watanabe's house had been real.

The blood work I'd done the week before had come back positive for some autoimmune disorder I didn't understand.

"Does it matter, Doc?" I'd joked. "That my DNA was screwed up we knew already."

"No, Ulysses, not your DNA. You are an epigenetic chimera—you express genes that are normally not expressed in other humans."

And, apparently, that was exactly the problem.

Homer's Ulysses had gone down to Hades to find out his fate. My fate instead had always been within me. In my blood. My oracle, my blind Tiresias, a Japanese American doctor who could read DNA like Ella Fitzgerald read a music score, told me my immune system was going berserk, attacking my own heart because it expressed genes the rest of my body did not recognize. It seemed surreal, almost a joke, yet Watanabe didn't share my humor when I laughed at the news.

So I thought of something smart to ask. "How do we make it stop?"

"There's only one way," he'd replied. "We suppress the immune system."

"What if we don't make it stop?"

The absence of an answer was as hard as an untold sin.

Right, I thought, getting out of bed. *Don't take the fucking medication and your heart goes. Take the fucking medication and your immune system goes.*

Watanabe's prescription rested on my nightstand, unused.

Look at the bright side, Ulysses.

You get to pick your own ending.

* * *

The door looked ominous. It was crossed in red "biohazard" tape. Pictures ripped off some manga comic book plastered the glass pane. Satish knocked.

"Why's the door closed?" I objected. "Every other office here at Electronics is open."

Satish gave me a look that meant, "Wait and see."

The door opened a crack. Loud rock music and the mildew-y smell of chilled sweat spilled out. A face emerged from the darkness—gaunt, unshaved, with a dark birthmark that sprawled from his right temple down to the outer corner of the eye. Somewhere, a Halloween costume was missing its face.

"Hello, Viktor," Satish said. "This is my partner, Detective Presius."

Viktor regarded us carefully, not moving a muscle except for the twitching of his ash-colored pupils. "Right," he said, pulled his face back into the darkness, and closed the door.

I smiled. "So. That went well."

Unscathed, Satish rocked on his heels. "Just remember not to call him Vik," he whispered. "Pisses him off."

The door opened again. The loud music had been silenced, not the smell. "I only have one extra chair," Viktor said, looking at me. "Grab one from Dan."

"Who's Dan?"

"Guy next door," Satish replied.

I found a metal chair, folded and abandoned in the hallway, and was then left with the arduous task of finding a spot in Viktor's office.

Viktor's office was dark, windowless, and filled with dust and the peculiar smell of old computers. Two long and narrow desks faced opposite walls, their surfaces completely buried with stuff. The only light came from a dim table lamp and the two side-by-side monitors that emerged above a general chaos of DVD cases, dirty mugs, programming books, and random pieces of electronics. Overhead lockers were open and stuffed with keyboards, laptop bags, and cases of Gatorades. I squeezed between the tables, unfolded the chair in the only free corner of the room, and sat down.

Viktor squinted at the code dribbling down his two screens, then turned to us, his smile as thin as paper. "You guys want the short answer or the long one?"

His voice seemed to brew somewhere at the bottom of his throat before coming out. It gargled in a shady, yet fluid way.

"Both," Satish replied.

He nodded. "'Kay. Short: it's not a language I recognize."

I chortled without being amused. Everything about the Byzantine Strangler was an enigma: the ligature was a mystery, the fibers he shed unidentifiable, the origin of the tiles unknown, and now Viktor from the Electronic Unit, was telling us that the code printed at the back of the tiles found next to Laura's body was yet another puzzle.

"I hope the long answer's going to be a bit more helpful," I said.

The thin paper smile evaporated. Computer experts can be as dogmatic as the Church and as obscure as the assembly instructions that come with Swedish furniture.

"I could elaborate," he magnanimously offered.

"Please do," Satish said.

"'Kay. It's not a high-level language. One—could be some kind of micro-code, which runs inside the CPU or control code. Two—could be a cipher text, an encrypted message. Could be a plain encrypted code or have something hidden, like steganography. Or both. The feds have the best tools to crack these guys. I'd contact the RCFL in Orange."

"The fibbies take their sweet-ass time with our evidence," Satish grumbled. "That's why we came to you instead."

Viktor ignored him with the smoothness of a polished floor. "If it's encrypted, there's not much anybody can do unless the guy is stupid. So let's assume it's something else for now. The characters remind me of the output of a disassembler between a high-level language and a receiving device. Like the old HP 42 plotter."

He pointed to a window on the screen, where he'd typed the symbols found at the back of the tiles. "This one, for example: #g 3 could stand for command group three, #cs .5 for a point-five character skew, and #lw would be setting the width. Problem is, those codes are no longer used. Today's machines have switched to G-code."

The hell of a long answer. He could've delivered it in Japanese, as far as I was concerned.

My partner scratched the white stubble under his chin. "Okay," he said. "Okay. Does this help us in any way?"

Viktor's computer started hyperventilating. It sounded like an airplane about to take off. "It helps some," he said, while typing. "It tells us our man feels comfortable around computers. Perps usually leave messages behind because they want them to be deciphered. So, either we find the key or, eventually, he's going to give us the key."

I snorted. "That'll work. How many murders do you think he'll need in order to hand it to us?"

The paper-thin smile resurfaced. "It's the reality of things."

Viktor's computer beeped.

I scooted closer. "Did it just exhale its last breath?"

"No, the machine's fine. It didn't find anything on last vic's hard drive, though."

"Laura Lyons?" Satish asked. "What was it supposed to find?"

Viktor paused the typing for a moment, then resumed. "The receiving device. I was looking for some kind of HPGL visualizer, like Visual Basic or similar. If I'm right, and this is the output of a high-level language, we should be able to find the receiving device. The obvious place to look would be the victims' computers, but so far no luck."

Satish leaned forward and stared at the screen. "I assume you looked at Amy's hard drive as well?"

"Yes. Both work and home."

"So, what now?"

Viktor's hands dropped from the keyboard. His eyes remained on the screen. The birthmark sprawling from his temple down to the corner of his eye was dark brown with lighter lines inside. It looked like a computer chip, really, which was sort of ironic.

"There *is* something," he said, at last.

"What?"

He pulled up the Internet browser and typed in a new URL. "This. *CoreProgramming.com,* a discussion board for programmers of all backgrounds. I'm pretty sure if I post the code somebody will recognize it."

Satish leaned back in the chair and crossed his arms. "If our man is familiar with this kind of programming, chances are he knows the board."

Viktor nodded. "Course. There's a good chance he's one of the users."

"Well, then, if he's on, he'll recognize the code."

I thought about that. And then I thought it was brilliant. And Satish must've thought the same—which happens a lot more than you'd think—because he looked at me and beamed.

"Is the board public or private?" he asked.

"Private. A guy based in Albany, New York, owns it. It checks."

"Good. That excludes him from being our man."

"It also means we'll need warrants," I said.

"It'll take a few days," Satish said. "We won't post anything until we have the warrants."

Viktor scratched his birthmark with the tip of one finger. "So, theoretically, we can throw our bait on the board and see what kind of fish we net through the IP addresses. But I'm ready to bet our guy's not going to use a static address. He's gonna use at least one proxy, and he'll do it anonymously."

Satish pondered. "Sounds far fetched."

Viktor shrugged. "Our man may not take the bait, but I'm pretty sure those guys will pinpoint what language this is. If it is some language."

"So that's at least one bird," I said. "As for the second bird—our man taking the bait—anybody who'll recognize the code and lives in the L.A. area is worth a close look at. I assume you already have an account that's untraceable to us?"

Viktor dropped his chin and looked at me like a Boston terrier. "Course."

"Good. Then as soon as we get the warrants, post the code from one tile. You pick the one. Every answer you get, you retrace the IP address, user name, and every bit of information you can get. Especially people in SoCal. Try to engage them in a conversation. We need to find out not only what the hell the code means, but also as much as possible from the responders."

Satish inhaled deeply. "Track, what are the odds?"

"Hey, if this guy is like the BTK killer Dennis Rader, that's exactly what he wants us to do. That's why he left us the code, so we can communicate. The code doesn't need a key, the code *is* the key."

Viktor rubbed his birthmark again. "Dennis Rader got caught because he did something stupid. He was playing with dolls and floppy disks. Our guy here is more advanced. He fiddles with computer code."

"Dennis Rader wasn't stupid," Satish said. "He just wanted to get caught. They all do, eventually. Road Runner has no fun if Wile E. Coyote stops chasing him." He sighed, got to his feet. "Let's do this."

* * *

A bartender in a tight, pinstriped vest stirred a Martini with wet, clinking sounds. He reached for a lemon with a well-rehearsed sweep of his arm, cut it in half, and squeezed it with both hands. The zesty scent of citrus reached my nose. It mingled with the fruity aroma of vermouth, the various melodies of human perspiration, the cantabile of kitchen smells.

A lady with brimming lipstick and a wreath of plastic beads around her neck sat at the other end of the bar, her party dress too old to be cheerful, and her glass too small to fit her sorrows. A couple flirted at a dimly lit table. They fit all possible clichés you can think of on couples flirting in a bar. He kept his fat wallet next to his plate. She eyed it from above the rim of her glass, while taking small, calculated sips. Three flat screen TVs hanging from the ceiling showed Quinteros from the Houston Astros homered to center. The L.A. half of the Dodger stadium looked disappointed. A couple of guys at the bar booed.

Satish talked. I nodded without paying attention.

I glazed over, and the meeting from the day before with Watanabe replayed in my head.

Take the prescription medication, Track. We need to stop your antibodies before it's too late.

What the hell is *that* supposed to mean?

Is it gonna kill me?

Please. A cougar attack followed by encephalitis didn't kill me when I was six. One month of juvi hadn't killed me when I was sixteen, two bullets in the chest a few years ago hadn't killed me either.

I'm tough, Doc.

A waiter with a thin mustache, feminine brows, and lips as tight as his posture stood in front of us. He described the specials on the menu like a doctor explains sex to his teenage kid.

Satish closed his menu with a loud slap. "Philly burger with fries."

The waiter nodded, scribbled, and then turned his supercilious stare on me.

"I'll have a—er, salad—a *steak* salad," I said. I almost choked on the words but managed quite well, all things considered.

The waiter scribbled, turned on his heels and left. Satish let out a shriek. "A salad? You ordered a salad in a place like this? That's like asking for a tie in a kurta shop!"

I shrugged. The TV screens panned over Rodriguez flying out to the right. The Astros crowd stood up in ecstasy. I squeezed the lime into my Corona and took a swig. "What d'you know, Sat? I might even turn vegetarian, one of these days. It's supposed to make you live longer, isn't it?"

Satish's face hung up in horror. "Salad ain't gonna make you live a minute longer. It'll just *feel* longer."

I tapped the Corona logo embossed on the bottle.

Satish's phone rang.

"You think too much," Satish said.

"Maybe."

He wobbled his head. "It's okay. You think too much, you screw up your own life. You think too little, you screw up everybody else's life."

"What a philosopher you are, Satish."

He grinned. His phone kept ringing.

"Sat."

"What?"

"Answer the damn phone."

He dropped his chin and looked at me. "It's *your* damn phone, Track."

"Huh."

It was Thomas Ellis, from the county coroner's office. "Detective! I didn't see you at the cut today."

My neurons skipped a synapsis. *What cut?* The only one still fresh in my head was *my* cut... from the nightmare I had this morning. "Unless you were planning on cutting *me,* I didn't have any autopsy scheduled for this morning."

He laughed. Glad *he* found it funny. "No, sir, not you. The infant corpses you found."

The infant corpses.

"I believe they were born full-term and alive," he added.

I felt a shiver swoop down my spine.

It wasn't a shrine. It was a dumpster.

"Dr. Ellis, that wasn't my jurisdiction. I notified the divisional detective on call, and—"

"Ganzberg. Yes, he was here for the autopsy. Well, I still think you'd be interested in seeing this. How about you stop by tomorrow morning?"

Diane had called me earlier to tell me she'd found something interesting on the fibers. "Can't in the morning—what's your schedule like in the afternoon?"

He checked. "I have a cut at one p.m. Come at four, then. You and your partner."

I hung up and told Satish. "That's perfect," he said. "We can swing by the shop before the meeting."

"The coroner office shop? What d'you need to stop there for?"

He grinned. "I'm getting one of their barbecue aprons for my brother's birthday. The front says, 'The L.A. county coroner has spare hands and spare ribs.' My brother loves ribs."

"That's tacky."

"Tacky? He loves that kinda stuff. You have to see the T-shirt I got him last year."

"What did it say?"

"The L.A. County Coroner is dying for your business." He chuckled. "Get it? *Dying?*"

"What a loving brother you are, Sat."

"I am, aren't I? I never forget a birthday."

The waiter delivered the mouth-watering burger to Satish—pinky raised, straight face and all—and flopped a heap of green, wilted leaves in front of me.

"What the hell is this?" I said.

The straight face wrinkled at the corners. "Your steak salad, sir."

I couldn't even see the steak part.

Sat smirked from behind his double burger.

I pushed the salad away. "Feed it to the chickens. I'm having rib eye. One pounder, rare, whole black pepper. Add a skewer of grilled shrimp and we're buddies."

One of the brows in the straight face rose about half an inch. It considered me very carefully, then slid back into place. "Very well, sir."

The steak salad departed. The Dodgers kept losing to the Astros: Loney singled to center; Hudson doubled to deep left center, Loney to third; Wolf grounded out to second. Satish squirted a blob of ketchup in his plate, dipped his fries, then stuck them one by one inside the big, fat bun.

"You think too much," he reiterated with his mouth full and his cheeks content. "You think too much."

NINETEEN

She looks like a gypsy bride. Black mars her wings like tracks of a tarred ocean on a white beach. She doesn't move. Her mate, smaller and darker, zigzags his serenade on the windowsill, nervously flicking his antennae.

Yellow light from the street pools inside the bedroom and casts long beams on the walls.

I should kill them, *he thinks.* I should kill them both.

He waited too long, though. The cocoon was empty when he got home tonight. And now they're everywhere.

Gypsy moths mate in July. They lay hundreds of eggs, wrapped in a wispy nest of silk.

The sounds of the city drone in the distance – the wailing of sirens, the swooshing of helicopters. Sounds he's gotten used to. That's not what's keeping him awake at two in the morning. It's the tingling, again. His feet are tingling. He rubs them against the sheets, but the tingling doesn't go away.

The male moth crawls up the wall. The female holds still and waits.

He tosses and turns, wishing he had no feet, wishing for a body with removable parts that he could wear on and off as needed, like pieces of clothing.

The soles of his feet sting. He bends his legs to his chest and slides a tentative hand down his calf, fingers creeping along his ankle, slowly brushing the side of his foot.

He holds his breath. He doesn't want to know. He just wants the tingling to go away.

He just wants...

There's a lump under his foot, and it's swollen and hairy. It's disgusting. He cups his hand around it, and the lump creeps between his fingers, wriggling away.

"Shit!"

He closes his fist around it and smashes it. His hand emerges from underneath the sheets, bloody slime and hairs plastered on his open palm.

"Argh!"

The tingling creeps up his legs and under his skin, hairy legs crawling all over his body. He shoots up, groping for the light. Bed sheets tumble on the floor.

A one-inch long larva pokes out of his belly button, its legs leaving a trail of blood on his skin. A handful of them squirms over his right breast, feeding off his flesh. He opens his mouth to scream, and larvae belch out of his throat. He yanks them out, and yet the more he pulls off his skin, the more they come out of every orifice in his body – his nostrils, his ears, his eyes...

The sirens ebb off, the helicopter fades in the distance.

The first rays of dawn sneak through the curtains, while up on the wall, the male moth finally reaches his white bride.

TWENTY

Friday, July 17

The door was open. I knocked on the jamb. Diane didn't even lift her eyes from the computer screen. "Close the door and switch the lights off."

I stood by the door and considered. "Right now? In the lab? I'd love to, Diane, damn I would, but it just doesn't feel private enough. People could walk in any time and—"

"Don't be stupid, Track, it's not funny." She tapped her heels across the room and closed the door. "Turn off the light, I have to show you something."

I obeyed and flipped the light switch. The lights and sounds from the hall ebbed off. In the dark, her scent wavered like a votive candle.

"You changed shampoo brand," I said.

She frowned. She didn't know I could see her frown.

"You don't like it?"

"No. I mean, yes. I just happened to notice it's different."

Diane bit her lower lip, thoughtfully. She was holding something, but her lip was more attractive, so I kept my eyes on it. "You liked the other brand better," she said, half teasing.

"D. I don't give a — What's in your hand?"

"A slide." She held it up for me to see. Flattened between the glass and the cover slip, two tiny filaments were coiled together, and they glowed like the Nokia Center at night. If the Nokia Center were made of tiny filaments squeezed in a microscope slide, that is.

Diane smiled and her smile was clever and delicious at the same time. "So, tell me, Track: do you know any African animal — with fur — that glows like this at night?"

A-ha. Touché. I looked around, found a lab stool, and dropped my ass on it.

"Where'd you go?"

"Right here."

Diane turned toward my voice, disoriented — her eyes couldn't see past the glowing filaments in her slide. She raised a hand and flipped the switches. The receding bulbs flickered and hummed back to life. The light washed down on the sleek workbenches, the microscopes, the centrifuges, the fridges, the biohazard bins, the trays of vials, the boxes of slides, and the stacks of empty tissue cassettes.

"What do you think?"

"I suppose that's one of the mysterious fibers from the Byzantine Strangler?"

She grinned and nodded.

"You dyed them?"

"Uh-uh. They naturally fluoresce." Her smile got cleverer. "So?"

"I think it's fabulous," I said. "All we gotta do is toss a

few suspects in a room, turn the lights off, and pick the guy with the glowing hair."

Diane expressed her disapproval with little staccatos of her ambrosial scent. "Very funny, Track." She walked back to her chair, set the slide on the desk and tapped the computer mouse. The monitor flicked to life and asked for a username and password. "These aren't hair fibers."

I scoffed. "Fine. They're not synthetic fibers, they're not plant fibers, they're not hairs. Are they alien fibers and that's why they fluoresce?"

Diane logged on to the computer, double clicked, and pulled up a picture. "What do you think of this?"

I leaned closer. The first thing I saw was her scent— spicy, intriguing, and playing hard-to-get with my nostrils. Past her glaring scent was the computer monitor, and on the computer monitor was a picture—black background with a thin filament all curled up onto itself and glowing like a fluorescent light bulb.

"Where's that from? Roswell, New Mexico?"

"No. From this website."

"Morgellons Disease Association," I read from the screen. "The fiber's a disease?"

Diane shrugged, which was something she didn't do very often, so that when she did, it became relevant. "A disease to some, a psychosis to others. And, to me, a theory on the Byzantine Strangler." She turned and looked at me the way women look at you when they want to see if you're still part of the conversation.

"Go on," I said. Her smile told me it was the right thing to say.

"Morgellons disease is a controversial condition. Patients report tingling and prickling of the skin, crawling sensations, rashes, and skin lesions. Some experience loss of concentration and fatigue. What's common to all, though—

and at the same time makes this condition so highly debated — is the presence of microscopic fibers that, apparently, come out of the skin lesions. Check it out, more pictures."

She scrolled down the web page. The images showed enlargements of curly filaments, some black like the ones we had found on the victims, and some transparent and entangled with portions of skin. Despite coming in different colors and shapes, all fibers shared one feature: they naturally fluoresced.

I rapped my fingers on the desk. "Can we compare our fibers with some taken from these patients?"

Diane shook her head. Her new shampoo wafted to my nostrils. I didn't say anything this time. "See, depending on who you ask, they'll tell you these fibers don't even exist. The Board of Psychiatry claims the condition is completely delusional. In fact, some patients believe they see bugs coming out of their skin, besides the fibers, so whatever condition they have, gets treated as delusional parasitosis."

"Somebody must think it's real."

"Patients do. And their families. They put up the website to spread the word."

I looked at her. "What do *you* believe?"

She let go of the mouse, brought a hand to her mouth, and nibbled a cuticle on the side of her thumb. I wanted to nibble her lips instead.

"Track, the lesions these patients experience are most frequent around the mouth, on hand palms, and on the feet," she said.

"Lesions on hands and feet. Interesting. Amy had lesions on her feet, Laura had them on her hands, too. The Byzantine Strangler is reproducing the disease on his victim."

She nodded.

"When are you getting the DNA results back?"

"*Mitochondrial* DNA," she corrected me. She sighed, turned to the computer screen. "I called the lab earlier this morning. They told me it's in the pipeline."

I got to my feet. "Put pressure on them. Tell them we got a serial killer on the loose."

"I call them every day."

She walked to the door with me, then looked down and tipped her head to the side. "Maybe we should talk to Washburn."

I stiffened. "Washburn? Why do you want talk to the shrink?"

She came closer, so close I could smell the warmth of her breath and it was as soothing as Aretha Franklin's voice. "The only reason you don't like Washburn is because you have to sit in his office every time you are in an OIS. And you tend to be in an OIS *a lot*. To everybody else, Washburn is one of the leading experts on criminal minds. If our guy has Morgellons, maybe Washburn can give us some hints on his next moves."

I didn't hear a word she said. Her lips moved, her eyelashes beat, her brows bent in the slightest frown. And all I heard was, *Damn it, Ulysses, kiss her. Kiss her now.*

She gave me a pale smile, one of those smiles you might consider putting on your lapel if you're that kind of old fashioned guy. She leaned closer, brushed a finger along the front of my shirt. "You look stressed," she pressed.

A shade of melancholy blotted her eyes.

Orpheus crossed Hades to get his Eurydice back. Except in this game called life, I was the one with the one-way ticket to Hades.

* * *

Ellis hadn't gained an ounce since last time I saw him. He was gaunt and lanky, with a face like a crow. He smoked like a chimney, and the smell of nicotine clung to his skin like glaze on doughnuts. It was almost refreshing in a place that reeked of cadavers and formaldehyde. He came out of the autopsy room, stripped off his gown and surgical gear, washed his hands and face, donned a lab coat, and dragged us down the hallway into the histology lab.

"Nice, quiet place to have a chat," he claimed.

The lab was indeed quiet, save the humming and tilling of the machines, milling around as if they had a life of their own. A technician stood in front of one of the benches, frowning at a microscope while jotting notes in his notebook.

Ellis pushed away a colorful stack of slide boxes, rolled over a couple of stools, and flopped a blue folder on the cytology bench, between a slide stainer and a tissue chopper. They both smelled suspicious to my sensitive nose. *Everything* smelled suspicious in that place.

"Mind you," he started, opening the folder. "This is all preliminary. Frank Devore, the forensic anthropologist— you know him, right? He came to the autopsy this morning. Couldn't tell us much, he needs to run more tests on the fetal bones. Some of his conclusions might be different than mine. I'm hoping he can help us date the remains." He forked his reading glasses and gave us both a quick glance from above the rim, before scanning his notes. "Anyhow. Various degrees of adipocere in all of the six corpses. The rest is completely skeletonized." One by one, he took out the pictures of the baby corpses and lined them on the countertop. I recognized the one we'd plucked out first because it was the most intact. All others looked like doll parts with bones sticking out, held together by exsiccated cartilage and tissue: a pelvis with legs, an arm, a torso.

And never a head.

Ellis's bony fingers swooped over the pictures. "You know the process, right? Because the bags were tightly tied, the anaerobic bacterial fauna turned body fat into what's commonly known as corpse wax or adipocere."

"I thought adipocere was quite rare," Satish said.

"It is, but less so in children who tend to have more body fat than adults. It's even likelier in infants. In my career I've seen it a handful of times. Now. The next thing you need, besides body fat, is water."

"The cistern was dry," I admitted.

"Yeah, but we can't assume it's always been dry, can we?" Ellis showed me his yellow teeth. It tempted me into offering a Listerine strip. "In fact..." One of his bony fingers pointed at me. "In fact, I think this can give us a clue to when these bodies were dumped."

That perked my interest.

Ellis arched over the countertop and rearranged the pictures. "Your colleague, Ganzberg. He took nice sketches. Way better at drawing than you, Track."

"Thanks, Doc."

"Not that I don't teach, him," Satish said.

"Thanks, Sat."

"Okay." Ellis stepped aside. "What do you think? I've rearranged the pictures according to the way they were found in the cistern. The adipocere corresponds to different levels of water. One level here," he tapped, "and a second one here. Possibly a third, though for this one we only had an arm and part of the torso, and that's hard to pin down."

I remembered a detail that had escaped me before. "There were water level marks on the inside of the cistern."

"Floods during rainy seasons?" Satish offered.

"El Niño," I said. "Brilliant, Sat. Last strong one was winter '97-'98."

Ellis bobbed his head. "That's what I was thinking. '91-'92 was the one before that, which could explain the second level. There might be a third one, if you look closely, dating back to the Eighties."

"Can you corroborate it by dating the corpses?" Satish asked.

Ellis took the reading glasses off his face and bit one of the tips. "That's not going to be easy. The flip side with adipocere is that it stops the tissue from aging. All we have for a TOD are the bones, and they're now in the hands of the anthropologist. We'll see what he can come up with. From what I can tell you, the bones unaffected by adipocere were completely disarticulated, non-greasy, and free of soft tissue. But as you know, with the kind of weather we have out here, you can get a body completely skeletonized in a matter of weeks. The remains were sealed so well in the plastic bags that, except for the torn one, animals didn't get to them, and soil erosion was minimal. We could be talking decades. All the clues we have are from the scene, like the El Nino hypothesis. I sent roots and dead vines that were interspersed with the trash bags to the lab. But foliage regrows every year, so don't hold your breath on that. Another clue would've come from clothing, but there's no trace of fabric in the bags, either."

"They were buried naked?" Satish asked. "Any chance they were buried right after birth, then? As in still births?"

Ellis bobbed his head. Over his long neck it looked like a crow pecking. He set his glasses down and tapped the first picture with a yellow fingernail. "This was the most intact one. I opened it up and looked at the heart. Detectives, I can tell you that this little guy was born alive and breathed at least once in his short life. The foramen ovale, an opening in the fetal heart, was closed. It closes at birth but remains open in still births."

"How old do you think the baby was when he died?"

Ellis shook his head. "Days. Hours. Maybe a month, but no more than that, if we believe gestational biometry charts. The length of the femur bones and the abdominal perimeter are compatible with full-term births. Unfortunately, we have no skull, not even a scrap of cranial bone. Usually those are the most informative in fetuses — in terms of age at birth and dating process."

Satish opened his mouth. "Which brings us to the question —"

"What the hell happened to the heads," I said, interrupting him.

Ellis stretched his lips into a smile. "Ah, now you ask." He reached for the blue folder and retrieved a new picture. It was an enlargement of the neck cavity. It reminded me of a thawed Thanksgiving turkey, and the association made me uneasy.

"As you can see from this photo," Ellis said, "the neck wasn't severed, or else the edges of the wound would be straight and clean. I sliced a section and put it under the microscope. The tissue looked scarred."

"Scarred?" Satish seemed surprised. "How?"

"I ran some tests. I was looking for meconium, to see if they'd been killed right after birth. Guess what I found instead?"

I said, "The reason why you called us here?"

"Exactly. Sulfates. Not just in this one. In all of the bags, from the dust retrieved inside. Lots and lots of sulfates."

"What's up with sulfates?" Satish asked. "Is it what I'm thinkin' it is?"

Ellis nodded. "Sulfate salts — what's left after sulfuric acid reacts with the water in the tissue."

I inhaled, long and slow. Satish brought a hand to his face and squeezed his cheeks.

235

Ellis crossed his arms. "If it makes you feel any better, I'm pretty sure it was postmortem. Newborns' airways and esophagus are so short it would've gotten into their stomach. There was no trace of sulfates in the lungs or stomachs—the ones I could analyze, at least." He sighed. "I've seen enough of this stuff to tell you that the most common way is a pillow on the baby's face. I guess in this case, the cowards didn't want to look at that face again, so they got rid of the problem."

"Would the sulfuric acid completely erase the baby's head?" I asked.

Ellis nodded. "Newborns are all soft tissue. Not much would be left."

Did Hercules look at his children's faces after he killed them in a fit of rage? Fate took revenge on him, as he burned alive, his flesh consumed by a centaur's blood, much like sulfuric acid on his skin.

Sometimes I wish real life worked the same way as mythology.

* * *

Jank Biologicals was founded in 2000 as a consulting service for manufacturers of biological products. After a few failed clinical trials, the company bought Lyons's patent in 2003 and developed his HIV vaccine. Their revenues had steadily grown since the first pilot study in 2005.

Though they boasted more than 40 consultants, the HIV vaccine was their biggest project. I flipped the report, trying to understand Lyons's role in the company's development.

"Lyons got one hundred grand for the vaccine patent," I said.

"Not bad," Satish replied. "My old man would be rich by now." He pulled the bank files on Lyons's assets out of the evidence cardboard box and dropped them on his desk.

"Your old man? What'd he do?"

"He invented the WYAO vaccine against poverty."

I clinked a paperclip against my teeth. "WYAO?"

"Work Your Ass Off. Worked miracles." He sniggered and spread the papers across his desk. "Let's see if Lyons ever bought any stocks from Jank." Satish licked his index and turned pages. "Bingo. He did, back when Jank started producing the vaccine—they were penny stocks at the time and he bought five hundred thousand shares. Hmm. PPS stayed the same for the first two years then started growing. And growing. By 2007 his net gain was—wait, am I reading this right? It was almost a million."

I almost swallowed the paperclip. "That much? So the company's been doing real well. That why he started recommending the wife to buy shares too?"

Laura Lyons had bought shares in 2007, Amy the following year. Laura had borrowed the money from her mother, except from what the mother had told me over the phone, she never returned it. The company's shares had been soaring since 2005 and more than quadrupled their value. Obviously, Laura didn't want to sell and return her mother's money.

Satish raised his palm. "Hold on. Not the end of the story. Lyons started selling back the shares last year."

"Last year? When?"

"Right after summer. He's now got only fifty percent of what he'd originally bought."

I slammed a hand on the desk. "So he's convincing everyone to buy stocks while in the meantime he's selling them?"

Satish shrugged. "He bought property in Malibu after he sold the patent. Maybe he needed the cash."

"Makes no sense. The company's revenues are healthy,

the vaccine study is going well..."

Satish scrolled down the bank statements. "Hey, look at this."

I got out of my chair and leaned against his desk. "What is it?"

"Jank's been bleeding into Lyons's bank account every six months since 2005: thirty grand, fifty, another thirty..."

"What for? Settlements? Wages?"

"Hmm. *Undisclosed work*. The hell's that supposed to mean?"

Lyons wasn't listed as one of Jank's employees. The money was filed in Lyons's tax return as "uncategorized income."

I lifted the phone from its cradle. "Let's find out," I said. I looked up Jank's contact number, dialed, and pressed the speakerphone button.

An operator picked up. We were put on hold for a good five minutes, passed on to one of the company's financial advisor, then put on hold again.

Finally, a young voice with a vague note of sympathy picked up the phone. "Er—Detectives? I'm told I can't disclose the information."

Satish's browses shot to his hairline. "Why? The recipient is under investigation. If the payments are legit I don't see why there's a need to keep them in the dark."

"Oh, I'm sure they're perfectly legitimate, sir. We have many MD's working for us on several clinical trials, and they are regularly remunerated for their consulting work. It's all under the sun, except—"

"Except you can't tell me the exact reason for these payments."

"I'm afraid not, sir."

I leaned over the speaker. "You do realize we can get a warrant signed in two hours and get the information anyway, right?"

"Yes, sir," the sympathetic yet helpless voice replied. "I'm afraid that's your only option."

We thanked him for nothing and hung up.

Satish sighed and rolled up the sleeves of his shirt. "Toss a coin?"

I shook my head, opened the laptop and logged onto the A.D.A. server to start the warrant process. "My turn to do it. Sheesh, it's four already."

Satish's eyes darted to the wall clock. He frowned then jumped out of his chair. "Time to go to Bob's."

I raised my eyes from the screen. "Isn't it early for dinner?"

Satish picked up cell phone and badge wallet from his desk, and slid them both in his pocket "Happy hour starts at four thirty. And clam chowder during happy hour is only five bucks." He winked. "I'm half Indian, Track. And I'm a cop. I never miss a good deal. Wanna join when you're done with those warrants?"

I made a face and started typing the warrant application. My appetite had run away from me again. "Go ahead. I might join you later."

Satish adjusted his holster. "As you wish. But don't forget happy hour's until five thirty. That's all you get at Bob's." He flashed me a smile that smelled of dental floss and cumin. I tracked the sandy scent of his skin out of the door, down the hallway, into the elevator. Then I lost it.

I submitted the warrant application, then closed the laptop and wondered what to do with my life. My eyes fell on the open murder book on my desk.

No matching ligature.

No matching code.

No matching tiles.

No matching fibers.

And now six infants, murdered, then marred with sulfuric acid.

When? And why? By whom? Same person who was teasing us with a handful of colorful tiles?

The connection with Jank was intriguing, though so far it had revealed nothing.

Lyons had ties with all three victims, but no knowledge of computers. From what his assistant told us, he even had her type and send his emails because he didn't want to bother with the mail editor. The hospital's bioinformatics department developed all the software and computer work needed for the vaccine design and data analyses. All Lyons did was give orders.

What if the symbols found at the back of the tiles weren't a computer code?

Maybe Lyons is right. Maybe the Byzantine Strangler is after him.

The murders so far could've been just practice. The killer was getting closer and closer to Lyons, circling him.

The photos of the baby corpses made me nauseated. I flipped through them until I got to the pics of the water tank. I stared at the corrugated metal cover and the cement structure, its interior lined by different floods.

The report had a full paragraph on the trash bags: "Seven pairs of black plastic trash bags (one inside the other), size large, no cinch tie, the handles tightly knotted, tied with a double loop and two loose ends. Detritus found inside included: dried vegetative material (roots, vines, and leaves), insect pupae, sandy dirt, spiders, and common beetles."

From the pictures, I could tell that the outer bags were all faded in color, but the inner ones still had the GLAD logo. The logos were all slightly different. The most informative had a "3-ply StressFlex" motto right beneath the company names.

No cinch ties. Those had appeared relatively recently, maybe in the last ten years? Back when I was a kid we'd tie the handles to close them. I still remembered hauling the trash bags to the bins outside.

The memory lit up a light bulb. I opened the laptop again and Googled "Tom Bosley." Wikipedia page, Facebook fan page, movie database. Hmm. I typed "Tom Bosley GLAD." The computer redirected me to YouTube. I watched a video of a kid bouncing around a trash bag and smiled. I used to be like that. *On a good day*. Bosley's friendly smile appeared on the screen after the kid. I paused the video. Both bags in Bosley's hands had the writing "3-ply StressFlex" on them. It was 1982.

One by one, I found all GLAD logos through the TV commercials on YouTube. They spanned the '80s and early 'nineties. It wasn't a time stamp, and it added nothing to what Ellis had already told us.

But it was something.

I moved on to my next item on the agenda and started a new search. This one was iffy, had to fill out a form that ensured the LAPD that my search was legal and motivated by an ongoing investigation. I entered one of Callahan's favorite Internet boards, assured the site that I was older than eighteen, and was rewarded with free advice on safe sex and the phone number of a bunch of clinics offering free HIV testing. Interestingly, Laura Lyons's one was the third one on the list.

I clicked enter.

The language was crude, the offerings bold (an understatement, really): top, bottom, cock pics, butt pics, undetermined hours of sex. I was only interested in screen names. I clicked on the archives and navigated all the way back to when Callahan was roaming the site. I found only two of his posts, both rants on same-sex marriage rights. I scrolled down the responses and the screen names they'd been posted under: *Ultimate Cock, AlwaysOnTop, mr_kam...* I clicked on the last one and found a few more posts.

I pondered. On the list, Callahan's screen name was "Code7," the police code for "lunch break." The mr_kam guy started posting right around Callahan's time, then vanished. KAM is the LAPD radio code for "end of transmissions." Was it all a coincidence?

I was going nowhere with this, so I closed the laptop and picked up the phone.

Ganzberg wasn't surprised to hear from me. "Life's a bitch, Presius," he said. "They told me to pull the patrol unit from the water tank post. The brass said it wasn't worth it now that the news leaked. I tell you, life's a bitch, dude."

"What about installing a camera?"

"We don't have that kind of technology, too expensive. The usual shit."

I propped a foot on the desk and stared at the tip of my shoe. "Was this after Ellis told you about the sulfates?"

"Yeah. He says the kiddos had been done a while ago. So my sergeant says, 'Let the RHD deal with it. They've got more manpower than us.'"

"Nice of him to mention."

"What d'you want me to say? You got your own problems."

One of the wanted faces hanging from the wall sneered at me. "What problems?"

Ganz's voice dropped. "Henkins, man. Don't tell me she's not all over you for taking her case."

The sneer on the wanted face spread farther. "She's not," I said.

I heard a rattle, then a faked cough. When he came back, his voice sounded normal again. "Well, I did a little digging in the neighborhood closest to the water tank, inquired about old tenants, rumors, and such. Same old, same old. People with short memory minding their business. Most of it is projects, built in the Eighties."

"That would fit the bill," I said. "About Henkins—"

"Problem is, people come and go. I got a list."

"Good thinking. Have one of your blue suits go there and interview people. As for Henkins—"

"Working on that. It's gonna take a while to go through the list. Did I mention life's a bitch? Good night, Presius."

He hung up and I never got a chance to ask him to clarify the Henkins statement.

I leaned back in my chair and chewed on a paperclip. I stared at my shoes, then at the sneering face on the wall. "What are you laughing at?"

The face stopped sneering and stared at the ceiling instead.

Things didn't add up. They never do, really.

I called Satish. He'd already had his chowder, along with some degree of alcohol, I guessed from the silvery cheer in his voice. Jazz played in the background—Dizzy Gillespie's *Salt Peanuts*.

"They pulled the patrol unit from the water tank scene," I said.

"Not surprised. The news is out. Catching the guy at the scene now is like catching a fly with a shotgun."

"Some people are good at that."

"People can do the strangest things."

The Jazz stopped. Clapping sounds rushed through the phone then quieted down. I considered corpse wax and body dumps, fluorescent fibers, big pharma companies, shotguns and flies. I considered my own life, dangling over a cliff called genetic fate.

If there is such a thing as genetic fate.

The Jazz resumed—Wynton Marsalis, this time. Satish was saying something. "So, what are you going to do about it?"

"Go home, load my gun, and pack my camping gear."

Silence, the clinking of silverware. And then: "Remember the boxer stance."

"What for?"

"For the shotgun, Track. Good luck." He closed the phone and the Jazz died.

TWENTY-ONE

The last rim of light outlined the profile of the mountains. Colors blurred in a grainy black and white, and scents blossomed like night flowers. The air smelled of sagebrush and toyon, of dry soil finally letting go of the heat of the day, of evening breeze tinged with a hint of humidity. It smelled of intimate things, wild scents that amplified and dispersed in the darkness, like melancholic tunes spilling down a deserted alley.

The noises were hushed, covered by the trilling of crickets and the hoot of a solitary owl.

The water tank looked like we'd left it. Despite my efforts to cover our tracks, the low trees still bore the signs of our visit. Green leaves were scattered all over on the ground. Freshly snapped branches drooped from where one of our men had stood the light boons. It had taken some effort to bring all our equipment up there and it still showed. I put down my backpack, got on my hands and knees and sniffed all around the corrugated metal. Will sniffed with me. Now that the reek of corpse wax had been unearthed, coyotes and raccoons had come to visit the place. The smell was still strong.

No unfamiliar smells, though.

That was disappointing.

The Pain coiled around my ribs, sharp, intense, and short. Just a friendly reminder that it wasn't gonna go anywhere without me. I let the wave wash off completely before moving again. Will came by my side and dropped something dirty and chewed and stinky on my face.

"Very thoughtful of you, pal, but I'm really not hun—"

I inhaled. *Bones.* I grasped it from my face and took a good look. It wasn't human, that much I could tell. It looked like a femur, maybe a cat or a small dog. I crawled to the hole Will had dug and found more bones.

In the meantime, the mutt had gone to work on a different site. "Will, wait! You're turning the place into a gopher nest."

I grappled with him and snatched another cracked bone out of his mouth. Still small, still nothing larger than a cat. Brittle and dry, with no traces of tissue left. Maybe a couple of years old, give or take.

I pondered what to do about the animal bones Will had dug out, decided I wasn't in the mood to keep them, so I buried them back and covered the holes.

Something clicked in my head.

The urge to follow the prey, stalk, chase, pound... kill and bury.

I know you, Byzantine Strangler. I know you very well.

I know you've been here, it doesn't matter how long ago.

I called Will, left the tank and walked farther up, past the growth of low sagebrush rimming the hillside. Humming softly, the familiar expanse of downtown glowed in the distance, a flat constellation of intersecting boulevards and freeways.

I followed the lit-up Five with my eyes, then the Ten west, then tried to picture exactly where South L.A. was. The night breeze blew in my face. It was mild and tepid and it smelled of wildflowers.

How hot was it in South Central right now?

I thought of Ricky Vargas, prowling, like me, but on different grounds, in a different jungle. On a different hunt.

I found a clearing surrounded by shrubs, unrolled my sleeping bag, and set the backpack as a pillow. I'd brought one gun only, the revolver, which I unholstered and slid under the backpack.

Will sniffed and marked the whole area before snuggling next to me.

Up in the sky Orion raised his bow. He pointed it to a lonely airplane that blinked its wake across the sky. Orion didn't really care. He kept his bow high toward Castor and Pollux and didn't pay any attention to what us humans were doing down below.

I thought of headless babies and cats and dogs buried under the water cistern.

I thought of Detective Henkins, how she was supposed to be *all over me* about the Callahan case, according to Ganzberg. I thought of Lyons's love affair, how he *still* loved his wife even though he regularly snuck into another woman's bed. Lyons, MD and scientist, either a killer or the next victim immolated in the name of science. I thought of the arcane code at the back of the tiles, each tile a different color — a clue, a teaser, a challenge.

And then I thought of my own life, constantly balancing between reason and instinct, between what I let myself be and what I should've been instead. Hanging between hunter and prey, angel and devil, life and death.

Your genes make you special, Ulysses.

You just told me my very special genes are going to kill me.

There's a possibility, yes.

Sometimes I wish doctors could legally lie.

I stared into the night sky, the low edges tainted by the yellow glow of the city. The rest was black vastness. Dapples of stars, like distant songs. They melted into Eva Cassidy's voice singing *The Autumn Leaves*.

Thanatos, god of Death.

Of all mortals, only one tricked Death, King Sisyphus, who slyly chained Thanatos with his own shackles. He was punished to eternally roll a boulder up the incline of the Olympus.

Eternity is the punishment for those who don't die, Ulysses.

And so, you too, Ulysses, shall die.

TWENTY-TWO

Saturday, July 18

Coyotes howled, crickets chirped, owls hooted and cicadas sang. And I tossed and turned and didn't sleep. The turd didn't show up, either. I dozed off at the crack of dawn only to be awakened by the buzz of my cellphone a couple of hours later.

"Yello?"

Nothing.

I sat up, hoping the cell would get a better signal. "Hello?"

Still nothing. I didn't recognize the number, so I hung up, lay down again and closed my eyes. The phone rang one more time.

"Yes?" I snapped.

"Detective?" A raucous voice, from far away. Tired, or maybe just straining through a bad connection. Spanish inflection. "It's about Ricky."

It took me a couple of synapses to connect the dots. I hadn't slept much and I hadn't had coffee either. *Ricky Vargas*. I was talking to his uncle, Vicente.

"What'd he do?"

"Nothin'... yet. He's hanging out with those guys again. His *amigos*." He put quotes around the words *amigos* and I heard the quotes through the phone. "Please help him drop those guys. You said you were his friend, you said—"

"Look. He's not a minor anymore. He's making his own choices."

"They're banging again. In the barrio. They don't know what they're doing, they—Help him, Detective. Please. *Me lo van a matar*."

I promised him I'd do my best. He gave me the address where he was staying now, made me promise again, and then hung up.

I looked down onto the basin and the view was already hazy and hot. I sat there, contemplating for a minute longer.

My cell phone rang again. I didn't even check the number.

"Yes?"

Nothing.

"Look, I can't hear you, but I promise I'll go talk to him, okay? I promised four times already!"

I waited for an answer. I heard a crackle and slow breathing. Something told me this wasn't Vicente Vargas I was talking to.

"Your genes," the voice said. Another long pause. "They'll kill you."

It took me a few moments to register the meaning. By then the voice had already hung up. Voices don't have smells, damn it. I looked at the number, didn't recognize it, dialed back. An electronic voice informed me that the number I'd called had been disconnected.

Damn quick, the bastard.

I closed the cell, pondered what to make of the last call and came up with nothing. So I packed up, went home, showered and had my usual couple of espressos. Satish called to let me know he was going to spend the weekend in San Diego for a family gathering to celebrate Karkidaka Vavu Bali. Satish was about as religious as Bill Maher, but when it came to Hindu festivals, he didn't miss one.

I snorted. "Sat, didn't you celebrate Vavu Bali last month?"

He chortled. "That's because according to the Malayalam calendar the festival could've fallen on either the new moon in June or the one in July, and since we're Indians and we prefer to celebrate rather than argue, we're doing Vavu Bali twice this year."

"At both new moons?"

"Yup."

"Go to hell, Sat."

* * *

I got out of my Charger and took a few minutes to let my body adjust to the sweltering temperature outside. It was late July and the thermometer was bound to hit the triple digits. The sky was yellow and the helicopters kept a close watch on the mountains—fire season was at the door. Perched on the hills, white houses sat in the sun like lazy cats. Skinny palm trees rolled up and down the sky, following the profile of the California landscape. Everything was fenced off: a vacant basketball court; a lime green house; a sandy condo.

And Satish is at the beach in San Diego.

A few trash bins from the day before were still lined up

along the sidewalk, slowly simmering reeks of leftover dinners, dirty diapers, and greasy food packaging. The streets had the noiseless emptiness of an afternoon siesta.

I walked to an apartment building painted in some new-age light blue: black railing, two stories, doors on the right side, car ports on the left side, and boxed hedges along the front, trimmed so evenly you could've stacked a deck of cards at the top. A loud TV shouted out of an open window, a phone conversation blabbered from somebody's backyard.

I followed the driveway along a row of car porticos while olfactory trails from different cuisines — Asian, Mexican, Italian — clashed along the way. The communal dumpster was tucked between a cinder wall bordering the next property and the side of the building. I donned latex gloves, scrunched my nose and squeezed behind it.

On Friday, January 30 a county pick-up truck came to pull out the apartment dumpster and found a body piled against the wall — Charlie Callahan's body. Six months later, I didn't have much hope to find anything. The place had been searched with a fine toothed comb by the SID field unit, washed off, then layered back with the weekly stinks of trash, gas exhaust, rain spatters. Charlie wasn't rich, he didn't have any priors and, as far as I could tell, he wasn't on anybody's radar. He had traces of meth in his pockets, but nothing turned up from his apartment or vehicle.

He was HIV positive.

He was gay.

Two paper bags stood in one corner next to the dumpster. I took a peek inside. Trash — the usual lazy ass who came yesterday after the pick-up had already hauled the bin to the curbside and didn't feel like walking to the street. I sniffed the edges of the bags and smelled something acidic. I poked a stick inside, moved a few cans, and glimpsed plastic bottles, bleach, a bottle of drain opener.

Acidic drain opener.

A vehicle turned into the driveway and parked into one of the carports at the back.

I hooked the handle of the drain opener with the stick and pulled the bottle out. From its weight, I could tell it wasn't completely empty. About a cup was still inside, I estimated. *A cup will do the trick.* I placed the bottle back, crouched by the wall, and followed the nooks and crannies of the cinder blocks, brushing my fingers along the edges.

I reenacted the events of January 30 in my head.

Charlie comes down on Thursday night, wearing slippers. One flight down the stairs to toss out the trash, and then back home, or so he thinks.

Death sneaks from behind, wraps a ligature around his neck and pulls.

And then death watches him, as he collapses, his head scraping the cinder block bricks.

He faces his assassin as he falls.

The assassin doesn't touch him, just watches.

And maybe glimpses a paper trash bag left and has an idea.

Erase a face.

Why?

Is this how the Byzantine Strangler got his first inspiration?

Somebody was standing behind me. Low threat, no adrenaline, no gun oil, mild brand of aftershave, clean clothes—still smelled of laundry detergent. Dandruff shampoo, a whiff of gas exhaust still lingering in the air. Just got back from the gym or equivalent, showered, came home. A hint of sweat and rubber from a duffle bag with dirty clothes inside.

I slowly turned.

Handsome, wide hands, straight posture—the stance of

a dancer. Not imposing, but not humble either. He smoothly ran a hand through his hair. It was a show, a man accustomed to the stage. The tilt of the head gave him away.

"Can I help you?" He licked his lips, making his smile glisten.

Smooth voice, too.

I smiled my cop smile. "How often do pipes clog around here?"

* * *

The espresso came in the right size cup. It had the right aroma, the right consistency and the right color. I poured sugar and it piled nicely on the surface and floated three seconds before flipping and sinking.

Not that I'm dogmatic about these things.

I stirred. He watched me stir.

I downed it in two gulps, enjoyed, smacked my lips.

"How did you like the espresso, Detective?"

"If I didn't see you make it, I would've said I'd made it myself."

David Labeaux's smile smelled of Colgate and it was perfect, much too perfect. After a while I grew tired of it. His fingers fiddled with the tassel of a runner. He chuckled softly. "Don't worry," he said. "I know you're straight. I could tell right away. I won't make a move on you. Plus—" He sighed, looked away. The tassel pirouetted in his wide fingers. "I'm building my life over, with somebody else. There's only so much mourning you can do. At some point you need to move on."

"I thought you and Charlie had split up."

David cocked his head again, in that peculiar genderless way that's neither masculine nor feminine. "We did. Last year. We stayed friends—after all, we were neighbors. And then, right after he got laid off, he came to see me one night, and — you know."

No. I didn't know and I didn't *want* to know.

He sat at the bar counter, opposite of me. Behind him, a window framed a cutout of acacia boughs wavering against a blue sky. Prisms of light brushed along champagne flutes and margarita glasses hanging upside down from ceiling racks.

"Don't you want closure?" I asked, admiring the color coordinated walls, the sleek droplights, and the modern design furniture, the kind you glimpse leafing through a home décor magazine while waiting at the doctor's office.

"What do you mean?"

A pool table stood askew between the bar counter and the entertainment center. There was a cue chalk on the far edge of the table. I plucked down one of the cues hanging from the wall and brought it to my nose. Nice quality wood. "Don't you want to know who killed him?" I said, chalking the tip. I like the smell of chalk. It's like a bass in a soul jazz tune. You hardly notice it, but if it's not there you miss it.

He let go of the tassel brusquely, as if it burned. He ran a hand across his hair, less smoothly than he'd done before, then came around the countertop, dance-walking. He smelled elegant and refined, like his apartment. He smelled of a life of Martinis and strolls down Paseo Colorado, of expensive clothes and cocktail parties, of a life lived to be enjoyed except when *real* life happened, and things like HIV and murder came to shutter your dreams.

"We weren't lovers in the literal sense, you know. I mean, he'd tested positive, and I—" He swallowed. "Ghosts find a way to haunt you even when you don't believe in them."

He brushed a hand along the edge of the table, dragged the rack toward the end rail and started filling it. I took aim and shot a couple of balls toward him.

He arranged the balls in the rack, then passed me the cue ball. "You break?"

"Sure."

We silently watched the balls scatter around the table, smacking against one another. I pocketed two.

"Good break," he said, reaching for a cue. He studied the kitchen carefully. "The press didn't treat him right. One of the most conservative journalists blew up the meth story. He described Charlie as some uber-tattooed freak who liked to shoot up his veins." He shook his head, sadly. "He wasn't like that, you know?"

"Who was Charlie Callahan?"

David stared vacantly at the kitchen. "A beautiful person. Young. Determined. Full of life."

I didn't pocket on my next shot, so I passed him the chalk. He handled it with care, his genderless movements somewhat natural on his frame. We're all chimeras in our own ways.

"Did things change after he got laid off?"

"He was devastated." Strong shot, pocketed two. He ran his fingers behind his ear and chose a new angle. "He was scared he wasn't going to find another job. And he needed a job desperately in order to afford the meds. That's how I learned he was positive. He hadn't told me before."

"You learned *then* that he was positive?"

He leaned with one hip against the table and nodded. "He'd enrolled in this experimental vaccine trial, and I'd just heard in the news the preliminary results had been very promising. He'd been careful, but sometimes—Anyway. You never think how vulnerable you are until it hits you."

He looked me over with large, wet eyes.

"Do you happen to know if he ever saw a Dr. Liu while he was on the vaccine trial?"

He positioned the cue and hit the ball hard in the middle. A straight shot into the pocket. "No. Thompson's the name I recall." He frowned, head cocked to the side. "Funny."

"What's funny?"

"His mom called me a couple of weeks after he died. She asked the same thing."

"About Dr. Liu?"

"Yeah. She wanted to know if he was her patient."

"What did you tell her?"

The corners of his mouth twitched downwards. "I didn't say much to her. I despised that woman. She and her husband—they never spoke a word to Charlie after he moved out here. I don't even know how she got my number. I asked her why she wanted to know. She mentioned some next-of-kin approval the doc needed, but she wasn't even sure if it was his doctor asking. And then she added, *You're all the same pack*, and hung up on me. Bitch."

Foul shot, my turn, ball-in-hand. I chalked the cue and repositioned myself.

"You're saying Charlie never mentioned a Dr. Liu?"

"Not to me," he said.

"Was he happy with Dr. Thompson?"

He shrugged in his feminine way—a fallen angel who no longer knew what to do with his wings. "He saw Dr. Thompson only once. After that, it was always the P.A. He wanted better care but he couldn't afford it now that he'd been laid off. He was determined to fight for his health. He told me he had a way, that he knew somebody who could help."

He bounced the cue ball off the side rail and pocketed two balls in one shot.

"When did he tell you this?"

"Hmm, let me think." He tapped his lips with two fingers. "It must've been early November, because I remember discussing plans for Thanksgiving over that same conversation."

The bi-weekly cash deposits started around the end of November. Some nice help, he was getting.

"Was he ever more specific about this supposed—help?"

"No. He seemed ok—for a little bit, at least."

My attention perked. "What happened afterwards?"

The question made him nervous. He hit the cue the wrong way and scratched it. He sighed, propped the cue stick on the floor and leaned against it. "Christmas came and he still hadn't found a new job. You know, the holiday blues, I suppose."

I rolled the cue ball in one hand. "David," I said. "I can smell people. I can smell when they lie, when they deceive, and when they simply hide something because they fear some kind of repercussions. You may have moved on, but you ain't gonna find closure until we cuff the bastard who killed Charlie."

He dance-walked to the wall and hung his stick. "Want another espresso?"

"No, I want the truth."

He swung his hips as he walked. Not as much as a woman, but still. He opened the small fridge behind the bar counter, took out two bottles of Coronas and a lime.

Perfect espresso and Coronas in the fridge.

The guy was starting to freak me out.

"I told you the truth," he said, uncapping the beers. "Just like I told the truth to the other detective, back in January. A woman, I forget—"

"I know her. Go on."

"She and her partner came only once. After that I heard on the news that they'd caught Olsen and he was killer.

They never came back."

"Did you believe it?"

"That it was Olsen? Could've been. He lived down the street. He yelled at us one time because we were holding hands."

David cut the lime, stuck a slice inside the neck of each bottle, and passed me one.

"But you don't believe it was him," I said.

He left his beer untouched on the counter and scuttled off to a room to the left. When he came back he was holding a picture. "He gave me this a few days before he got killed. *In case something happens*, he said. Why would he say something like that?"

I took the picture from his hand and sniffed it. It smelled of paper—he'd kept it in a book. I recognized the same scents I'd detected when I went through Charlie's personal belongings: passive smoke, cheap aftershave, cologne. I looked at the photo. It was Charlie, sitting on a beige sofa and smiling, one arm on the back of the sofa, the other on his leg, crossed over his knee. He was wearing jeans and a green T-shirt, and he seemed relaxed and happy. On the right corner I spotted one end of a coffee table, with two beer cans, an ashtray, and a pair of reading glasses. Behind him, was a poster of what looked like the Niagara Falls.

David said, "It's a cell phone shot."

"Where was it taken?" I asked.

"No idea," he replied. "It's not his apartment."

"And he never said why he wanted you to have it or who took it?"

David plucked the lime out of the bottleneck and took a swig. "I told you all I know, Detective."

And now it was my job to connect the dots.

TWENTY-THREE

Detective Courtney Henkins opened a battered cabinet that smelled of alcohol, old wood, and overall stale. An eclectic assortment of bottles at various stages of aging and consumption twinkled in a shaft of afternoon sun. Perched on a chair at the other end of the room, a Yorkshire terrier showed me her teeth and growled.

"Jameson?" Henkins asked, squinting at her collection.

"D'you happen to have a Barolo in there?"

A scratchy sound came from the depths of her throat. Some people would've called it laughter. "What's that, a table game?"

"I'll settle for Irish whiskey, then. Probably half your dose, though." I picked up a centenarian raincoat from a shaggy recliner, tossed it on a sofa that appeared to function also as bed, desk, and closet, and sat down. The recliner welcomed me with the desolate tang of thrift store.

The high-pitched drone of a NASCAR race blabbered

from the adjacent unit, the voice of the ESPN commentator rising with every lap. From the street came the giggles of the people walking down to the beach, and the smells of those who instead had nothing better to do than sit on the porch and watch them go by.

The terrier snarled and gave me a leery eye.

"Pearl's not used to guests," Henkins said. She set the bottle of Jameson on the chipped coffee table in front of me and padded to the kitchen—a square of linoleum that hosted an anachronistic stove and a whining fridge. The kitchen table was buried in cereal boxes and canned soups.

Henkins went through her cabinet doors as if it were somebody else's house. She emptied an ice tray in the sink, distributed the ice cubes between two glasses, and, despite my request, she filled both to the rim. I hoped by the time I left the place I still remembered my way home.

"So. Where's your handsome partner?" she slurred, handing me the drink. She took the first swig while slumping on the sofa-turned-closet, on top of the pile of clothes. The sofa whined, the clothes didn't complain. Pearl jumped down from the chair and ran on her mama's lap.

"Not that I couldn't fancy you," she added after the first mouthful of whiskey.

"Sure," I said, lifting the glass. "Be my Circe, I'll be your Ulysses."

She laughed, gulped down the rest of the drink, and smacked her tongue. And then she leaned backwards like a wilted plant, peering at the ice in her glass, eyes already filmed with the first signs of intoxication.

So there she was. Balls of steel drowning in a glass of whiskey, solitary companion of the lonely. Guessing from her age, she'd sailed through a few rocky marriages and survived the roughest times with the LAPD, back when Affirmative Action was but a joke among the brass circles, and discrimination against women and minorities was considered a form of machismo.

She'd tamed the testosterone but not her addictions.

I set the glass on the coffee table and asked, "Where's the restroom?"

She peered at me through skeptical eyes. "Door to the left. The one to the right's a closet. That's all there is, can't get lost."

I didn't. I knew exactly where to go and what to look for. When I came back, both ladies were where I'd left them, Henkins on the sofa, her glass refilled, and the sour terrier on her lap, eying me sternly.

Friendly company.

I flashed them a smile—it went unnoticed—and as I resumed my post on the battled recliner, I leaned forward and clonked a little something on the coffee table. The little something caught Henkins's attention. Her half-lid stare popped open. "What were you—"

"Your doctor's name's Andy Liu."

"That's none of your business," she snapped.

"You made it my business, Courtney, by slipping one of those prescription bottles in Callahan's evidence box." I pointed to the bottle I'd retrieved from her bathroom cabinet. It was identical to the one we'd found in Charlie's evidence box, except the name wasn't scratched off on this one. The patient's name was Courtney Henkins, the doctor's A. Liu, and the office number was the office number I'd called after I left David Labeaux's house, where they told me the only Dr. Liu in their practice was Andrew, not Amy.

Pearl snarled. Henkins pushed her away, sat up and poured herself another drink. I considered how many more minutes of her lucidity I had left. She drowned her face in another glass of whiskey. "We busted our asses over the Callahan case," she drawled. "You spoiled RHD dicks—

everything's set on a silver plate for you. You grab it, run, and get the glory." She ended the spiel with a hiccup.

"Bullshit," I said. "That's what you wanted us to think." I leaned forward and leveled her eyes. They were tired eyes. They may have even been pretty in a previous life. "Satish and I found a prescription bottle in Callahan's evidence box. It was from an A. Liu doctor. We thought of Amy Liu and made the connection. Problem is, the prescription bottle was never logged as a piece of evidence. You wanna know what I think? That's a rhetorical question, I'll tell you anyway. I think it wasn't logged because *you* put it in there, after Amy Liu had been murdered and the case got transferred to us. You took advantage of the fact that your doctor's name is A. Liu, scratched off part of the label, and sneaked down to Property as soon as you got a chance."

I leaned back and watched her eyes struggle not to droop.

"You planted evidence, Courtney," I pressed on. "I don't know why you did, but I have a theory. Somebody wanted the case out of the way. A young gay man brutally murdered. Some got outraged, some didn't, it got political. The pressure to catch the killer mounted, they caught one, not quite the right one, but close enough to let the moods cool down a bit. Maybe not forever. Maybe just for a while, like the Sherri Rae murder. Bury it for a while, and let a few people retire or leave. People in this country seem to have a short memory. And the few who do remember find it damn convenient."

She said nothing, so I went on with my theory. "Until June all precautions had been taken to keep Charlie Callahan all hushed up. Then Amy Liu dies in a similar way. What's the connection? Copycat or serial killer? A serial killer picks his victims at random. They're the hardest fish to get. No pattern, no motive. But you provided a pattern, Court, by making us believe that Callahan was Amy Liu's patient. You gave us a connection because you couldn't tell us there was a connection. Why?"

"He was—" she started, then closed her mouth and bit her lip. She came forward and went for the bottle. I was faster. She hit her hand against the coffee table and cursed. Her eyes strayed to the Jameson now nestled on my lap. No amount of alcohol was going to smear the glare she sent my way. She flopped back on the sofa and sighed.

"He was *her* patient. In a way. They found Amy Liu on June 19. As soon as I heard sulfuric acid had been used, I went to see my captain. I told him I wanted a new task force on the Callahan case. There was a chance this could be the same killer and we had to reopen the case. He told me the case was going to the RHD. He said, 'Henkins, file your request to retire.' I told him I didn't have enough benefits. He said, 'We'll make sure you do." She laughed bitterly. "I couldn't believe my ears. I gave my life to the agency. That's how they pay me back."

She looked at the bottle, languidly, then pushed her empty glass toward me. "My mouth is dry."

I poured some more whiskey. "Keep talking," I said.

She took a swig, swished it, then examined her reflection in the glass. "The name Amy Liu was familiar. I knew there was a connection. When I saw that she was an HIV doc I remembered."

"Did you interview her over Callahan's death?"

She shook her head. "I knew nothing about her until she showed up at the morgue."

"At the morgue?"

Henkins sloppily nodded her head and tittered. "Don't you love coincidences? I just love coincidences."

"I don't believe in coincidences. What did she want at the morgue?"

She gulped down another mouthful of whiskey. "Samples, she said. She had to get consent from Callahan's estranged family. She got it, collected her samples, and we never heard back from her."

I turned the bottle on my lap. The reek of alcohol was starting to annoy me. Henkins drained her third glass. Her eyes were slippery. She licked her lips and gave me a lopsided smile. "You're cute."

"Talk to me, not the bottle. You never went to see Amy Liu, then? You never asked her why she needed those samples?"

She shrugged. "We got Callahan's killer, didn't we? Malcolm Olsen. Violent, homophobic—he fit the bill. When they cuffed him over a domestic violence call, they called me down to the joint, told me, 'This is your suspect, grill him.'"

"And instead of reporting what was going on, you ducked your head, complied, and forgot all about Amy Liu. I bet your memory got refreshed when you heard she'd been murdered."

She tilted her head and stared at me. "You think you're a smart ass just because you're RHD?"

"I don't think much until I hear the whole story."

"Jesus." She clonked the empty glass on the coffee table and sprang to her feet. She stood there, thinking, then flopped back on the sofa. The terrier jumped back on her lap and sent me a disapproving glare. "Of course it became important after she was killed. Thing is, it was no longer there."

"What wasn't?"

Her forehead corrugated. "Her request. She'd filed a request for the samples, with the father's consent and all, and it wasn't in the murder book. I called the morgue. They didn't have it either. Then the captain called me in his office.

He said to forget the Callahan case. He said to pass everything onto you guys and keep my mouth shut."

"So you kept your mouth shut instead of reporting the fact that you had been harassed to silence. Was it a change of heart that gave you the idea to slip one of your prescription bottles into Callahan's evidence box? I guess at that point it no longer mattered whether the evidence was fake or real."

The monotonous drone of the NASCAR race on the neighbor's TV ebbed off, replaced by the loud music of the commercials. The terrier chewed her paws. Henkins's eyes glazed over again. She brought the glass to her lips, but there was no more whiskey and the ice cubes had reduced to pebbles. I set the bottle back on the table. I was done with her. I was done with everything. She could drown herself in a pool of alcohol if that was what she wanted.

"We never had this conversation, did we? Hell, I'm drunk. You never came to my house, I never opened that door."

I got to my feet. The terrier snarled at me, I hissed and walked away.

"Presius! We never had this conversation, did we?"

I opened the door, walked out of the thrift store smell, out of her miserable life, and closed the door behind me. I walked down a flight of side stairs framed by walls so close there was hardly any room to spit. Rusty metal letters hung on the white façade, forming the writing "Sea View Luxury Apartment." It was old and faded and I wondered when it stopped being true.

The ocean hummed its scent into my nostrils. The sky was blue and the air balmy. This close to the sea, the temperatures were in the seventies, and the sweltering heat from Silver Lake, where Callahan lived, was but a memory. It was Saturday and the whole world was headed to the beach. Three-generation families strolled down the sidewalks in flip-flops, sun umbrellas, and Hawaiian shirts. Kids ran holding their sand buckets. Divas in smoked shades and skimpy bikinis drove by in their cabrios. They kept circling the block looking for a parking spot.

A low beat rapped from the beach, where dwelled distant sounds of happiness and oblivion. I walked down a block, and then another, and then another, until I rapped my knuckles on the front door of a familiar Venice bungalow.

* * *

The Venice Boardwalk in a late summer afternoon is full of people and solitudes. Psychics read tarots and cheap fortunes, even happy endings if you can afford the extra charge. Doctors in green slacks and white smiles offer marijuana prescriptions, though they aren't real doctors and their smiles aren't that authentic either. The smell of hot dogs, beer, and fried sugar overwhelms the ocean breeze. Music spills out of car windows and lingers over the lost beat of the waves. Across from the shops selling plastic junk and derogatory T-shirts, bums the same color as the sidewalk beg for a coin, a word, a smile.

On the Venice Boardwalk people slur instead of talk, cheap sex waits for you on a doorstep, and genderless faces can either date you or rob you with a stare.

The Venice Boardwalk is where Hortensia lived and painted. I watched her stop at a coffee van to buy an iced latte, washing off the seller's greedy stares with a casual tip of the head. She rose on her toes to reach for her change, and the hem of her gypsy skirt offered a glimpse of taut calves and slim ankles.

We walked silently for a while, her hip brushing my

side.

"I'm liberated, you know? All that sexual angst—I've always thought it was all religious crap, instead—I mean, abstinence can be quite cathartic once you get used to it. You should try it."

Surfers came out of the water and propped their boards against the palm trees. Tanned kids played Frisbee on the beach. They looked young and healthy.

I felt neither.

"Track?"

"Hmm?"

"I broke up with Gary."

"I figured."

Hortensia shook her head and her hair fanned in the breeze like red sails. "All that sex. I mean, it was exhausting. And after all, it's just sex, you know? Just another addiction."

She beamed, the sun glimmering off her sunglasses.

A puzzled me stared back from her lenses. "Yeah. No. I think you're crazy."

A lady in a camping chair and a strip of cloth barely covering her underwear waved a manicured hand at me. "Your future for ten bucks, handsome," she said.

"I already know my future."

Hortensia clinked the ice in her cup. "Have you told her?"

"Told who?"

"Your girl. Don't you have a girl?"

I didn't reply. My legs kept walking.

"She'll want to know."

"Know what?"

"What you just told me. What your doctor said."

I said nothing. She sipped her drink until there was nothing more to sip and dumped the empty cup in the first trash bin. A bum sitting next to it gave her a toothless smile.

"So? Are you gonna tell her?"

"Jeez, Hort. What's there to tell? Docs say all sorts of stuff. Doesn't mean they're always right."

She stopped to pull a hairpin out of her skirt pocket. She held the pin between her lips, gathered her hair up and collected it at the nape of her neck. Her hair smelled warm under the sun. Her white hands still carried the scent of acrylic paints and turpentine. "Your doctor told you what he should've told you from the beginning: you've got a genetic condition and nobody really knows what's going on. That's all there is. Now, if you'd listen to me, you'd turn vegetarian, do yoga, and go see a homeopathy practitioner."

I laughed. "Right. And convert the Pope to Islam. Anything else?"

The hair bun came undone and she didn't bother pulling it back together. "You should quit your job. That life style of yours—it's just insanely stressful. Think of all the toxins it adds to your system. Go on a detoxifying diet. I have a friend who drinks a gallon of cranberry juice every day. It's done miracles for her."

I acted on instinct as soon as it darted past my peripheral vision. I grabbed her arm, pushed her away, and caught the Frisbee midair, half a second before it would've split her forehead.

One of the tanned kids playing on the beach came running toward us. "Hey, that was a great catch! Wanna join us?"

Hortensia beamed. "Why not?" She shook the flip-flops off her feet and stared at me.

I gave her the Frisbee. "You go ahead. I'm not in the mood."

She stepped closer and brushed her lips against mine. I felt like basking in that kiss a minute longer but she didn't let me. "You'll be fine," she said. She picked up her flip-flops and ran in the sand, red hair fanning and skirt flapping in the breeze.

I watched her play for a couple of minutes, then left.

You'll be fine.

The tarot lady had found a client with matching piercings and complementary tattoos. She held his hand while talking around an unlit cigarette. Whatever his future held, it must have been hilarious, because they both laughed heartily, their faces golden in the afternoon sun.

The rappers had started their show, the line at the hotdog stand had doubled. The sun was coming down, blinking through the frazzled tops of the palm trees, and yet the evening was still young, naïve, and careless.

I thought of going home, but my car thought otherwise.

And cars are like women. You can try and say no, but once they make up their mind there's nothing else you can do but tag along.

* * *

Diane didn't answer the door right away. The house was dark and silent, but I knew where she was and what she was doing. I could smell her from the door, in her white jogging sweats, nursing a tub of ice cream in front of the TV.

I rang the doorbell again. A couch spring sighed. Fuzzy socks brushed on wood floors. I stared at the shut door, waiting. A bolt turned, once, twice. The security chain slid and dangled with a clink against the jamb. She opened slowly.

"Hey," I said.

A smile cracked through her shell and tinged her voice. "Hey," she replied.

She stood there, chewing the inside of her cheek, making

me want to chew the other side. And then she opened the door all the way, and when she did, I inhaled her fully, her clothes, the familiarity of her pheromones, the intimacy of her body. I stepped inside, closed the door behind me and pulled her to me. She didn't hold back, not when I kissed her, not when I slid my hand inside her shirt. The scent of her naked skin enveloped me, snippets of me entangled in it.

Her voice crooned in my ears, her words mingled into a melody of verses, was it real? Or was I dreaming, when I heard her whisper, *I want to be part of you, part of your thoughts, your gestures, the funky way you raise your brow and tilt your head whenever I say something you don't approve of. The way your jaw tightens when you feel strongly about something, the way you fiddle with your fingers when something's bothering you.*

I want to be part of every nook in your brain, every breath you take.

Every one of my breaths... If only she knew... How densely she inhabited every breath I swallowed...

I can smell everything of you: the root of your hair, the arch of your eyebrows, the locks tucked behind your ears, the flesh of your lips. I can smell the air you breathe in and breathe out, the different gradients of your skin, like different textures in a quilt, salty on your face and lips, sweet between your breasts, and spicy on the inside of your arms.

I watched her make breakfast the next morning with a strange lightness in my head, a forgotten familiarity encoded in her gestures. How long have I been lost in my Odyssey before finding home in this one moment?

TWENTY-FOUR

Sunday, July 19

I stepped out of the shower, stuck my nose into my armpits and grinned. I'd used Diane's body wash and now I smelled like her. I towel-dried my hair, wrapped the towel around my loins and walked to the bedroom. Diane's voice rang from downstairs. On the phone, I thought. I picked up my pants from the chair and slid them on.

"Can you call him, Ma'am? We really need to talk to him *now*."

I froze. Male voice. At the door. Too far away to smell him. The way he said "now"... *A cop*. I ran to the window and looked down. A gray sedan was parked in the driveway, behind my Charger. A plainclothes cop stood by my vehicle and leaned to peek through the windows.

"Hey!" I yelled.

He looked up at me. "This your car?"

272

"Fucking is!"

"Can you come down and unlock it?"

What the hell?

I clipped the pancake holster to my waistband, slid in the Glock, and took a peek down from the top of the stairs. I could only see Diane's back, at the door. She hadn't let them in. The guy she'd been talking to was still holding his badge.

Diane protested. "It's Sunday. And he's not even on call."

"Sorry, Ma'am. It's an emergency."

She sighed, asked them to wait, and closed the door. Her temper preceded her up the stairs in angry whiffs. "You didn't tell me you were on call!"

"I'm not. Where are they from?"

"Pacific Community."

I stormed back into the bedroom, grabbed my shirt, back-up and extra mags.

"What happened?" Diane asked.

"No idea. But they didn't call my cell phone or my watch commander. I don't even know how they found out I was here. They just showed up—something's wrong."

"So then you don't have to go."

"You don't get it, D. If they wanted to call me on duty, they'd call the watch commander. There's something else going on, and it doesn't look good. I'll call you when I find out," I said, and kissed her.

* * *

"Sorry to ruin your party, pal."

Detective John Sakovich smelled of menthol aftershave and Kool Blues. His hair was wavy, prematurely white, and disguised in a light blonde dye. He had a dull nose, equally dull eyes, and curly lips—lovely feature on a woman, disturbing on a man.

He said sorry again without meaning it and shared a sneer with his partner, Detective Chris Lang, a kid's face on a short, burly body. They were both wearing plain clothes — shorts and polos — the butts of their firearms bulging underneath their shirts.

Lang was driving, Sakovich attempting civilized conversation without trying too hard.

As I rode along, I stared at the back of their heads and simmered.

"I wish you'd tell me what this is about," I said.

"You'll see when we get there."

"I could've followed you with my own vehicle."

"No worries, no worries," Sakovich reassured me. "We'll drive you back to your girl."

Lang snickered. "Which one, the gal or the car?"

They laughed. I didn't share their sense of humor.

It was a hazy morning. Traffic into town was fluid until we hit the Ten westbound and merged into the crowds of beach fanatics and Sunday surfers with their boards piled up on the car roofs. The skyline of downtown came in and out of the haze and was soon forgotten. For a long stretch of time there was only the intermittent blabbering of the radio and the monotone views of the Ten: billboards, gas stations, frazzled trees, electricity poles, more billboards, more gas station signs, sprawling malls, clustered apartment buildings, more billboards, and more gas stations.

Then the curbsides became higher and greener and Detective Lang merged into the right lane and onto the Lincoln exit ramp and suddenly it was clear where we were going. I still didn't know why but I had a hunch it wasn't to throw a surprise party.

Henkins's apartment building looked grayer than I remembered and the "Luxury" word in the wooden sign saying "Sea View Luxury Apartment" looked even more concocted. Two LAPD cruisers were parked along the curb, and two officers stood at the bottom of the stairs to Henkins's apartment. I looked up and a streamer of yellow tape hung from the doorjamb, gently flapping in the breeze.

Damn it.

I'd just been hit by a full load of shit.

* * *

Henkins was still where I'd left her, on the couch, hands wrapped around the glass of Jameson. The glass was empty and the dog was gone. She was smiling. A strange, you-think-you've-fucked-me-but-I-really-fucked-you smile. There was a hole in the middle of her forehead, about half an inch in diameter. Small caliber, certainly not a hollow point, which would've blown her face off. She went peacefully, in a way. Probably saw the gun but was too drunk to react. Or maybe she no longer cared.

The glass I'd used was where I'd left it, with my nice set of prints and DNA. The kitchen was in the same mess as the day before. The carpet stunk, the cabinets reeked, the place was a shack. Yet, I couldn't see a sign of a struggle, forced entry, fight—nothing.

Killer comes, killer smiles, Henkins smiles back, killer shoots, killer leaves. The neighbor's NASCAR speed race covers the blast of gunfire (or maybe a silencer does, if the killer's that conscientious), and the crowds coming and going from the beach camouflage him as one of many—the best disguise of all. And if said killer doesn't make mistakes, he even has a nice scapegoat who's happened to leave fingerprints and DNA on the scene.

Great.

"When?" I asked.

"Sometime yesterday," Sokavich replied. "She's already as stiff as a board. Couldn't get the glass off her hands."

Within character. Not even when dead she'd let go of the booze.

"You've called the M.E., I suppose?"

"On his way." He leered, I leered back.

Henkins didn't smell too bad—all the alcohol she'd downed must've preserved her well—just ripe enough to be one day old, as Sakovich had guessed. I smelled the dog, the alcohol at the bottom of the empty glasses, and the menthol of Sakovich's Kool Blues impregnating his clothes.

"Damn," I said. Maybe she wasn't one of our finest, but she was still a cop. *One of ours.*

Sakovich narrowed his eyes. "Always fucking enraging when a cop killer walks away like this." He sat on the recliner, crossed his legs, reached for his breast pocket and produced a cig. He stuck the cig in his mouth and stared at me. "Have a seat."

Lang grabbed a chair from the kitchen. I could've grabbed the other chair but I didn't want to get too cozy with these two. So I leaned against the wall next to the window. "Thanks, I'll stand." At least I could peek a strip of ocean from the window.

Sakovich nodded and lit his cig.

"You guys aren't gonna call the SIDs?"

"In due time," he replied and puffed out smoke. The acrid reek of burnt menthol filled the room.

"When did you find her?" I asked.

Lang's chair squeaked. "Hey, partner," he said. "I thought *we* were gonna ask the questions."

Sakovich pushed smoke out of his nose, lips curled around the cigarette butt. "My partner's right, Presius. We're gonna ask a couple of questions, you're gonna answer, and if we like the answers, we're done. If not, we go on asking more questions."

"What do you want to ask?" *Like I didn't know.*

I'd called the watch commander yesterday, right after leaving David's house to get Henkins's address. From there, how many people got ahold of the fact that I'd seen her? From the looks of it, the killer and I were the last ones to see her alive.

I thought of the anonymous call I'd received yesterday morning. *Your genes are going to kill you.* Was I being stalked, framed, targeted, or all of the above?

"When did you last see her?" Lang asked, baby face bobbing over a taurine neck.

I smiled, looked out the window. Red roofs peaked here and there from a green sea of treetops. "Look. Let's cut the crap, okay? You dragged me here because you got wind I'd come to see her. I'm no cop killer and I'd be a hell of a stupid killer to let my watch commander know where I was going and then show up and whack her in the head."

Sakovich's curly lips stretched. "Things don't always go as planned."

Punching him in the face wouldn't have gone as planned either, yet it would've given me a considerable amount of pleasure.

I said, "You really think I'd cold-bloodedly shoot a fellow cop for no apparent reason?"

Sakovich chewed his cigarette butt and said nothing. Lang flexed his biceps underneath his tight shirt, and Henkins sat on the couch, smiling, the cold glass of Jameson snuggled in her hands. Maybe we should've asked *her* who the hell did her in.

Down the street, an engine roared and then was killed. Lang got out of his chair, pushed the door open, and looked down the landing. "Coroner's office," he said.

Sakovich didn't move. "Great," he said, squinting

through the last billows of his Newport. "Means we'll have to take Detective Presius for a visit to Pacific."

* * *

Pacific Station is the artsy station. There are roses in the parking lot, pretty murals in the hallway, and a mosaic along the perimeter wall outside. Built in 2008, the mosaic says, "Through these gates pass great officers."

Two of those great officers escorted me to the squad room and had me sit at one of their desks. An officer with a "Hell, it's Sunday" face came to take my guns for fire testing. The squad room was quiet except for the intermittent ticking of an electric typewriter. A hefty detective was sitting behind it, at an equally hefty desk. He gave me a quick once-over and then went back to his typing. At the end of the room a door with the plate "S.A. Zoltak, Captain III" stood ajar. A quick glimpse of a movement told me somebody was in there, probably keeping an ear on us.

My hosts confabulated while I sat and twiddled my thumbs. They decided on a Dr. Pepper from the vending machine in the lobby. Sakovich gave Lang a dollar bill and asked me if I wanted one too. I replied I had plenty of dollar bills, I wanted a c-note instead. He didn't look amused. Lang scuttled off, Sakovich slumped in his chair and stared at the papers on his desk with a face hung somewhere between boredom and annoyance.

My thoughts reeled back to the events of Saturday, searching for a detail I could've missed.

I'd seen David Lebeaux in Silver Lake in the morning. He'd given me an enigmatic photo of Charlie Callahan, which had an even more enigmatic story attached to it. The photo was fairly normal—the guy sitting on somebody's couch and smiling—but what he'd said when he'd given it to David—"In case something happens"—puzzled me.

From Silver Lake I'd gone to Venice to see Henkins. Venice was the usual chaos of people coming and going. Anybody could've followed me, anybody could've gone up to Henkins's apartment, anybody could've shot her and left unnoticed because that's what anybodies are—unnoticeable. Sakovich had probably already knocked at every door in the building and come out blank.

The most disturbing part was what I'd learned from my chat with Henkins—likely the reason why she'd been shot. Somebody wanted the Callahan case closed, and closed quickly. How did the Byzantine Strangler fit into this? Was Callahan his first victim, and if so, why the pressure to close the case? Callahan must've been a very inconvenient victim, one that was bound to open up an old can of worms. Amy requested autopsy samples from Callahan's postmortem, and now the request, according to Henkins, had vanished— the only link between Amy Liu and Callahan. So Henkins had thought of reproducing the connection in the form of a faked prescription bottle. She had succeeded, in a way, but it had also cost her life.

I'd despised her actions and now I felt sorry for her.

Lang came back with the Dr. Pepper, dragged a chair closer, uncapped the bottle with a hiss and brought it to his mouth. "So," he said. "Where do we start from?"

The question seemed to awaken Sakovich from his momentary daydreaming. He rapped a hand on the desk. "From the beginning." He opened a drawer, retrieved a brand new pack of Kool Blues and unwrapped it, oblivious of the "No Smoking" sign hanging behind his head. "According to the conversation you had with the watch commander, you asked for Henkins's address on Saturday July eighteen at 1:05 p.m. You said your current location was in Silver Lake. So, assuming Saturday traffic and all that, you should've gotten to Henkins's place between 2:30 and 3:30."

"Quarter to three," I said.

He tore the wrap open and tapped the packet on his wrist to produce a cig. "How long were you there?"

"About forty-five minutes."

Sakovich reached for the lighter in his breast pocket. "What did you talk about?"

I looked at the pillar behind him. "There's a sign behind you that forbids you to smoke."

He grinned around the cigarette butt. "It's Sunday," he said, clicking the lighter. "We don't follow rules on Sundays. Go on, we're all ears."

"You already know why I wanted to talk to Henkins. It's been all over the news."

Sakovich held the cigarette between two fingers with the grace of an Adonis. He blew smoke at me and I held my breath and kept my face straight and pretended I was inhaling Diane's hair instead. "The Callahan case," he said.

"Correct."

"Share that conversation, if you please."

"I don't."

Lang tossed the empty bottle of Dr. Pepper into the bin. "You don't what?"

"I don't please."

Sakovich's smile was as heartfelt as the welcome greeting on an ATM screen. He made a high-pitched sound to go with it, something between the screech of a jay and the whistle of a parakeet. When he was done, he popped the cig out of his lips and said, "Presius, you do realize that you're withholding information relevant to a murder investigation and your refusal translates into insubordination—a firing offense."

A plume of menthol smoke curled up from his cigarette.

"I do realize," I said. "I also realize that my conversation with Henkins does not pertain to *your* murder investigation, it pertained to mine."

"Until I hear it I'm not sure I believe it."

Lang slid forward in his chair and crossed his arms. The tight sleeves of his polo strangled his bulging biceps. "Why did you go to her house on a Saturday? Why not talk to her at the station? Why not go with your partner? You better have a very good answer to each of these questions."

Sakovich sucked wistfully on his cig. "You have two options, Presius," he said. "You can stand by the Fifth Amendment and go find yourself another job, or you can take the Lybarger admonishment and run with it. Me, I'd have no second thoughts."

The Lybarger rule was a California State ruling from the Michael Lybarger case, an officer with the Vice Unit who, under investigation for false arrest and bribery, refused to cooperate and was fired for insubordination. It boiled down to what Sakovich had just told me: I could choose to keep my mouth shut, in which case I'd face insubordination charges and lose my badge. Or, I could spill the beans and, under the Lybarger rule, anything I'd say would not be used to incriminate me. Which is bullshit because any cop with a bit of gray matter in his mind knows that if the brass decides he has to go down, they will simply find some other ballast to make him go down.

Given the circumstances, I decided to spill some of the beans, choosing my beans very carefully. By the time I was done, Sakovich had smoked two cigarettes and was tapping a third one, still unlit, on the chair armrest. "You think Callahan was killed by the same person who killed Amy Liu and Laura Lyons?"

"That's what I'm trying to find out."

"Did you ask Henkins?"

"Henkins told me I was nuts to still be looking into this. She said to give it a rest because Olsen whacked Callahan and we were all wasting our time."

I stared at him. If somebody overheard my conversation with Henkins, my lie was out. But here's the thing. There was only one person who could've overheard our conversation—the killer. Sometimes it's a good thing to share a secret with a killer.

The officer who'd done the ballistics returned my guns and declared them clean. I tucked them back into my holsters without a word.

Lang got up from his chair and stretched his legs. Sakovich curled his lips and pondered. I stared at the wall clock. It was close to four p.m. The hefty detective in the corner had long stopped typing. The door to the captain's office was still ajar. I pushed my chair backwards and got up.

"I'm not convinced, Presius," Sakovich said.

"That's my statement," I replied. "You've got a fellow detective dead and a cop killer on the loose, Sakovich. I suggest you start working on this case." I turned around and walked to the Captain's office.

Lang shot to his feet. "Where the hell d'you think you're going?"

I sprang the Captain's door open without knocking. A sad little man looked at me with sad little eyes. He stood up and was no longer little and his eyes weren't that sad either. They glared from above the rim of red reading glasses.

He took the glasses off, rested them on the table, and asked, "And you are...?" His gesture had purpose, his voice entitlement. The frames on the wall behind him told me he was a family man and a decorated officer. The look on his face told me I wasn't welcome.

I walked to his desk and offered my hand. "Presius," I

said, as if he didn't know already. "My sincere condolences. You lost one of your best officers."

We shook hands. His were knotty and cold despite the room temperature. He smelled of nicotine, a different brand than Sakovich. Dunhill, I guessed.

He let go of my hand and dropped back in his chair. "Thank you," he said, in a dismissive way. He picked up the reading glasses he'd left on the desk and perched them back on his nose. A famous logo at the side of the frames had the only function to let me know that those glasses alone cost as much as my weekly salary.

I agreed that was no place for me and left. I bumped into Lang's biceps on my way out of the Captain's office.

"We've got your prints in her apartment."

I smiled and walked away.

"You can't leave," Sakovich yelled after me.

"Of course I can," I replied. "It's Sunday. We don't follow rules on Sundays, remember?"

They didn't stop me. They didn't offer the ride back they'd promised either. I didn't care. I'd had enough of their company. I walked through the exit gate and read once more the writing on the mosaic. "Through these gates pass great officers."

I shoved both hands in my pockets, walked through, and whistled. I'd just been promoted to great officer.

TWENTY-FIVE

Monday, July 20

"Hmm. That would explain the smell," Satish said.

"What smell?"

"All the shit you've been wading through. I mean, shit happens, but somehow it seems to happen to you more."

We exited the restaurant on Ramirez Street. A couple of black and white Crown Vics were parked in the lot across the street, the flyover from the One-Oh-One swooping above with its steady flow of vehicles. Downtown loomed on the right, wrapped in a blanket of haze.

Over lunch, I'd recounted the highlights of my rough weekend: the meeting with David Lebeaux and the photograph of Charlie Callahan he'd given me, my conversation with Courtney Henkins and the planted prescription bottle, the piece of information on Amy Liu's request of Callahan postmortem samples and how the request had vanished, and finally my lovely acquaintance with John Sakovich and Chris Lang from Pacific Station.

On Saturday I'd despised Henkins for resorting to subtle means to send us a message instead of stepping forward. Now that she was dead, she'd suddenly turned into a hero. Death can do things like that.

"How did you get home from Venice?"

"I flagged a patrol car and had them drop me off at Diane's—my Charger was still there. When I finally got home, I found my house ramped. Will was at the neighbor's, unharmed. My neighbor feeds the mutt every time I don't show up at night."

We crossed the street and waved our badges at the guard behind the entrance booth of Piper Tech, a red and gray building made of brick and cement. It housed the Electronics Unit and the Hooper Memorial Heliport. To access the labs you had to walk to the back of the building through the loading docks. I wasn't quite done recounting the events of the weekend, so we sat in the shade, over yellow metal stairs, behind a pillar where somebody had painted he words "Loading only."

"So they searched your place," Satish said. "That's to be expected. They're not gonna trust you and you shouldn't trust them. Are you sure they didn't plant anything while they were there?"

"Unless they're stupid, if they want to fuck me that bad they won't plant anything in my house. Too obvious, somebody would smell a rat. They checked my vehicle when they picked me up. They wanted to nose into Diane's house, too, but she told them to fuck off."

A helicopter—the third in the last hour—took off from the roof of the building. The swooshing roared in our ears and then ebbed off.

"Did you tell Gomez everything?"

"No. I told him what I told Sakovich and Lang."

Satish regarded me with small chocolate eyes. "That means you won't even try to make Henkins's case."

I fiddled with the restaurant receipt. "Look," I said. "This is a jam."

"It's called shit."

"Fine. Let's call it shit. We're sinking deeper and deeper in it. If the brass comes down to tell Henkins the Callahan case is closed, some big fish is dipping. Big fishes and serial killers don't usually go hand in hand, so I'm starting to think the serial killer thing is all bullshit shoved in our face to cover somebody's ass."

"Just to remain within topic."

I sighed. A truck turned into the driveway, stopped, and then backed into the loading deck. The beep hammered in my ears. We got up and shuffled to the elevators, hands in our pockets, shoulders slouching, and hearts as heavy as a morning hangover.

* * *

"What the hell happened in here?" The blades of a standing fan swallowed my voice and digested it. The fan was swooshing, the AC was hissing, and the computers were whirring. I counted three on Viktor's desk alone, with monitors lined up one next to the other. There were more on the floor. Even the tiny spot for my folding chair was taken. We had to crowd around the monitors and stand.

"This is what I'd call a cyber warfare," Satish said.

Viktor's desk looked like a Tower of Hanoi of computer screens, each displaying its different jargon of white code over a black background. Hunched over the laptop, Viktor waved a busy hand. "Never mind the mess. Just watch your step. Some bogus Internet business in Orange County got pinched for Internet fraud. The bunco squad delivered the hardware this morning."

I tried to watch my step but the cables were in the way.

The birthmark on Viktor's face looked more ominous today. "So," he said.

"Let me guess," I ventured, looking over my shoulder to make sure that whatever I was leaning against wasn't going to cause a domino fall of computer towers. "You've got short answers and long answers and neither will make any sense to us."

Viktor's gray eyes looked at me vacantly.

Satish leaned against the doorjamb and crossed his arms. "In which case, let's hear the short answer first."

Viktor swiveled his chair around and surveyed all computer screens at once. "The code at the back of the tiles are snippets in a language called XYPlot. It's a graphing program, no longer supported."

Satish smiled nice and wide. "And what exactly are we talking about?"

Viktor grabbed the laptop, set it on his lap, and swiveled next to Satish moving his legs like oars. Funny how easily we forget we can walk once we're on wheels. "XYPlot is a source language. People use it to create graphs. It's an old generation tool, so our guy is either not fresh out of college or not up to date with his software."

"Or maybe he just likes to muddy things up," I added. I kicked away the cables on the floor, unfolded an old metal chair that stood abandoned against the wall, and saddled it.

"Killers tend to do that," Satish said. "What's the long answer?"

Viktor scratched the back of his shaved head. "Well," he said, dragging the word a second longer. "As soon as I posted the inquiry on the board, the answers came in pretty quickly." He typed the URL on the laptop and pressed enter. I noticed then that the keyboard on his laptop had no letters.

"What happened to your letters?"

"What letters?"

"The ones usually found on keyboards?"

He shrugged. "They distract me. Had to make a special order to get a blank keyboard. They charged me extra."

How inconsiderate.

He pointed to the screen. "See this? That's my post, right there, and you can see all the replies in the order they were posted." He scrolled down the screen. "This couple of guys here, linux_nerd and MacWiz are everywhere, even in forums they know nothing about. The usual big-mouthed egos—after a while on a board you learn to ignore them."

"Wait. We shouldn't be ignoring anybody here—"

"Relax. I'm tracking everybody, just ignoring the answers. I'm also tracking the page loads and keeping an eye on the rubberneckers. All dynamic IPs, but their providers, routers, and locations came in loud and clear. Comcast, Rogers Cable, Road Runner… A few from India, Singapore, Russia. Many from Europe. I store the IPs as they come in, here, see?" He clicked on an Excel sheet and showed us the table.

"We're interested in California providers."

"Assuming the one we're after doesn't use a proxy, that is. I got a few, mostly the lurkers. Let me show you the posters first. A lot of dudes love to fly by and sell smoke, so I had to filter the right answer from all the junk. Now, this guy here—he's got the first crack at it, see? Here's what he says: 'Is this a full code? The way you wrote it makes no sense to me. Looks like XYPlot source code. It's nearly extinct but a few dinosaurs still use it.' I clicked on the link he added and it checked. These other users posted a few minutes later and confirmed it."

I leaned forward and squinted at the screen. There were acronyms I did not understand, and a lot of the jargon only Viktor could understand. Some of it seemed to have sparked a flurry of aggressive responses. "Are they always this friendly?"

Viktor sneered. "This particular board tends to be a little testosterone-driven. A lot of trolls lurking. Some of the threads get so heated they turn into cock-fighting pits. There are moderators, but you never see them."

Satish said, "I would assume our guy — if he ever got into the discussion — would keep a low profile."

Viktor nodded. "Right. Which is why, frankly, I don't think any of these guys fits the bill. I've analyzed most of the IPs and only a couple track back to L.A. County."

The laptop beeped and a window popped up on the screen.

"What's that?"

Viktor frowned. "We just got a new response."

Satish squeezed in, I pulled the chair closer.

"Hmm, that's interesting. I haven't had responses in a few hours now. The thread's activity has gone down once the question has been answered, and — "

The new post came from a guy with screen name g-cat. Satish read it: "*Why ask?*" He scratched his chin. "That's not very useful."

"Hold on." Viktor blindly typed on his unmarked keyboard. "Shit."

"What's wrong?"

"This dude is giving me a useless IP. Let me run it one more time."

He opened a new window and typed. Code dribbled, chips crackled, detectives waited. Minutes went by, until Viktor shook his head and gave up. "See?" he said, as if we could actually see. "His IP is dynamic, class C, either residential, a small business or a wi-fi hotspot. The MAC is untraceable, probably due to a security vault running on the originating computer or router. In other words, can't get his footprint."

"But the guy just posted, right? Is he online right now?" Satish asked.

Viktor switched back to the Internet browser. "He is."

"Post something, then," I said. "Anything. I don't know, 'Who the hell wants to know? Who the hell are you' —"

"Calm down, let's think," said Satish, the voice of wisdom.

"Yeah, and while you're thinkin' the guy's gone," I protested.

"Hold on," Viktor said. " He started typing again.

Satish and I scooched closer.

Just curious about this code, I read on the screen. *Why do U wanna know?*

"He'll reply to that," Viktor said. "I know these guys."

I rapped my fingers on the back of the chair. The fan swooshed, the AC hissed, the computers on Viktor's desk whirred. Detectives waited.

Then the laptop beeped.

Satish and I spoke almost at the same time.

"Did you get it this time?"

"What did he say?"

The frown across Viktor's forehead didn't look encouraging. "No, same bogus IP. He writes, 'You asked a stupid question. A kindergartener can recognize XYPlot.'" Viktor shrugged. "Typical answer. At least he bothers to spell correctly. Most everybody else doesn't."

His fingers didn't leave the keyboard.

"What are you doing now?"

"Looking up his profile on the board. Hmm. Not one of the regulars. He has only two other posts, totally unrelated to this. That's strange, he's a member since 2006. He probably lurks a lot."

"Can you Google his screen name?" Satish asked.

"Sure thing." Viktor's fingers clacked on the keyboard.

I said, "Some of these guys are easily traceable. Hell, some of these people are everywhere—Facebook, LinkedIn, Wikipedia—you name it."

Satish chortled. "Hail to Zuckerberg for inventing a public outlet for rants and drivels."

Viktor squinted at the screen. "Hmm. Not this one. Screen name's too common. I got a boat, a construction company, a videogame." He clacked some more. "On Facebook I get studios, clothing, a singer—"

I exhaled in frustration. The constrictive space around us made me feel claustrophobic. I got out of the chair and started pacing in the hallway, just outside the door.

"There's one gmail account under g-cat, but no public profile."

"Can you send him an email?" Satish asked.

"No way to tell whether it's the same guy. Damn it, he's no longer online."

There was a moment of mourning silence in which the blades of the fan seemed to snicker sadistically at the three of us.

"What are the odds he'll be back?" I prodded.

"To lurk? Absolutely. To post again? Who knows. I can try and contact him privately on the board."

"What are you waiting for?"

"Wait, wait, wait." Satish held out a hand. "Let's think this time before we jump into things, okay? Damn it, Track, let's just take a breather and think. We need something smart, something to engage this guy to talk to us."

Viktor's lip hung low. "Since we're doing some thinking, you do realize this may be a dead end? The packets connecting to the board came from some public hotspot. The info was hidden, but it doesn't mean the guy's got something to hide. He could've logged from a federal computer. This dude could be working for the feds, the government, or any private company with an umbrella policy of security vaults on all laptops."

Satish and I were silent for a few seconds.

"Why the attitude, then?" I objected.

Viktor didn't seem impressed. "Computer programmer attitude—it's all over the map."

That was easy to believe. Still.

I shook my head. "Haven't you worked long enough with us cops, Vik? Guy leaves no trace, he's automatically flagged."

"Fine," Viktor said. "I'll PM him on the board. What do you want me to say?"

Satish crossed his arms. "How about a blunt: 'Did you write the code?'"

I raised an eyebrow. "And what do we hope to accomplish with that?"

"Stroke his ego. If he wrote it, he wants us to know. He thinks he's safe, armored behind—what did you call it? A vault, and a fluke IP address."

Viktor bobbed his head in approval. "Yeah. Stroking egos is good in this field. Let's see what he comes up with."

"He might tease us just for the hell of it."

"Worth a try. He wouldn't leave these clues if he didn't want some of the crumbs to get to him. He wants to talk to us. And we're giving him the opportunity." Satish peered at me through dark eyes. "This ain't the BTK killer, Track. He's as evil, but way savvier."

TWENTY-SIX

The sky was heavy with layers of evening heat. The trail of vehicles along the One-Ten was a headless snake of boxed humanities. Dave Brubeck in the car stereo wasn't helping this time. The rhythm of *Take Five* is best enjoyed with either a woman or a Bloody Mary. I had neither with me, so I turned the stereo off.

The brake lights of the cars ahead of me blinked. My impatience simmered in the afternoon heat.

Diane called, the usual note of disappointment in her voice. "I thought we had plans for tonight."

"I'm stuck in traffic."

She pouted.

"Go ahead and eat," I said. "I'll call you when I'm off the Two."

There was a pause of silence heavier than a drowning man — the drowning man being me. "Fine," she said at last. "But do come. There's something important I need to tell you."

She hung up. I pulled down the window and stuck a hand outside, just to feel the air. Heat sweltered from the pavement and crawled inside the car. The back of my shirt melted against my skin. I closed the window. The left lane toward the junction with the Five was clogged. I came to a complete stop, cursed, and swung the car out of the lane, causing a trail of loud honks to follow me downstream. I honked back, forced my way to the right lane and took the Solano exit.

I drove through North Broadway and then turned onto Elysian Drive, the whole time thinking about the investigation. I had four murders—Charlie Callahan, Amy Liu, Laura Lyons, and Courtney Henkins. I had six unidentified infants killed sometime between the Eighties and the Nineties. I had two sets of hairs, one from Amy, and one from Laura, both identical. They fluoresced and didn't match any known type of hair except for some weird disease that may or may not exist. I had seven tiles, four found next to Amy's body, and three next to Laura's, and the last three were marked with some XYPlot code at the back that nobody knew what it was useful for.

That covered bodies and evidence.

As for suspects, that was a whole different yarn to disentangle. The killer, or killers, didn't fit any standard profile I could think of. The victims ranged in gender, sexual orientation, racial and socioeconomic background. The scalp and skin harvesting were sophisticated trophies. Could be the usual drive to amputate the victim, or could be something else. The tiles, on the other hand, pointed to something completely different. An artist, I'd thought at first, except now we had a code and a possible suspect roaming a board for computer geeks.

Lyons was in this up to his neck. Could've been the

killer, could've been, like he claimed, the next victim. He didn't strike me as a cop killer, though. How did Henkins fit in all this? Henkins's mouth had to be shut because of Charlie Callahan. The more I thought about it, the more I realized Charlie Callahan's death held the key to everything.

I wandered. My Charger wandered with me. The hills of Ascot Park unfolded on my right, yellow, dry, and thirsty. Dusk fell, pink tainted the sky. Tired silhouettes of palm trees bowed to the sunset.

I found myself back in El Sereno, cruising the winding road to the water cistern. I pulled to the curb and rolled down the window. The air had the dull scent of hot summer nights.

Downtown twinkled in the distance.

I pondered. The engine idled.

And then the Charger roared again and I left the narrow winding road and drove back downhill. Lampposts pooled yellow light onto the blue hour sky. Silent homes with dimly lit porches gave way to spread-out parking lots and blinking neon lights advertising psychic reads, twenty-four-hour drug stores, and booze shops.

I stopped at the red light between Valley and Eastern. To my right I spotted a grayish banner that said, "Café Allegro Espresso Bar," under a kinky gutter that leaked old tears of rust. The brick wall had layers of gas exhaust and pollution, and the door stood half-hidden and unnoticed in a little alcove beneath a white sign bearing the picture of an espresso cup and the writing, "Free Wi-Fi."

Free wi-fi two miles away from the cistern – a public hotspot.
What are the odds?

Just outside the café, an old bum in a green, frayed sweater sat on a bench. He flashed me a one-toothed smile and pointed. I ignored the smile and the pointing. He did it again. The car behind me honked. The bum laughed.

The light had turned green.

I screeched out of the intersection, whipped the car in one of the parking spots by the street, and grabbed my cell phone. It was past working hours, yet Viktor picked up immediately. When I asked him if he could locate all Internet cafés within a two-mile radius from the cistern, the man didn't utter a word. All I heard was the clacking of an unmarked keyboard. Thirty seconds later came the verdict: "The cistern is up in an isolated area, Detective. All I see is an old joint called Café—"

"Allegro," I interrupted him.

"That's exactly the place."

I thanked him and hung up.

The bum was still on the bench, smiling. Beer and urine had brewed a soup of ancestral smells on his skin. I gave him a dollar and pushed the door open.

It was warm inside, the air laden with a fog of cigarette smoke and caffeine. A kid with a guitar sang from a stool in a corner. The song was soft and melancholy and I didn't know anything about it except that it was soft and melancholy and it made me think of Diane having dinner by herself.

By the window, a fragile-looking man with ruffled ash-blonde hair was hunched over a laptop. The wall behind him was plastered with a decade worth of flyers: theater plays, yoga classes, music classes, rentals, sales, lost pets, wanted. At the back of the counter, a blackboard displayed a range of espresso drinks, sodas, smoothies, and their prices. The melancholy song came to an end and the kid with the guitar bowed his head. The man at the table in front of him clapped his hands. Nobody else took notice.

A weathered dame with heavy eyelids and skeptical eyebrows came to the counter to ask for my order. Her hair sat quizzically at the top of her head and came down at the sides of her neck in little static question marks. She was as true a blonde as the Italian sodas she sold were true Italian.

"A single shot espresso," I said. "In a ceramic cup."

The heavy lids came down a notch. The skeptical eyebrows remained skeptical. "All our cups are ceramic, hon. But I've shut down the espresso machine for the night. I got drip." She pointed a hard chin toward the pot and then, to show me how much she cared, she took a rag from her apron and started wiping the counter.

"Not my lucky night."

The lids rolled up a bit and gave me a look-over. "That could change," she said, and her lips tweaked into the flash of a smile, so quick it looked like a nervous tic. Not even the eyes joined in.

I wasn't going to stick around to find out.

I thanked her, walked away, and fished out another dollar for the kid with the guitar. My eyes fell on the hunched back with the ash-blonde hair. The tall paper cup next to his laptop smelled of coffee polluted with some sugary syrup. Something shone on the table next to the cup. Something round and silvery, change, aligned in a perfect row of one quarter, three nickels, and two dimes.

Coins aligned in a perfect row.

Just like in Lyons's kitchen, just like on Amy Liu's console.

I inhaled. I could only smell coffee, cigarette smoke, and heavy breathing. The air was stale and saturated.

Damn it.

The Italian soda blond had already left the counter. I walked back and rattled my knuckles on the empty display case awakening sugary scents of long gone pastries. The blonde took her sweet time to come back.

"What roast is it tonight?"

"Guatemalan, Hawaiian, or Spanish."

I dropped a five-buck note on the counter. "Spanish. In one of your ceramic cups."

The tic flew over her lips again.

"I don't drink in paper," I added, for whose benefit I don't know.

Her blood red nails went fumbling for a mug. She turned, filled it, came back. "The pot's fresh," she said, handing me the change. "You bus when you're done."

The music resumed. A giggling pair of girls got out of their chairs and left the place. Now it was just me, the Italian soda blonde, the guitar player and his lonely fan, and the ash-blond man with the aligned row of coins next to his open laptop. There were plenty of empty tables, but I took my mug and sat at the one next to him. I picked up a two-day-old newspaper, flung a leg over my knee, and sipped the drip coffee while swaying my foot. My eyes focused above the rim of the paper, my nose beyond the gasoline smell of the pages. I could see his profile, now. It looked vaguely familiar, but I couldn't place it. Tall forehead, long and straight nose, the way Michelangelo liked to paint them, and ashen, borderline-sick complexion, studded with old acne scars. The hint of pale stubble on his unshaved chin.

The guy seemed oblivious to my presence. His nostrils widened slowly as one finger brushed the laptop pad in gentle strokes. Whatever he was staring at, it had his full attention.

Hard to percolate the thick scents of the place. Something vague came to me, as faint as a thread of cobweb—a dry, aseptic smell that reminded me of tired hospital rooms.

If only I could smell the coins.

I swung my foot faster, hit one of the table's legs, bumped it, and spilled coffee on the floor.

"Damn it," I shouted. "I'm so damn sorry." I bent

forward, armed with napkin and wide-open nostrils. He was fast. He swept the coins in his pocket, shut the laptop closed, and jumped to his feet. Not a drop of coffee had reached him, and yet his eyes widened with the alarm of a drowning cat.

"It's—okay."

My nose was fast too. I caught a whiff of nitrile gloves, laced with the decaying sweetness of rotten flowers.

He was at the door before I could take a second sniff.

Italian Soda popped behind the counter like a silhouette at a carnival shooting game. "No refills for spilled coffee."

I smacked the half-full mug on the counter in front of her. "You can spill the rest of it."

It took a moment to readjust to the smells outside. The stale air, laden with coffee grounds and cigarette smoke, kept lingering in my nostrils. I whirled my head looking for the stranger with the nitrile glove smell. The bum sitting on the bench lifted his lids and his eye whites peered at me as if coming out of the brick wall. He grinned like the Cheshire cat and pointed to a lanky figure quickly disappearing in the wavering lights of the urban night, his back still hunched, and the laptop folded underneath his arm.

I broke into a run, then thought better of it, and resolved to a quick pace. Deep inside my body, something complained. I told the something to shut up. My man reached an old station wagon Volvo, copper colored and dinged to the sides.

"Hey!" I yelled, fishing out my badge.

He didn't even turn. He opened the front door, slid inside, and tore off.

I double-backed, ran for my Charger, whipped it into traffic, and gave chase. Somewhere between dodging oncoming vehicles, flattening the gas pedal, and reaching for the radio, I remembered to turn on the siren.

Everything around me swirled into a blur. The southbound traffic on Valley spread apart and the dinged Volvo appeared about four hundred yards ahead of me, its dark shadow lit up intermittently by the streetlights.

The fucking license plate light was out.

The speedometer needle hit home. I reached for the radio mike as I entered the big bend on Valley. One hand on the wheel, tires screeching and smoking, and the radio jumped to the passenger floorboard.

Damn it.

No time to think.

No time to see, smell, react. No time to even shit myself, as I entered a tunnel of blurred lights and Mach speed in which the sound of the siren wobbled and wavered struggling to keep up with me. I don't care if that's not even possible, it's what you feel when you get sucked into high-speed pursuits.

The light at the North Soto crossing flickered above me.

Can't stop.

We both ran a red light, the Volvo and I. Then the Volvo, too, became a blur. Pain shot up my arms.

No time for pain either.

The Pain didn't listen and spread its icy tentacles around my shoulders.

The Volvo blur spun to a ninety-degree turn on San Pablo and crashed through lowered rail crossing bars. My Charger followed. Red lights flashed. A loud whistle shrieked in my ears—the Pain, no, something bigger. I spun over debris, tires skittering, then regained control. The train, the Pain, the Charger.

I lost control.

My fingers remained tightly clasped around the wheel, but the wheel now had a mind of its own. The train hit the back of the Charger. The vehicle spun and toppled. My face hit the airbag, the windshield spidered. Shards of glass rained over me.

I saw red.

Red oozed all over my face, warm, with its soothing, metallic tang. I smelled something else, too.

Gasoline burning.

Shit.

Clicking the buckle release and whamming the door open came all in one reflex.

I dove out of the car onto hard concrete, rolled, tried to get up, staggered, rolled farther away.

The blast illuminated the night. The palm tree I'd hit lit up like a torch, flames whipping high into the sky. Chunks of tree trunk flew in all directions. One bounced inches away from my face, smoldering.

The train was no longer in sight, nor was the Volvo.

I heard a distant siren and felt a strange sense of relief.

It's over. They sent a patrol car. It's over.

Seconds slogged by. They felt like weeks, months, years.

I fought the urge to pass out.

The Pain had made me numb to smells, sights, everything.

Only the metallic tang of my own blood stuck to my palate.

The siren came to a stop. Boots crunched the gravel. A radio crackled. I recognized the call for an ambulance. The voice I didn't recognize.

"Are you all right, sir?"

He crouched over. I saw myself reflected in the shine of his helmet.

A CHP. Brilliant.

At that point, I figured I might as well pass out.

TWENTY-SEVEN

The room was full of nothing. A view-box window, a retractable surgical light, biohazard bins, racks, cabinets, monitors. A TV screen. A gaudy curtain disclosed a slice of brightly lit hall where voices came and went like ocean waves. Next to a defibrillator, a box of tissues looked innocent and rather unsophisticated. Above it, a dull painting in dull colors depicted a dull mountain.

I smelled the gray flatness of the linoleum floors and the apathy of the walls. The cloying scent of cumin and saffron from Satish's Indian-spiced perspiration hummed softly in the background. He sat quietly in a chair by the wall, staring at the ceiling as if it were a starred night. "Nice hospital," he said. "Good thinking to crash half a mile away."

"They gave me the within-mile special rate when I checked in," I mumbled, unconvincingly.

Satish jingled something in his pocket and looked at me rather pitifully. "Tell me again how you got yourself pursuing a guy you had absolutely nothing on."

"I did not—"

I held an icepack against my right temple and looked emptily at the mint green walls. The mint green walls looked back and said nothing. The fluorescent lights in the ceiling did all the talking. They hummed at the syncopated rhythm of the *Waters of March.*

I got to the end of the road all right.

I closed my eyes and squeezed the bridge of my nose. "It was an Internet café," I said, very slowly and very carefully. "And it was the only Internet café within a two-mile radius from the water cistern. Same neighborhood. Viktor said Internet cafés—"

"Do you know how many people use laptops in those places?"

I kept my eyes closed. "There were coins. Next to him. Aligned. Just like I saw at Amy's house and in Lyons's kitchen."

This time Satish said nothing.

And there was that smell. On him.

The sweet and rotten smell mixed with nitrile gloves.

"I sat at the table next to him. I wanted to take a peek at his computer screen." I swallowed. My tongue felt like a dead piece of meat in my mouth.

"Did you manage to?"

"I dropped my coffee cup so I could lean close enough to see. As soon as I did, the guy shut the laptop closed and jumped to his feet."

"So the guy was staring at porn."

I sprang my eyes open. *Shit.*

The possibility hadn't even occurred to me.

"That would explain why he ran," Sat went on.

"Sat, you know the drill. Guy runs, cops chase."

He scratched his chin with one finger and shot his eyes

up at the starry ceiling. I did the same and all I saw was scraped panes and fluorescent lights. Still humming, still *Waters of March.*

"I glimpsed some kind of graph on his screen."

He didn't look convinced.

"What the hell, Sat. Fine, say he was peeping porn. You're right, could've been child porn, given the way he fled. Guy runs, cops chase. It's the way things are. And it's never wrong."

He kept on scratching his chin. It made a soft, whispery sound that laced nicely with the tune in my head. "You know, once in a graveyard shift we stopped a guy carrying a large duffel bag in a residential neighborhood. The guy ran, and—"

"And the duffel bag was full of empty cans. Yes, you told me the story, Sat. This is not the same thing. It was his computer he was nervous about. You gotta admit, a computer can hold a lot more interesting stuff than a duffel bag."

"Did you show him your badge, or could he claim he was running away from a lunatic stalking him?"

"He saw the badge all right. And he heard the siren once I blasted it. He never stopped."

Satish bobbed his head and jingled coins in his pocket. His phone started buzzing. He checked his watch. "How much longer are they going to keep you?"

The throb in my head pulsed faster. My car had turned into a cube of melted metal. I'd suffered a concussion, won two stitches on my right brow, and the net result of all this was that my suspect was still on the loose. I'd been stuck in this hospital room for over two hours now, with a short field trip to the lab to have an MRI taken. Once they'd established I was low priority, I'd fallen in the *forgotten* category.

"Let's see," I said. "I got three people ogling at me when I got here. One to check scratches and bruises, one to stitch my brow, one to come back and stick a Band-Aid on my face. I could've read *War and Peace* in between their visits."

Satish was no longer listening. He answered the phone with a corrugated look on his face.

A nurse pulled the curtain all the way and sent a glacial stare to Satish and the phone screwed into his ear. "Please take the call out to the lobby, sir," she said, with a deliberately strained voice. "No cell phones allowed in the ER."

Satish briskly nodded and went out.

We stared at each other, the nurse and I.

She walked over, set the tray she'd been carrying on a cart by my stretcher, then propped a pair of hands on her wide hips and looked down on me, her thick eyelids fluttering over me with the grace of windshield wipers. "How we doin', hon?"

I lay back and smiled real nice. "Can't speak for you, but I'm kinda bored."

She took the icepack from my hand. "I'm never bored here, hon. Let's liven up your night with a tetanus shot, then doc's gonna talk to you about your MRI, *then* you go home."

She delivered the shot with chilling precision, gave me a fresh icepack, and when she was done, she pointed an opinionated chin to the cart next to my stretcher. "That's your dose of Ibuprofen. You better drink it."

My head throbbed. "How about the Margarita I'd ordered?"

Her codfish eyes didn't blink. The windshield wipers fluttered a few times. "Sorry, handsome. We went through the last bottle of tequila after a patient puked barbequed ribs all over the OR table." She laughed, her coarse voice sounding bitter rather than amused.

She wiped all humor off her face and asked me sternly: "How's your neck, hon? Can you move it all right?"

"Of course. Why would I want to move it, though?" I lifted the small plastic cup, said, "Cheers," and gulped it down.

The nurse dusted her lips with the hint of a chortle, smacked a clipboard on her round hips, and flashed a condescending smile to Satish, who emerged right then from behind the curtain. "Is he always this charming?"

"Oh, no," Satish said. "That's the concussion. The asshole part, instead? That's him."

She took the medicine cup from my hand and the stainless steel tray from the cart. "The doctor will be with you shortly."

I'd been in hospitals often enough to know that "shortly" had a completely new meaning in a place like that. Her clogs squeaked away, and the curtain rod rattled its farewell.

Satish dropped in the chair by the wall.

"I could really use some booze, pal," I said, holding the fresh ice pack to my head. "Johnny Walker cures all maladies."

Satish didn't reply. He casually tapped the cellphone on his thigh, as trying to catch an afterthought.

"Who'd you talk to?"

"Gomez. He says hi, by the way. And that you're an asshole."

"Thank you."

"You're welcome. Mixed news. Air Support is patrolling the area. They've got one aircraft on a perimeter with the FLIR, and one checking the river bottom for car dumps. They've got your description of the suspect, assuming you were lucid enough to get his clothes right."

"Course I did! You think I'd forget a guy that sends my

Charger flying at an intersection? How long did it take for the chopper to pick up the chase?"

Satish sighed. "The problem is that you lost precious seconds with the radio. Had you initiated the call—"

"Hell, Sat, I'm fully aware of what went wrong, okay? Do you or do you not have some good news to report?"

"Yes and no. The bad news is that even though it's night, this time of the year the FLIR is not as efficient as in the fall or winter when temperatures cool off. The good news is that they picked a 'hot' vehicle in an almost empty parking lot here on campus, one block away from your car accident."

The FLIR was the Forward Looking Infrared, a special camera that converts heating sources into images. They're so sharp they can pick a man hiding under a vehicle or a marijuana crop growing in a garden.

"And?" I prodded.

"*And* we've got campus security checking it out. No word on the make yet, but Gomez said he was going to call back as soon as he'd find out." Satish shrugged, ran his tongue carefully over his teeth. "Could be some doc working a night shift."

"Don't they have designated parking? Why would the lot be almost empty?"

"It's not too close to the hospital."

Out in the hallway, the background level of voices went up a notch. Clogs squeaked, heels tapped with a nervous beat. A familiar spice wrapped its fingers around my nose. It was tainted with tiredness, anger, frustration, and it had the melancholy sex appeal of Billie Holiday's singing.

Diane pulled the curtain all the way to the wall and stood there, catching her breath. "What happened?" Her voice was a couple tonalities off-key. "Last time I talked to you, you were on the One-Ten about to merge into the

Five!"

From his chair, Satish straightened up.

I cleared my throat. Even the throbbing in my head quieted down. "I uh—had a couple detours. *Unplanned* detours."

Her eyes blinked over me. They flickered around my head, pondered over the bandages, slid down my scraped chin, took in the whole me—not very dignified in my underwear, but the parameds had taken my guns and clothes when I was too weak to protest.

Her pursed lips loosened up and tweaked down at the corners. Her brows rotated a few degrees outwards. Her walk lost all of its gall as she came to me, flopped on the edge of the stretcher and touched my stitched brow with the tip of her fingers. "Goodness! Are you in pain?"

I swallowed. "A little," I said. Given the circumstances, it felt appropriate to complain. And I liked the hint of worry in her voice. It had a mellowness I could easily get used to.

Satish cleared his throat a little too harshly to sound spontaneous. He shoved both hands in his pockets, not sure what to do with himself, and jingled whatever it was that was jingling in his pockets. "Track's fine," he said after a little while. "He just needed a new car and decided to play cops and robbers with the first guy he found. The guy happened to be dumb enough to run."

Diane looked at him then back at me.

"We think the killer's a computer pro," I said.

She squinted. "Who? The Byzantine Strangler?"

Satish started pacing. "Yes. But we still don't know the meaning of the code he left behind the tiles."

"Right. And wasting time here doesn't get us any closer to finding the truth." I tossed the ice pack at the foot of the bed and got up. When the wave of dizziness and nausea passed, I grabbed my shirt from the rack where an intern had left it, and slid it on.

Diane stood up and squeezed her purse. "What programming code is it?"

Satish shrugged. "Something called XY—"

"Plot," I said. "XY—fucking—plot."

Her lips repeated the name, minus the French. "Sounds familiar..."

I buttoned my shirt, then pulled on my pants.

"Of course!" Diane squealed. She yanked open her purse and fished out her phone. "I got back the mtDNA results today," she said. "And I was looking for some easy viewing tool to compare the babies' DNA to the one from the fibers."

She tapped her iPhone and pulled up the browser.

Satish stopped pacing. I tucked the shirt into my pants. It carried the reek of my own perspiration, sweat and adrenaline from the high-speed chase.

"There." Diane turned the iPhone around and held it up. "See this? It's a DNA viewing tool. Now, if I upload a sample—" She tapped some more. Sat and I flanked her like guardian angels. I squeezed a little closer and sunk my face in her hair. Her breasts would've been nicer but less appropriate. A graph appeared on the small screen, a bunch of horizontal lines with colored ticks.

And it clicked into place. I smacked a loud kiss on Diane's head. "That's exactly what I glimpsed on the turd's laptop at the Internet café!"

"Wait, it gets better." Diane scrolled to the bottom of the page, pointed to a button that said "XYPlot" and clicked on it. The link opened a window of code—line after line of jargon of which I only recognized one thing: the pattern of hashes, numbers and letters the Byzantine Strangler had left at the back of the last set of tiles.

Satish clicked his tongue, rocked on his heels for a bit, then resumed pacing. "Viktor said many scientists use the code for graphing."

I sat on the edge of the bed. "This is the kind of graph the guy was staring at when he shut his laptop and ran."

Satish turned to me abruptly. "What was the guy's name on the board?"

"G-cat."

Diane's eyes sparkled. "G, C, A, and T—the four DNA nucleotides. The guy's a DNA freak."

My girl was on fire. "You're a genius, D! And four-colored tiles," I added.

"That was the first set. The second set only had three."

"But four colors," I insisted. It was clear. Suddenly, it all made perfect sense. The tiles, the coins, the guy's ashen, almost sick face, as he stared at me for a split second and then ran.

"The guy is obsessed with DNA," I said.

Satish pointed at the phone in Diane's hands. "The graph. It's got the same colors—green, red, orange and aquamarine."

Diane drew in a sharp intake of air. "Oh my God, it's the code! See? The color ticks in the graph represent nucleotides. Green for A, red for T, orange for C, and aquamarine for T."

Satish looked at me. "There's your code. Cracked."

I tried to smile but I wasn't very convincing. "I found g-cat and let him run."

* * *

The moon was a pale smile across a starless sky. The foothills rolled to our left, speckled by the occasional twinkle of a house or the looming silhouette of an antenna farm. To our right, downtown stood quietly and impassively.

You're out there, you son of a bitch.

I'll find you. I swear I'll find you.

"Track."

"Hmm."

"Do you get it, now?"

"No."

Diane clenched the wheel of her VW and sighed. A vehicle passed us in the right lane.

I felt small, weak, and mortal. *Very* mortal.

"What is it you don't get?"

I brushed a finger along my stitches. The nylon threads poked out of my skin like whiskers.

"I don't get any of it," I said. "We established the hairs came from the killer. They fluoresce, and that's how you figured the Byzantine Strangler has this weird condition—what's it called again?"

"Morgellons disease."

"Right." I rapped the window with my knuckles. "And these hairs have DNA."

"*Mitochondrial* DNA, Track. A very special kind of DNA."

"Fine. They've got *some* DNA. And you compared it with the DNA from the kiddos."

"That's right." Diane was going fifteen miles over the speed limit. She barreled up on the slow poke ahead of us and waited until she was five feet away from him before swerving into the left lane to pass him. I wanted to ask how much her insurance premium was, but there were more pressing matters.

"We found the hairs on the victims, yet you tell me the DNA nails them to the babies. The DNA from the hairs *and* the babies is a match, is that what you're saying? Are the babies the ones with the disease, then? And how the hell did hairs from the babies end up on the victims? Hell, babies don't even have hairs!"

The head concussion must've made me very stupid.

She whipped the VW back to the middle lane. "You keep missing the fact that it's *mitochondrial* DNA, not the regular DNA from the nucleus. I told you before, mtDNA is not unique to one individual. Get it? Related individuals can have identical mitochondrial DNA."

"Well, if it's not unique, it's not informative."

She jerked her head sideways and yelled at me. "Track. Shut up and listen, okay?"

I shut up. My head wasn't throbbing anymore, but it was hard to listen. My thoughts were running around like chased rats.

"Mitochondrial DNA is inherited from the mother's side. It doesn't undergo recombination like chromosomes do. That's why in most cases a child has the identical mtDNA as her mother, unless a mutation happens, which is rare. So, you're right, it can't nail a person, but it can tell you how closely related two individuals are. On the mother's side, at least."

I pondered. The rats in my head partied. I scrunched my forehead—stitches pulling and all—and pondered harder.

"The DNA from the hairs found on Amy and Laura was identical to that of the kiddos?"

"All but one, which had one mutation."

"The babies all share the same mother."

She nodded her head up and down. "Yes."

"As does the Byzantine Strangler."

"Or, he's a she—the mother."

"G-cat is a guy."

"And you have no proof this g-cat guy is the Byzantine Strangler *or* the guy you chased tonight."

"Don't piss me off, Diane. I didn't whack my Charger for nothing."

"Don't spill your ego, macho man. You're not always right."

That killed the conversation for a while. We got off the Two on Mountain and wound up the hills of Chevy Chase. It was two a.m. Darkness enveloped us like silence, the VW's headlights carving small cones of light on the pavement. The stale smells of hospital clung to my skin like leeches. I rolled down the window and inhaled. The air was scented with fir needles, sage, and night flowers, and it was warm, as warm as a lover's unmade bed. Clusters of homes peeked here and there through the blanket of the hills.

I thought of Charlie Callahan's body, strangled and mauled behind an apartment dumpster. I thought of Amy Liu, who wanted to know something about Charlie, something that likely killed her. I thought of Fred Lyons, who lost a lover and a wife, and whose involvement in either murder was still very much suspicious to me. I thought of Henkins, a lifetime spent measuring herself up to the boys, only to give up at the end, when she stumbled upon something bigger than her career—somebody else's career. I thought of David, Charlie's friend-slash-more-than-a-friend, of one-night stands turned into Russian roulettes, a life gamble much like car racing or shooting vodka up your veins.

I thought of a mother killing her babies and burying them one by one, naked and lonely.

Give a life, take a life.

And then I thought of the Byzantine Strangler and tried to give him a face, any one of these shady figures, all of them, or none of them at all.

Diane yawned. She pulled into my driveway, killed the engine, and then yawned some more, rubbing her eyes with the tip of her fingers. I kissed her on the head and got out of the car.

There was a high-strung olfactory note in the air, like a guitar playing a familiar melody with one of the cords out of tune.

Somebody's been here.

My muscles stiffened. Soreness clumped in my back and legs, soon washed away by a new wave of adrenaline. Diane mumbled something. She slammed the car door shut and clicked the locks. I walked up the driveway, then around the garage. The gate to the walkway was unlatched. Past its metallic tang, the latch smelled rotten and sweet and diseased. It smelled of my guy.

I kicked the gate and yanked the Glock out of its holster.

Diane ran after me. She found me standing by the picnic table at the back, Glock in hand, and cold sweat weeping down my jaw. Something glistened on my table under the pale light of the moon.

At the back of the property, the eucalyptus trees whispered their minty scent and washed the foul smells away.

He's gone.

Diane's side brushed against mine. She gasped and brought a hand to her mouth.

He'd left them on the picnic table. Two rows, three tiles each. Aquamarine, red, green the first row. Orange, red, aquamarine the second.

She rummaged in her purse, got her phone out, and opened the browser to the DNA tool. She moved her index finger quickly, her thoughts in line with mine. "T, A, G for the top row," she said. "C, A, and T for the bottom."

"Tag cat," I said.

Tag cat.

"He's after me, D."

She frowned. "You? Why?"

"Because he's obsessed with DNA, that's why."

TWENTY-EIGHT

The screams. He couldn't stand the screams. And then the blood, afterwards. Lots and lots of blood.

"Go dig, Hector. Go."

"Why?"

"Because your mama said so, that's why!"

She'd hand him the bloodied bag and tell him to bury it. One, two, he forgot how many.

Too tempting not to look inside. He did once, and never forgot. Never understood.

The bags kept coming.

One, two, he forgot how many.

He found the perfect spot. Over the years, bushes grew around it, and trees, and wildflowers. Sometimes a coyote would come too. And he killed the coyote. By then, killing had become easy.

But the screams. Those never were easy.

It became worst when he understood.

"Why, Ma? Can't you make him stop?"

"Stop? No, baby, why? Your mama would be so lonely without him."

"Then tell him, Ma. Tell him."

"He's too young. He wouldn't understand."

So Ed would still come over for dinner and stay for the night and everything would be fine until Ma would start puking again and growing and Ed wouldn't show up for a while until the time came and the screams and the blood and Hector would hike up the hill and dump another bag.

One, two, he forgot how many.

* * *

His hands bleed, his feet hurt. He peels off the nitrile gloves. His palms are veined with blood. He rushes to the bathroom to wash it off. His hands, his feet, his face.

"Hector! You're late. Again! I haven't had the Roxanol, or my dinner, or — "

Everywhere. Gypsy moths everywhere. It's an infestation. They crawl out of the walls just like they crawl out of his skin, nostrils, ears.

" — my bag needs to be changed, and my tubes disinfected, and — "

He lets hot water run until it scalds his skin.

Scalding is good. It will kill the bugs.

He lost the car. The computer is safe, though. He couldn't afford losing the computer.

How did the cop find him?

Maybe it was all a coincidence. The cop couldn't possibly know.

The cop couldn't possibly know about him, but Hector Medina knows everything about the cop — his name, his face, his address, his phone number. His genes. The wonderful epigenetic switches taking place in his body. It's not perfect. The cop's going to die. That's okay. All he needs is a few samples of his tissues and then he can work on fixing the problem.

He needs time.

Medina closes the faucet.

"Hector! Are you listening to me?"

More time.

He comes out of the bathroom and cranks up the AC. Chilled air blows down from the vents in the ceiling.

"Hector! I don't like it this chilly. Come change my bag, it stinks!"

He walks into the kitchen, grabs a fresh pair of gloves from the pantry, the formula jars, the medications, the measuring cups.

A gypsy moth crawls on the tiles above the stove.

He stares at it.

They're everywhere.

"Hector!"

His heart starts pounding. He's killed cats, coyotes, humans, and never in his life he'd smashed a gypsy moth. Yet gypsy moths ruined his life more than anything else.

"Hector! Are you listening?"

More than anything else.

He takes the measuring cup and smashes the bug with the flat side. It leaves a splatter of white powder and black hairs on the kitchen tiles.

"Hector! What do you think you're doing? My bag. You need to change my bag. And I'm past due my dose of Roxanol. It's hurting all over, can't you see? Get that thing off my face, Hector. You think I'm scared of you? You pussy cat. You think this thing is gonna kill me, don't you? I'm not dying, Hector. I'm not dying. Despite all the crap those big doctors colleagues of yours tell you. What did they tell you? Weeks? Months, at most? Bullshit. I'm not dying. I refuse to die. There's nothing you can do about it. So now put that stupid toy away and change my — "

The gypsy moth.

He stares at the feathery wings, all crumpled up, and the cloud of white, sparkly powder spilled over the kitchen tiles.

And he likes what he sees.
Today, for the first time in his life, he smashed a gypsy moth.

TWENTY-NINE

Tuesday, July 21

I sprang my eyes open and then closed them again. Every muscle in my body was sore. It wasn't the Pain. Strangely, the Pain was quiet. I brought a hand to my face and rubbed my eyes. My vision spotted like burning camera film. Then shapes reemerged, one by one. An old dresser, the colorful painting of a red, naked woman lying languidly in the forest, the open door of a closet, a few shirts clinging to hangers, ties, pants, a chair, a plastic rack of shoes hanging at the back of the closet door. An open window, the smell of eucalypti softly drifting inside.

"It's almost noon." Diane's voice came from far away, even though she was sitting on the bed, next to me.

"Noon, huh?" I drawled. Will's tongue came to my face, warm and moist.

Diane called him to her side and patted him. "You slept

through the morning."

"You stayed the whole time?"

She flashed me a deliciously malicious leer. "I've been watching you. The doctor said to keep an eye on you."

I groaned myself out of bed and sat on the edge. I needed a shower, a shave, clean clothes, and possibly a new head, one that didn't hurt this much.

Diane pressed a cold finger against my temple. "Are you feeling any better?"

"I'm great," I mumbled. "Stop spinning the ceiling, though. It's making me dizzy."

She smiled, kissed me, padded to the bathroom, came back with a bottle of Advil in her hand. Hell. In juvi you could bribe the guards into slipping you acid. A double sawbuck bought you a couple trips and the happiest five hours you could remember.

"Satish called," she said, handing me the medication.

"When?" I shook two Advil tablets out of the bottle and downed them.

"A couple of hours ago. He was running VIN numbers through the DMV database."

Blood rushed to my head. "They got it? They got the vehicle, then? When, how?"

"He said the parked vehicle picked up by the FLIR was a Volvo and it matched your description. The VIN on the doorjamb was scratched off but they got the hidden one instead, and the plate turned out to be from a dump. They towed it early this morning."

I stood up. The ceiling behaved and stayed put. My shoulders and neck ached, and I let them ache and I didn't care. My heart thumped wildly. "What did you say about the plate?"

Diane shook her head. "Probably bought illegally from a car dump."

"Fine. The VIN's all we need. Glad they got the hidden one."

The news energized me. I got to my feet and headed to the bathroom. I started undressing. "Where's Satish now, at the Glass House? Can you call him and tell him I'll be there in twenty minutes?"

"Track, wait." She leaned against the bathroom door, a question hanging from her eyes. "A Doctor Watanabe called."

I started the water and let it run.

Watanabe.

"Thanks," I said, stepped into the shower and pulled the curtain. Her scent melted in the hot water vapors. The door clicked closed. Rivulets streamed down my face, neck and shoulders.

They found the hidden VIN.

The son of a bitch may be good with computers, but he's an idiot with cars.

When I got out of the bathroom, Diane was sitting on the bed, the silent question still hanging from her lips. I tried to ignore it but it kept following me around as I went through hangers looking for shirt and pants.

"Don't you want to know why your doctor called?"

"He heard on the news that I'd totaled my car and wanted to make sure I didn't total my neck as well."

I tossed a set of clothes on the bed, toweled dry my hair and ran my fingers through it. I could've used a comb but then it wouldn't have matched the bags under my eyes, the stitches on my brow, or the two-day stubble shading my cheeks. The mirror smiled at me proudly.

Diane leaned back on the pillows — Will snuggled next to her — and laced the hem of the top sheet around her fingers. "I told him you were okay. He wanted to know what caused the accident."

Her eyes came on me. I zipped up my pants then slid the belt on. "I got into a high speed chase and lost control of the vehicle. What's so surprising about that?"

"I told him you were okay, but he still sounded concerned."

"Well, yeah. You told him I was fine, so that should've taken care of his *concerns*."

"Why do you see a geneticist?"

The question irritated me. Why it irritated me I couldn't tell. In a perfect world a perfect me would've answered, "Because I have some kind of genetic issues." But my world has always been far from perfect. So instead I snapped, "Hell, D. Why d'you go about answering my phone?"

That didn't go down easy. She hopped off the bed and stormed out of the room, a totally unaware Will scuttling happily behind her.

"D!" I grabbed guns and holsters and followed her to the kitchen.

She dropped a breakfast dish in the sink. It clonked on top of the two-day old pile I'd left in there. The aroma of the coffee she'd brewed two hours ago was still in the air. I set my guns on the table, pulled a chair, sat down, and adjusted the ankle holster. "Are you coming to Parker Center?" I asked.

Diane opened the dishwasher and started filling it like her life depended on it. "I got an offer from Harvard."

Something in my head went silent. I pressed the mag release button on the Glock and let the magazine slide into my palm.

"The job at the Public School of Health I'd interviewed for. I got it," Diane went on. "It's a good offer. Good hours, good salary."

"You get good hours and a good salary here, too."

"Great benefits."

"The LAPD has great benefits."

She transferred all dirty mugs from the sink to the dishwasher top rack and ignored my comment.

I pushed a new magazine inside the Glock's well. "It's in Boston."

This time she turned and locked eyes with me. "Yes. It's in Boston."

There was sour in her voice. It stung like the morning chill on a wintry day.

I stood up, secured the pancake holster on my waistband and slid the Glock inside. "We're on a hot trail," I said. "We're gonna catch this guy."

She slammed the dishwasher closed. "You're not listening, Track. I'm taking the job."

I stood there, in the middle of the kitchen, no more expressive than a chipped statue in a forgotten church.

"You're going to Boston?" I said.

"Give me a reason *not* to go."

Her statement hung like an unfinished sentence in a blank page. I wanted to put a period at the end of it. Yet I was nothing but a pen whose ink had all dried up.

I tilted her chin up and kissed her. And then I left.

* * *

The midafternoon sun cast a layer of dullness on everything. Skinny palm trees staggered against a hazy sky. Chafed one-story houses overlooked thirsty lawns circled by metal fences and cinder block walls embellished with wrought iron railings. Faded apartment buildings dominated each block, their gray, barred windows as welcoming as a pit bull growl.

Satish drove slowly and methodically. Eyes followed us from the sidewalks, faces as old as time chewing cigarette butts on a staircase, their undershirts stained with grease and sweat. Dark-skinned kids played soccer with an empty can in a sweltering parking lot. Street names like Harmony and Amethyst and Topaz and Onyx glistened at the corners of lonely crossings, next to a rusted leasing sign or a lost cat flyer pinned to a telephone pole.

I said, "We were here two minutes ago."

"I know."

"Need extra mileage?"

"No. Just thought we'd take a look at the neighborhood first."

He finally pulled the vehicle over and killed the engine. I felt a little prickling at the back of my neck. "Which house?" I said.

He cocked his head. "Number 5130."

"Number 5130 Celestial Drive?" I repeated.

"Correct."

"Lyanne Norris, age fifty-nine?"

Sat hid his surprise behind black shades. "Correct."

"Diagnosed with gastric cancer five years ago, two surgeries, three rounds of chemo, confined to bed since last February. She the one who supposedly owns the Volvo I saw fly over the San Pablo intersection last night?"

Satish leered at me from behind the shades. He swallowed, slowly slid the shades off, and then leered some more. "Have you been practicing mind reading over your sabbatical from the police force?"

"No. I've been sniffing out missing people. And one in particular I'd sort of given up on, until her path led me to six dead infants."

Katya Krikorian, the missing persons case I took on over my short stint as a P.I., had gone missing last May. She had just visited Lyanne Norris the day she disappeared. Katya left Lyanne's house, parked her car a couple of miles away, and never made it back home. I'd come to 5130 Celestial Drive twice. The first time nobody answered the door, while the second time I managed to talk to Lyanne's nurse. Had I known what I knew today, I wouldn't have contented myself with the brief chat we had at the door. Damn it, had I known, I would've found a way to get into the house and sniff the whole place inside out. But what reason did I have, back then, to suspect a harmless woman confined to bed? The nurse told me Lyanne was sleeping and confirmed that she had terminal cancer and had not left her bed for the past five months—same story painted by the police report filed under the missing persons.

Satish tapped the steering wheel with the side of his thumb. "Obviously the woman doesn't drive. She either loaned it or it got stolen and she didn't report the theft."

I swallowed, feeling like a complete idiot. "She has a son," I said, bitterly. "Lyanne's nurse told me she hardly sees him, but he's the one taking care of Lyanne when her shift is over."

"You didn't interview the son?" Satish asked.

I shook my head. "The officers who investigated the missing persons did. The report didn't raise any flags, and the nurse said he'd never been there during Katya's visits. He seemed pretty innocuous, just an average joe who took care of his ill mother, and—Damn it."

It was clicking into place. I just remembered that his job description in the report was "medical researcher."

"Let's go," Satish said.

We stepped out of the car and crossed the street. The air was hot and viscous. It slowed down everything, even sounds. An inflatable pool simmered in the sun in front of the house next door. A rubber duckie bobbed its head from the shallow water.

Number 5130 stood at the top of a driveway that led to a

one-story cottage house in cracked pink stucco, with tacky plastic awnings hanging over the front windows. The exterior needed a paint job, the window frames begged to be replaced, and the roof had seen better days. A mop of unruly ivy choked the sidewall to the right, crawled around the edge, and sprawled across the garage door. It promised to be an interesting garage, one that hadn't seen fresh air in a long time.

Two trash bins were amassed against a metal fence. Sickly dandelions infested what was left of a lawn.

Satish walked to the door. I stayed back, inhaled, and didn't like what I smelled.

Satish knocked. Nobody answered. He knocked again, louder.

"Sat."

"Hmm."

"There's a smell."

Satish rocked on his heels. "Don't look at me, Track. I fart Indian." He chortled and tried the door again.

I shook my head and looked around. A little boy stared at me from behind the fence next door. I waved. He showed me the rubber duckie he'd retrieved from the tub. A door slammed from his house and a woman too old to be his mother and too young to be his grandmother marched out and padded across the front yard barefoot. She picked up the child and quickly turned away.

"Ma'am," I called.

She turned with deliberate effort. I cocked my head toward the pink cottage. "Noticed any activity at all today?"

"She's sick," she spat. "She no longer comes out."

"Who takes care of her?"

The boy squirmed in her arms. She narrowed her eyes, studying me. I slid out my badge wallet and held it up for her to see. That loosened her tongue a bit but not too much.

"They had a home nurse." She shrugged a shoulder, tweaked half a lip. "She couldn't take it anymore and quit. Her son takes care of her now. Nice fellow. Doesn't talk much, but puts up with a lot of crap."

"What about today?"

She shook her head. "Haven't seen a soul today."

"Heard anything at all?"

She shook her head again, and then she was gone. Satish was staring through one of the windows. He turned and shook his head. "Let's try the backdoor."

We waded through a strip of high weeds between the sidewall and the metal fence and came to a scrawny backyard mottled with patches of naked dirt. A clothesline strung a mellow note in the dull afternoon air. A swarm of flies drew persistent circles on a white screen door.

The reek grew stronger. It was sweet and rotten and it reminded me of wet rust. It lingered in the air like thick morning fog.

Satish smelled it too, this time. "This ain't farts," he said, wistfully. He banged a fist against the doorjamb. The flies bounced off the screen like spit, pirouetted in and around our faces, and then settled back.

No answer. There wasn't going to be any.

I opened the screen door and drew my Glock. "Hold the screen door."

"Track—" He sucked in air through his teeth but held the screen door just the same.

Flies tickled my face like a feather duster. "When was the last time I was wrong about this?"

He smiled despite himself. "I just hope we can find a link between all these cadavers we keep finding."

I kicked the door open. The frame splintered and chips of old paint flecked off.

"Police!" I yelled.

There was no answer.

The door swung open onto a dark hallway that had the distinctive smell of things too old to care. The walls were yellow with no windows, the carpet was dingy and stained. Dark doors with brass knobs stood silently along the way, waiting. I stepped inside.

Behind me, Satish muttered, "Man, it's bad."

"That's not the methanol," I replied. It was the sweet and rotten smell of disease, the reek of decay slowly taking over the body long before it's dead, of an open wound refusing to heal, of a liquid death seeping through the last shreds of life. I knew that smell, and I cursed at myself for not picking up on it earlier, the first time I detected it on the tiles.

"Ms. Norris?" Satish called. He tapped my arm and passed me a pair of gloves.

I turned the knob on the first door to the left. It smelled of old metal, the kind that stays on your hands long after you've touched it. The door opened to a bathroom, a strip of space between a wall and an ancient vanity, no windows, slate blue linoleum floors, a white sink with two spouts, a large mirror just not to feel claustrophobic, and dark cabinet doors that smelled of medicine. I opened one. Cleaning supplies on the bottom shelf, medicine organizers on the middle one, medical supplies on the top one. There was a year's worth of nitrile gloves supply. Everything was clean and orderly. Something I'd not expected, given the outside look of the house.

In the hallway, bi-fold closet doors opened to an alcove with an outdated washing machine and drier. I closed the doors and turned to look for Satish. The smell of detergent and aged fabric gave way to a new tang. Something acrid, pungent, with an aftertaste of burnt…

"Satish!"

"Over here."

It was in the past. Everything was in the past. The drawer chest with clawed feet, the oval mirror with the scroll frame, the smell of camphor lingering in the air, the black and white pictures, the golden tassels at the corners of the pillows... the reek of gunpowder, the Walther PPK pistol in her knotted hand, probably a mint edition, one of those things you still see in old James Bond movies.

Sprawled in a bed too large for her size, Lyanne Norris gawked with pale, vitreous eyes. They looked like the bottom of a green bottle. Her brows flexed together with anger, her lipless mouth hung open like a forgotten drawer. Her skull was sunken at the temples, with long flecks of white hair that looked like sticky cobwebs. A pale arm rested along her side, loosely covered in paper-thin skin, the other bent over her chest. Blue fingers wrapped the butt of the Walther. The barrel sat slightly askew on top of her bulging stomach.

The hole in her throat hadn't bled too much. It was crimson red, the size of a quarter, with blackened edges. It smelled of dried blood and burnt skin.

"She's gone," Sat said. "Cold, no pulse."

"You had your doubts?" I leaned over close enough to smell the gun and the inside of her palm. "Not sure she fired it herself."

"Even if she did, somebody had to pass her the gun."

There were tubes coming out of the bed and connecting her to all sorts of things. The feeding bag was half full. The sharps disposal box on the floor next to the nightstand contained no syringes—it must've been emptied recently. The medical waste pedal bin in a corner had a fresh liner.

I lifted the side hem of the sheets. Still warm, the acidic reek of urine drifted to my nostrils, the bag hanging like a ripe mango from the bedframe. A clear catheter wound up from the bag to the top of the mattress, under Lyanne's jutting side.

"Hey, Sat. Come over to this side."

He came, thoughtfully holding his radio as if he tried to remember what to say.

"Look at this. Does it remind you of anything?"

He scrunched his forehead together. "When I had my appendix removed?"

"Jeez, Sat. Look at the catheter. It's smooth and thin, not too thin, but not too thick either, would leave a nice, uniform indentation except if you hold it too much to the side then the two-way fork leaves a slightly funneling mark, which would fall"—I rose back to my feet and touched my neck—"just about here, close to the ear."

Satish looked at me skeptically. "The telltale mark we found on Laura Lyons's neck," he finally agreed.

He nodded then held the radio to his mouth and called for backup over a dead body. He walked to the dresser and started opening random drawers as he explained the situation to the dispatcher. I let the sheets fall back down and walked out of the room. Clean kitchen, clear Formica countertops, a white fridge with empty shelves save a couple of open medicine bottles, more drugs in a corner between the stove and a metal toaster that could've come out of a vintage sale. Jars of formula in the cabinets, ordered by expiration date. They had the sweet, gooey smell of the tiles—the rotten bit being the disease decay. No other food item visible anywhere, not even crumbs. There was no dishwasher. The sink was empty and dry, a few items rested in the dish rack: two bowls, a wooden spoon, a measuring cup. I found one-year's worth supply of catheter boxes in the pantry. They came in two options, sixteen French and twenty-four French. I picked one of each, closed the pantry, and moved to the last room in the house.

THIRTY

Black tarp covered the only window, duct-taped all around the frame. There was a folding bed against the wall, frugally made, and a metal desk covered with papers, a black swivel chair, a waste basket filled with used nitrile gloves that smelled of decay mixed with feeding formula—sweet and rotten like the Byzantine Strangler's tiles. The first desk drawer contained a box of paid bill stubs—electricity, gas, phone—all in Lyanne's name. I removed the box and something rattled at the back of the drawer—a ring with two keys. I sniffed them, didn't notice anything particularly interesting besides the usual key smell, placed them back and closed the drawer. An Internet cable was sandwiched between two piles of papers, looking for the computer it'd once connected to. I looked too—in the remaining desk drawers, under the bed, in the closet, but the computer had vanished with no trace.

It didn't really matter. All I needed to know was on the wall. Scientific journal articles and paper clips, photos, some cut, some neatly torn by hand, all stapled on a cork board, and when the corkboard had run out, he'd continued taping them on the wall, on the tarp covering the window, on the closet door. In one clip, Lyons was the featured researcher of the month, in another he was at a lab bench, unconvincingly holding a pipette, his name highlighted in the text below the photo. Lyons in his lab coat at the hospital, Lyons in his office, a younger Lyons smiling at the camera, a hand around his deceased wife's shoulder.

The younger Lyons was praised in most clips. He'd won the Medal of Science in recognition for his work on HIV. A photo of him shaking hands with Mr. Clinton had the caption, "Dr. Frederick Lyons makes stunning discovery on the origin of HIV."

The clips with the older Lyons had mixed reviews. "Dr. Lyons's grant shrunk over the past five years," an NIH grant reviewer was quoted saying. "Dr. Lyons left the International Immunology Meeting in the midst of controversial critiques." It looked like in the past couple of years, famous Dr. Lyons had lost his stamina. I skimmed over the rest of the clips and moved over to the next portion of the quilted mural.

A chrysalis was pinned to the corkboard, on top of a paper on gypsy moths.

Diagrams of chromosomes populated one side of the wall, genes and position numbers annotated in blue marker. And then the graphs — the ones Diane had discovered. They were plastered in the middle of the wall, sets of horizontal lines occasionally peppered with colored ticks, always four colors — red, aquamarine, orange, and green — line after line of As, Gs, Ts, and Cs. I leaned against the wall and examined the printouts closely. They were pasted together so that the lines continued from one graph to the next, with penciled marks at the top. Words had been scribbled below, words I couldn't read at first, until my eyes adjusted to the spidery handwriting and started deciphering letters, then sounds, then names. Gloria Weiss, Katya Krikorian, Amy Liu, Louis Gallegos, Laura Lyons.

Gloria Weiss was a twelve-year-old run away girl who'd gone missing two years earlier. I didn't recognize the name Louis Gallegos. Katya Krikorian, though, I did recognize. I'd finally found her — albeit too late.

The graphs were taped together, like tiles in a mosaic, a mosaic of DNAs, gene after gene, chromosome after chromosome, after… I froze, gloved hands flattened against the wall. The last graph was blank, the name scribbled at the top written in a hurry, a pencil stroke to the last letter running off to the edge of the paper.

Presius. Ulysses M. Presius.

Sweat chilled at the back of my neck.

The phone call.

He'd called me to tell me about my genes.

The bastard has my lab results. That's how he got my phone number, too. He left the tiles at my house to tell me he's after me.

My eyes strayed over the neat piles of papers blanketing the desk. Research papers, drafts, lab notebooks — one for each victim whose DNA he'd collected. I searched through the pile until I found the one with Katya's name written in caps on the spine and opened it. It read like a journal — a lab journal. Samples he'd collected, thawed and tested, DNA typing, PCR amplification, RNA matching, even the mitochondrial DNA Diane had mentioned, gene expression arrays, the whole nine yards. The details were beyond me, all I understood was the lucid and chilling details with which he documented everything, from the tissue excisions to the extraction of strings of letters — DNA, RNA, amino acids.

The guy wasn't just obsessed with DNA. He was *after* DNA, the whole package in fact, the full genome, the way it worked in every tissue, what genes were expressed and why.

These weren't victims. They were his lab rats.

He kills *because of* DNA.

From the bedroom, I heard Satish talking to the dispatcher, frisking the room as he talked, opening and closing drawers and closet doors. I closed the lab notebook and started digging through the pile of scientific papers.

I found the paper I'd spotted on Lyons's desk the time we interviewed him in his office. I recognized it from the penciled corrections, a feminine calligraphy that matched the different annotations on Callahan's graphs. There were new marks, in red ink this time. A side note read: "Medina, this is BS. Check Amy's notes and make sure this doesn't happen again." The tone was Lyons's. The penciled notes had to be Amy Liu's, then.

Medina. My memory rewound to the day we interviewed Lyons at the hospital. Medina was the skinny guy stuttering about alignments. I concentrated on his face, drew a blank. An anonymous face, scarily pale, the hint of a stubble... like the guy I'd chased on the Volvo.

"What's this, a shrine?" Satish was standing by the door, a weary look on his face.

"A shrine, a lab, a hell." I caught myself grinding my teeth. "What have you found?"

He dropped a closed checkbook on the desk for me to see. "This. Two names on the account—Lyanne Norris and Hector—"

"Medina. Hector S. Medina."

"You been reading minds again?"

"No. Papers." I held up the one with Lyons's note and

336

pointed to the list of authors. Hector S. Medina was the first one. "Amy Liu had found some kind of flaw and Lyons ordered Medina to clean up. That's how her DNA ended up right…" I rotated my hand up in the air, found the graph with Amy's genes and pinned it with my index finger. "Here."

Satish frowned. "That what got her killed? Her DNA?"

"Maybe. Or maybe the DNA was the trophy." I rapped the paper with the back of my fingers. "It sounds like she exposed some kind of crap Medina did in this paper. I'm guessing the guy wasn't too thrilled."

Sirens howled from the street.

"That's our party," Satish said. He tilted his head, took in once more the wall and its gruesome trophies, and left the room. I picked up the checkbook and the paper and followed him to the front door. A cruiser and the coroner's van were parked in the driveway. Satish stepped out to talk to the responding officers.

The entry way smelled of shoes and Febreze. A faint reminiscence of gasoline clawed its fingers around my chin and turned it to the door to the right. The usual brass knob with ancient black dents stared at me and told me to try it. It was locked. I walked back to the office turned into shrine, opened the first desk drawer, removed the box with the bill stubs, retrieved the ring with the two keys, returned to the entryway, inserted the first key, didn't work, inserted the second one, unlocked the door, and stepped into another world.

* * *

The smell of gasoline was still there, lingering in the background. It's one of those smells that never fades, no matter how long ago the garage stopped being a garage and turned into a storage locker. I blinked, waiting for my eyes to adjust to the darkness.

It was a large, L-shaped room, and I was standing at one end, with the garage door around the corner at the other end. The floor was made of cement and the walls were unfinished, with yellow layers of fiberglass insulation rippling between wood studs. Trusses and exposed pipes crammed the ceiling. Dried up halos of mold retraced past roof leaks and poor repair jobs. A rusty bicycle hung from a hook in the ceiling. Around the corner, a sheet of thin light pooled from the glass panes at the top of the garage door and pooled over randomly assorted items: a three-legged chair, a rusty oil drum, a standing freezer.

A *modern* freezer, a relic in reverse, a glimpse of modernity in a world stuck in the past.

Satish's voice came from the other side of the garage door. He was talking to the medical examiner. An engine ran in the background. The beep of a truck backing up hammered in the distance. And yet in this garage fallen in disuse everything seemed eerily still and quiet, as if watching the world from a remote spot.

Dust motes fluttered in a golden sheet of light. Mold ringed the walls and tinged the air with a sweet stench of mushroom. Camphor, old wood, mildew, and something vaguely human, vaguely animal, vaguely dead.

The freezer gave out a loud sigh and started to whir. I squeezed between the skeleton of an upholstered recliner and a battered dining table covered in cellophane, and shuffled cautiously to the freezer. It stood next to a rusty oil barrel.

I opened the freezer, the hair at the back of my neck standing up as if I was opening a coffin. Breaths of gelid air blew in my face.

I inhaled.

I *had* opened a coffin.

Yellow and white tissue cassettes were piled on the top shelf, as orderly as the closets and pantry I'd seen inside the house. Ziploc bags layered the next shelf—white, black and yellow. Each bag contained hair—a nice, thick clump clinging to dried shaved skin. I took in a sharp breath, squatted, and braced myself for the bottom shelf.

Bones, each set sealed in a transparent bag, fairly fresh, dried tissue clinging here and there. An ulna, maybe, one could've been a metatarsus, another a shoulder blade. I knew neither Amy nor Laura had been deboned, so this had to be Katya and maybe the twelve-year-old girl. There had to be more of them somewhere else.

I stood up, closed the freezer, and looked in the next obvious place. *Obvious to my nose.* The lid of the oil drum didn't yield. It still smelled of oil, rust, metal, chipped paint, methanol, cadaverine. I looked around, walked through the turbulence of dust motes, back to the metal racks. Hammers, an old drill, empty glass jars, dried up paint cans, brushes, a toolbox. I opened it, retrieved a flat screwdriver, went back to the oil barrel, stuck the screwdriver between the lid and the top edge of the barrel. It yielded this time. I pulled the lid up slowly. Respectfully.

Katya's skull stared at me with a disdained and empty look. It sat on a substrate of sand mixed with laundry detergent and soda. A few strands of white hair precariously hung at the top of the forehead. Black skin, like charred wax, clung to the skull's jawbones and left out the teeth to flash me an eerie grin.

The grin said, *You idiot, it took you this long to find me.*

Satish banged a hand on the garage door. "Track. You there?"

I lowered the lid. "Yup. Got company, too. Tell the M.E. to get ready for another one."

"Jeez—another stiff?"

"Or two."

I heard him blow air between his teeth. "Sheesh."

A radio blabbered.

"Sat?"

"Yeah. I'm sending the guys inside. And uh—Viktor just called."

* * *

The sharp light of a July mid-afternoon hit me like a sudden graveyard call. I slid on my sunglasses, hooked hands around my belt and stared at my partner.

"I'm going," I said.

Pearls of sweat beaded Satish's salt-and-pepper temples. He dipped a hand in his pocket, pulled out a handkerchief, and patted his brow. "Track. We've got at least two cadavers in this house. We've got Katie at Parker Center trying to track down everything we can possibly track down on this Medina guy. He hasn't reported to work this morning—no surprise there—and they're interviewing every coworker they can find, including Lyons. We've got two patrol cars down in Hollywood looking at the area indicated by Viktor, but—"

"Sat, the guy's there and Viktor's got his location. Do you need anything else?"

"We don't know it's the same guy, and Hollywood's not exactly the best place to spot a fugitive. It requires a lot of man power that—"

"I know it's the same guy! The guy I chased down Valley, the guy who made me slam my Charger and who killed the two ladies in this house and the two others. He's fucking dangerous and we can't take chances."

"It's like chasing a ghost!" Satish raised his voice. In six years we'd been partners, he'd never once raised his voice. He was my senior, so I shut up. "Do you have any idea how many people there are in downtown Hollywood this time of the year?" he pressed on. "Let the blue suits canvass the area. If we go too, by the time we get there Viktor might have lost the signal and all we got is a cloud of dust. We've got two cadavers here. Let's finish up at least one job properly."

One of the uniformed officers appeared at the door, a red face on a boxer's body. He shot a nervous glance at the two of us, cleared his throat, and then mumbled, "The M.E. says he's ready to bag the lady."

"Coming." Satish patted his brows again, shoved the handkerchief in his pocket, and shuffled back to the door.

"I know the guy's face," I said. Satish froze, one foot on the doorstep, the other hanging behind. "You saw him too, way back, when we interviewed Lyons. He was standing by the door. Tall, lanky stutterer? Do you remember him, now? Viktor said he'll keep him talking. He's using a disposable cell, and as long as the cell is on, he's traceable. Viktor's got signal from two towers. Our guy hasn't been moving for the past twenty minutes. I can see him, just like the other night, sipping his coffee and browsing the Internet. He thinks he's safe, the son of a bitch. I can spot him out of a million faces. I've got his face, his clothes, his damn smell. The blue suits ain't got any of that."

We looked at each other. Two cops, two partners, two dicks butting heads.

I turned around and walked to the car. I opened the door, slid behind the wheel, and jammed the key into the engine.

I let the engine roar, my last word on the matter. As I shifted the stick onto driving, the passenger's door opened.

"Viktor's got the location right around the Hollywood

Vine station," Satish said. "Plenty of people, peak of the day, four cruisers patrolling. A needle in a haystack. *But* the signal's loud and clear."

He sent me a sideways glance. I grinned, put out the sirens and screeched into the street.

THIRTY-ONE

Decked in sunglasses, mikes, radio earplugs and black formal suits, Sat and I strode along the Hollywood sidewalk looking like the Men in Black. I told Satish that if some dorky tourist was going to stop us for pictures I'd pull out the Glock. He laughed and replied they'd think we were shooting a movie.

Above us, one of the Air Division choppers was on a perimeter, ready for a possible chase. We had the cruisers on the street, Viktor on the radio, guns in holsters, and roughly thirty thousand people roaming the Hollywood Walk of Fame. I'd dragged Satish on a one-in-a-million mission. I was still sore from the car accident. My brains simmered in the heat. Awakened, the Pain stirred around my loins.

We walked briskly, westbound on Hollywood Boulevard, from Vine toward the Kodak Theater. Past the shady smoke shops with loud rock music spilling out, past the drag queen store displays with whacky wigs and strip club costumes. Viktor's voice crackled in my ear bud. "Got a somewhat longer message, this time. He's definitely in the Hollywood and Highland area."

"Getting there. What did he say?"

"I asked him about XYPlot and DNA. That got him going. He thinks he's safe, the bastard, but the tower signal is pretty strong."

"Can you get an exact location?"

"As long as he keeps the wi-fi connection open I get regular updates on his location from the cell tower. The minute he turns it off we lose him."

"Shit, we're so close. Keep 'im talkin'."

"Sure thing."

The chopper's blades swooshed above us. The buildings got gaudier and taller, the billboards larger. They portrayed perfect smiles and fake lives. Right as we reached the escalators to the Hollywood Metro Station, Viktor croaked on the radio again. "I've got him within twenty feet from your location."

I felt the excitement of the chase. *Twenty feet.* I spun around and inhaled. A cacophonic blend of smells hit my nose.

"Help!"

The crowd parted. A few rubberneckers stood ogling without uttering a word. One of the many fake Michael Jacksons froze in his walking robot pose.

"Help!"

Olive skin in a yellow summer dress, black hair tied up in a thick ponytail, well-shaped ankles balancing over high wedges, and dark eyebrows shot up in a high frown. Red lipstick matched the painted fingernails clutching anxiously to a pink teddy bear. The pink teddy bear didn't match.

"My child!" She brought a hand to her forehead. "Somebody took my child! Please, help…"

Damn it!

Satish shot his badge in the air. "Who took your child, ma'am?"

"I don't know —" She swallowed, turned around toward the escalators and waved a hand in a vague direction. "We just got out of the metro. We were holding hands and then she suddenly squirmed away. Oh God, it all happened so fast—" She started hyperventilating. Satish grabbed her arm and walked her to a bench. I tuned the radio to our frequencies and flagged down a cruiser.

"Did you see somebody take your child?" Satish asked.

The woman squeezed the teddy bear on her lap and rocked back and forth. "Her hand slipped out of mine. I turned but she wasn't there anymore. I barely saw her walking away, there was a man next to her, I think—I think the man was dragging her away, I tried to run, but… but… too many people, I just lost her! Oh God." She broke into tears.

I squatted down next to her. "What man? Do you remember him? Can you tell what he was wearing?"

She shook her head. "Not too tall. Blond, I think—"

The radio crackled in my ear. "I lost him!" Viktor's voice broke off. "I fucking lost him. He turned off the cell, the bastard!"

Jesus.

I yanked the teddy bear off the woman's hands and brought it to my nose.

"Sat," I yelled, "Cover the metro!" And then I ran.

* * *

The Kodak Center is a labyrinth of smells, a haystack where the faint trace of a five-year-old is a very fine needle. I crouched and sniffed, searching for her scent. Kids brush their hands along walls, stair railings, posts. I smelled everything, the delicate scent of her palms still strong on the teddy bear I was holding.

The sun glared, the crowds packed the sidewalks. I swore, jostled the German tourists in Hawaiian shirts and flip-flops and the flocks of Japanese with twelve-inch-long camera lenses and flowery sun umbrellas. I found a trace on the railing of the Highland staircase and swam upstream against a tide of loud Italians drenched in expensive perfumes. I sauntered across the stands in the shopping plaza, looking for the trace. A young man with a putty crest offered me a cell phone. An artificial blonde in high heels and low skirt disapproved of my pink teddy bear.

The fountain jets swished up from the middle of the plaza and gargled. Kids in their bathing suits played tag with the water, shreds of laughter floating up like bubbles. Up on the walkways across the three-story archway, between the standing elephants of the Babylon set, tourists elbowed one another to take pictures of the Hollywood sign. I ran to the bottom of the stairs, sniffed, found no trace, came back, picked it up again in the alley down to the Grauman's Chinese Theater. A tiny hand had brushed along the wall at about my waist's height.

Down the stairs I went.

Tourists buzzed like bees in a beehive. Heads, baseball caps, feet in sandals, jeweled arms, naked shoulders, too much cleavage, too little clothes.

A child's face emerged and smiled at me.

Wrong scent. Her mother gave me a scornful look and pushed the child away.

The trace, damn it.

I lost the trace.

I peeked down the street but there was nothing to see or smell except gas exhaust and the scent of the flowers and candles people had left at Michael Jackson's star.

I stood in the middle of the plaza, hands hooked on my belt, sweat pooling around the small of my back and trickling down my forehead. Panting. The sun glistened in my face, teasing. The Pain sneaked up on me, one short flare, and then it was gone.

The airy voice of a flute soared from a corner, shyly at first, as if looking for its way through the crowds. It came with a faint, delicate scent.

A child's scent.

I craned my neck.

Sitting on a bamboo stool, between the white lion statue and the orange pillar, was a small man with a long, white beard, and a hat made of balloons on his head. A plastic flower poked out of the breast pocket of his long, linen blazer.

The girl was sitting on the ground in front of him, mesmerized. She watched his fingers move up and down the flute keys, her lips slightly parted, her thin brows pinched with admiration, oblivious of her desperate mother, of the cops scattered around looking for her, of the world loudly spinning around her.

And right there, under the scorching sun, watching this little girl completely transported by the music, I had an epiphany. One of those moments that only happens once in a lifetime, when suddenly you see it all with such sharp clarity it hurts. The catharsis of the truth, after which emptiness sneaks up on you like a mugger, like the silence that comes after the last note of *Autumn Leaves*.

That's when it hit me. Hard.

What a fool I'd been. A fool who'd been fooled so well. The solution had been in front of me all along and I'd failed to see it.

The music stopped, the man smiled and offered the girl

a balloon.

I smelled my partner behind me a moment before he spoke. "That the girl?"

I nodded.

"No kidnapper?"

"Don't think so. She probably got lost and started wandering on her own." I gave him the teddy bear. "I'd double check on the clown just in case."

Satish walked to the girl and stooped down. She took the teddy bear nodding her head up and down, big tears rolling down her cheeks. Satish picked her up and she wrapped her arms around him. As they turned, the man with the balloon hat waved at her. She waved back. Brave little kid.

An officer stayed with the man to ask him some questions.

Satish walked past me.

"Sat," I called.

He kept walking and didn't reply.

"I know where to find him, Sat."

He stopped, turned, and gave me a hard look. "I don't care what you *think* you know, Track. We're done chasing ghosts."

THIRTY-TWO

Moonbeams blinked over the pool surface like pale smiles. All around, banana and eucalyptus trees whispered scents of cool summer nights. Water lapped with the monotony of silent prayers. The ocean echoed it with its distant roar.

An engine whirred noiselessly at the end of the road. Headlights bobbed up and down, vanished for a moment, then reappeared. A yellow light flashed, the gate opened. Tires tore up the driveway. The gate rattled and closed. The light at the gate stopped flashing.

The engine died and the headlights faded, their halo lingering in the night one moment longer.

A figure stepped out of the vehicle, locked it, walked over to the door. Decisive steps, a brisk, solid tap thrumming in the night. The tinkling of keys, the clicking of a lock. The moon pooled down the man's head and shoulders in different shades of silver. The squeak of a door opening.

I stepped out of the shade. "Good to see you, Dr. Lyons."

He jumped, the key bunch fell off his hands.

His face squirmed. "Detective..." I smelled panic. A whiff, then it was gone and the cool Doctor Lyons was back. He kept his eyes on me as he stooped down to retrieve the keys. When he leveled me again he looked over his shoulder.

I smiled. "It's just me, Doc. Didn't bring company."

"How did you get past the gate?" He didn't sound angry. Just surprised.

I showed him the key. I wondered if he recognized it. "Unfortunately, you didn't leave the door open for me, so I had to wait outside. I waited quite a while, in fact. Drink?"

He agreed because he didn't have a choice.

The house was cooler than I remembered. It looked emptier, too, even though all it appeared to be missing was a wife. Her things were still there, where I'd seen them last time. A handful of women fiction books on otherwise empty shelves. A vase of wilted flowers. Sporadic knick-knacks of feminine taste. Her photographs.

Lyons flipped the light switches as he crossed the first living room, then the second, then the dining room with the see-through fireplace. Our images reflected off the glass panes, the pitch dark outside broken by an arch of garden lights and the lampposts looming behind the property wall. The face of the moon emerged from a thin shroud of clouds and glimmered over the fringes of the palm trees.

It was a peaceful sight.

Lyons swung his black briefcase on the kitchen countertop then stood there rolling up his sleeves while covertly examining me. "All I got is scotch," he said, coldly.

"That'll be fine."

He studied my face—I held his gaze—then slowly

walked to the wet bar. I watched him wash his hands, pull down the glasses, fill them with ice. The Venus replica watched him too, from her corner. She seemed to lean farther than last time, her stone eyes harder. Or maybe she was just trying to get away from the recessed light that beamed in her face. I gave her a sympathetic look. She didn't reciprocate.

Lyons turned, two drinks in his hands.

We sat, he on the couch in front of the fireplace, I on the recliner at the other end.

He sipped then asked, "What brings you here tonight, Detective?"

I clinked the ice in my glass. "We're looking for a colleague of yours."

He looked into his glass. "Medina. I've heard. His mother shot herself — is that so?"

I nodded — that was the story given to the press.

He took another swig, smacked his lips. It was good scotch. "Didn't show up at work today. But that much you know already." He scratched his temple. "It's uh — a bit of a shock, really. Medina's one of my best people. Associate researcher, I should say. He's got a Ph.D." He stared at me as if the information should've made a difference. I tried to look as if it made a difference. He sighed and leaned back on the couch, the glass of scotch snuggled in his hands. "I don't understand why he'd vanish like that. Something really grave must've happened. I trust him."

"Of course you do. He does all your dirty work."

He dwindled for a moment then quickly regained his temper. A nervous titter surfaced between the sides of his goatee. "Yes," he said. "Indeed. Sequencing and aligning DNA can be one of the dirtiest and most tedious tasks you can think of."

I joined his titter like a good ol' pal, drained my glass,

then clinked the ice a bit more. "Seriously, Doc. You have no idea where he could be hiding?"

He frowned, all humor suddenly drained off his face. He cocked his head backwards. "Hiding? You think he's implicated in his mother's death? Medina was devoted to his mother. Her days were numbered, she was holding to a thin thread. I'm not surprised she killed herself, given the circumstances."

I tapped a finger on the glass. "Maybe I should reword the question. Where are *you* hiding Hector Medina, Dr. Lyons?"

His brow shot up. The rest of him remained still. I inhaled. *The spice of adrenaline.* Could be fear, could be deception. The same finger that had scratched his temple came down to the corner of his mouth and brushed the sides of his goatee. Slowly, thoughtfully. Then the leer came back, not fully, like a minute earlier, more cautiously, rather. Testing grounds.

"I see," he said. "That's why you came here. You think Medina came to me." He brought the glass to his mouth, took a long drag, then cupped it with both hands and smiled a sad and thoughtful smile. "Why would I be *hiding* my lab assistant, Detective?"

That was an easy question to answer. "Because you still need him. Because you're nobody without him. You don't have a vaccine, you never had one. Medina did it all. I saw his lab notes. I saw more than I ever wanted to see."

I watched him take the news, his body posture, the change in perspiration. He sat with his elbows propped on his knees, staring at the ice in his glass. His jaw twitched. Then, suddenly, his eyes darted to the wet bar.

I pressed on. "You had one brilliant idea, Doctor. Fifteen years ago. It made you famous. You finally proved what had been controversial for so many years. HIV causes

AIDS. You had it. It was all yours. And then, after that, your muse dried up. Grant money shifted to other groups, your lab shrunk. Lyons wasn't coming up with good research any more. The papers you published afterwards were flops."

He listened quietly. "So?" he said. "Year after year the NIH has continued to cut funds. Every lab in this country experienced the hardship, not just mine." He shot his eyes to the wet bar again, coupled with a spike in adrenaline. His hands tensed around the glass. His jaw twitched. He looked away from me, and, rolling the glass between his palms, asked, "What are you getting at with this?"

"I'm getting to a killer. More than one, in fact."

He shot to his feet and so did I. "I need another drink," he said, sharply.

Before he could come around the coffee table, I stepped in front of him and took the glass from his hands. "Let me do the honors," I said. Whatever he'd eyed at the wet bar, I wasn't going to wait and find out.

I didn't fill the glasses. I set them on the edge of the sink, turned around, and kept my eyes on the man. He flopped back on the couch and rubbed his face. He didn't make eye contact. He just sat there. Maybe he knew what was coming.

"So, you teamed up, Medina and you," I pressed. "He was the brains, you were the authority to endorse the ideas and make them happen."

"What's wrong with that?" he mumbled, without effort.

I thought I smelled something. Vaguely. I inhaled. It was gone. I focused on my speech. "Nothing's wrong with that until it crosses paths with murder."

His shoulders shook, his head with them. He was laughing, a sad, dry laughter that had long lost all its amusement. "It's the second time you've said that, Detective. I think I've made it clear that I've been the victim in all this. I lost a patient, a wife and a dear colleague."

"That was the plan." I leaned against the wet bar, right hand close to my holster. I knew he was unarmed but I also assessed him for a solid man, in good shape, and quite capable of putting up a good fight. "If anything were to go wrong, you were going to play the victim and Medina was to take the blame. Of course, Medina didn't know this."

The smell came back. A fluttery, vaguely sweet, vaguely rotten wisp of a human scent.

Lyons stood up, shoved a hand in his pockets, and walked toward me. Casually, as if trying to think things over. "And this plan of mine, as you call it," he said, one finger drawing a circle in the air. "Where exactly did it go wrong?"

My turn to leer. I bobbed my head. "Oh, it was perfect. The weapon, the set-up, the whacko killer motive. A French catheter—who would've thought of that? Strong, smooth, kills fast with virtually no telltale. Very clever, Doc."

He looked amused. I'm sure, deep inside, his ego felt flattered. I could smell it. He stood close to the Venus replica and put a hand on her waist. It was a sensual gesture, as if he were about to invite her to dance.

"Very clever, Doc," I repeated. "Almost perfect."

The "almost" jarred him. His fingertips pressed hard around the marble of the statue and became white.

"It takes a strong, steady hand to strangle with a French catheter," I said. "A hand Medina didn't have."

He kept his eyes on Venus's feminine navel. He caressed it, softly. "No?"

"No. Medina has Morgellons disease, a mostly psychotic condition that causes his hands to bleed. He's in constant pain. He wouldn't have the strength to hold the ligature for so long. No, Doc. Medina didn't strangle the victims. *You* did."

The sound was almost imperceptible to human ears, but

not to mine. The smell drifting to my nostrils—I finally recognized it. Medina had been hiding in Laura's home office. The door opened a crack, enough to release his scent. I turned to face him, and it was a mistake. Lyons grabbed the Venus by her waist and shoved her toward me. The statue hit the wet bar and split in half. The gracious goddess of love weighed a ton on me. I stumbled back and fell on the floor, my limbs still wacky and sore from last night's car accident. I heard a noise, like a drawer slamming. I rolled the lady over, and as I pushed myself up there was a flash and then sharp pain shot up my spine and took hold of every nerve in my body. I coiled, my limbs as tense as wrung rope, and yet I couldn't stop shaking, an invisible wire tied around me, squeezing.

Click, click, click, click, click.

I flopped on my stomach like a curled leaf.

No, it wasn't The Pain.

The fucker was hiding a Taser behind the wet bar.

THIRTY-THREE

"Damn you, Medina. You almost fucked up everything."

A door slid open. Medina's smell came in full view. More rotten and more sour. He was scared, now. "You k-killed him?"

"You think I'm nuts? He's a cop!"

I groaned. A few of my nerves went on shaking on their own. The rest of me refused to move.

I smelled Lyons hovering over me. Then I felt his cold touch.

"Got a good blow to the head," he said. "He's tough, though. He'll come back soon."

He went right back at it with the Taser, the bastard. Five more seconds of hell. This time I didn't even bother groaning. I figured I was pathetic enough. He dropped the Taser, stooped down again, and slid my Glock out of the holster.

Medina's heavy breathing, approaching from the other

side. A fist took ahold of a chunk of my hair. It pulled. "You know, his DNA —"

"Forget it." Lyons's steps, brisk, business like, moving away.

Medina let go of my hair and stood up. "Where are you going?"

Lyons's voice, from a different room. "Keep an eye on him!"

Water rushing — a bathroom. The tip of my fingers tingled.

Medina's steps, softer than Lyons's, tentative. More noises, clinking of glasses, rolling of drawers. Cabinet doors slamming closed.

"What are you doing?" Medina whispered.

Funny how he was no longer stuttering.

"I'm doing what I should've done all along. Potassium chloride. He's going to have a heart attack, nice and smooth. We'll call nine-one-one, and by the time he gets to the hospital he'll be happily knocking at heaven's gates."

"What? Waste him like that? Don't you get it? I saw his expression levels, from some blood tests he had done a few weeks ago. It's amazing! I've never seen anything like that. His sense of smell, his eyesight, everything. The number of pseudogenes expressed in his tissues is comparable to that of a —"

"I don't give a fucking shit, Medina!" Lyons's leather soles tapped out of the bathroom. "I'm done playing your games."

"They're *not* games. My HIV vaccine —"

"*Your* vaccine, Medina? Yours?" The voice turned, sharply. "You fool. You're nothing without my money and my name, Medina. Nothing. Your ideas are worth two cents without the money to implement them."

A sharp air intake. The acrid smell of rage. A snap —

latex gloves.

The tingling spread to my arms. I rushed it and moved a muscle. He saw it and zapped me again. Ten seconds, this time. Ironically, I was getting used to it. And I learned my lesson.

They stood, watching me cringe. Like they watched Amy and Laura.

"We could still use him," Medina said. "Let me have some hair sam—"

"Shut up!" A smack vibrated in the air like a strung cord. A thump, the drag of furniture. "I don't give a shit about his genes, okay? I should've used potassium chloride all along. You and your stupid super-human ideas. You had to harvest your fucking samples." Lyons walked away then came back. "Let's make it look like a wacko did this," he said, in a falsetto voice. "Nobody will suspect accomplished medical professionals! Look where it got us. All I wanted was to shut their mouths, and the potassium would've done that. A poke and we were done."

"You're deluding yourself." Medina, his voice low, near the ground. "The M.E. would've found the poke."

Lyons laughed. An evil, perverse laughter. "You're so naïve, Medina. You wanted hair? I'll tell you what you do with hair. You hide the poke, you fool. A nice, tiny poke at the base of the skull." His steps came toward me.

"The tox results will find it!"

The voice's temperature dropped below freezing. "How the hell did I ever think you were so smart, Medina? Potassium chloride is naturally found in the blood, that's anatomy one-oh-one, you stupid fool."

A pause. Soft, unidentified noises, like nameless colors. Then Lyons's voice, again. "Check your watch. We'll call the parameds ten minutes after the shot."

Lyons walked around me to the wet bar. His shoes came

into view, shifting by the sink, as if he were rinsing something. No water was running, though. Behind me, Medina didn't move. He whined like a little boy. "I could've used his bones. His hair at least, the lining of his nose for the olfactory receptors..."

No more noises. Only Medina's relentless whine. "His heart, his muscle tissue. The brain, imagine what we would've found in his brain..."

Lyons's feet turned and spread apart. After that, they stopped moving. A subtle click.

"Every neuron would've been — what are you doing?"

"You're annoying me, Medina. You're a genius but too much of a whiner."

The pop was loud. A second one followed, then deafening silence and the smell of gunfire. Medina wasn't whining anymore.

"There, you traitor. For planting Amy's photo in my kitchen."

Lyons's shoes walked toward me. He stooped down, checked my pulse. I saw his knees, his crotch. I fantasized drilling a full-metal jacket in that crotch of his.

"Nice job, Detective," he said. He wrapped my fingers carefully around the Glock's butt. "You caught Medina *in flagrante*. You shot him, all right. And then you got so excited, you had a heart attack." He clicked his tongue in pity, his face so close to my back I felt his breath down my neck. "Too bad, isn't it?"

Lyons made sure the gunpowder from my Glock transferred to my hand, then slid it out of my fingers and took it away.

His shoes went back to the wet bar, then came back. His gloved hands held up a syringe. He grasped the hair at the crown of my head with his left hand. A drop of chilled liquid from the needle fell on my skin. I held my breath.

It felt like hauling a rock, but it was just my arm. I swung my elbow in his nose — it wasn't a hard blow, but the surprise effect covered where I lacked. I sent him rolling off, then slid the revolver out of my ankle holster, pulled the trigger and blew his face off. And then fired again.

"There," I said. "Two for Medina, and two for you. Next time remember that cops always carry a backup gun, you idiot."

And then I collapsed backwards, tension washing off from my body like summer rains. My jaw started chattering. It was an eerie sound. Kinda funny, actually. *Idiot forgot to check for my backup.* I tittered. My teeth rattled.

I rolled on the floor and laughed my head off. And that's how Satish found me.

How much later, I couldn't tell.

THIRTY-FOUR

Wednesday, July 22

There were two loud pops, then a thump, then the crackling of static.

It was more of a *rattling* rather than a crackling, but the recording was bad enough that nobody but me noticed. Which was good.

Lieutenant Gomez pressed the STOP button, removed his reading glasses, and rubbed his bulging eyes. His pate shone under the fluorescent light. The little hair he had at the sides of his head stuck out. He smelled of chamomile and interrupted dreams.

A fan spun silently on the ceiling. From the top of a dented metal filing cabinet, the fax machine whirred and spit out the ad for a one-in-a-lifetime Hawaiian dream vacation.

Satish sat in the chair to my right, one leg bent, the other stretched ahead of him. He rested his chin on the L between his thumb and his index finger, so he could look straight ahead at the Lieu and not at me.

To my left, cozily settled in the two chairs against the wall, were my old pals, the FID officers—Force Investigation Division. They smelled of nicotine and doughnuts and convenience store shaving cream. I got to spend some quality time with them last year, over another couple of officer-involved shootings. They were my guardian angels. Every time I squeezed the trigger, they came down from heaven.

One sat with his arms hooked at the back of the chair, his legs crossed, and a sneer plastered on his face. He rocked slowly on the hind legs of the chair. The recording of the Taser clicking made his sneer widen. His pal took notes throughout the recording. From time to time he lifted his head, pointed his pencil and asked Gomez to rewind the tape. He had some issues when Lyons and Medina walked off to the bathroom. Their voices came and went in distant barks, so I had to repeat to him the conversation as best as I could recall it. He took notes, tapped his pencil, took more notes.

At the end of the recording there was a moment of silence, after which Gomez swiveled back in his chair and inhaled. His wide and short hands clutched the edge of the desk. "The wire?" he said to me. "Good idea."

I offered a smile.

Unsurprisingly, he didn't smile back. "Confronting the suspect by yourself?" He leaned forward across the desk and locked his eyes into mine. "Fucking dumb."

The FID dicks snickered. The taller one pushed the chair backwards and leaned it against the wall. He wasn't wearing a tie, only an electric blue shirt, the collar unbuttoned to show a thick, bull-like neck that widened into flaps every time he flexed his muscles. Specks of dandruff glistened on the electric blue.

Gomez's eyes shifted to Satish. My partner didn't look at me. There comes a time when your partner is not allowed to cover your ass. Satish cleared his throat. "We had a— divergence of opinions."

Gomez's brow shot up in his bald forehead. "You advised your partner against this—" He waved his reading glasses at me. "—suicidal mission of his?"

"Correct."

Gotta love my agency. You can do a thousand things right, but if you make one mistake, sure as hell, it's the one mistake they'll never forget. I didn't know what was worse, the FID dicks snickering behind my back, or my partner tale-telling me to the LT.

To hell with all of them.

"I was right about Lyons," I said. "And Medina *was* the Volvo driver I'd chased down Valley. I'm sure when our people crack Medina's computer at the hospital, they'll find—"

"Two men down, Track!" Gomez's face turned the color of red beets. "You could've been one of them!" He swallowed, slid on his reading glasses, then took them off again, pinched the bridge of his nose and squeezed his eyes closed. "Will you ever—*ever*—be able to close a case following the usual police procedural, Detective Presius?"

I opened my jaw then closed it again. "Is that a rhetorical question?"

The tall FID dick stopped leaning backwards and the chair's front leg came to the floor with a loud thud. "That's how cowboys conduct investigations," he said.

Gomez's sense of humor was significantly impaired at two in the morning. Not that it was much better during the day.

I didn't care either way. In a little over twenty-four hours I'd slammed my car into a tree and torched it, found one and a half cadavers—plus bits and pieces here and there—got slammed to the floor by a faithful replica of the Venus de Milo, been Tased three times, and got this close to being poked with a lethal injection.

My sense of humor was so primed I could feel myself dropping to the floor and rolling in laughter all over again any minute, just out of sheer joy for being alive.

Gomez pushed his chair backwards and got up. Four sets of eyes rose with him. He scratched his bald head, looked down on his desk, found nothing of interest, pulled the chair back behind his ass and sat down again. Four sets of eyes lowered.

The FID's pencil resumed squeaking on paper.

Gomez grabbed a pen and rolled it between his fingers. "We've got two medical professionals down," he said. "Together, they cooked up a serial killer M.O. and perpetrated heinous crimes." He paused, swallowed, rolled the pen. "Medina was a sociopath. The body parts found in the freezer of his mother's house fit the bill. Lyons, though—Lyons was a big shot. A recipient of the National Medal of Science. The press is going to howl at us. And all we have on him is—this." He tapped the handheld recorder I'd worn inside my shirt.

I shifted forward in the chair and clutched my knees. "And the paper draft," I said.

"What paper draft?"

"The paper that Medina wrote and Amy penciled all over because it was wrong."

The paper missing from Amy Liu's home office, the one I'd later found in Lyons's office, and then again in Medina's shrine. I couldn't understand Amy's corrections, but I knew exactly who could. *Diane.*

"Amy Liu was a young MD in Lyons's group. She also happened to be his lover, but that's a different story. People like Lyons use sex like us dicks use cigarettes. Anyway, Amy was collecting data for a vaccine trial, a vaccine that Lyons had patented based on ideas spurred from the sick, yet brilliant mind of Hector Medina. The two sold the patent to a company named Jank Biologicals. The vaccine yielded terrific results in monkeys, yet the FDA wouldn't approve the vaccine until Lyons made the brave move of injecting himself and attracting a lot of attention. The vaccine was finally approved and Jank started producing it for the clinical trials. The patent money barely scraped the surface. Lyons and Medina were in for the big bucks—shares. Lyons had become a hero, his study was featured all over the media. Jank shares soared. Lyons was finally collecting."

I looked around me. They were all listening, so I went on. "Phase I went smooth—all they had to show was the vaccine was safe, which they knew already. I think the problems started with phase II. The pilot study showed that the vaccine wasn't working—that's what Amy found out when she reviewed the data in Medina's draft."

The FID taking notes raised his pencil. "Was the vaccine harmful?"

I knew the answer because Diane had explained it to me. "No. They would've halted the study if that were the case. It wasn't harmful, but it wasn't working either. Amy tried to prove it, when she requested Callahan's samples—she wanted to see what went wrong in his case. She confronted Lyons with the data in her hands. Lyons, though, had other plans. He'd started selling Jank's stocks. He had already made millions, but he wasn't quite happy yet. He'd bought a house in Malibu and a bunch of luxury cars—the expenses were adding up. He wanted more money, money that he knew he could squeeze out of the Jank's stocks—which kept soaring—for a little bit longer, at least until the truth about the vaccine came out."

"So Callahan's death tipped Amy Liu?" Satish asked.

"No, Amy found out on her own. She needed samples from Callahan to prove it, and she used them to confront Medina and Lyons. Lyons of course knew what needed to be done: shut Amy's mouth for good. Medina, though, had his own ambitious plans. The freak wanted to apply the same powerful idea behind the HIV vaccine to human genetics. He wanted to create a super-human by tiling together DNAs from different individuals. So, instead of wasting cadavers, why not enact a lunatic serial killer and get some experimental samples while they're at it? Two pigeons with one stone. In fact, as we'll find out a little later in the story, Medina's had a little practice of his own already."

There was a tap. I turned, and the FID taking notes pointed his pencil at me. "Why fake data? That's stupid if the vaccine turned out not to work."

"The truth was going to come out eventually. Lyons would've had to admit that the vaccine wasn't working. Things like that happen all the time: great results in monkeys that do not reproduce in humans. All Lyons wanted was more money from the Jank stocks. He wanted to push the trial longer so he could sell more stocks, at a higher price. He had Laura on his side—who'd borrowed money from her mother to buy shares—and he probably tried to convince Amy, too. Maybe he offered her money. Amy didn't want to hear it, though. She wanted to halt the trial, start over with a new vaccine, one she'd designed herself."

I paused, looked around. They were all quiet, staring at me. The pencil scribbled on the notepad. Gomez rolled the pen and bulged his eyes. The fan swooshed, the crack in the open window let the night breeze drift in, together with the distant snore of a half-asleep freeway. I resumed my account. "The night of Amy's party Lyons leaves with all other guest. He then comes back. Amy's waiting for him, waiting for her lover. Little does she know, she's meeting her assassin instead. Medina attacks her with the acid, Lyons finishes her by strangling her with a French catheter — the perfect ligature, leaves virtually no telltale mark."

"How do you know it was Lyons?" FID dick again. Had to keep up the pace for his notes.

"You heard it on tape. Medina had a skin condition called Morgellons disease. His hands and feet bled regularly. His lab notes were spotted with bloody fingerprints. His hands hurt, he wouldn't have had the strength to strangle a woman. Lyons didn't deny it when I confronted him."

"He didn't admit it, either."

I held his gaze and decided to ignore the remark. "Medina flees, Lyons has a change of heart and calls nine-one-one. Maybe he panics. Maybe it's part of the plan because he's such a die-hard macho he thinks he can tease us and never be caught. I thought of asking him but as you know things got out of hand. His voice is on tape. That word he uses — abraded — is his signature."

"Why kill the wife if she was in on it too?" Gomez asked.

"Laura freaked out after Amy died. She was in for the money, not for murder. Amy had left a message on Lyons's voice mail about Medina's paper, a message that Laura picked up instead of its intended recipient. I found out one night when I examined Amy's phone logs. Of course, at the time I didn't know the kind of message Amy had left on Lyons's machine. When Amy was killed, Laura must've guessed that both Medina and her husband were behind the murder. So now there was another woman who needed to be shut up. By now, the show had been well rehearsed. Lyons steps out of the house to take his daily swim, leaving the front door open. Medina has both a key and the passcode to the property gate—same key I used to get through Lyons's property gate. I found it in a drawer at his mother's house. Medina attacks her with the acid, Lyons strangles her, then Medina does his sampling thing—something I believe he enjoys very much."

Satish rapped his knuckles on the armchair. "He kept all that stuff in his garage... why?"

"Because in his sick mind, Medina was a genius," I said. "He wanted to create a genetic super-human by piecing together the genomes of all his victims. A *mosaic* of genomes, which is probably what gave him the idea of the mosaic tiles."

And that's why he came after me, I thought, but didn't say out loud. Me, the chimera, the one who impersonated his genetic dream.

The best of trophies.

"What about the babies?" Gomez asked. "They also had been attacked with acid. By whom?"

"Right. The babies." I looked at the wall clock ticking above Gomez's shiny head. It was two thirty a.m. I was tired, very tired. My muscles felt numb from the Taser. I slowly got up, walked to the water fountain by the American and Californian flags, filled a paper cup, then returned to my chair. "So, now we get to Medina's pathetic story and why he enjoyed playing the part of the whacko serial killer."

The FID leaning back against the wall let go of the chair again and again the front legs hit the floor with a thud. "He *was* a serial killer."

"He had a good teacher—his mother. Lyanne Norris was a single mom when she had Medina. She gave him his dad's last name, but the dad never came back to meet his son. Several other men came back instead, at various times, and enjoyed Lyanne's company under the sheets. Maybe there were some regulars who lasted long term, I've no idea. Lyanne got pregnant regularly, killed the babies, and dumped sulfuric acid on their faces. Medina must've assisted to some of the killings. I don't know what that can do to a child's brain—watching your mother kill your own siblings. He visited the dumpsite regularly. There were animal bones scattered around. I'm guessing he killed them, pets and wildlife, before he graduated to humans. Maybe that's how he got the idea of killing his first victim, Gloria Weiss, a twelve-year-old run away gone missing two years ago."

"Two years later, he struck again: this time he chose an elderly woman, Katya Krikorian. Katya's son hired me to find her when she went missing last May. She was a friend of Lyanne's, her only friend, in fact, according to Lyanne's nurse." I turned over to Satish. "The neighbor yesterday told us the nurse had quit, remember that?"

He nodded, wearily. "I spoke with her over the phone. Apparently Lyanne was no palsy-walsy. The nurse couldn't take it no more and quit last week. She'd left a note for Medina but never heard back from him."

I resumed my story. "When I interviewed the nurse the first time, I asked her if she had any idea why Katya would leave her car one mile away from Lyanne's house. The nurse didn't know but told me that she'd overheard the two talk about hiking places in the area. Katya liked to hike and Lyanne, for some awkward reason, had suggested the trail to the water cistern. The nurse also mentioned that Katya had on numerous occasions complained about the state

Lyanne was in and recommended calling social services — at the time I hadn't made much of the comment, but it's easy to see now how that would've pissed off Medina. He must've been happy with a nurse who minded her own business and only had limited time in the house."

Gomez rippled his wide forehead. "Why would Lyanne recommend hiking up to the cistern? Regrets?"

"Her days were numbered and Katya was her only friend. Maybe it was her attempt to a confession. She probably had no idea her son was a regular visitor at the cistern. Medina, on the other hand, was worried Katya would've called social services. Maybe she even threatened to do so that at some point."

I took a breather and drained the water in my cup. Nobody talked. A chair squeaked, a loud thud followed. The tall FID dick was back on four legs, staring at me.

"You satisfied?" I said.

He twitched his jaw. "For now," he replied.

His partner tapped his notebook. "We'll write a report on the incident and call you when it's ready for you to review. We need to include the autopsy reports, the gun residue analysis, and all the likes. You know the drill."

Hell I do.

They got to their feet and scrambled to the door. Electric Blue Shirt saluted me before heading out. "Till the next one, cowboy," he said with the usual smirk.

"Asshole," I mumbled, and met Gomez's flaring glare, eyes bulging underneath two rolls of scrunched forehead and brows. He was still rolling the pen between his fingers. Had it been an axe maybe he'd already have thrown it at me.

"I'm not satisfied, Track."

"I figured."

Gomez steered his bulging orbs to Satish. "How did you

370

know where to find him?"

Satish straightened up. "Forensic scientist Diane Kyle called me."

"I'd left the paper with her," I said.

Sat nodded. "That's what she said. She also said that together you figured out about the faked data. And that you left in a hurry and she could no longer get ahold of you. She worried you'd do something stupid."

Gomez's frown relaxed for a fraction of a second. "What do you know? He *did* do something stupid."

We fell silent, the word "stupid" bobbing in the air between us like a buoy. The pen rolled, the fan swooshed, the freeway droned. And then, all of a sudden, Gomez shot to his feet, walked to the door and opened it. "Out," he said. "I need to get some sleep. Report to me in the morning."

We shuffled out of his office and across the deserted squad room. It looked even more squalid in the middle of the night, with the scratched Formica desktops and the polyester ceiling panels. In the elevator lobby Satish jingled his car keys and rocked on his heels.

"Something's missing from your account," he said.

I frowned.

"Who killed Charlie Callahan and Courtney Henkins?"

The elevator doors rattled and opened. I stared into the small space that smelled of lubricant oil, old metal and dirty secrets. I shook my head and stepped inside. "I'm afraid we'll never find out, Sat. Or maybe we will. In twenty years, when the next Stephanie Lazarus will be unveiled without too many heads having to roll off."

* * *

The first sunrays were blinking through the treetops when I finally drove home. Chevy Chase was quiet, save the hissing of the garden sprinklers and the screeching of the jays. The morning air was still cool. I got out of my truck and inhaled the scent of oak bark, eucalyptus, and sage. I was exhausted, drained, and happy to be alive. I almost fucked up my job but that seemed no longer relevant.

Will was happy to see me alive, too. The King went as far as to hop down his windowsill to come meet me at the door. Life was back to normal.

I sang in the shower and hummed as I shaved. I dropped on the bed naked and fell asleep instantly.

A noise awakened me—the stupid sparrow that'd been trying to get through my window since the start of the summer. He'd littered the windowsill with his droppings and dented the screen. One of these days I was going to shoot him, but regretted having to pay for a new windowpane. I groaned, rolled over and something poked me in the stomach. I sprang my eyes open. It was noon, and I'd slept six hours straight over my own pile of dirty clothes. I sat up and picked up my pants. The holsters were empty, of course—the FIDs had sequestered both my guns pending the OIS investigation. I turned the pockets inside out. A long, white and cold, marble shard fell on the bed. I smiled. Had to bring a piece of Venus home—my latest trophy. I lifted it and caressed it. I tried to remember which part it belonged to but couldn't quite place it.

An image flashed before me. A lizard's red eye, ogling from a man's shoulder.

Vargas.

I'd completely forgotten about Ricky Vargas.

I jumped out of bed, pulled on a pair of briefs and picked up the phone. I was about to hang up when I finally heard a click. I heard nothing else so I shouted into the mouthpiece, "Hello? Detective Presius here."

"I hear you, Detective," Vicente Vargas replied. "But

you're too late to save my Ricky."

* * *

Friday, July 24

The sound of bells tolling is like a sad memory you can't manage to forget.

People spilled out of the white church in black dresses and suits. They filed down the stairs, the men looking grave, and the women crying. The air was hot and humid for California weather, the faces red and sweaty. They were all heavily scented, a blend of aftershaves and fragrances as loud and gaudy as a flock of parrots.

Maria Espinoza Vargas leaned on the arm of a young girl and almost collapsed. Two men held her from behind. The crowd got thicker around her. Maria shook her head and waved them away. She had strong bones in her face, and deep eyes that had seen everything and weren't as terrified of death as they were of human beings. Her heavily made up face had creased and smeared and melted in black tears.

The pallbearers emerged from the depths of the church and brought the coffin outside.

Maria shrieked, "Mi hijo!"

The coffin bobbed down the stairs. Parked in front of the church, the hearse's engine whirred. The bell tolled, and the white wreaths withered under the sun. A layer of haze lingered in the air like an incoming migraine.

The pallbearers pushed the coffin inside the hearse, placed a wreath of white carnations at its foot, and closed the vehicle's door. A man waved and the hearse started moving. Behind it, Maria walked and shrieked. Two men walked beside her, holding her arms.

The rest of the crowd followed.

Vicente Vargas limped his way down the stairs, one eye looking at me, and the other following the hearse. He stood with the helpless dignity of a disarmed man in front of the enemy. I wasn't the enemy, but I was too late to prove it.

"That's my sister-in-law, Ricky's mom," he said. "She's a widow. My brother died when the kids were five and three."

"A shooting?"

He nodded, his head heavy on wide shoulders. His lazy eye looked lazier than I remembered. I wasn't sure which eye to stare at, so I watched the procession instead.

"I'm sorry," I said. I would've said more, but I didn't know what.

He looked down at his hands, wide and cracked and still caked with cement and hard labor. The cuffs of his blazer were worn out and a button was missing from the front. It smelled of weddings, baptisms, quinceaneras and funerals — too many funerals.

"*No paran,*" Vicente said quietly. "*No van a parar hasta que se maten todos. Dicen que fue un nene de trece años.*" He shook his head heavily again. "*Trece años,*" he repeated, shuffling away.

"I'm sorry," I mumbled again, but he was no longer listening.

I don't speak Spanish, and he never asked me if I did. Some things don't need translation.

A thirteen-year-old had shot and killed Ricky Vargas in a drive-by. In South Central, where life is survival, your first shooting marks your entrance to adulthood, and your first step toward the tomb.

In South Central, young lives were expendable, debts were paid through retaliation, and gangs haunted the streets, looking for a deal, a rock, a buck. Looking for trouble. Somewhere in South Central, somebody tonight was celebrating and Maria was crying. Somewhere in South Central, good and evil blurred, hunters and prey mingled, and today's killer became tomorrow's victim.

That's the soul of L.A., the city of angels and devils, of richness and poverty, of fires and mudslides. The city of opposites.

I walked back to my truck feeling the heaviness of defeat against a faceless enemy. I longed for revenge and yet I had nobody to hate but myself.

Ricky Vargas. Courtney Henkins. Charlie Callahan.

The bell stopped tolling. I started the engine and let it idle. My eyes strayed to the glove compartment. I popped it open and slid out Callahan's photo. After they'd ramped my house and I'd found the Byzantine's tiles in my backyard, I'd hidden the photo in my truck. I still didn't know what it meant, but I was fairly sure Charlie's killer knew.

I stared at the photograph.

Talk to me.

It didn't. Charlie Callahan smiled his happy, innocent smile. The beige couch, the meaningless poster behind him, the side table with the lamp, the ashtray, the reading glasses.

The reading glasses.

Red, with a famous logo on the temple. I knew I'd seen them before. And the ashtray. I brought the photo to my nose and inhaled. It wasn't just passive smoke. It was *expensive* passive smoke.

My thoughts rewound back. How did it all start? Callahan's dead body, a suspect, a conviction. The *wrong* conviction, yet after the incarceration of Malcolm Olsen, the case was closed.

Malcolm Olsen.

You hate it here, Detective, don't you? You hate it just like me, he'd said.

And then he'd given me a clue. *Nail polish.*

Something clicked at the back of my head.

Menthol. Kool cigarettes. Gas exhaust. Nail polish smell.

Reading glasses with a famous logo on the frame.

I placed the photo back in the glove compartment, backed out of the lot, and left the cemetery. Blood was pulsing to my head. I wanted revenge. I'd failed Ricky Vargas and I wanted revenge. And I knew exactly where to find it.

THIRTY-FIVE

Sunday, August 2

Runyon Canyon Park sprawls at the top of the Hollywood hills, above the growling belly of the city. From the south entrance, the main trail snakes up to Inspiration Point where people sit and watch the sun rise behind the San Gabriel Mountains. The sky turns pink and the clouds tumble over the basin like lost shreds of happiness. Noises are muffled and the air is crisp and smells of eucalyptus and sage and yucca. The steep incline is mottled with scrub oaks, toyon, red shanks, and sugar bush.

Not that Detective John Sakovich cares. He likes to come up here before anyone else does, so he can jog without worrying about his boxer getting into fights with other dogs. On his way home, he buys flowers for his wife. He showers and heads to work, stopping at Dunkin Donuts for his free coffee first. Such is the life of Detective John

Sakovich. A date, from time to time, to be kept strictly secret among his own circles. Circles of people like him, people who understand.

Like Captain Zoltek. He understands. Of course he does. Because Captain Zoltek has his own little problems that need to be fixed. Problems like Charlie Callahan. A mistake, rather. And Sakovich can take care of such mistakes. Tit for tat, one hand washes the other. A little harder when Henkins had to go too. The timing was perfect, though. Should things turn murky, the stupid RHD dick will go down. He'll make sure of it. No more mistakes.

The stupid RHD dick who's watching him now.

Only, he doesn't know.

I donned latex gloves and followed. One last star twinkled in the sky. A pale moon close to the rim of the mountains smiled. Detective John Sakovich hiked up the dirt road, his headlight headband bobbing in the last remnants of darkness. His boxer scuttled ahead, sniffed, peed, left his trace of odors for me and Will to follow. Covertly, unseen.

By the time Sakovich reached the top of the ridge the first light of dawn had started rimming the mountains. Scraped by palm treetops, the Hollywood hills blinked. The freeways hummed in the distance. Just out of LAX, an airplane scratched the sky.

The boxer barked.

Will leaped ahead and off the trail. I followed Sakovich's acrid sweat, impregnated of the one too many beers from last night, his menthol aftershave, his pack of Kools.

Nail polish.

There was a car that night. I saw it when I walked the dog. An Oldsmobile Alero, black, one of the older models. A guy was inside, smoking. When I walked back he was still there. Rolled up his window and left. And I smelled nail polish after the car.

Only somebody with a refined sense of smell would notice. I'd stopped at a 7-Eleven the night before, purchased a pack of Kools, lit one cigarette, left it burning on the pavement, by the car exhaust. The engine ran, the cigarette burnt. Combined with the gas exhaust, the menthol contained in the Kool cigarette, as it burnt, took on an acrid, synthetic tang.

Nail polish.

The boxer kept trudging behind.

"Come on, Max. Move on, buddy," Sakovich called.

Some persistent scent nagged Max's nostrils. Sakovich stopped to wait. The boxer didn't budge, his nose pointed to a bush off the trail. He sniffed, barked, then delved down the incline and disappeared in the brush.

"Fuck. Max!" Sakovich jogged back to the edge of the trail and looked down, the beam from his headlight lost in the vegetation. The incline was steep, an intricate mess of wild bushes, scrub oaks, and laurels.

"Max! Come back!"

Somewhere down the hill Max growled.

Sakovich bristled. "Coyotes!" he muttered, unholstering his revolver. "Fucking coyotes!" He left the trail and sauntered down the incline, gingerly at first, his path blocked by branches and twigs. Max yelped, Sakovich broke into a run, his large body wobbling over a rugged terrain of rocks and twisted roots.

It wasn't coyotes. It was Will, growling and gnarling, he and Max going in circles, flashing their teeth. I snapped on latex gloves. Sakovich raised his gun and aimed.

I pounced on him from behind, slammed him on the ground and crunched my boot over his hand. "Let go of the gun! Now!"

He squealed in pain. The minute he let go of the gun I picked it up and dug the barrel in the middle of his forehead right as he was trying to get up. He froze.

"Presius... What the hell you think you're doin'?"

"Avenging a fellow cop, you bastard! Get down!"

I made him lie down, face on the ground.

Eat dirt, piece of scum.

The dogs barked. I flew one round on the ground to scare them away, then got on Sakovich's back, knees planted on his ass and legs, and sunk the gun barrel in his neck.

The dogs scrammed.

"You'll pay for this, Presius," Sakovich spat.

"Did you look up my package, Sakovich?" I hissed.

"I — what?"

I twisted his right arm, pressed the gun harder. "My package!"

Dry leaves stuck to his mouth as he spoke. "I'm gonna ruin you, I swear. I'm gonna have you destroyed. Your career —"

"Did you look up my package?"

"Yes! I did! Fucking mental you are!"

"So then you know what I did to Danny Mendoza."

He didn't reply this time. His muscles tensed. I'd killed Mendoza when I was sixteen, carved the eyeballs out of his skull with a penknife.

I bent over and whispered in Sakovich's ear: "I'm gonna do the same thing to your pretty little dick."

He froze. I smelled a little bladder release. "You won't get away with it, Presius."

"You're a cop killer, Sakovich. You deserve to die."

Once a killer, always a killer.

The voice echoed in my head and gave me a chill. For a moment, the gun in my hand faltered. Sakovich sensed it and tried to buck. I kept him down and sunk the barrel deeper into his neck.

His voice cracked. "What—what the hell do you want, Presius?"

I stared at the gun in my hand. "Smart ass," I said. "You didn't bring the one you used to whack Henkins. Course not. Did you dump it in the riverbed? Or better even—down at the harbor?"

"What—I didn't—argh!"

"You bastard. You killed a fellow cop, fucking traitor." I pressed the barrel so hard the vein in his neck almost popped. "I wanna hear the whole story. Nice and slow, we got time. Sun's not even out yet. Start from Callahan and don't stop until I hear where you dumped the gun you used to whack Henkins."

He spat, almost choked on his words.

"Sorry," I said. "Didn't hear you. I believe we were talking about Callahan. Your Captain, Zoltek, found him on Craigslist. Nice find. Or were you the pimp? Whose screen name is mr_kam, yours or Zoltek's?"

KAM is the radio code for "end of transmissions." Only a fellow LAPD would've come up with that one.

Sakovich grunted. "That's bullsh—ARGH!"

I twisted his arm harder. "You saying?"

"H-how did you—"

"I did my homework, Sak. You see, there's a certain photo of Callahan in my possession, a photo taken at your boss's house. Nice red couch with the Niagara Falls hanging on the wall behind?"

"I've no idea what you're talking about."

"Fine. I'll give you a few hints, then. I'm gonna guess mr_kam was Zoltek's screen name on Craigslist. He hooked up with Callahan, had fun while it lasted, then Callahan got laid off and things went a little sour. Callahan needed money and decided to ask for some financial help from Zoltek. When Zoltek refused, the request turned into blackmailing. Zoltek complied for a while—pouring about five hundred bucks into Callahan's pockets every other week—until he got tired and hired you to get rid of the problem. Am I doing well so far?"

He squirmed. I held him down, gun pressed nice and hard to his jugular vein.

The bastard kept his mouth zipped, so I went on talking. "Getting rid of Callahan turned out to be fairly easy," I said. "You made sure Callahan's cellphone disappeared and planted a little meth in his pockets just to muddying the waters. Even got the perfect suspect to nail—the homophobic neighbor Malcolm Olsen. You forgot the picture, though."

"W-what picture?"

"The picture that connects Callahan to Zoltek. Let's assume Zoltek's wasn't as stupid as to bring Callahan to his house. He still made a mistake. He left his glasses on the coffee table next to Callahan. Extravagant glasses, the expensive kind. The kind I couldn't help but notice when I offered my condolences to Zoltek the day you guys interrogated me at Pacific Station. I'm sure the Captain appreciated the gesture, given he was the one who ordered you to shut Henkins up."

"Oh, come on. All this based on some glasses that anyone could—"

"I blew up the photo, Sakovic, and got a serial number on the frames. Did you know glass frames had serial numbers? Nice feature. Had to make about a dozen phone calls, but I finally found the legitimate owner of the glasses."

Sakovich screeched. "You can't—I don't believe you. It's private information, you need a warrant for—"

"Zoltek's glasses are in a photo with Callahan. Callahan gave the photo to a friend when he started fearing for his life. Zoltek fucked Callahan. Maybe you both fucked him, wouldn't be surprised by that. You both had fun while it lasted, then dumped him when you found out he was HIV-positive. And when Callahan threatened to become a problem, Zoltek ordered you to get rid of the problem."

"Can't prove it." He swallowed. "You're nuts, Presius. You're gonna pay for this."

I held him down at gunpoint and twisted his arm until the collarbone cracked. "I don't give a fuck, Sakovich. You're done. Say bye-bye to the world, you don't deserve to live a minute longer."

"No," he cried. "No, please. I'm sorry. I really am, Presius, I swear. What I did was wrong. Now don't be stupid and let me go. I'll turn myself in. I promise."

Now he was talking.

"Did you kill Callahan?"

He hesitated. I cocked the gun. His bladder released completely this time. The smell repulsed me.

"Yes! Yes, I killed Callahan. I strangled him that night. Snuck up from behind and strangled him."

"What did you do next?"

"What d'you think I did next?"

I clicked my tongue. "Did you look into his eyes, Sakovich? Did you watch him die as he—"

"Shut up! Fuck, Presius, he was a fag. Just another stupid fag who—"

"Who died looking straight into your eyes?"

He groaned, his forehead scrunched in pain. "I couldn't stare at his face, okay? There was a bottle of drain opener right there next to the trash. I grabbed it and poured it on his face. I—I just couldn't... I couldn't stand staring at his face."

His police badge was tucked in his arm sleeve, together with his cell phone. I yanked the strap off his injured arm, making him roar in pain.

"You don't deserve an LAPD badge, you bastard."

"I'm going to turn myself in! I swear! Just let me go and—"

"Not until you tell me where you dumped the firearm you used to kill Henkins."

"What? I didn't—"

I slammed his face down and pressed the gun harder against the back of his neck. He whimpered, bits of dead leaves stuck to his lips.

"Fine," he croaked, and then he told me. He'd sawed the barrel off the gun and then dumped it in a septic tank. The bastard. I thought of Henkins, slouched on her couch, sunken in her failures and her pride; Henkins who'd helped cover up a murder and then regretted it; Henkins who'd falsified evidence but never admitted her own mistakes.

You've been too harsh on her, Ulysses.

And now she's dead.

"Fucking bastard you are, Sakovich," I said. "She was drunk and unarmed. What kind of vicious snake are you to kill a fellow cop like that?"

His body tensed under mine. The reek of his perspiration peeked, his rage overcame his fear. "The vindictive bitch," he spat. "She deserved to die."

I inhaled, pulled the gun away from his neck.

"Finally," he said. "Now, gimme back—"

He never finished the sentence. I squeezed the trigger and shot him in the head. A single round, straight to the temple. His body jolted. His muscles twitched for a few more seconds and then slackened.

The roar of gunfire ebbed off and all I could hear was my heart, thumping.

A strange calm took over me. I looked down on Sakovich's body, his nose plastered with dirt, and a trickle of blood wiping down his temple.

"I was going to turn you in, Sakovich," I said. "But you made one mistake." I got off his back and snuggled his gun back into his right hand. "Next time show a grain of remorse."

I slid off the latex gloves and plucked my cell phone out of my arm strap.

"You still there?"

I'd dialed Satish's number one second before pounding on Sakovich. I had no idea if he'd picked up, no idea if he'd stayed on the line the whole time. I squeezed the phone against my ear, heart thumping in my chest, and only heard static.

"Fuck," I muttered.

"I'm here," Satish finally replied.

I exhaled. "Did you hear everything?"

"I did."

I breathed heavily, pain coiling around my lower back. "Then my task is done," I said, and hung up. I left it up to Satish to call the Force Investigation Division and turn me in.

Once a killer, always a killer, I thought, bitterly.

Maybe the shrink was right after all.

I heard the dogs howl in the distance. The sun had finally come out, and the golden light of sunrise twinkled through the leaves and whispered in the breeze.

The piece of scum had killed a fellow cop. He didn't deserve to live another day. He didn't deserve to live another hour, another minute.

I didn't look back. I just left.

THIRTY-SIX

Diane's breath had the intoxicating aroma of the Barolo I'd served over dinner. A shaft of yellow streetlight sneaked through a crack in the curtains and pooled over her face. She was beautiful, her hair spread over the pillow and her eyes tainted with a note of sadness. I sipped her lips and inhaled her breasts, my hands on a mission to untangle the bra clasp. One by one, I undid the front buttons of her shirt and kissed her skin as I uncovered it, little waves of goose bumps rising and falling along my path.

"You sure you don't want to go with me?" she whispered.

Traitor of a bra clasp bit my finger. "Where?"

She turned and looked away. "You know where. To Boston. To help me look for a new place."

It was midnight. Her flight was leaving in six hours.

"I'm not an East Coast kinda guy."

She sighed and slid a hand down my chest. "What kind of guy are you, Track Presius?"

"The kind that doesn't like to talk while making love."

I kissed her and she kissed me back and we stopped talking and made love instead.

We didn't talk while she made coffee, four hours later, or when she closed her suitcase. We didn't talk much along the drive to LAX, either. Small talk. The weather, how expensive it was to rent a place in Boston, where she was going to start looking. Cambridge, most likely. I nodded and said nothing. I walked her to the terminal just so I could kiss her one more time.

"Are you going back home?" she asked.

"No. There's something I need to take care of."

She got in the security line and turned one more time to smile before she disappeared in the midst of people, deodorants, morning breaths, and badly assorted fragrances. I left the airport with the odd feeling that there was another life I could've lived as an East Coast kinda guy and I would've enjoyed it and been happy, but the other life had closed its door and all I was left with was my West Coast kinda life.

* * *

Ricardo José Vargas's gravestone lay in an uneven patch of overgrown grass, underneath the wide shadow of a sycamore that looked old and wise the way some old and wise sycamores do. The gravestone was a rather inconspicuous piece of white marble with a plain cross and the dates 1990-2009 engraved underneath the name. It smelled peaceful and earthly. There were fresh flowers on it, carnations and white roses that the shade of the tree had kept away from the August sun. All around, scattered with no apparent order, were other gravestones, some as inconspicuous, and some as tacky as they come, sharing company with angels and Maries, and blue-eyed Jesuses.

Not even in death there's equality.

The expanse was partly enclosed by a two-foot-tall black metal railing that ran behind the tree and stopped at the top of a green mound with no apparent reason. From there, the green slope tumbled all the way down to a row of dogwoods covered in white blooms. A fat crow was having its morning breakfast with the berries scattered on the ground. Nobody else was around. It was just me, the crow, and the dead.

Quite a nice crowd.

I kneeled by the stone, took out my penknife, and traced a small square in the ground a little off to the right. I dug along the edge and cut the grass below the roots, removing the square as a whole. I looked over my shoulder and inhaled. The crow cawed. The wind carried no scent other than the grass and the sycamore leaves and the dogwood blooms. And the scent of the dead, which was probably in my head only, but I could smell it nonetheless. From my pocket, I took out a white handkerchief, unfolded it, took Sakovich's police badge, dropped it in the hole in the ground, and covered the hole again with the patch of grass.

I'm sorry, Ricky. I promised your uncle I would protect you, instead I failed you.

Ricky Vargas had made his first gang kill at age fifteen to prove he was a man. I looked at my life, at all the second chances I'd had, and now, standing in front of Ricky's tombstone, all I felt was regret.

I should've helped you get a second chance too.

The wind changed and brought new scents. New and familiar at the same time. I heard Satish's steps approaching a few seconds later. He stood next to me, held his hands together behind his back, and didn't utter a word. I kept my eyes on Ricky's tombstone.

"FID looking for me?" I asked.

The Force Investigation Division was going to have a blast with me this time.

Satish rocked on his heels, his perspiration coming and going in gentle waves. "No."

I pondered. "What about Sakovich?"

Satish looked down at the tombstone. "Suicide." His mouth was straight, his eyes hard, and yet I swear the man was smiling.

"You knew he wasn't going to turn himself in," he said.

I nodded. "I saw it in his eyes when I mentioned Henkins' name. He was going to bring me down on armed assault and hope to walk away with it."

Satish bobbed his head. He licked his lips, thought of something smart to say and came up with nothing.

"Listen to the radio, when you get the chance," he said at last. He saluted me, spun on his heels and walked away.

I stood there and stared at the grave for a long time and after I'd stood and stared for a long time, I turned around and left. Somewhere up on Olympus, Nemesis, the ruthless goddess of divine retribution, looked down on me and smiled. I'd just given up my trophy. It made me feel uneasy and a little lightheaded but somewhat proud of what I'd just done. I wondered if it made me any less human than I already was. I came to the conclusion that I didn't give a shit either way. Individuals like John Sokavich, Captain Zoltek, and Frederick Lyons weren't any more human than I was, and neither one was more of a nemesis to me than myself.

Myself.

My true nemesis.

My own genes. Attacking me.

After all, there was an inner justice to the universe.

The One-Ten was crammed in both directions, but there wasn't a single cloud in the sky, and the haze was as good as it gets in August, and all together it made for a glorious day in the crowded City of Angels. Somewhere up in the San Gabriel Mountains the first fire of the season had set off, and the acrid smell of wildfires was just starting to tinge the air. I slugged along, my beautifully assembled Porsche engine useless in the morning commute traffic. Straight ahead, the glass and steel towers of Bunker Hill loomed like a modern Colossus of Rhodes. To my right careened the fifty-four-story scaffolding of the Marriott, next to the Nokia Plaza, the city's attempt to bring life back to downtown. As if traffic wasn't bad enough already.

I turned on the dispatch radio and tuned in to the Hollenbeck radio frequency. I didn't have to wait for too long. After the usual ten-twenty-sevens, a couple of disturbance calls, a "flagged down for robbery and a domestic violence" call, Unit 4-A-53 tuned in for a Code Six in Santa Paula, followed by a Code Robert. Two officers from the Santa Paula PD had retrieved an H&K P-30 in the septic tank of a rural home just off Ojai Road. The watch commander told Unit 4-A-53 to follow procedure and bring the gun into LAPD custody as the anonymous call had connected it to the Henkins murder.

I grinned. The warrants had come in pretty quickly, considering Satish made the call only twenty-four hours earlier. I wished they'd find Sakovich's prints on the gun, but I knew the bastard had been smarter than that. At least they had the slug retrieved from Henkins's skull and I was pretty sure they were going to match the ridges with the barrel. Hopefully, the fact that the Santa Paula home belonged to Sakovich's brother-in-law was also going to raise some flags.

I tuned to KJazz and B.B. King's scratchy voice rasped my ears. An airplane roared over the skyline of downtown and I wondered if it was heading to Boston and if it was Diane's plane.

B.B. complained he needed some love so bad. His voice got lost in the morning traffic.

Thank you for reading MOSAICS.
Please consider writing a review on Amazon.
It will help the author as well other readers.

ACKNOWLEDGMENTS

Just like with the first book in the Track Presius Mystery Series, for MOSAICS, too, I'm mostly indebted to my patient, smart, and supportive beta-readers: my heartfelt thanks go to Cristina Rinaudo, for putting up with me; Cindy Amrhein, for being there whenever I need you; Karen Alaniz, for being the first one to believe in my writing; Rowan Greene, for your constructive criticism; Nancy Matuszak, for patiently reading and supporting me; and to Heather Lazarus, Carolyn Fahm and Janice Hackney, for being my faithful proof readers and copy editors.

Many thanks go to my team of experts: Christianne Lane, for escorting me around Los Angeles County; Elizabeth Lund, George Marquardt, and Michael Bunker for teaching me how to fish bass, even though only fictionally; Steven Halter, for help with programming languages and lingo; Michael Galassi, for tips on how to put together a Porsche engine; award winning author and cardiologist D.P. Lyle, to whom I owe the accuracy of my autopsy scenes; Deepa Nadiga, for useful conversations on psychiatry; and of course, a huge thank you to the one and only, retired officer Tim Bowen, who patiently walked me through all things LAPD, checked the police procedural, and whose memoir inspired Satish's stories.

Many of the scientific topics discussed in this book arose from inspiring conversations with my amazing mentor, friend and role model, Bette Korber, the beautiful mind behind the mosaic vaccine, and with my dad Franco Giorgi, professor of developmental biology at the University of Pisa.

Finally, these acknowledgments would not be complete without mentioning my supportive family. My parents always knew I was restless, though I'm not sure they ever anticipated to what extent. *Grazie babbo e mamma!* My husband is my harshest reader and I love him to pieces for that. And to my kiddos I ask for forgiveness as for years they've been wondering what mom was doing tied to her laptop until the wee hours of the night. I love them to pieces, too.

ABOUT THE AUTHOR

E.E. Giorgi is a scientist, a writer, and a photographer. She spends her days analyzing HIV data, her evenings chasing sunsets, and her nights pretending she's somebody else.

BLOG: chimerasthebooks.blogspot.com/
PHOTOGRAPHY: elenaedi.smugmug.com/
GOODREADS:
goodreads.com/author/show/7954733.Elena_Giorgi

www.ingramcontent.com/pod-product-compliance
Lightning Source LLC
Chambersburg PA
CBHW061922170626
46813CB00006B/2269